... HAD A
ONE-WAY TICKET TO AMERICA
IT TOOK THEM ALL THE WAY
TO THE TOP!

"A dynamic novel that begins during the 1916 uprising in Ireland and crosses the sea to New York and San Francisco. Simultaneously it accounts for the lives of two inhabitants of the same part of the Irish countryside who have a common peasant background but go their separate ways in the new world. One is Nora Shannon, who had been betrothed to Tom Cassidy before he was killed by hated British troops putting down the revolt. The other is Tom's brother, Patrick, who after being at the heart of the trouble and incarcerated in jail, escaped to make a fresh start . . . the author succeeds in meshing their stories and maintaining suspense throughout. The result is a compulsive and satisfying book."

The Seattle Times

PASSAGE WEST

DALLAS MILLER

AVON
PUBLISHERS OF BARD, CAMELOT AND DISCUS BOOKS

For my Irish grandfather and grandmother,
who could neither read books
nor write their own names,
yet came to America because it was their only hope,
and the last hope of the world

AVON BOOKS
A division of
The Hearst Corporation
959 Eighth Avenue
New York, New York 10019

Copyright © 1979 by Dallas Miller
Published by arrangement with Harper & Row,
Publishers, Inc.
Library of Congress Catalog Card Number: 79-3982
ISBN: 0-380-50278-X

First Avon Printing, May, 1980

AVON TRADEMARK REG. U.S. PAT. OFF. AND IN
OTHER COUNTRIES, MARCA REGISTRADA, HECHO EN
U.S.A.

Printed in the U.S.A.

Contents

THE AMERICAN WAKE

1

As Nora Shannon opened the huge double doors of the drawing room, her hands were trembling. She caught a fold of her dress beneath her starched white apron and pulled her hem an inch or so off the floor, then hurried across the Persian carpet in slippered feet.

"Did my lady call?" she asked in a shy voice made strident by fear, dipping her knee respectfully as she did.

Lady Wingfield smiled serenely at the girl's discomfort, then turned toward her brother and sister-in-law, who were guests at the house, so that they might share her amusement.

"Yes, Nora," she replied with wonderful ease. "Sir Richard will be sitting late today in Assize Court at Skibbereen, and tea will be delayed one hour. Would you please advise the kitchen staff, and also find Harry and inform him. I'm sure that I saw him not too long ago turning into the *boreen* that leads to the strand."

Nora dropped her knee ever so slightly, then turned and rushed noiselessly from the room. She closed the doors behind her and walked across the marble floor of the great hall toward the kitchen.

The *boreen*, she repeated to herself. It was so like the English to appropriate an Irish word and make it their own, just as they had appropriated nearly everything else in Ireland. If it was "the little road" her ladyship would be meaning, couldn't she have said as much? Nora had never heard her utter it before and could only guess that it was done for the benefit of her English guests, the Monteagles, who owned property in Kerry near Kenmare and visited Ireland only once a year to collect their rents.

In the cavernous kitchen, Nora made her way to Hannah, who stood at an immense black stove, and announced, "Sir Richard is after being late in town today, and we're to hold tea until half-seven, ma'am."

From his corner next to the hearth, Redmond McCarthy, one of the footmen, spoke up. "Sir Richard can starve for all I care."

Hannah shook a wooden spoon at him. "You have an uncivil tongue in your head, Redmond. If it weren't for Sir Richard taking you in, you'd still be living in a hedgerow."

His eyes opened wide with outrage. "I'd be living in a house of me own if Sir Richard's father hadn't pulled it down on top of me father's head."

Hannah looked at him as if he were a madman. "Sure and that happened years and years ago."

"It feels like it happened yesterday. And me stomach's no fuller than me father's was."

"Nor your head, either," she retorted smartly.

The fact that the Wingfields had settled in Ireland in Cromwellian times, two hundred fifty years before, was quite ignored by the kitchen staff, who discussed their arrival as if it had just occurred. But then the toppling of the McCarthy cottage, torn down stone by stone for non-payment of rent, the family driven into the fields, dated from 1870, and the year was now 1916. In Ireland, time did not lessen grievances; it enlarged them.

"Mark me words, Hannah," Redmond said, "Sir Richard will have a hearty appetite today, with all the sorrow he's bringing to young Cassidy. He's sending the lad to prison, they do be saying in town."

To Nora, it was unthinkable. The boy was only seventeen—her age. How could such a youth be plotting insurrection, as the Crown had charged? True, he had been caught rowing a currach from Whiddy Island to the strand beneath the Earl of Bantry's property with two kegs of gunpowder in his narrow boat. A foreign schooner had been sighted off the coast just the week before, and the British were of the opinion that a great store of gunpowder had been buried on the island, wrapped in canvas sail.

But if traitorous and blackguardy acts had been committed, surely those responsible were the men who had delivered the gunpowder in the foreign vessel, not the boy who had been persuaded to row it, keg by keg, to the mainland. Why condemn a lad to prison for having participated in something he scarcely understood?

But what troubled Nora most was what would happen when Patrick Cassidy opened his mouth in court. Some people were born with the gift of gab, but Patrick's gift was for defiance. He had no love at all for the British.

Once, when Nora had accompanied the Wingfields to Dublin on a shopping expedition, Lady Prudence had bought a souvenir china plate for her in a shop on Sackville Street. On it was the face of a noble lady. It would look grand, altogether, Nora thought, on the shelf over the hearth at her family's cottage.

The following Sunday, when she walked the four miles along the coast road to the fishing village where she had been born, she carried the precious plate with her. When her mother and father saw it, there was no end to their admiration. And when the neighbors were called in to look at it, they sang their approval.

Everyone except Patrick Cassidy. His eyes darkened as he gazed at the portrait on the plate.

"No honest man could sleep in the same house with the likeness of that old whore and villain," he said about the woman whose face was in cobalt blue on the commemorative plate.

The fisherfolk were properly astounded.

"Do you know who that is?" he asked them. *"That* is Queen Victoria."

There was a hum in the small room that was something less than reverential.

"During the Great Famine," Patrick Cassidy began, "when one *million* of our countrymen died of starvation, that woman dug into her purse and gave two thousand pounds for the relief of the starving Irish. *Two* thousand pounds! Less than a halfpenny for every dead man, woman, and child!" His voice very nearly broke under the burden of emotion. "The English provide one kind of relief for themselves, and another for the poor Irish."

Patrick contemplated the queen's Hanoverian features.

"That plate is not fit to hold an Irish brime," he declared.

Nora had gasped. To Patrick, even an Irish turd was too good for Queen Victoria!

In the end, to preserve the peace, Nora had removed the plate from the shelf and hidden it in the cupboard, but the following week, when she looked for it, it had gone. She knew better than to ask where.

Nora's father, like Patrick's, was a fisherman, as their families had been for centuries, which helped explain why they had survived the famine of 1847-1848. Mackerel taken from Roaringwater Bay had sustained them when other Irishmen, who lived inland and subsisted on potatoes, died because their crops had rotted in the ground. During those years, the Cassidys and the Shannons had shared everything, and survival was an exceedingly strong bond. Almost nothing was stronger. Nora had grown up thinking that the Cassidys were an extension of her own family.

Like all the young girls of the area—except those who were dwarfed, clubfooted, or light in the head—Nora was put into domestic service at a very early age. She was only ten years old when she first left home to work in the Wingfields' vast house. The advantage of being employed by a gentleman's family, her parents had said, was that she would be able to acquire skills that would be useful later on in life. During her first week at Doonmara House, she had learned how to make a bed. The necessity had never occurred before, as Nora, her nine brothers and sisters, and her mother and father all slept in one room on straw mats that they laid out each night on the floor in front of the hearth. As Hannah put it, neither the very rich nor the very poor knew how to make their own beds —the one through indolence and the other through want. But in time, Nora became quite proficient at it.

After two years as a chambermaid, there occurred a vacancy in the kitchen, and Nora requested to be transferred. At the Shannon cottage, preparing supper involved little more than baking bread in a cast-iron pot and boiling potatoes. Perhaps once a month, there would be a few rashers of bacon. Nora knew nothing about

6

cooking the fine food that gentlefolk ate, but she proposed to learn. With Hannah's guidance, she helped prepare joints of beef or lamb, roasted chicken, salmon, duck, or pheasant. Vegetables and fruits were carried by steamer from the continent for the Wingfields' table, and rich, many-layered French and Viennese pastries were baked for them. As Hannah worked, Nora watched until in time she could duplicate the cook's skills.

Nora did not learn the culinary arts to satisfy her gluttony or curiosity, but to guarantee survival. Her cousin Mary in New York had written and said that no Irish girl need beg on the streets of that city if she could cook a decent meal.

And it was Nora's intention to go to America, as it was Patrick Cassidy's intention as well. More important, his brother Thomas, who had been keeping company with Nora, would be going with them. Though Thomas had not yet formally declared himself—how could a man propose until he could support a wife?—it was understood that they would marry as soon as they reached the New World.

But now all that was in jeopardy.

As she left the *boreen,* Nora saw young Master Wingfield walking with his two greyhounds at the water's edge. The wind was lively even on this mild day, and as Nora hurried toward him across the sand, her skirt ballooned out behind her.

"Master Harry?" she called.

At the sound of her voice, he turned. At his side, the two lean hounds bent their heads downward and shivered, as they did even on the warmest day of the year.

"Hello, Nora," he said when she was abreast of him. "Have you come to walk with me?"

A blush inflamed her cheeks. "You always do be teasing."

He smiled when he saw her color rise. "Do you think I would hurt you, Nora?"

"No, Master Harry," she replied truthfully.

"Yet the minute you come near me, you're as nervous as my two hounds. You shouldn't be, Nora. Be at your ease with me. Consider me a friend."

7

At last, Nora smiled tentatively.

He was not the usual Englishman, to be sure. Locally, in fact, he was considered something of an oddity because in fine weather he would often row out to Cape Clear and there draw the natives into conversation. Then, to their astonishment, he would write it all down.

"He do be putting it in a little book he carries with him," they said about it, not without suspicion.

And afterward, Nora had heard, he would take his notebook with him when he visited Lady Caverly and her daughter, Lucy, whose immense Palladian house sat on lands adjoining the Wingfields', and there he would read to them the tales told to him by toothless old crones in their tiny cottages on Clear Island. It was all very daft, if Nora was any judge.

She let the words spill out of her mouth: "My lady says I am to tell you that tea will be kept back till half-seven."

A smile lifted his lips. "You are to tell me that, are you?" he asked. "Well, you have told me very well, Nora."

Without warning, he leaned over and kissed her on the cheek.

She pulled away. "You're very bold," she said.

"That I am, Nora."

Distracted and giddy, she turned and ran across the sand to the house in the distance.

2

Although Sir Richard Wingfield considered himself a kind man and a fair and astute one, it was also true that he was an Englishman, and while kindness, fairness, and astuteness served an Englishman exceedingly well in his own country, they did nothing but incite wrath once they were taken abroad to Ireland.

Sir Richard, who had often contemplated the problem, had come to the conclusion that there were two explanations.

The first was that Englishmen who owned property in Ireland were, more often than not, absentee landlords who rarely visited except to collect rents from their tenants. And if there was a single lesson to be learned from history, it was that the landless class invariably despised their landlords, particularly those whom they enriched without ever seeing.

The second explanation was that the Irish were ungovernable.

Today, at the sitting of the Assize Court, Sir Richard saw still one more instance of it.

The youth standing before him was certainly not unattractive. It was uncanny that the Irish could produce such lavishly beautiful creatures on a diet scarcely enough to keep a medium-sized dog alive. Patrick Cassidy was strikingly good-looking: dark-haired and dark-browed, but with creamy white Celtic skin and cerulean blue eyes. As he stood before Sir Richard, he held his head high, as if he were about to dine at Dublin Castle with a duchess on his left and a countess on his right, and not about to be sent to Mountjoy Prison.

In the courtroom behind him, Sir Richard could make

out Cassidy's family. They were rude and humble people. The inevitable manure still clung to the Wellington boots that Cassidy's father wore, and from experience, Sir Richard knew that he should not be too surprised to find a louse or two in the room after the pack left. Just looking at them made Sir Richard's ankles itch.

On the other side of the courtroom sat Lady Caverly and her daughter, Lucy, dressed in their smart London frocks and their wide-brimmed hats. Sir Richard had nodded in surprise when they entered, thinking they were waiting to see him, but then he saw young Cassidy acknowledge their arrival with a slight inclination of his head. Sir Richard deduced that Cassidy must be one of the native curiosities that Lady Caverly had unearthed, perhaps even in concert with Sir Richard's own son.

Both Lady Caverly and Harry Wingfield were madly interested in Irish culture, though so far as Sir Richard could see, there *was* none.

He now gently repositioned his sweating haunches on the woolsack beneath him and listened to the summing up by a member of His Majesty's constabulary.

The constable extended his arm and pointed a finger at the prisoner.

"He is a ruthless and an obdurate lad, Sir Richard, and no good will ever come of him. I have little doubt but that a fearful and dastardly act was planned by Cassidy and his allies, a threat to concord and peace on this island. We must set examples, Sir Richard, lest the rabble be encouraged to emulate this rascal. He is a threat to British sovereignty and to the Crown itself."

The constable stepped back from the bench in order to allow the magistrate an unobstructed view of the prisoner.

Sir Richard adjusted his spectacles. "It is my understanding, Cassidy," he began, "that you admit to nothing other than being illegally on the Earl of Bantry's strand?"

"I do not even admit to that, begging your pardon, Sir Richard. I rowed to shore on God's water and came to rest on God's land. May I remind the court that the Earl of Bantry has no more than temporary use of either."

Sir Richard scrutinized the boy more closely. "You are

surprisingly articulate for a young man of your station in life," he said.

Cassidy met his eye without blinking. "And you are for a man of yours," he replied with equal condescension.

A slight color rose to the magistrate's face. "Your people are fishermen, I believe."

"They *are*," Cassidy answered, pressing hard on the verb, as the Irish do.

"And are you able to read and write?"

"Despite English neglect, I *am*, sir."

There were no schools in the area for Catholics, and small landowners of the Protestant faith were forced to send their children to Cork City for an education. Large landowners sent theirs to Dublin or to England—if, in fact, they ever left England in the first place. Literacy was not considered desirable among the native Catholics. What need did they have of letters if nothing was required of them but to scrub floors and empty slop jars?

"And how have you learned, might I ask," Sir Richard said to the prisoner.

"A very kind English lady has taken an interest in me and has supplied me with books and elementary instruction. If I am now an embarrassment to her, I humbly apologize. She had no way of knowing"—he paused to look at the constable—"that I would become a ruthless and obdurate lad."

"You are a cheeky fellow, Cassidy."

"I have no talent for crawling, sir."

"An assault against His Majesty's government cannot pass unpunished, despite your youth. You have willfully sought to incite revolution among these poor, ignorant people, even though you were well aware that your attempt was bound to fail. You have a lust for martyrdom, you Irish do."

For lack of tea, Sir Richard's stomach rumbled loudly. He cleared his throat to create a conflicting noise.

"It is my opinion, Cassidy," he went on, "that your patriotism is in want of tempering. I know of no better place than that to which I am now about to sentence you."

He paused to wet his lips.

"Patrick Cassidy!" he roared. "It is hereby decreed

that you will serve a period of no less than five years of penal servitude, confined to His Majesty's prison in the city of Dublin, and that you will be transported thence, Monday next, the day after Easter. This court of law is now adjourned."

There was a sharp cry in the courtroom, then a sudden keening.

Expectedly, the keening came from Cassidy's black-shawled mother. To everyone's astonishment, the cry came from the Honorable Miss Caverly.

Quickly, Lady Caverly collected her daughter and began to lead her from the room. As she passed the Cassidy clan, she leaned over and whispered to one of Patrick's three brothers, "Thomas, may I have a word with you outside?"

While the elder Cassidy remained with his wife and two other sons, in hopes of being permitted to see the prisoner, Thomas followed the English woman and her young daughter up the aisle to the door.

Once on the steps, Lady Caverly turned to him and said, "Thomas, I shall do all I can to rectify this mistake. In the meantime, will you convey to Patrick our deep-felt sorrow."

"I shall, my lady."

Miss Lucy Caverly touched each eye with the tip of her handkerchief.

"My daughter and I shall take it upon ourselves to supply him with food as long as he remains here in Skibbereen, so that you and your father will not have to make the long journey into town."

"We're very beholden to you, my lady. And Patrick is, as well. He thinks the world of you and of Miss Caverly."

"I wonder if it isn't all an attempt to destroy the Gaelic League," she replied. "Sir Richard must have known that Patrick is very active."

It was through the Gaelic League that Lady Caverly and her daughter had met Patrick Cassidy. They had heard that Gaelic was spoken in the fishing village not far from their house, and that John Mary Cassidy was the most proficient speaker of all. Thus, they began to

12

visit the tiny cottage during the long winter months, and in time grew fond of the entire family. Quite by accident, they discovered that not one of the children could read or write English. So it was proposed that in exchange for Gaelic lessons, the four Cassidy lads would be instructed in reading and writing by Lady Caverly.

But two of the boys, Lambi and Eamon, lost interest, much preferring to spend their time with their father in the hide-bottomed rowboat. The third, Thomas, was an earnest and dogged scholar but lacked brilliance.

Patrick—as Lady Caverly often said—was dazzling.

Or, as Harry Wingfield said, "He's at least as clever as a second-year man at Trinity," hastily adding, "though that may not be the compliment I intended it to be."

It was not unusual to find the four of them—Lady Caverly, her daughter, Harry Wingfield, and Patrick Cassidy—tramping over the fields through the prickly gorse in search of antiquities. Patrick knew where every round tower in the neighborhood was, and every stone fort. Sometimes on a fine evening, Lady Caverly would pack a hamper and they would picnic at an ancient Druidic fortress while she read Yeats to them, or Thomas Moore or Synge.

"Oh, it is so gorgeous," she would say, eating breast of chicken and sipping French wine as she read.

And Patrick, for whom the supper was even more gorgeous than the poetry, would be the first to nod his head in agreement.

"We will miss him most awfully," Miss Lucy said now to his brother before the court of law.

"It is unthinkable that Patrick is involved in any plot," Lady Caverly declared.

"It *is*," Thomas agreed.

"I am bringing it to the attention of the Chief Justice of Ireland," she continued. "It is an outrage that such a splendid youth should be sentenced to prison for what I am sure was only a harmless prank."

"I am as sure as your ladyship," Thomas replied.

While Patrick's mother waited in the courtroom, his three brothers and his father were brought to the small cell to which he had been taken. They were instructed to do their talking through the iron bars.

"It's mean lodgings the King has given you," John Mary said to his son.

By way of reply, Patrick said urgently, "Can we talk?"

Thomas looked over his shoulder. "Your man is at the end of the hall. He won't hear."

"What news of Casement?" Patrick whispered.

"He has bent the Kaiser's ear."

Under the burden of emotion they felt, no one was at once able to speak. There was reverential silence.

"Thank God," Patrick sighed at last.

To the Cassidys, and to other Irishmen too, an enemy of Britain's was an ally of Ireland's. It was because of this that Roger Casement had journeyed to the Continent to enlist the aid of the Germans, who thought even less of the English than the Irish did.

"Casement has got his Mausers," Thomas said. "They come to Tralee on the twentieth."

"What day is that?"

"Thursday."

"And the Rising?"

"Easter Sunday is the day, the twenty-third."

"You are sure?"

"As sure as man can be. We rise on Easter Sunday."

They crossed themselves, each one, from forehead to breast. On the day of the resurrection of Christ, the people of Ireland would rise against their oppressors after centuries of torment and abuse.

"And what of me?" Patrick asked.

"Until then, you will be guest of the King," his father answered.

"And Cork will rise?"

"And Kerry, too," said Thomas.

"Dear God in Heaven, please grant our cause success."

After his father and brothers had left, Patrick felt a keen disappointment, not only because he would be of little use to them between now and Easter Sunday but because he had deceived his Anglo-Irish friends, Lady

14

Caverly and Harry Wingfield, and on Easter Sunday his deception would be revealed.

It was peculiar indeed that ancient Ireland could attract the sympathy of Lady Caverly while modern Ireland could not. Patrick himself had seen her sit for hours enraptured by the carvings on a giant Celtic cross, yet she would fail to notice a family living in squalor no more than a hundred feet away. She had been among the first to champion the use of the Gaelic language, but for her, the language was to be used to croon thousand-year-old legends, not to create new ones.

Patrick and his brothers saw things quite differently. When they had learned, at last, that they could speak the language of their fathers openly and with pride, the first thing they had asked was: If their language was Irish and their culture, too, why in God's name was their land owned by foreigners?

Patrick's two older brothers, Thomas and Lambi, had been the first in the family to join the Volunteers, and they in turn recruited their father, then Patrick, and finally Eamon, who at fifteen was the youngest. Originally, the Volunteers had been established to protect what few rights the Irish still possessed, not to agitate for new ones. But when England went to war with Germany in 1914, another peril presented itself. The English Parliament began to cast a covetous eye across the Irish Sea with the hope of conscripting Irish manhood to serve in the British Army.

For Patrick and his brothers, it was the final outrage. After centuries of shameful servitude, only the most abject of slaves would give up their lives in order to protect the welfare of their hated masters.

If Irish blood was to be shed, it would be shed for holy Ireland, not for England.

Yet as a military organization the Irish Volunteers left a great deal to be desired. For one thing, no one had any clear notion as to who, if anyone, was in charge. For another, the communication system between different units was frequently subject to interception. Worst of all, the men were virtually without arms. The Cork Volunteers were desperately in need of the rifles Roger Casement

15

had won from the Kaiser, which were due in Tralee on the twentieth. Without them, it would be difficult for the Corkmen to rise. They had nothing but small caches of arms hidden throughout the county, the movement of just two kegs of which had already cost Patrick his freedom.

He wished with all his heart that he could go to Tralee with his brothers and help them carry the good Kaiser's Mausers back to Cork. But after all the years of longing, on the day the nation rose he would be in jail eating cold roast beef and red wine supplied by Lady Caverly and her daughter, sustained by them at the very minute his father and brothers were attempting to destroy their class.

3

Harry Wingfield would not be having tea with his family after all, but would be riding at once to Castle Caverly. Understandably, Lady Prudence asked why he couldn't have a bite to eat before he left.

"Because I can't sit at the same table with that man," he said about Sir Richard, who had just returned from Skibbereen with news of Cassidy's conviction. Harry was certain that his father had imposed the severe sentence on Cassidy only because Patrick was his friend and both were involved with the Gaelic League.

When he said as much, Sir Richard replied, "I am not at all opposed to your spending time with wild Irishmen, Harry, and even taking an interest in that mumbo-jumbo they call a language. What annoys me is that you would defend their acts of aggression against the Crown."

"I don't believe it was," Harry replied. "In fact, it's impossible. Patrick isn't that sort at all. He's harmless."

"There isn't a harmless creature on this island. And with a little bit of drink taken, as they phrase it, they are all maniacs, every one of them."

"How can you say that! You don't even know them!"

"*Know* them? I know them better than you, Harry. Who do you think officiates in court when they half kill each other? They are the most fractious people in the world. There isn't an Irishman in Cork who wouldn't like to hit every other Irishman over the head with a club. They have not *evolved* sufficiently, Harry. The mistake we British made when we first laid out plantations here was that we didn't transport all the native Irish Catholics to Australia, like *convicts*. If we had, Ireland would be a much better place in which to live."

17

Harry was speechless with rage. At no time in the past had his father gone quite so far.

"I don't think you feel anything at all toward these people," Harry cried at last.

"So long as they keep their distance, I find them quite tolerable." He waited, then added, "For people who are fundamentally incapable of self-control."

"And *you* are self-controlled?"

"It is the mark of an English gentleman, Harry."

Harry shook his head. "You were born in Ireland, and you have lived here most of your life. You're an *Irish* gentleman, not an English one. And if you don't face up to that fact very soon—" Harry fought for words but could not find them.

"No," Sir Richard said to his son at the door of the great hall. "I was born an Englishman, and I shall die one."

For Harry, it was a stunning revelation. He looked at his father as if he were seeing him for the first time. The difference between them was almost beyond healing.

For though Harry himself was born an English gentleman, he knew with certainty that he would die an Irish one.

As Harry was led into the drawing room of Castle Caverly, he saw Lucy standing by a long window, looking across the grounds that led to the edge of Roaringwater Bay. In the distance, gulls swooped in and out of Kilcoe Castle, roofless and derelict, the Caverlys' home from the twelfth century to the eighteenth, when the Georgian house had been built.

When she heard his footsteps, she turned. "Mother is writing a letter to the Chief Justice," she said.

"A hell of a lot of good that's going to do. He's my father's cousin. I've just had a terrible row," Harry continued. "I can't go back to the house."

"Stay with us. Mother would love the company."

He waited, then asked, "And not you?"

"Of course, Harry. You know how fond I am of you. We're fixing a hamper for Patrick's supper, which I'll take

18

down to him. You're free to come with me, if you like."

"I think I'm going to return to Dublin."

"But why so soon?"

"Perhaps I can talk to Mr. Yeats and persuade him to come to Patrick's defense. He's very influential." Harry threw himself into a chair. "Now aren't you sorry you came back from London to this benighted place?"

"London's really quite horrid. Soldiers everywhere. All you have to do is mention Flanders and everyone starts crying."

"I almost forgot the war."

"In London it's impossible to forget. It's everywhere. My cousin Arthur was killed. Did I tell you?"

"Vanessa's brother?"

She nodded her head. "Soon there will be no one left."

Lucy had spent a year with the Somervilles, her English cousins, who had a good deal more money than her mother.

The Caverly house was enormous and badly in need of repair: the roof was rotted, the gutters were gone, and the furniture was all a bit shabby and old. The lands might have been productive had there been someone to supervise such matters as drainage, but Lady Caverly was widowed and had an unfortunate knack for choosing inept managers. All she hoped to do was to keep a roof on the place until Lucy married Harry Wingfield; his family would be able to restore Castle Caverly to its old splendor.

They were counting on Harry, but he hadn't proposed yet. Lucy and her cousin in London had talked about it often. If a girl lacked money and had nothing but debts, she was obliged to marry a man who could correct such deficiencies.

"But I don't really love Harry all that much," she had said to her cousin.

"What a lot of piddle. That isn't important. You'll adjust in time. And don't forget that after the war there won't be any Englishmen left—virile ones, anyway—so consider yourself lucky. All the Wingfields *I've* met are very comfortable."

Certainly the Irish Wingfields were more comfortable than the Caverlys.

"What if I should move in here?" Harry said suddenly to her from the chair opposite. She looked alarmed. "I don't mean just for the night till I patch things up with my father. What if I should move in here permanently? What would you think of that?"

She thought it prudent not to answer.

"Of course I would marry you," he continued. He waited. "Would that be acceptable?" Lucy took a breath, then replied, "That would be acceptable, I suppose."

"I'm really getting tired of being a child. Do you know what I mean? Being my father's son and my mother's son. This way, I'll be independent, and so will you. Do you think your mother would approve?"

"Oh, I'm sure she would. Would your father?"

"He'd be glad to get me out of the house. He doesn't think very highly of me. He's very stingy with his money, too. But if I marry, he'll be obliged to increase my allowance. We could take a house in Dublin for part of the year, and the rest of the time live here."

"I think the whole roof has to be replaced," she said with surprising candor.

"You mean rafters and all?"

"I think so. They didn't use pitch pine, the way they did at Doonmara House, and the wood is filled with worms."

"Well, if it has to be done, it has to be done. We don't want the roof blowing away in a gale." He bit his lip thoughtfully. "You know, the more I think of it, the more satisfactory it seems."

"It's really quite a nice house, and the roof isn't going to cost that much."

"No, I meant getting married and being independent. I really do think I'm ready for it. Why don't we announce it as soon as I get back from Dublin and conclude my business with Mr. Yeats?"

"That would be lovely. When would that be, Harry?"

"I should think I would be back by Easter Sunday." He waited, then added, "Or at latest, the following day."

*　*　*

Thomas Cassidy stood in his rough homespun, his cap in one hand, and knocked at the kitchen door of Doonmara House.

In less than a minute, Redmond McCarthy opened the door and barked, "And what would *you* be wanting?"

"A word with Miss Nora, if you please."

As McCarthy retreated into the kitchen, Thomas turned to nod at his brother Lambi, who stood at the lawn's edge, holding the tethered horses. Lambi had not approved of the delay, as they had hard riding before them, but Thomas had insisted.

Suddenly, Nora was at the door.

"What brings you here, Thomas?" she asked.

"A friend is in need in Kerry. Lambi and I must leave at once."

"Have you food for your journey?"

He patted his bulging pockets. "We have spuds and oat cakes."

"Stay," she whispered. "I shall get you something."

Nora hurried into the kitchen to the table, where tea things taken from the dining room had been placed. In a napkin, embroidered with the Wingfield crest, she placed several slabs of lamb as Hannah watched.

"For Thomas," she said softly. "He is to go to Kerry."

"Sure an' it's the last place God made," Hannah replied. "He'll need more than that, girl, or he'll perish on the way."

The older woman heaped meat into the napkin, then filled a second with sliced bread. She was most generous when dispensing the Wingfield food, it being her opinion that they did not suffer from deprivation. In fact, Sir Richard, whose belly was huge, was grossly overfed and as a result had a liver ailment. A little misappropriated food would serve to prolong the man's life.

Nora hurried back to the door, closing it behind her. As she stuffed Thomas's arms with the napkins, she saw a gravity in his face she had never seen before.

"You have no people in Kerry, Thomas," she said at last.

"We have acquired some recently," he replied, smiling.

21

"You mustn't do anything desperate. It won't help Patrick, nor yourself, either."

He touched her hand. "You are right, Nora."

"Do nothing rash or bold. You must promise me, Thomas."

"I shall do my best, but as you know, I am a weak man, Nora."

She knew its significance as well as he. She felt the color rise to her cheeks.

"God bless you. And safe journey," she said.

She watched him stride across the lawn to where Lambi held the horses, and as she did, she was afraid.

As she waved to him, she felt giddy, and all the strength went out of her legs. She should have told him before he left, but she did not know how. She had told no one, not even Father Daley in confessional. Hannah might have advised her, but she couldn't bring herself to ask the old woman.

Nora had not bled this past month on schedule, and it had never occurred before since she became a woman.

God knows, she was no fool. She had lived in close quarters with her family, and as a child when she heard rustling at night, then thrashing, she knew that her father was lying between her mother's legs and doing what men do to women. She had seen the bulls in the fields, too, and the donkeys. And she knew the consequences: her mother giving birth, or her father helping to draw a calf from the womb of a cow or a foal from a mare.

She should have known better. The Devil must have possessed her.

Thomas wasn't even to blame. It was as much her fault as his. He had tried to stop. "Nora, are you sure?" he had asked, and she had answered, "Yes, yes." A fever had come over her. A madness.

It had been a Sunday afternoon in late February, and she and Thomas had gone for a walk down by the crooked bridge. Bluebells by the thousands were blooming already on the bank by the stream, and Nora had lain back in them. They had embraced before, but this time Thomas was more daring. He touched her in places no one ever had, and though she wanted to move his hand away, a frenzy had overcome her. She had even helped draw him into her.

It was wrong. She knew it was. In the eyes of God it was a mortal sin. Yet she'd had no mind. She could do nothing but conclude what they had begun.

Afterward came the shame, and she had quickly covered herself. Thomas had tried to explain to her that it was all right because they would soon be man and wife, but Nora was not convinced and neither was he. Before she returned to Doonmara House that evening, they had agreed that it must never occur again until they were married.

But now there was no blood when there should have been. No one had ever told her what it meant, but she divined that a change was taking place in her body. Her breasts felt different already, fuller somehow, and she had been sick one morning the week before.

She would have to tell Thomas soon so that they could at once plan their marriage. It would be too shameful— she could not bear it—if they waited till she was big-bellied.

A hand now touched her shoulder, and Nora looked up at Hannah.

"Are you after being ill?" the old woman asked.

"A little, ma'am," Nora replied almost inaudibly.

"Go to your room and rest a few minutes, girl. I'll get Susan to do your work for you."

"Thank you, ma'am."

Nora rushed through the kitchen and up the back stairs to the third floor, where the staff was lodged. Her tiny room was furnished with a narrow cot, a chest of drawers, and a crucifix on the wall.

She threw herself onto her knees and began to pray that all would go well—for her, for Thomas, and for their unborn child—then waited for the ecstasy that would reveal that God had listened, but nothing came.

4

I t will be thundery weather," Lambi shouted over the
wind as they reached the crest of the hill, then began
the descent to Bantry town.

In the distance, rain was already falling. The weather
would not hinder them, though the roads could, as the
mountain pass between Cork and Kerry was narrow and
easily flooded. But by the time they reached Glengariff
the storm might be over.

Thomas was more concerned about the German ship,
the *Aud,* sailing offshore in unfamiliar waters. If it had
difficulties or went aground, the rifles would be lost. Even
to get this far was a phenomenal achievement, as the British Navy regularly patrolled the coastal waters and chal-
lenged any German vessel. The *Aud* lacked a radio, so
there was no way of keeping in touch with it. The only
message the Cork Volunteers had received came directly
from Germany, advising them that the ship would arrive
in Tralee Bay on the twentieth. Thomas could only suppose that the Kerry Volunteers had been similarly notified.

It would be touch and go, all the way. If everything
went well, he and Lambi had but three days to return to
Cork with the arms, and they would be coming back in a
horse-drawn wagon at half the speed and facing twice the
hazards. At any point along the route they could be intercepted by the Royal Irish Constabulary.

Thomas had known from the beginning that it would
not be easy. A few thousand men, without training or organization, were attempting to seize control of their homeland from the strongest, most powerful nation in the world.
Many of the Cork Volunteers had never even fired a rifle

before except while poaching on lands owned by English lords, and certainly they lacked any sort of military discipline. But what unsettled Thomas more than anything else was the lack of planning and the uncertainty. Even now as they set out for Kerry, they did not know what to expect. All they had to go on was the name of an Irish Volunteer—his last name was Stack—and the date of arrival of the ship.

It was going to be very chancy. First they had to find Stack, then wait for the ship, and finally transfer the arms to shore without being detected. Once having done that, they would have to journey back to Cork, not to bed, but to revolution.

Now, as they rode through the narrow main street of Bantry toward the Glengariff Road, Thomas could not even think of insurrection. It was Nora who propelled him, the sweetness of her, the softness of her thighs. Oh, to lie with her again, this time as man and wife! How fine that would be!

"A careful eye, Thomas lad," Lambi said to him as they rode abreast through the street. Ahead of them, on a corner, stood a member of the Royal Irish Constabulary.

"Fine day!" Thomas shouted as they passed, unable to contain his excitement.

The man looked sullenly at the two riders, then turned his back to them.

"Did he recognize us, do you think?" Lambi whispered.

It was a valid enough concern. Only today their brother Patrick had been sentenced in Assize Court, and that very man had testified against him. Had he remembered them from court, and would he take notice of their journey northward?

"You were brazen," Lambi declared. "I wouldn't have said a word, meself."

"And it would have been fatal," Thomas replied. "Had we said nothing, he would have seen conspiracy on our faces. So I gave him a hearty greeting instead."

"That you did, Thomas. It almost took the hair off his head."

They laughed, then urged their horses to an easy canter through the street to the town's edge.

* * *

Beneath a threatening sky, a handsome trap drew up in front of the courthouse in Skibbereen. In a minute, the Honorable Miss Lucy Caverly emerged, tethered her white horse, then reached back into the carriage for the hamper that she had prepared for Patrick Cassidy.

"Miss Caverly, I believe," a constable at the door said to her, bowing his head respectfully. A reek of old perspiration rose from his uniform. His face was purplish-red from drink.

"I have come with supper for Mr. Patrick Cassidy," she said. "Could you deliver this to him? I shall wait for the basket."

"Of course, my lady."

The stoop-shouldered man carried the hamper down the hall toward the rear of the building where prisoners were kept. As for his drunkenness, it was common knowledge that members of the Royal Irish Constabulary were given to drink. At the same time, members of the Irish Volunteers, the patriotic organization, were compelled to abstain. Patrick himself had said that only a drunken Irishman could serve an English King.

"*Mis*-thur Cassidy!" the constable howled before Patrick's cell. "Stand on yer feet!"

Patrick rose from the wood-slabbed bed as he was instructed. The constable opened the cell door and handed him the basket.

"Miss Caverly has brought you a feed," he said. "You'll be obliging me if you remove it be-fahr me eyes, as I am to re-tahrn the basket to Miss Caverly."

Whatever it was, it was far more appetizing than the gruel Patrick had been offered an hour ago and had declined, saying at the time, "I shall not eat the King's swill." As the constable waited at the door, he dug into the basket and pulled out a portion of cold pheasant.

"Pheasant," he said with undisguised delight.

"It will take more than a pheasant to make a gintleman out of the likes of youse," was the constable's sharp retort.

Cassidy continued. "A heel of bread," he announced, holding it up for scrutiny, "done in the French style."

27

He reached into the basket once more. "And a tart. Raspberry, if I'm not mistaken." As he said it, his hand felt something cold and metallic at the bottom beneath a linen napkin, and his heart almost skipped a beat.

The tart met with the constable's immediate approval. "I wouldn't mind having that, meself," he said.

"If that is the case," Patrick replied, "it's yours. Consider it a gift."

With one hand he lifted the tart from the basket and handed it to its admirer, and with the other withdrew the napkin and the object it enclosed. As the constable's teeth sank into the tart, his eyes shut blissfully and rapture swept over his face. Quickly, Patrick placed the napkin and its burden on the three-legged stool next to his bed.

The constable sighed. "God save us, it's lovely!" he exclaimed, wiping his mouth with the back of his hand.

Patrick returned the hamper to the man. "My compliments to Miss Caverly," he said.

"I shall deliver them, *Mis*-thur Cassidy."

With that, he was gone, and Patrick was left with the snub-nosed French pistol Lucy Caverly had provided him. He opened its chamber and found that it was loaded. Miss Caverly's intentions were unmistakable: it was to be put to use. Yet surely he couldn't attempt an escape, as it would serve only to alert the authorities to what was planned for Easter Sunday. Then he recalled that she knew nothing of the plan. All she knew was that he was to be sent to Dublin the following Monday.

Absentmindedly, he began to nibble at the breast of pheasant. It was rich fare, to be sure. As he chewed, he tasted something unfamiliar and gradually worked a shred of paper to his lips. More of it had been lodged between the skin and the flesh of the pheasant, and most of it was still intact. Patrick now joined the severed piece to that which had not been disturbed and formed a note.

Dearest Patrick,

A single constable will accompany you on the train to Dublin, and this gift from me might distract his attention long enough for you to leave his

28

company. Seize your opportunity one mile beyond the stop at Clonakilty, where a horse will await you. You will be supplied with false papers and passage to America.

Not a word to my mother or to Harry! They know nothing of this.

Yours,
Lucy Caverly

It was a reckless thing for her to have done. Dangerous and illegal. Had she been caught, she would have been severely compromised.

Beyond his window a horse neighed, and as it did, Patrick stood and looked down upon the street. Dressed in her splendid London clothes, Miss Caverly sat in the open carriage, the empty basket in the seat at her side. As she saw Patrick's face, she smiled.

Patrick did the same, then watched as she drove off, and long after she had gone he was overwhelmed by a feeling that was, he was certain, far more complex than patriotism.

Steam shot from beneath the coach, the train convulsed, then finally stopped, and as it did, Harry Wingfield stepped down to the platform of Kingsbridge Station in Dublin and made his way through the tumult and the crowd toward the street. Hawkers of shriveled apples and bruised plums howled their wares as he passed, and importuning porters bore down on him, arms waving, as he continued through the ornate station, carrying his own satchel.

Outside, horse-drawn hansom cabs were lined up at the curb's edge. He hailed one.

As they set off for the College Green, Harry leaned back and looked to his left and his right. Already his nostrils detected the heady odor rising from the River Liffey, blended with a malty aroma from the Guinness Brewery. Lamps were lit on the streets and the bridges, and people hurried along the walks next to the quays.

Harry had more than a passing acquaintance with both

Paris and London—he had spent the early part of his life in England at Harrow, his father's school—but much preferred Dublin. Of the three cities, only Dublin was untouched by the nineteenth century. It remained an eighteenth-century capital, and though some of its buildings were seedy, others were downright gorgeous. It was, above all, a city of people rather than buildings, and Harry could never tire of Dubliners. They were the most outgoing and public people in the world, convivial whether you wanted them to be or not.

He had been miserably unhappy in England because the other boys had looked upon him as something of a colonial. They poked fun at his speech, which had an Irish lilt to it, and asked on occasion if his parents kept chickens in their drawing room. Moreover, his character and sexual orientation was different from most of the English lads. He could not recall the number of times that older boys had attempted to crawl into his bed with him, though each time he had declined. They themselves thought nothing of it, and more than one had accused Harry of being a priest-ridden moralist, though, in fact, he was as Protestant as they were.

Dublin was a manly city, sure of its gender. Men did not sleep with other men. Either they slept with women or they did without and "played with their puddings," as local wags put it. It was in Dublin where Harry had acted out his own manhood for the first time at a brothel—kips, they were called—and found it very satisfactory indeed.

Now, as he sat in the cab as it turned onto Westmoreland Street, he considered how lucky he was soon to be married to Miss Caverly. He would have his degree from Trinity at the end of this term, and if things went well, they could be married by late summer. If he had his way, they would spend the first three months of their married life in bed.

Yet until he was married, he would have to make do. Thus, in addition to calling on Mr. Yeats in Merrion Square, Harry also hoped to visit the kips before he returned to West Cork.

"The Lincoln Gate? Or is it the front gate you'd be wanting, me lord?" the driver yelled at him.

"The front gate."

The hansom now pulled up before it, and Harry could see the welcoming statues of Oliver Goldsmith and Edmund Burke.

"Two shillings would suit me fine," the driver said as Harry stepped out.

"Then you are due for three, I'd say."

"God bless you, guvnor."

Guvnor indeed. An Irishman never used the term except to an Englishman or an Anglo-Irishman. No matter how he tried, Harry could not escape his class.

He picked up his satchel and walked over the cobblestone pavement under the arch into the square beyond. The place seemed deserted as he made his way past the Campanile toward his room.

"I say, Wingfield!" a voice shouted at him. "What are you doing here?"

Harry turned to find himself face-to-face with John Ormond, who was a year behind him.

"I thought you were in Cork, corrupting all the local girls," Ormond continued.

"I was," Harry began. "I mean, at least I was in Cork. But I had to return to Dublin on business. Is anyone else around?"

"Almost everyone's home. *I* would have gone home but no one's there—they're all in Italy, doing it from top to bottom, and who wants to spend a holiday in an empty house?" He waited. "You're looking very good, Wingfield. Cork has agreed with you."

"I'm engaged to be married."

"I say, that's wonderful, Wingfield. Really splendid. It calls for a tune, don't you think? A little celebration?"

"I wouldn't mind at all. Just so long as you don't allow me to drink too much. I've come to Dublin to talk with Mr. Yeats, and I don't want to do that with a monstrous headache and a thick tongue."

"He's much too precious for me. He makes me feel like such a dolt. I don't envy you."

"I want him to champion someone's cause. A local fellow in Cork."

"A rustic?"

Harry laughed. "You might describe him that way. I have a feeling that he would take exception to it."

As they walked past the Examination Hall, Ormond said, "You didn't mention the young lady's name."

Harry took a deep breath, then sighed. "Lucy Caverly. I've known her most of my life, but I've never paid much attention to her until this year. She and her mother live next to my family in West Cork."

As they entered the hall and bounded up the stairs, Ormond asked, "Who's her father?"

"Sir Anthony Caverly. He died about four years ago."

"I think I know who they are. Good family, but not much money."

"You *do* put it baldly."

"I'm just being realistic, Wingfield. I have to consider such matters. I've got two older brothers, and I'm doomed to poverty unless I marry a rich girl."

"If I hear of any likely candidates, I'll mention your name."

"*Would* you? That's very good of you, Wingfield."

Harry pushed open the door to his room, and as he did, two figures inside quickly rose from where they were seated on the floor. Desmond McAuliffe, who shared digs with Harry, was clearly embarrassed—it was strictly forbidden for girls to visit a student's quarters—yet the young lady standing beside him was remarkably composed.

"I'm awfully sorry," Harry stammered. "I hadn't expected anyone to be here. I thought you went to visit your family in Galway, Desmond."

"I changed my plans at the last minute," Desmond replied, then cleared his throat, which did not appear to be functioning properly. "May I introduce a friend of mine. Miss Kitty O'Neill . . . Harry Wingfield . . . and John Ormond. We were just—just studying. Weren't we, Miss O'Neill?"

She smiled bountifully. "Of course. What else?"

Harry found himself beginning to blush. "I'll just leave my satchel here on the bed. You wouldn't by any chance like to join us for a drink? I'm celebrating my engagement."

"But how wonderful, Harry. Who is she? A Dublin girl?"

Ormond smiled. "Harry isn't hearty enough for a Dublin girl. He's found one in Cork."

"We hope to be married this summer."

"It's stunning news. I'm so glad for you, Harry. Kitty and I—Miss O'Neill and I would love to have a drink with you, but we're going to be busy this evening. Will you still be here tomorrow?"

"I'll be staying until Easter. Or possibly the day after."

Something like confusion crossed McAuliffe's face, but he quickly recovered. "If that's the case, I'm sure we'll be seeing a great deal of you during the next few days."

Harry began to back out of the room. "Well, we'll leave you for now. It's been lovely meeting you, Miss O'Neill."

"Lovely!" she echoed.

The door closed behind them as Harry and Ormond made their way down the stairs to the courtyard. When Ormond at last spoke, it was almost a whisper.

"That's most extraordinary," he said. "Did you see what they were doing?"

They stood in the courtyard now and looked up at the solitary lighted window on the second floor.

"The lights were on, Ormond. They couldn't have been doing anything too indecent."

Ormond shook his head. "You didn't see what was under Desmond's bed. There were guns there. There must have been four or five."

Harry hadn't seen anything of the sort. "It's quite possible that he's going to do some hunting," he suggested. "Though at this time of year, he'll find lean pickings in the fields."

Ormond turned to Harry. "I shouldn't think that those guns would be appropriate for grouse or pheasant."

Harry looked up in alarm. "What were they?"

"They were Mausers," Ormond replied. "I'd bet my life on it."

5

As quickly as it had begun, the squally weather was over. A thousand stars filled the night sky.

In the distance, off Baltimore Harbor, Nora was able to make out the sweeping beacon of the lighthouse, guiding ships away from Ireland's rocky southern coast. In the dark waters of the Atlantic, German and British warships were sure to be cruising, and she had heard tales of silent submarines lurking beneath the surface.

Her eyes scanned the water's edge for signs of the war in far-off Flanders, but, thank God, she found nothing there, no bloated bodies of once-fair German youths or laughing English lads, eyeballs plucked from their heads by the fish. More than one had already been washed ashore, to be discovered at first light shrouded by sea grass, face down in the wet sand. The English were repatriated and the Huns given hasty burials by the fisherfolk lest the constabulary learn of their arrival and defile —so it was thought—their bodies. Many a pagan and many a Lutheran were given proper Catholic interments far beneath Ireland's green grass.

Death at sea was no novelty to the people who lived along the coast. Brothers and fathers, uncles and cousins —all had been lost to the raging waters, no matter how skillful they were in their currachs or how wary. One minute they could be fishing peacefully, enjoying the fine day, and the next, their tiny boats would be riding waves as high as hills. Sometimes they could be identified only by the clothes they wore, knit by loving wives or mothers, and often their bodies would be carried great distances up the coast to Kerry or Clare.

Sure and it was a hard life, whether one fished the seas, tilled the soil, or made the beds and cleaned up after

English lords. Nora began her work at sunrise and never retired from the kitchen until bedtime. Except on Sundays she had no life of her own. Her life was given to the Wingfields in exchange for her board, her narrow bed, and a few shillings each week, which in time would pay for her passage to America. She considered herself lucky, however, for without the work she would be dependent upon her parents at home, and they had scarcely enough spuds to keep themselves alive.

Yet Patrick had told her that the Irish themselves had once been kings and great lords, and that when Europe was at its darkest and most ignorant during the Middle Ages, the Irish were scholars and wise men. Nora could not conceive of it. She herself could write nothing but an X in lieu of her name. How could she be descended from kings and princes when, in fact, she spent her days in slavery?

Even now, Nora had left work in the kitchen to rush to the fisher village, yet had promised Hannah and Susan— upon whom her work would fall—that she would make it up to them the following day. It was most urgent that she see her ailing mother, she said. She would return before morning.

But it was not her mother she was concerned about. After the tea things had been taken from the dining room, Redmond McCarthy had drawn her to one side of the kitchen and whispered, "Nora dear, it's me big ears that are troublin' me again. Me lady's brother has said to Sir Richard that there may be more to Patrick Cassidy than meets the eye. He's after saying that the lad may be part of some grand conspiracy about to take place." He waited to see the effect his words created, then added. "Sir Richard is to telephone the Lord Lieutenant's man at Dublin Castle in the morning to warn him that something might be afoot."

"He is to telephone tomorrow?" Nora repeated.

"It's what I'm saying, girl."

Nora needed to hear no more. With Thomas en route to Kerry and Patrick in jail, John Mary Cassidy would have to be told at once. Whatever was about to take place, Nora was sure that the Lord Lieutenant's man ought not to know of it. There were few telephones in West Cork—only one in Skibbereen and one in Clonakilty, both at the railroad stations—and perhaps some accident might befall them or Sir Richard be prevented from reaching them.

Nora hurried now over the crooked bridge and looked into the teeming water that was salmon-filled, though no one was allowed to fish them on penalty of fine or imprisonment. The bridge, built during the Great Famine by starving men who received a penny a day for their labors, was owned by the Wingfields, and the salmon as well. And if an occasional Wingfield salmon wound up in an Irishman's net or at the end of his line, it was never eaten, as it was much too dear. It was sold at one of the inns and fed to commercial travelers.

On the other side of the bridge, a lean gray pony stretched its head far over a stone wall and neighed with pleasure as it saw Nora approaching. She stopped to stroke its neck. It was after being lonely, she supposed.

No lonelier than Nora herself. The last time she had walked along this road Thomas had been at her side and they had talked of America. In America, he had said, you did not have to take off your shoes on rocky roads in order to save the leather as they were doing then and as Nora was doing now. In America, a man who worked hard, and a woman, too, could own several pairs of shoes. To go barefoot was unthinkable unless you were a wee one.

At the rise of land, Nora looked down to see the village built along an inlet of the sea. Turf smoke rose from all the chimneys, and the pale light of kerosene lanterns shone through the windows. Only a thin strip of sand separated the cabins from the water, and in the fierce gales of winter, sometimes the tide crept almost to their doors.

They were small, two-room houses with hard clay floors, and the wonder of it was that so many lives could be contained within their walls. Yet some cabins housed as many as thirteen or fourteen souls. Intimacy was inescapable, and the bonds formed were lifelong. If a brother or sister died, or a mother or father, part of you yourself died, as they were extensions of you. They lived at your fingertips. Their hungers were your hungers, and their sorrows were yours, as their joys were, too. To be separated from them provoked a sadness beyond telling.

Yet Nora knew that she would have to leave her beloved mother and father, and it was doubtful that she would ever see them again, as the ocean voyage was long and costly. On the occasion of leaving, families did not restrict their emotions to mere farewells, but instead held wakes. American wakes, they were called, as children were sent into the unknown, never to return. It was very much like death itself.

At the door to the Cassidy's cabin, Nora knocked, and as the door was opened by Thomas's mother, she stooped her head to enter.

"God bless everyone who do live in this house," she said.

"You are out late, Nora."

"I *am*. It's John Mary I'm after coming to see."

Thomas's mother drew up a stool close to the hearth. "Himself is mending his nets. Sit you down, Nora. Have you had your tea?"

"I *have*, thank you." Nora was almost ashamed of the rich leftovers she'd had in the Wingfield's kitchen, knowing that the Cassidys had to make do with potatoes and tea.

The woman went to fetch her husband through the half-door at the rear of the cabin. As Nora waited, she looked up at the smoky rafters, where three sides of bacon were curing. Except for the stools, a few chairs, and a large cupboard, the room contained no furniture. A curtain at one end concealed the bunk where John Mary slept with his wife, and the boys slept in the loft next to the warm chimney. The room was aromatic with peat smoke, locked in by the thatched roof.

John Mary Cassidy bent nearly in two to enter the low door, then stood beside Nora. He was a giant. Six feet one, Thomas said, and Thomas was only an inch shorter.

"Bedad, it's you, Nora."

At once, Nora stood. "I have news." Without further

preamble, she repeated what Redmond McCarthy had overheard.

Thoughtfully, John Mary considered it. Eamon now looked through the half-door.

"She do be saying Sir Richard will convey his suspicions to Dublin Castle," John Mary whispered.

"Sir Richard will do that, will he?" Eamon asked. "The man will have to have a hearty voice, I'd say."

"But the telephone!" Nora protested.

He smiled. "What telephone, Nora? The 'little people' will be up early in the morning, I'm thinking, to dance on the wires."

Even Ireland's leprechauns, the magical fairies, would serve the cause of freedom.

In the low-ceilinged pub on Poolbeg Street, Harry stared into his empty glass as John Ormond snapped his fingers and shouted at the barmaid, "More porter, please, and be quick about it, my good woman. We have had a nasty shock."

Not one, but a brace of them. Stumbling onto Desmond McAuliffe's small arsenal would have been shock enough for one evening, but Harry had also learned from Mr. Yeats's housekeeper in Merrion Square that the great man was out of town and not due back until the following day. Harry had made an appointment to see him shortly before noon.

"He's rooting around the bogs of Sligo for rhymes, I'd say," Ormond declared.

"He doesn't rhyme if he can help it," Harry observed. He would be unable to ask him to intercede on Patrick Cassidy's behalf for at least another day. And in the meantime, Desmond McAuliffe was about to do something mad that would bring shame to Trinity College. Perhaps—as Ormond has suggested a minute ago—he and his friend were planning to shoot off a nipple or two from Queen Victoria's statue, or a hand or a foot from Lord Nelson's. It would not be the first time such acts had been attempted.

"Of course, Desmond is a Viking," Ormond added by way of explanation, "so what can one expect?"

"A Viking?"

"His family dates from the ninth century, and they've been creating havoc ever since." McAuliffe's name, he said, derived from "son of Olaf."

"Whatever his name is, it's damnable if he and that shop girl friend of his take pot shots at the local statuary."

"What else could they be up to?" Ormond demanded. "Besides, I heard him grousing about Lord Nelson's pillar not too long ago. He said it was out of proportion and interfered with the vista along Sackville Street. Not that there is much of a vista to be interfered with." He held up his foaming glass of porter. "Cheers, Harry."

Harry gulped his drink.

"They're such asses, people like McAuliffe," Ormond said. "What good will it do poor old Ireland to blow off Victoria's nose or sever Lord Nelson's penis once again? This is the only city in the world, Harry, where the people's wrath is regularly inflicted on harmless marble."

It *was* peculiar, Harry conceded. Nowhere else did people complain as much, yet do so little about it. His father's explanation, of course, was that the Irish were too simpleminded to protest. Harry disagreed. To him, they were the kindest, most civil people in the world. They lacked the ingrown evil and inherited lust for blood that characterized the Prussians. And, unlike the British, they had no desire to be masters, even of themselves.

"I'll say this for the damned savages," Ormond continued. "There is no better place to own land, as the people are too meek ever to attempt to seize it. How many acres do you have down there in Cork, Harry?"

How much land did the Wingfields possess? It took a moment's accounting. "Three thousand or so, I expect."

"And does your governor have armed soldiers protecting it?"

"Not a one."

"The people are content with just a few yards of soil for themselves. That's all they want. They plant their spuds, as they call them. They consume their spuds. They procreate once a year. They're on their knees in church every Sunday. It's all they need to be happy. They're weak

40

and characterless people, Harry. We should consider ourselves lucky that they are."

Ormond's family owned huge estates in Kilkenny, and his father had a reputation for being a ruthlessly competent landlord. If his tenants did not work the land to his satisfaction, they were put off it. Ormond himself had boasted that his family had done more to increase the populations of Boston and New York than any other family in Ireland.

"The war is bound to thin them out a bit," Ormond now said. "I heard today that they'll soon be conscripting here in Ireland."

Harry looked up in alarm. "Who told you that?"

"I learned from someone who dined recently at the Castle."

Harry shook his head. "They'll never fight for England."

"We shall give them no alternative. My God, Harry, hundreds and hundreds of Britain's finest are being killed every day in Flanders."

"It's Britain's war, not Ireland's."

Ormond looked offended. "Your logic leaves something to be desired. They are British subjects, Harry. They will serve the King as they have in the past."

Suddenly the porter in Harry's glass was bitter. "I wouldn't count on it, Ormond. Not this time."

"And on what do you base your conclusion?"

Harry couldn't say. It was a feeling he had. Now, the more he remembered it, he was sure that the temper of the people had changed within the last few months. Something was in the air.

"I think we have pushed them too far," he now said to Ormond.

"Nonsense," Ormond replied. "Some people are born to be slaves."

Harry's senses tingled from the porter, but he distinctly heard his classmate order another round. "I really shouldn't. I've been drinking far too much lately. It's bad for the liver, you know. Besides, I was thinking of going to the kips tonight."

"There's a new girl on Tyrone Street. From Liverpool,

I gather." Ormond leaned over and whispered, "They say she does it French-style, Harry."

Harry's knees almost buckled. If is was true, it was very alarming. Most of the girls were not the least bit innovative. "Molly is the one I generally see," he said sheepishly.

"Ah, yes, Molly. She's the one with the remarkable cunt, isn't she? Put a half crown on the floor and she'll sit over it and pick it up, neat as a whistle."

Harry had not been aware of her talent, but he was looking forward to testing it. Nervously, he sipped from his glass. "You must promise to see me home, Ormond. You know how I am when I've had too much to drink."

"It happens to the best of us."

"Just don't let me do anything outrageous. I have to be in good form when I see Mr. Yeats tomorrow."

A man really did need to get drunk now and then. It relaxed him most wonderfully. The world became more interesting, too. Even Ormond, who was sometimes an ass, was quite attractive when he was drunk. Better still, when Harry was drunk.

God, whatever would become of him? Himself, he meant. Another two months at university, then marriage to Lucy Caverly. After that, what? They would settle down and become elderly. They would join the West Carberry Hunt and ride to the hounds. They would go to London once a year and to Paris every second or third. From time to time, Harry would sneak away to Dublin in order to visit the girls of Tyrone Street.

As fond as he was of Lucy Caverly, he wished there were more to life than that. Nothing exciting ever happened to him, and perhaps nothing ever would.

After only a few hours' sleep in the shelter of a glen, Thomas Cassidy and his brother approached Tralee just as day was breaking. As luck would have it, it was market day, so their appearance in town was not likely to alarm the authorities. The road was crowded with horse-drawn carts.

They stopped a farmer who was driving two young calves with a stick, and asked for directions. "We are in the market for bonhams," Thomas said, "and we're after hearing that you have among you a man named Stack, who raises them."

"That he do," the farmer replied. "He will take a fair price for a piglet, too, I warn you."

"We are particularly interested in those that are German-born. They are very hearty, we've been told."

The farmer assayed them carefully. "Ah, yes, it's that Stack you'd be wanting. Come with me and I'll show you where he may be found."

Yet the minute Thomas and Lambi rode into his farmyard and told him who they were, he scowled.

"So you are Volunteers?" the man called Stack said to them. "Well, you have come too damn early! What is wrong with you men of Cork! Have you minds of stone?"

Breathlessly, Thomas answered, "We learned that the German ship is due today. It is the instructions we were given."

"You have learned incorrectly, you Corkmen. The Kaiser's ship does not arrive till Easter night."

Thomas could not hide his confusion. If the rifles didn't arrive until Easter night, they would be of no value to the Corkmen on Easter Day.

Stack explained it. "The Rising has been postponed."

"Postponed?" Lambi asked incredulously.

"Till Easter Monday. The plotters in Dublin were of the opinion that Sunday would be too soon, as we would be unready. At our request, the Germans have been asked not to deliver our twenty thousand rifles until the night before."

When Thomas spoke, his voice was filled with mockery. "The night *before!* Do you know what that means, man? Cork will have no arms. It's a two-day trip by wagon from here to Cork! *Whose* minds are made of stone, I'm asking you!"

"Be reasonable, man! What would you have us do? Send twenty thousand foreign rifles into those hills three days before they're needed? If even one were lost, the constabulary would be alerted. No, we had to make a choice, and we chose the prudent route. The rifles will remain at sea until the night before the Rising."

Thomas shook his head sadly. "You made a choice,

to be sure, and you sacrificed the Corkmen, who will now be without arms on the day the nation rises."

"It couldn't be helped," Stack said.

Thomas spat on the ground. "And where is Casement himself?"

"They say he do be coming under the sea like the fishes."

"By submarine?"

"By submarine."

The color rose on Lambi's face. "And will he have his Norwegian sailor boy with him, locked between his buttocks?"

Stack's eyes narrowed. "Who the man lies with is no concern of mine. We shall take his rifles no matter what his persuasion in bed."

"A man who dallies with other men should never have been entrusted with such an important mission," Lambi said angrily.

"Stack is right," Thomas replied. "No man can judge another solely on what he does in bed. We are all of us two-legged beasts, Lambi, the minute we pull our trousers down. And if Casement brings happiness to his Norwegian lad, and the Norwegian to Casement, I have no quarrel with the manner by which it is obtained." He waited. "It isn't that. There's no harm there. The harm is that we are not to rise till Easter Monday."

He looked across the fields at the gold-and-lavender clouds scudding past the morning sun. "We were to rise on the day Christ did. It was to have been our resurrection, as it was his. And now we have thrown it away."

"We shall still succeed," Stack replied.

"I hope so. For your sake and for mine, as well as Ireland's."

In the end, the Kerryman could not persuade them to stay. The rifles would arrive too late to be carried to Cork in time for the Rising, and it was unthinkable for Thomas and Lambi to be away from their father and their brothers on that day.

"And what will ye fight with?" Stack asked.

"With pitchforks and spades and fists," Lambi answered, "as we have nothing else."

6

By the time he returned to Doonmara House in mid-morning, Sir Richard Wingfield was in a rage. He had wasted half the day, traveling first to Skibbereen, then to Clonakilty, only to find that the telephone lines were down.

It was so like the damn Irish. They could do nothing right. If they were asked to build a wall, it would lean; to tile a roof, it would leak; to lay a road, it would flood. It was folly, in the first place, ever to have expected that they could operate a telephone system whose wires did not blow down at every second gust of wind.

To make matters worse, the loutish clerk at the railroad station in Clonakilty could not even find a decent piece of paper on which Sir Richard could scribble a hasty note to the Lord Lieutenant that could be sent to Dublin on the next train. The only sheet of paper in the place had been used as a coaster for a teacup, but Sir Richard considered his message to be sufficiently important for the mark to be overlooked. He advised the government that a youth had been apprehended transporting gunpowder in West Cork and perhaps it was a part of some greater plot against the Crown.

Privately, Sir Richard felt that the Irish could no more stage a rebellion than they could build a wall, and that Lord Monteagle's fears were exaggerated. Still, he had done his duty; no one could say that he had lacked vigilance. The letter was now on its way to Dublin, or at least he hoped that it was, though he knew for a fact that the train service was sometimes even more deplorable than the telephone system.

He had promised his brother-in-law, Lord Monteagle,

a day's shooting, but it was almost eleven when they left the house, dressed in Wellingtons and hunting jackets, rifles on their shoulders. They made their way across the park surrounding the house and into the fields, following two red setters. It was late in the year for pheasant or partridge, but they might find quail or a wild goose or two.

As they turned into the field, they saw a young servant girl arrange tea towels on the limbs of a primrose bush for them to dry.

"Good morning," Sir Richard said, unable to remember the girl's name.

"Good morning, my lord," Nora answered, then quickly retreated toward the kitchen door.

"I wouldn't mind a piece of that," Monteagle said after she had gone.

"They need cleaning up, some of them."

"Are they"—Monteagle searched for the word—"accommodating?"

"Some of 'em. We had a young one about a year ago —can't remember her name—she used to let me visit her in her room from time to time. I gave her a couple of shillings for her trouble, as she was saving boat fare to Australia. After she left, I developed a fearful rash. Thought it was the clap, you know, but it must have been something I ate, as it soon disappeared."

His brother-in-law nodded his head sympathetically. "One has to be careful."

"I'm getting to be too old for much of that."

"Nonsense! The more you do it, the longer you'll preserve the capacity. It's like a rusty nut and bolt. If you don't turn it from time to time, you'll never get it open again."

"Hadn't looked at it that way."

Ahead of them, the two setters had stopped and were now frozen in the pointing position. From within a clump of gorse came the distinctive sound of a bird.

"Corncrake," Sir Richard said. "Bad luck to shoot them, the natives say."

"They do, do they? If that's the case, I'll defer to their superstitions."

46

After Sir Richard called off the dogs, they continued through the stubbly furze. It was a glorious morning. The air was effervescent, the sun shone through the hurrying clouds, and it was neither hot nor cold. A finer day for shooting could not be imagined.

From where he stood against the wall of his cell, Patrick Cassidy considered the inadequacies of Irish jails. His back ached from the wooden bed. His neck and hands were spotty from bites that had persisted until, on his knees, he had found and squashed four fleas. He felt dirty, cold, and damp. The stone walls were mossy, and he now saw that a waterline—from where the River Ilen had flooded in the past—reached almost six feet above the floor.

Bedad, he said to himself, if a hard rain fell between now and Easter Sunday, sure and he would be drowned! For like all Irish fishermen who spent most of their lives on water, he didn't know how to swim. After all, as he had explained to Lucy Caverly, if God deserted an Irish fisherman in a stormy sea, it was damned unlikely that He would take the trouble to help him to shore, no matter how much thrashing he did with his arms and legs.

In the distance, he heard shuffling footsteps approach, and in a minute a constable appeared at the door. Behind him was Patrick's younger brother, Eamon.

Impatiently, the constable declared, "He says he is to talk to you about agricultural matters, and you are to limit yourself to that." He moved to one side of the hall. "I'll keep me ears open, so youse will have no chance to try something cagey or cute. You've got three minutes."

Eyes wide, Eamon stood before him, and Patrick could hear him swallow, then see his Adam's apple work. "We are having trouble with the ducklings," he whispered.

"Talk louder so that I can hear!" the constable commanded. "What ducklings can bring you all the way to Skibbereen just for a chat with this felon?"

"It's the Muscovy ducklings, sir," Eamon said to the man. "Them's we ordered to replace the ones the fox ate."

The constable harumphed. "The trouble with ducks in

this damn country is that if you turn your backs, the fox will have them."

"Sure and it's the truth," Patrick declared easefully to help his brother. "What news of the ducklings, Eamon?"

"They have miscarried. They will not arrive, so our nest will go unused."

Patrick's heart beat wildly. "But we were to have them by Sunday."

"They say we will have no need for them till Monday."

"The nest will be empty till Monday?" His eyes indicated disbelief.

Eamon nodded his head. "It's what I'm saying, Patrick." He waited, then added, "So we have canceled the order from Kerry."

There would be no rifles in Cork for the Rising, which would not take place until Monday. Patrick comprehended that much. But to cancel the order? What did he mean by that?

"John Mary says I am to tell you that we will make the best of it. Our nest will have some other use."

It was insane! Patrick couldn't permit them. They were planning to do something by themselves, quite apart from anything the Volunteers did in the rest of Ireland. And without arms. It was insane!

"No," Patrick said sternly. "The fox will only get them."

Eamon inhaled a lungful of air, then let it escape. "John Mary says we are to trap the fox."

Almost inaudibly, Patrick asked, "When?"

"On Christ's Day, this Sunday."

From across the hall, the constable folded his newspaper and looked toward the cell, his face puzzled.

Quickly, Patrick asked, "And how is the cow?"

"The cow is keeping good."

"And how are the pigs?"

Before Eamon had an opportunity to reply, the constable walked toward the two of them. When he spoke, it was in the whine of an old lady. "And-how-is-the-birds? And-how-is-the-cats? And-how-is-the-bumblebees? Come along with me now. I have no time for the likes of you."

48

He took Eamon by the arm and began to lead him down the hall.

Eamon yelled behind him, "John Mary says that we shall be here on Sunday with an Easter feed for you."

Patrick answered him, "Tell him I shall have a ready appetite."

So John Mary and his sons were going to remove him from the jail before he was escorted to the station.

It would be perilous; no doubt about it. If they carried if off and if the Rising succeeded, they would have to hide and be isolated, without help, for twenty-four hours.

And if the Rising failed . . .

For the very first time, Patrick acknowledged that there was such a possibility.

"Open your mouth. That's a dear," a voice cooed next to Harry's head. "I've got a lovely little sausage for you, 'arry."

His mouth felt as if every tooth in it had been yanked. It was unthinkably sour as well. Only minutes before, when he woke up, he had found himself struggling for breath, and the naked girl who just spoke to him had hurried him down the hall to the jacks, where he emptied his stomach.

He studied the girl who was holding the sausage. Her pendulous breasts hung onto his bare chest.

"Don't you remember me, luv? It's Bridgit."

Harry's memory was stirred. He recalled that before he had passed out they had made love and she had been very robust and imaginative.

"You said you're from Liverpool, didn't you?" he asked.

"You see? You remember. Now open your mouth, 'arry. You'll feel much better once you have a wee bit of sausage inside you."

She rubbed the sausage sensually over his lips until they opened, and he took first one tiny bite, then another.

"I don't even know where I am," he said when he had finished.

She smiled, then whispered, "You're not in Stillorgan." With one hand she reached down and slowly began to knead him between the legs. Involuntarily, he became alive again.

"No, I shouldn't think I would be."

Effortlessly, she moved her hand until it contained his testicles. "You're not in Ballsbridge, either."

"It doesn't seem that I could be."

Suddenly her head was sliding down his bare chest and belly. "And you're nowhere *near* Bullock Harbor." Her mouth enclosed a single gonad, as if it were a grape.

Harry didn't know if he should shriek or sigh. "I suppose I must be on Tyrone Street," he said at last.

She released him, then rested her chin in the wiry hair at his groin and looked up at his face. "Last night, you told me you'd never forget me, 'arry. It's how you were saying you would make me a duchess."

"I must have been very drunk."

"Flaming drunk—both you and your friend who was with Molly."

Ormond! Of course, Harry had been at Mulligan's on Poolbeg Street with Ormond until someone behind the bar had said, "Time, gentlemen." Then they were on the street. He had a vague recollection of having been placed in a taxi and taken somewhere.

"Is my friend still here?"

"He left. He said your health was too fragile for you to be moved, but he'll come back for you as soon as he can locate a pair of trousers."

Trousers? Harry squinted until he made out what little furniture there was in the room. On a chair he saw his shirt and his suit coat, and on the floor his drawers, his socks, and his shoes.

"Where are my trousers?" he asked with apprehension.

"He borrowed them, your friend did. You see, 'arry, Molly was doing her trick for him, and it's how she was saying he owed her another half crown, and when he refused, she seized his bloody trousers and threw them in the jacks."

"The *privy?*"

"That she did, 'arry."

"And I am to stay here until he returns?"

"I have nothing to offer you but a frock."

"But I am to see Mr. Yeats this morning!"

In despair, he struck his head with the palm of his hand. He had come to Dublin to persuade Mr. Yeats to intercede on Patrick Cassidy's behalf, and all he had succeeded in doing was getting drunk, spending the night in the kips, and losing both his money and his trousers, for Ormond had used the last of Harry's money to convert to half crowns for Molly to pick up. It was his allowance for the rest of the term, meant to last him all of April and May. Unless he could borrow from someone, he could not even afford the train fare back to Cork.

With resolution, he turned to Bridgit. "I need a pair of trousers at once. I'll make it worth your while if you can furnish me with them."

Bridgit pondered the assignment. For a reason that was self-explanatory, most of the tenants in the house were girls. Yet there was, she seemed to recall, a gentleman on the first floor. He was in the building trades.

"A plas-therer," she said. "I've done him a favor or two, 'arry," she added inscrutably. "P'raps he would let me have the use of his trousers."

She scurried from the bed, removed a flannel robe from the bedpost and wrapped it around her, then rushed out of the room in her bare feet, leaving the door open. Harry covered his nakedness with a pillow, as he could find no blanket. In a minute or two, she had returned, holding a pair of white-spotted navy-blue trousers.

"It's 'is spare, 'e says. Will they do, do you think, luv? He needs 'em back by tomorrow."

As he dressed, he thanked her for everything. For the evening, for the breakfast, and for the trousers. If it were humanly possible, he would be glad to make her a duchess, but it was beyond his powers.

At the door, she said, "It's all right, luv. You're a darlin' man just the way you are."

Harry was buoyed by the information.

He made an exotic figure as he sprinted down Sackville Street to Bachelor's Walk, then over the bridge to West-moreland Street. Beneath his London-tailored suit coat

51

and elegant cravat, his spotted trousers attracted a good deal of attention.

He was breathless by the time he reached the College Green, but ran up the stairs to his room and flung open the door. Desmond McAuliffe was seated at the desk, reading.

"Oh, it's you, Desmond. I'm in a most awful rush."

McAuliffe turned to watch Harry drop his trousers to the floor and reach into a wardrobe for a substitute.

"You *are* in a hurry," McAuliffe said, returning to his book.

"I'm to see Mr. Yeats, and if I'm late, I shall never forgive myself."

He found a pair of gray trousers that nearly matched his suit coat, then attempted to put them on without removing his shoes. "Damn!" he said, struggling to the edge of his bed. He sat down, pulled off his shoes, then drew his trousers on.

"I say, were those rifles we saw last night, or did we imagine them?"

Desmond stopped reading and raised his head, but did not turn to face Harry. "They were for a parade."

"A parade?"

"Yes. This Sunday, but it's been canceled."

Harry secured the buttons of his fly, then arranged his braces. "I'll tell you one thing, Desmond. This city could certainly use a parade over Easter. Dublin can be deadly on holidays."

Desmond smiled. "Those were our views too, Harry."

When the Cassidy brothers returned to their home in West Cork, tired from the long journey through the mountains, what they learned from John Mary was far more catastrophic than what they told him.

"Cork will have no rifles for the Rising," Thomas said dejectedly the minute he slid down from his saddle.

"She will have no less than Kerry," his father replied. "The British have intercepted the ship, and even now it's on its way to Queenstown."

The news had just come from Baltimore Harbor, whose lighthouse was equipped with a radio.

"Do they know yet in Dublin?" Lambi asked anxiously.

John Mary shook his head. The Corkmen had learned only because they fished near the lighthouse and were comrades of the men stationed there. The radio report indicated merely that an enemy ship had been intercepted in British waters; yet the Cork fishermen knew at once that it was the *Aud*, carrying their rifles.

"Then that's it," Thomas said in disgust. "We have done all mortal man can do, but luck is against us."

It was fifteen-year-old Eamon who spoke up. "And what of Patrick?"

"We will free him. And when we do that, we will be wanted men," John Mary explained. "So let us finish what we have begun. Let Kerry sleep if it wishes, and unarmed Cork as well. But *we* shall rise."

They looked at him, dumbfounded. How and against whom? Thomas at last wanted to know.

"Our landlords," Eamon replied manfully.

They would rise not against the King nor against British soldiers, who were abstract and unknown, but against the Wingfields, whose every rage and cruelty they had felt for almost three centuries. The Cassidys had been slaves kept alive at the Wingfields' pleasure, dying when they became inconveniences. They had scratched the earth until their fingers bled to extract another shilling's rent, for fear of being driven off the land. They had crawled and begged for mercy when they were starving and destitute, and been answered with an increase of rent and the walls of their cottages knocked down if it couldn't be paid.

"And what are we to use against them?" Thomas asked breathlessly.

"The little that God has given us."

In his hand, John Mary unfurled a horsewhip and snapped it sharply against a wall.

7

While the others sat at the crude table in the cabin and had their tea, Thomas saddled a fresh horse and set off down the coast road to Doonmara House. He had promised Nora to see her the minute he returned, he told his father, and he must keep his pledge.

Nora would have to be warned of what was about to take place, and also of the consequences if the plan were to miscarry. Thomas had with him in a small leather purse the twenty pounds he had saved for the trip to New York; it was his intention to give it to Nora for safekeeping. It was altogether possible that she would have to go to America by herself.

What John Mary proposed was futile and perhaps suicidal, Thomas thought. A blood lust. His father felt compelled to thrash the Cassidys' centuries-old tormentor. The Wingfields would be fools if they didn't reply with rifles. At least Thomas could attempt to remove what rifles were at Doonmara House. Otherwise, John Mary's gesture to correct ancient outrages might very well result in new ones, even more horrible.

The sky was luminous and iridescent, like the polished shell of an oyster. Over his head, huge clouds flew at dizzying speed, blocking the sun; yet behind them it shone as it did on the day of creation, throwing off a clear and perfect light, more blinding than if it were cloudless. Now and then, shadows raced across the blue waters of the bay joining the green islands, and in the distance Mount Gabriel rose serenely into the air.

Travelers with jaded eyes had said that Ireland was God's most favored land, yet it could not even afford to keep its children from birth to death. It was wrong, to be sure. It was an offense against reason and nature.

Unlike Patrick, who looked forward to America and a new life there, Thomas would as soon remain in Ireland; yet because he and his brother were the ablest of the Cassidys, they had been chosen to go. To stay in Cork would mean that he would be unable to marry Nora until her father died or John Mary did, perhaps twenty or thirty years from now, as there would be no place for them to set up housekeeping. Besides, the money he would send from New York was sorely needed.

Yet he worried about the kind of family he would raise in America. Cities sometimes corrupted people, he knew, and it was said about the Irish that many became gross, indolent, and drunken in their New York and Boston tenements. They filled the jails because of their disorderly conduct, and they became public charges. To Thomas it was a puzzlement that people who, though desperately poor, remained noble in their homeland, became savage and base in the cities of the New World. They did not carry it with them, he was certain.

If God only looked after him for the next few days and kept him out of an English jail, within the month Thomas would proceed to New York with Nora and Patrick, where he hoped to persuade them to leave the city as soon as they were able. He did not want children of his to grow to manhood in a place where they never saw the sky. In New York, he had been told, there were tenement windows that looked out on brick walls only inches away. It would shrivel a man's heart to live in such a place.

Ahead of him on the road, he saw the Wingfields' Daimler approaching. He pulled his horse to one side, close to the hedge. Sir Richard was driving, and next to him sat the English lord; in the back seat were Lady Prudence and the English lady. Respectfully, Thomas removed his cap until the car had driven by. Lady Prudence smiled, but the others did not appear to see him.

Well, he was grateful that they were going for a spin. It would simplify his task. He hurried the horse to a gallop so that he could conclude his work before they returned. In time, he reached the high wall that enclosed the park around Doonmara House, then the ornate wrought-iron gate, which was open. He made his way up the long avenue to the rear of the house, tethered the horse, then stood at the kitchen door and lifted its knocker.

The cook Hannah answered, and behind her Thomas could see Nora standing at a table, her hands floury, laying out small loaves of bread in pans.

"May I have a word with Miss Nora?" he asked Hannah.

"Sure and you can have more than one."

Hannah retreated to the other end of the kitchen, where the huge black woodstoves were located, and as she did, Thomas stepped up to Nora.

"Nora, sit ye down. We must talk."

As quickly as he could, he explained why he had come and what had taken him to Kerry. She listened in disbelief. When he asked for her help in removing the guns from the house, she covered her mouth with both hands in horror.

"I have no choice," he said. "John Mary has waited too long for this, and he will complete the task with or without me. I have come for the rifles so that there will be no bloodshed."

Momentarily, Nora was speechless. "But why you, Thomas? Why your family? Why not other men?"

"Because Patrick is in jail and we must prevent his going to Dublin. We will be hunted men when we do that, so John Mary says we are to give them good reason to hunt us."

It was an effort for her to speak. "And will you hurt people?"

"So help me God, we won't." He waited, then added, "Except for Sir Richard."

"You will kill him?"

He shook his head. "We will whip him."

Nora gasped at the enormity of the undertaking. If the Rising on Monday did not succeed, Thomas would be jailed.

"And what will become of *me*, Thomas?"

He handed her the small purse and told her what it contained. If he were captured, she was to go to America by herself and he and Patrick would join her later.

Something like fear crossed her face, and her lips trembled. She could not speak for the emotion she felt.

"What is it, Noreen? Don't you worry. It will work out. Even if everything fails, no jail will hold me for more than a year, I promise ye."

How could she find the words? To tell him that she was carrying his child would only make it harder for him. "What your father is doing, Tom—will it fill the bellies of the starving dead? Will it lift them from their graves?"

He admitted that it would accomplish no such thing. Yet it was a grievance that had to be settled.

She brushed her eyes with her hands and left a floury smudge on her cheeks. In resignation, she said, "Sir Richard is after keeping his guns in the gunroom, and I have no key."

"Who would have it, then?"

"Redmond McCarthy."

Thomas's eyes narrowed. "Is he trustworthy?"

"He's a patriot, but likes his port wine and brandy too much, Thomas, to give them up. He's a weak man. If he has to choose between you and the Wingfields, you would be the loser."

"And is there no way to get the keys?"

She covered his hand with her own, drawing courage from its warmth. "I shall try," she said, then hurried from the kitchen.

Whether Hannah had overheard them, Thomas couldn't say. She looked at him with disapproval, but said nothing, then turned away.

On the wide staircase, Nora held up the edges of her long skirt so that she would not trip in her haste. In the distance, she heard several hall clocks begin to toll the hour, and she hoped that they would not wake Redmond, who napped at this time of day. He had served table for the midday meal, and it was hard for him not to help himself to generous portions of wine and brandy as he did. He would rest for two hours before serving tea.

As Nora opened the door to his small room on the

third floor, she heard his light snoring. He had removed his jacket and shirt and lay on the bed in his flannel underwear, his trousers, and his shoes. His ring of keys was on the dresser. She crept across the creaky floor and picked it up, holding the keys together lest they make a sound. Slowly she backed out of the room, looking at his sleeping face as she did, then closed the door after her.

She ran down the halls to the staircase, the keys hidden in a fold of her dress. Thomas was waiting inside the kitchen door.

"Come with me," she said. "I shall show you where they are kept."

The gunroom smelled of oil and cartridges. As they entered, a red setter rose to meet them.

"It's only Finnbarr," Nora said. "He won't harm you."

The guns were secured in a long walnut cabinet at one side of the room, and Thomas now began to try the keys. With the fifth try, he met with success. He turned the lock and drew open the doors.

Five rifles lay in the racks. Thomas lifted them out, one by one, and placed them on a table, then removed his belt and tied it firmly around them so that they would be easier to carry. At the bottom of the guncase were several half-empty boxes of shells.

"Redmond McCarthy was after saying he must go to town to buy shells, as Sir Richard and Lord Monteagle have been hunting almost every day."

Thomas scooped up what he could find and filled his pockets, then relocked the doors.

He turned to Nora and held her in his arms.

"I am afraid for you, Thomas," she said.

"Aye. And I am for myself."

"I wish this terrible thing would not have to be done, but it is your decision, not mine."

"Nor mine, either," he answered sadly, "but it must be done." He embraced her, then again, unwilling to leave her.

At last he broke away and picked up his awkward bundle. He would not use the coast road, he told her, as he might run into the Wingfields. Instead, he would travel through the glen and the woods. "And I shall be back on Sunday."

"They are having people in. We are setting a large table."

He nodded. "Then you may lay extra places for us as well."

After he had gone, Nora climbed the staircase to the third floor and replaced the keys on the bureau in Redmond McCarthy's room. Not until she had left the room and was in the hall again did she feel giddy and faint. She leaned against the wall for support.

If Thomas had removed the guns from Doonmara House to prevent bloodshed, she asked herself, why, then, had he taken the shells?

Harry stopped at a pub on Duke Street to collect his thoughts. He would much prefer to make his plea in stirring Gaelic, but he was sure that he didn't have adequate Irish, as the native speakers put it, to rouse anyone, least of all Mr. Yeats. English would have to do.

As he sipped his whiskey at Bailey's, he withdrew a pencil and sheet of paper from his pocket and began to scribble his thoughts. More causes had been lost by bad prose than through lack of supporters, he felt, and he would have to be careful with the words he chose. He was composing an advert for the *Irish Independent,* which could be signed by the great man and by other members of the Dublin intelligentsia. He wrote a headline: IS THIS ONE MORE ATTEMPT TO DESTROY THE GAELIC LEAGUE?

Very slowly, he began to argue Patrick Cassidy's case. The young man had been singled out for persecution by the constabulary, he wrote, only because he was a member of the league and championed the old language and customs. If Patrick Cassidy's sentence were permitted to go unopposed, the Gaelic League itself would soon be threatened.

He reread it. It wasn't memorable, but it wasn't bad for improvisation, and the use of an advert had occurred to him just minutes before. It seemed to him that Mr.

Yeats was more likely to support the cause if his duties could be kept to a minimum. A simple signature would do the trick; a flourish of a pen and—presto!—it was over. As for financing the endeavor, Harry would have to persuade the people at the *Independent* to accept his credit. As soon as he returned to Cork, he would dispatch money by the next post, provided that Sir Richard renewed his allowance.

His parents, he remembered, were planning to have the local gentry in for a dinner party on Easter Sunday. What better time to announce his engagement to Lucy! It might even soften his father's heart. Yes, of course, it would be a perfect time. All their friends would be there to hear the news.

Harry was ebullient by the time he left the pub and made his way to Grafton Street. He had just begun to practice his first words to Mr. Yeats—"I have long been an admirer of yours, sir"—when he saw a young girl step off the curb, then cross Duke Street and continue on Grafton. Harry dashed along the sidewalk until he had caught up.

"I say, Miss O'Neill," he began, "do you remember me? You're Desmond McAuliffe's friend."

She studied him coolly. "I'm dreadfully sorry, but you've apparently mistaken me for someone else." She turned toward the avenue, then hurried in and out of the horse-drawn carriages and motorcars to the other side of the street.

It was most peculiar. Harry was prepared to swear that it was Miss O'Neill. He held up a hand as he walked in front of traffic to the opposite sidewalk, then ran until he caught up with her once again. He took her by the crook of the arm.

"I'm *not* mistaken," he said to her.

She measured him glacially. "You're such a fool," she said, then broke away.

Harry felt too annihilated to give chase. He watched her disappear in the crowd. What an incredibly unkind thing to say about someone she scarcely knew. It was really very shabby. He intended to bring it to Desmond's attention.

You're such a fool, she had said.

Why was he a fool? What had she meant? Was there something that had escaped his attention? A connection?

Like Harry, Desmond was a member of the Gaelic League and had attended meetings at the college until three or four months ago, when he had explained that he was far too busy with other matters and couldn't be bothered. Desmond was an odd duck. Until recently, his interests had been directed toward Celtic poetry and art. Now he had Mausers under his bed, and had remained in Dublin for a parade on Easter Sunday, a parade that had been canceled.

As Harry passed a newspaper kiosk, he picked up a copy of that day's *Independent* and paid for it. Quickly, he leafed through it, not knowing exactly what he was looking for, but convinced that he would recognize it when he saw it. And there it was!

NO PARADES!

Irish Volunteer
Marches
Canceled

April 22, 1916

———

Owing to the very critical position, all orders given to Irish Volunteers for tomorrow, Easter Sunday, are hereby rescinded.

It was the parade Desmond was to have marched in! At some point within the last year, he had become a member of the Volunteers without telling Harry. Miss O'Neill must also be a member. As was Patrick Cassidy! Everything was now perfectly clear. There was about to be an insurrection, by God, and Harry had almost been caught napping.

It was past time for a signature on a petition. He needed to do something himself.

In great haste, he rushed across Nassau Street and was very nearly knocked down by a tram. He pushed past a porter emerging from the door of his residence hall and leaped up the stairs. He threw open the door to his room.

Desmond stood next to Kitty O'Neill.

"Now I understand!" he heard himself say. "And I have come to join you."

8

Easter dawned gray and showery.

In West Cork, fog blew off the sea and settled over the valleys and the glens, covering the golden gorse and the blooming hedgerows. Rain pelted against the roads and into foaming gutters.

On the coast road, four horsemen could be seen traveling toward town, heads bent into their jackets. At Kilcoe, they passed the small Church of Ireland chapel where, two hours later, the local Protestants—the Wingfields, the Townsends, and the Caverlys—would arrive in their elegant motorcars and carriages for the holiday service.

The horsemen continued until they reached the Catholic church on the windy and exposed hill, and as they passed, each rider made the sign of the cross from forehead to breast. They hurried by without going in. Before they left their cottage, they had knelt in prayer, as John Mary did not want to alarm Father Daley at the church by arriving so early on this Easter. He would at once suspect the cause and attempt to prevent them, saying, as he had before, that Christian life was one of acceptance, not defiance.

Few people were on the road to Skibbereen. For the natives, Sunday was a day of minimum work—the milking of cows and the feeding of animals—and a great deal of devotion. On a fine day, they would set off early to church in order to gossip on the steps with neighbors they saw only on Sundays. Following the service, if the weather held, the men would return home for their meal, then meet at the crossroads for bowling. They would pitch an iron ball all the way from Kilcoe to Ballydehob and back, sometimes making small wagers on who could throw the ball the farthest along the road. Finished, they would adjourn to the pubs and tell tales.

But John Mary knew that today would be different. Even if the rain stopped and the sun burst through the clouds, there would be no bowling in West Cork this Easter Sunday.

Because it was a holiday, there would be but one guard on duty at the jail, and he would not be relieved until evening. By that time, the Cassidys agreed, the constabulary would have more things to worry about than the disappearance of a prisoner, and it would be Monday, at the soonest, before the hunt would begin. And by then, please God, Dublin would be in the hands of its citizens and the British routed from the Castle.

Like others in Ireland, the Cassidys had been perplexed by the events of the last few days. The notice in the *Independent* canceling the day's parade had not escaped their attention; yet they had expected that. What worried and vexed John Mary and his sons was that there seemed to be no alternate plans. John Mary was afraid that the Dubliners' action would be slapdash and ineffective.

The news he was bringing to his son Patrick was not auspicious. The *Aud* had been scuttled in Queenstown Harbor, and its rifles consigned to the sea. Yet that loss could be borne, the Cassidys concluded, because the British would not be aware of the cargo until they made an effort to recover it. Far worse than that was the news that Casement had been captured.

The notice in Saturday's *Independent*, published in Dublin, read merely that a stranger had been apprehended by the constabulary in Kerry near Tralee, and that his presence there was thought to be suspicious. Late Saturday night, John Mary had learned that at least one of Casement's companions who had come with him from Germany by submarine had also been captured.

"Aye," John Mary had said when he heard, "and someone will talk to save his skin."

In Ireland it was said that a single patriot could be lost to the enemy and the cause would not necessarily suffer.

But if two or three were captured, it was almost inevitable that one would betray the others. The fatal weakness was thought to be peculiarly Irish and as ineradicable as the lust for drink to sweeten their sorrows.

So that as John Mary and his sons rode into Skibbereen on Easter morning, it was with the knowledge that perhaps the British had already learned what the Volunteers hoped to accomplish the following day in Dublin. And if the British were prepared, it was doubtful that the Rising could succeed.

Yet the Cassidys did not turn back.

In the town, the rain-washed streets were deserted and the shop windows shuttered. Early Mass, which would bring the people out of their snug houses, was an hour away, and as a result the Cassidys passed no one as they rode to the jail and tethered their horses.

It was Thomas who pounded on the huge door, his father and brothers on either side of him. In a minute, an unshaven constable appeared, suspenders over his underwear, his eyes pinched from sleep.

"We have come for Patrick Cassidy," John Mary declared.

Before the constable could take issue, Lambi had swooped him up and carried him across the room. He flung him to the floor, where Thomas sat on his chest as Eamon bound him.

"I have a wife and wee ones," the man begged.

"Sure and we would be doing them a service if we murdered you," Thomas replied, "but we have more important things to attend to."

Patrick had been waiting since before sunrise, his heart hammering, his palms wet. When his cell door was unlocked, he flew into his father's arms.

"Now we begin," Patrick said.

"If it please God," John Mary replied.

While Lambi removed the constable's pistol and slipped it inside his belt, Eamon searched the jail for other arms. The rifles were stored in the arsenal, the constable told them, and only his chief had keys. He would not return until Monday morning, as he was spending Easter in Limerick.

"I have a pistol as well," Patrick volunteered, showing them the French gun Lucy Caverly had given him.

"We will have no need of pistols," John Mary said.

Thomas nodded in agreement. It was his hope, too, that arms would not be used. He had hidden the rifles taken from Doonmara House in the loft under the rafters of the cottage. It would not do to be too brazen until news came from Dublin that the Republic had been proclaimed.

They secured the constable in the cellar and left the jail, locking it after them. As they rode from town, Patrick and Thomas shared a saddle.

"What do he be thinking?" Thomas whispered to his brother. "It's daft and filled with peril. We are to rise against the Wingfields."

Patrick knew that he could not contest his father's wishes. "If we have no weapons, what harm can come of it? It's how he wants to settle an old grudge, Thomas."

"And what if the lads in Dublin disappoint us and we find we're all alone?"

"We shall manage somehow. At least no one will say that we're cowards."

Thomas was clearly apprehensive. "Brave fools will not help old Ireland, Pat. Nor dead ones, either."

They rode in silence along the River Ilen, each deep in thought. For Patrick, there could be no solution in Ireland until the stolen land had been returned to its rightful owners. The hated landlords would have to feel the people's wrath. In that respect, John Mary was right.

"There must be no bullets," Thomas said, "until we learn how the Rising goes in Dublin."

"Aye, Thomas. No bullets."

Thomas waited, then added, "And if I should have bad luck, will you pledge to look after Nora?"

Patrick's eyes glistened. "I pledge," he said.

By the time they mounted the last hill before the fisher village, the fog had risen, the rain had stopped, and a pale sun shone through the gray clouds. At the hill's crest, they saw below them all the men and women of the village, standing in front of their thatched cottages, looking

68

up the road. And as they perceived that Patrick was once again free, a cheer went up, then another and another.

At shortly before noon, the first of the polished motorcars and carriages began to drive through the gates leading to Doonmara House and park in the raked white gravel before its columned portico. Lady Prudence had told her guests that Easter dinner would be served between twelve-thirty and one o'clock, the former if the weather was inclement, the latter if it was fair enough to stroll through the gardens behind the house before sitting down to table.

The Wingfields' gardens were known all over the south of Ireland, and had been since the eighteenth century when they were first laid out. Because of the mild climate, tropical flowers and shrubs grew with the same abandon as they did in Ceylon or Hindustan. Jasmine, bougainvillea, and pineapple trees grew near huge boxwood, ten-foot-high rhododendron, and hundreds of flaming azaleas.

Because the day had turned fine, Lady Wingfield's guests made their way leisurely along the paths through the blooming shrubbery, parasols extended over the heads of the ladies to protect their creamy skin.

They talked of the war in far-off Flanders, of crops and horses, and of recent trips to Dublin and London.

Lucy Caverly walked with Clive Townsend, home from Oxford for the holidays. In June, he said, he would accept a commission in the Royal Grenadiers, and he hoped to be sent to France shortly afterward. He asked if Harry would soon be enlisting.

"I quite doubt it," Lucy replied. "You forget, he's more Irish than you are. He considers it England's war."

"I wouldn't miss it for anything." He paused to admire a flowering shrub. "I suppose all this will be yours someday. Terrible thing to keep up, though."

Lucy was very familiar with the requirements of gardens. Those at Castle Caverly were overgrown with nettles and strangling ivy, as there was no money to hire gardeners. Everything would be solved, of course, as soon as she married Harry.

Harry was a decent enough fellow, she felt, though

69

naive and unexciting, overly mothered and held in contempt by his father. She knew for a fact that he drank too much. In time, he would go bald, as his father had done, and would develop a paunch.

Yet, so far as she could see, she had no alternative but to marry him. On occasion, girls of her class defied their parents and bolted, but it happened rarely, far less often in Ireland than in England.

Just the day before, when she had gone to Cork City to purchase passage for Patrick Cassidy from Queenstown to America, she had realized how lucky he was to be getting away from Ireland. The Irish themselves considered it a punishment to leave their beloved homeland, but Lucy was sure that many of them, once they reached New York, wouldn't return for anything in the world. She *envied* Patrick and the adventures he would have. The busy streets, the exotic people, the challenge of it all. How much preferable it was to living in Doonmara House and worrying about nettles in the garden.

If Lucy had been a man, she would have told her mother to go chuck it all, but she couldn't. She had no skills and couldn't earn a living. She could read books, write letters, oversee a staff of servants, and little else. All she had to look forward to in life was to be married, become pregnant, and have children.

"Well, I don't know about you," Clive Townsend was saying, "but if you ever do come into possession of all this someday, I hope you know more about flowers than I do." He leaned over and plucked a lavender bloom from a bush. "Now what in heaven's name do you call this?"

Lucy didn't have the foggiest. "You'd have to ask Harry what that is. Flowers have always bored me."

Clive smiled. "I hope *Harry* doesn't bore you."

She was unable to answer because at that moment Lady Wingfield began to shepherd her guests back toward the house. They crossed the glistening lawn to the terrace to where a footman held French doors open for them.

Because the dining room was on the north side and did not benefit from sunlight, the two huge cut-glass chandeliers were ablaze with candles, even though it was midday. Two immense white marble fireplaces stood at either end of the room, and the red damask walls were hung with paintings. Twenty-eight places had been set at the table, and the guests now made their way to their seats.

As they sat, the staff rushed on slippered feet across the carpet, carrying the first course. The salmon had been caught that morning, Lady Wingfield explained, and she hoped it would meet with their satisfaction.

They began to eat with a passion. It was astonishing how a stroll through the garden could put the edge on one's appetite, Lord Monteagle remarked.

Only Lucy seemed to toy with her food. As the others ate gluttonously, she studied them. Someday, she herself would be sitting at one end of the long table, entertaining people very much like them, Harry at the other end. It was all such a bore.

Lucy noticed the draft even before Lady Wingfield did. First, the prisms on the chandeliers tinkled, then the candles flickered. In the distance, there was a faint sound almost like waves. As Lady Wingfield summoned Redmond McCarthy to close the windows in the drawing room, Lucy looked across the room and into the hall.

She placed her knife and fork on the edge of her plate, awed by what she saw.

In the hall stood the local peasants, and in their hands were spades and pitchforks. John Mary Cassidy, whom she knew from the Gaelic lessons she had taken, now entered the room, a horsewhip in his hand.

Lady Monteagle screamed.

Sir Richard pushed back his chair and glowered at his unexpected guests. "What is the meaning of this?"

"We have come to claim our land," John Mary answered.

There were sighs and gasps. "You have come to claim a thrashing, is what you have done," Sir Richard replied, standing. "Redmond, fetch the guns."

Redmond was stopped at the door by Lambi Cassidy.

"You will leave this house at once, Sir Richard," John Mary said to him.

Sir Richard ranted and sputtered. "You're madmen, the whole lot of you. Redmond! Get the guns! We shall teach these bastards some manners!"

71

As the horsewhip struck his ankles, women screamed and ran from their chairs. Suddenly, the room was filled with peasants, howling and shaking their pitchforks. The dinner guests tumbled through the French windows onto the terrace.

Sir Richard rushed across the lawn, somewhat behind the others, as he was grossly fat and short-legged, and whenever he paused for breath, a pitchfork touched his haunches, urging him on.

"You are maniacs!" he shrieked. "You will pay for this!"

"No," John Mary answered. "We shall drive you homeless into the fields, as you did our people when you stole our land." He cracked the whip smartly against Sir Richard's buttocks.

"You will pay, you bastards! You will pay!"

At night, the revels began.

Despite John Mary's efforts to prevent them, the villagers stampeded through the vast house, flinging themselves onto Chippendale sofas and jumping up and down on featherbeds. The women slipped out of their worn clothes and into Lady Wingfield's elegant London dresses, wrapping silken furs and strands of pearls around their none-too-clean necks, while their husbands and sons exchanged mackerel-reeking homespuns for Savile Row suits, bowlers, and top hats. Thus dressed, they rolled back the huge Persian rug in the drawing room and danced rude jigs and reels on the polished marble floor beneath a glittering chandelier.

Thumping feet set rare Ming vases shivering on table-tops of French marquetry. Fiddles sawed the air and squeeze boxes creaked and groaned. A farmer boy found an armless marble Venus de Milo and danced a heady reel with it, smacking its cold lips with wet kisses.

The liquor closet had been liberated. Vintage champagnes, aged brandies, and fine whiskies were passed from hand to hand.

"*Up the Republic!*" they toasted. "Long may she live, God bless 'er."

Nora was hiding in the kitchen, where she had been

when the first wave stormed through. They had over-whelmed the tables and stoves like starving men, digging into tureens of souffléed vegetables with bare hands, tearing at the carcasses of chicken and geese. When they finished, they had thrown the empty platters onto the floor or smashed them against the walls.

Even when Thomas found her, she would not leave the corner where she hid. "They do be like animals," she said.

He attempted to justify it. "They have waited for seven hundred years, Nora. Allow them this night's celebration. Come dance with me, love."

Gently, he led her into the drawing room. Emboldened by liquor, the fishermen and farmers danced like dervishes, upsetting tables that Nora had so often painstakingly dusted. The women's faces were smeared with rouge and powder from Lady Wingfield's dressing table, and the air stank of French perfume.

"Where have the Wingfields gone?" she asked.

"They are sleeping in ditches tonight," Eamon replied, "where they belong."

Eamon's eyes were glassy from drink. Next to him, Lambi's face was ashen, and a smell of vomit rose from his shirtfront.

"You all do be drunk," Nora said. Patrick alone looked sober and clearheaded. "Can you not stop them, Patrick?"

He shook his head sadly. "God Himself could not stop them."

A lusty girl grabbed Patrick's arm. "A jig, Pat! Ye'll have a jig with me, lad."

Her huge breasts burst from the top of one of Lady Wingfield's dresses, and her eyes looked at him wantonly.

Patrick backed away. "One man among us must sleep tonight," he replied. "Dublin rises in the morning, and we must have our wits about us."

"Sure and a little brandy will put a fine edge on me wits," Eamon said. "Come, Pat. Tonight's no night to be too thoughtful."

Patrick's thirst was as great as the others', but he didn't dare drink. Far too much was at stake. By morning, a steady trigger finger might be needed.

"The Wingfields will be back," he cautioned them, "and

it's my thinking that they aren't drinking and dancing tonight the way we are."

"Aye, and they're halfway across the Irish Sea by now," Lambi said, "swimming the way the dogs do in the bay."

"Talk to John Mary," Nora implored Patrick. "They will listen to him."

Patrick hurried across the floor to where his father sat drunkenly in a damask wing chair, his head held up by one hand. "Bedad, is that you, Thomas?" John Mary asked. "We do be having a fine hooley, don't we, Tom?"

"It's Pat," he said, then sat close to him. His father's face was leathery from gales and salt spray, and his knuckles were gnarled from arthritis. He was old and tired, much older than a father of four young sons ought to be, but he had married late in life. Patrick was just seventeen; his father was over sixty.

"And we've had a fine day," John Mary continued, slurring his words. "Me own father can rest in his grave for what we have done today."

"But we should leave now," Patrick urged him. "Make the people go back to their homes before they bring grief on themselves."

John Mary's eyes blazed. "*This* is their home. They are here because it is rightfully theirs."

"No. It is the Wingfields' until it legally becomes ours. The law is against us."

"Tonight *we* are the law. Have a drink, lad. Compliments of Sir Richard."

Patrick declined the bottle, then watched as his father raised it to his mouth. Afterward, a smile crossed John Mary's lips and his eyes closed.

"Leave him be, Pat," Eamon said over his shoulder. "I shall see him home. But he is right. This is a night for rejoicing."

Yet Patrick could feel nothing but impending sorrow. As much as he loved his brothers and his father, what they were doing revolted him. To redress injustices was one thing. To recreate them was another.

"Come have a wee drink, Pat."

"No, it is the Wingfields' whiskey. As long as I have a penny, I shall buy my own."

From behind him, Patrick now heard wheels move across the marble floor of the great hall, and when he looked he saw a white donkey pulling a cart laden with plunder. It moved slowly beneath the Georgian fanlight of the opened door and into the night.

He rushed to the hall, and as he did, two men he had never seen before walked down the staircase with a long brass-faced hall clock between them, its pendulum clanging wildly against its mahogany case.

"Put that back where you found it, by God!" he shouted.

"Fook off," one of them responded. "We're taking no more than what belongs to us, mate."

They rested it against the wall, then remounted the stairs. Everywhere in the hall were piles of goods waiting for transportation: a huge bedstead, oil lamps, paintings in gilded frames, carpets, chairs, dishes, and even a red setter chained to the balustrade.

Patrick was sick at heart. What use did they have for these things? Would a rare Persian rug laid on the bare earthen floor that oozed water in wet weather make their lives more comfortable? As few of them knew how to tell time, what good was a long-case clock—especially one that was too high even to fit under the low ceilings of their rooms? What need did they have for an antique pitcher except perhaps to store buttermilk, and wouldn't a tin pail do as well?

"Goddam you all to hell," he said, turning to leave.

"Where are you going, Pat?" Thomas asked, Nora at his side, still in her starched black uniform.

"Look what they're doing. Stealing like common thieves. Is that all they wanted, Thomas? We've risked our lives for Ireland and freedom, and all these villains want is a carpet on their muddy floors."

"You expect too much."

"I expected more than this."

"We shall clear them out of the house before morning, Pat."

"I won't be here to help you."

"Where are you going, lad?"

"I'm going home. I can't bear the sight of them."

He hurried from the house and made his way down the avenue toward the road. In the darkness, he passed two donkey carts heaped high with precious goods stolen from Doonmara House, moving at a snail's pace toward the fishing village. When their drivers hailed him, Patrick spat on the ground and continued.

He hoped that God was not watching Ireland this night, for if He was, the country would be forsaken. Sure and there was a terrible weakness in men. Possessions were valued more than ideals. Slavery they didn't mind. It was deprivation of material comforts that troubled them. Goddam them! They had sullied all of Patrick's valiant dreams.

He set his shoulders against the wind and walked, head bowed, along the coast road. In the morning, first thing, he would try to make his peace with Lucy Caverly. At the moment, he felt closer to her than he did to his own countrymen.

"Wingfield," Desmond McAuliffe said to Harry, "I think your best bet is to stick close to us tomorrow."

They sat in the chill room at Trinity College, Kitty O'Neill huddled in a greatcoat on McAuliffe's bed. She looked pathetically small to be a revolutionary. Harry listened first to her, then to Desmond as they unfolded the plot.

They were not members of the Volunteers, but of the Citizen Army, and in the morning they would be helping Countess Markiewicz defend St. Stephen's Green. Harry would be able to help them dig trenches, they said.

"I know her," Harry exclaimed. "She's a Gore-Booth. Married a Polish chap."

"She's a rabid patriot," Miss O'Neill answered.

"But is she a military strategist, and if so, why in the devil is she proposing to dig trenches in a city park?"

"She's had experience in Flanders, I believe, where she went as an observer," Desmond replied.

"I shouldn't think there would be any similarity at all between Flanders and the middle of Dublin. There are high buildings all around Stephen's Green, and British soldiers will take potshots at anyone in the trenches."

"I'm sure that the Countess Markiewicz has considered that."

Well, Harry wasn't. It seemed to him a lot of foolishness. Moreover, he considered it an effrontery for anyone to ask *him* to dig trenches. "I'll dig one if the countess does," he said antagonistically, "but otherwise I won't. I really resent taking orders from a woman."

That set Kitty O'Neill off. "If you don't want to cooperate, you can jolly well go home to your mother and ask for a change of nappies."

Harry's face colored. "I don't see that it's necessary to be insulting. I've merely questioned the countess's wisdom in choosing to defend Stephen's Green."

She scrutinized him with her black eyes. "And what would you defend?"

He considered it. "I wouldn't *defend* anything. I would take the offensive and attack."

"We have very few rifles, Harry. What we're using were landed two years ago at Howth, and since then we've received no others," Desmond said.

"The soldiers will have machine guns," Kitty reminded him.

"The element of surprise is equal to hundreds of machine guns," Harry explained. "The British are not expecting anything. Tomorrow, most of the soldiers will be on leave for the day, as part of the Easter holiday. They'll be at Bray or Greystones, dipping their feet into the water or cavorting with the local girls on the sand. I wager that just a few of us could take Dublin Castle itself."

Both Desmond and Kitty were astounded at the boldness of his suggestion. It left them breathless.

Harry continued, "Countess Markiewicz may dig up the tulip beds in Stephen's Green if she so desires, but it will accomplish nothing. It is an assault against horticulture, perhaps, but not against the British Empire."

Desmond recovered himself. "The Volunteers are to seize the General Post Office."

"The G.P.O.?" Harry repeated. "And for what reason?"

"Because it occupies a prominent position on Sackville Street."

Harry arched his eyebrows. "And after they have seized it, what do they intend to do with it?"

"Hold it and wait for the Lancers to attack."

Harry turned away in disgust. "They're fools. They'll do nothing but impede the flow of mail. Where do you think the orders will come from for the Lancers to attack?"

There was no reply.

"Dublin Castle," he answered. "And if we are in control of the Castle, the Lancers will be paralyzed. Soldiers are not trained to think or to make decisions. They are trained to carry out orders. Without them, they can't function." He wet his lips. "I can understand why the Volunteers have chosen to seize the post office. It's a coward's choice. No cunning will be required. At the outset, it will be no more difficult than buying a halfpenny stamp. But once it has been taken, it becomes a liability. And if they wait for the Lancers to attack, in time it will become a charnel house."

Kitty looked at him with suspicion. "Do you think we should bring this to the attention of Countess Markiewicz?" she asked Desmond.

"Nonsense," Harry said. "If we do, we shall argue all night. I disagree with almost all of my father's points of view, but with one I'm in sympathy. He is fond of saying that if more than two or three Irishmen are involved in a scheme, it is impossible to get unanimity of opinion. It is second nature for an Irishman to contest and disagree. In the end, the countess may go so far as to let us dig trenches in the Castle Yard, in full view of the soldiers on duty, but nothing else."

"Then what would you suggest?" Desmond asked.

"That we take the Castle ourselves."

Even Harry was stirred by what he had said. Dublin

Castle was a fortress, and had been since the thirteenth century. Its ramparts were very nearly impenetrable and could not be scaled. Entrance would have to be made through the main gate on Dame Street, always guarded by sentries. It would be difficult, if not impossible, to pass through the gate.

"Just the three of us?" Kitty asked.

"The three of us."

"We have five Mausers among us," Desmond observed. "How will we ever get them through the gate?"

Harry's eyes met Kitty's head-on. "Under her skirt. Perhaps we can leave two with the Countess and tie the other three to her legs."

She set her mouth firmly, then barely opened her lips to reply, "I don't think I should like that, thank you."

"Whether you like it or not is unimportant, Miss O'Neill. You are not going to a garden party." Abruptly, he turned to Desmond. "It was a mistake to recruit her, McAuliffe. All a woman ever thinks about is how she can look pretty."

"Go to hell, you little dandy," she shrieked.

"Please," Desmond interrupted, "can't we be civil?"

"Not when a fool like Wingfield is about to ruin everything," she persisted. "Can't you see, Desmond, that he's nothing but a dilettante who thinks that this is all very droll? We should send him home to his mother at once, before he becomes a greater menace than he already is."

Harry had never in his life been so abused by anyone except his father. "Why is it, Desmond," he replied with wonderful calmness, "that every second woman born on this island is a shrew? It's little wonder that so many Irishmen are driven to drink."

"Stop it, both of you!" Desmond cried. "You have neglected to tell us, Harry, how you propose to get through the Castle's gate. Or are you suggesting that we climb the wall?"

Serenely, Harry answered, "We shall merely tell the sentry that we are calling on Lord Wimborne."

"You *see!*" Kitty exclaimed. "He is an ass!"

As patiently as he could, Desmond asked, "And it

is your opinion, Harry, that Baron Wimborne, the Lord Lieutenant General and Governor-General of all Ireland, the *Viceroy,* would admit us?"

"Of course he would," Harry replied smartly. "He wouldn't think of turning me away. He's a cousin of mine."

9

All night long, Nora could hear the wagons creaking down the long avenue toward the coast road and the sounds of fiddles and accordions drifting up the staircase from the drawing room. Drunken laughter came from the dark lawn, and shrill cries and running feet could be heard outside the door of her small room on the third floor.

Thomas's head lay against her breast, and his smooth, silken body half covered her. He was resting. Against her thigh, she could feel his manhood. Minutes before, he had ridden her, driving into her until she had screamed out in ecstasy; then rapture followed until he had finished.

And this time, afterward there was no shame. On the flowered banks of the stream in February, it had been hurried and furtive. She had been afraid that someone would see them, and as embarrassed at his nakedness as she was of her own. But tonight it was different. He had removed her clothes, article by article, and kissed each part of her body as it was uncovered. Still, she'd been reluctant to touch him by way of reply, for fear that it would be unseemly. At last, he took her fingers and held them against his penis, filling her hand with it.

"There be no harm to it, Nora, if it be done with love."

Thomas was right. Distinctions had to be made. Indeed, there could be no evil to what they were doing, because they loved each other far too much. Moreover, they were very nearly man and wife.

"Thomas?" she began. "Are you sleeping?"

"It's dreaming I am."

He raised his head to look upon her face, then bent down to kiss her lips once more.

"You should be talking to Father Daley tomorrow," she said. She waited, then added, "I'm carrying your child, Thomas."

He cocked up his head as if he could not believe what he had heard; then a smile lifted his lips.

"You keep a good secret, Nora."

She turned away, eyes glistening. "I was afraid that you would hate me, the way the people do be hating the dwarf."

At the edge of the fishing village lived an old man with his daughter, a cruelly misshapen dwarf. He used her as a farmhand and a drudge, and she was often seen in their mean little field, working as hard as a man. Two years before, while in the meadow, she had given birth to a baby, though no one had even known that she was pregnant. When pressed by Father Daley, she could not recall ever having lain with anyone, though she had a dim recollection, she said, that a drunken man, passing the cottage one day on horseback, had stopped to talk to her and had perhaps thrown her on the ground. He may have touched her, but she could not be sure.

The baby was taken away from her and given to a foundling home in Cork City, and thereafter, whenever the natives saw her, they made the sign of the cross from forehead to breast to ward off the evil she was thought to possess. Because of her transgression, Father Daley did not permit her to attend church anymore.

"Hate you?" Thomas asked. "Sure and I love you all the more. But you are right. We must marry before we leave for America, not wait till we reach New York. I have heard it told that single girls who are carrying children are turned back at Ellis Island. The Yanks will not have them."

Nora had heard similar tales of young girls who had left their homes in disgrace, hoping for a new life in America, only to be rejected at Ellis Island and sent back to Queenstown or Liverpool because they were pregnant. Nora herself was almost two months gone, and there was little to reveal the condition, but in another month or so—when they hoped to sail for New York—a sharp eye at the immigration shed would be sure to catch it.

"I have spoiled everything for you," she said sorrowfully.

"Spoiled? But I am the happiest man alive!"

"It will be much harder for us in New York," she exclaimed.

He understood her meaning. The two of them had planned to work before they married, in order to lay aside a little money to set up housekeeping. Now Nora would not be able to contribute. She would be a burden, she thought. She told him as much.

"You will be no burden, Nora," he declared. "To live without you would be a burden impossible to bear. We shall make do with what we have. Patrick will help us."

They knew no one in New York other than Nora's cousin Mary McNamara—Mary Mack as she was called—who worked as a domestic for a rich American family that spent part of the year in New York and part in Europe. They were Jews, and Mary Mack's letters were filled with wondrous accounts of them. "They do be eating fish with their heads still on, their eyes looking up at you from the plate like a puppy dog. Their ways are curious, but they are very generous and kind."

Yet because Mary Mack lived with her employers and traveled with them, she would not be able to offer hospitality to Nora or the two Cassidys. They would have to find a place of their own to live, though she promised to help them.

"I shall speak to Patrick," Thomas said, "and tell him what has happened. We shall manage somehow. Pat is a good lad and will never let us down."

What Thomas proposed was that they leave Ireland within the next few weeks, once the Republic was established. They would marry first, as soon as Father Daley gave them permission.

"I want my child to enter the New World nobly, Nora, carrying my hopes and my name." He caressed her face with his fingertips. "I shall talk to Patrick and Father Daley tomorrow evening."

All night long, the three debated, and by dawn Desmond could still not be persuaded to join Harry in his scheme to seize Lord Wimborne and hold him prisoner.

"It's not that we think it's a bad plan, Harry. But you see, we're committed to helping Countess Markiewicz, and if we let her down, she'll be raving mad. I'm afraid we shall have to take a vote on it. Kitty? Are you with Wingfield or with me?"

The young girl scrutinized Harry's face, then McAuliffe's. "I think that we owe the countess our allegiance," she replied resolutely.

"I hope to God that at least some Dubliners love their country more than they love a countess," Harry remarked acidly.

Desmond's face flushed. He stuttered and stammered in embarrassment as he said, "To hold Lord Wimborne a prisoner just doesn't seem quite cricket to me. In fact, it's bloody damn sneaky. We would prefer to meet the British soldiers face-to-face."

"But you're outnumbered," Harry exclaimed. "People will be killed."

"Of course," Desmond agreed. "Some people will have to die in order to make a blood sacrifice."

"But for what reason?"

"To attract the attention of the world," McAuliffe replied. "Perhaps then pressure will be brought on Parliament for the restoration of home rule."

Harry had to catch his breath, it was so absurd. McAuliffe wasn't about to strike for Irish freedom at all. He wanted a continuation of British rule and a Dublin Parliament that would do as the King bade it. McAuliffe wasn't proposing a Republic, but a Commonwealth government.

"So we move backward into the nineteenth century," Harry said in disgust.

"Ireland isn't ready for a Republic, and perhaps never will be. You must remember, Wingfield, that there are Protestants here as well as Catholics, and Catholic rule would be unacceptable to the Protestants, just as Protestant rule would be unacceptable to Catholics. The Crown alone can serve as arbiter between the two fractious elements. What I have in mind is an Irish Parliament, away from Westminster, and a benevolent monarch."

"Monarchs are benevolent only after they have been beheaded."

"Your opposition to English rule is unjustified."

"The Irish would still be slaves."

"In time, perhaps they might adjust to self-government, but not yet. They're too irrational and headstrong." He waited, then added, "Like you, Harry."

Time was being wasted. It was midmorning, and in some fashion or other, Dublin was to rise within a few hours. Harry could see no future in quarreling about approaches. He asked Desmond for the loan of a rifle.

"Then you propose to do it without us," Desmond replied.

"I shall try, anyway."

Reluctantly, they provided him with a rifle, then watched as he concealed it beneath his greatcoat. At shortly after ten-thirty, he set out from the college.

He could have taken a hackney, but he preferred to walk in order to settle his nerves. In the bright sunshine, shoppers hurried along Dame Street, and bankers and clerks rushed to their offices. At one point, a company of British Lancers passed by on smart-stepping black horses, but they moved without urgency.

Harry tried to imagine how his family would react to what he was about to do. His father would hate him all the more, he was sure, but might perhaps be moved by the swashbuckling quality of it. His mother—it was she who was Lord Wimborne's first cousin—would be embarrassed and annoyed. Lucy Caverly, he hoped, would respect him for his dedication to principles. And Patrick Cassidy, for whose benefit Harry had made the journey to Dublin, would now perceive that there was more to Harry than met the eye.

By God, he murmured to himself as he sailed down Dame Street, I am not the superfluous fellow my father thinks I am. I will have to be reckoned with yet.

He couldn't resist a smile as he peered into a plate-glass window at his reflection. If only he could carry out his plan, he would carve a niche for himself in Irish history, along with Lord Edward Fitzgerald and the valiant Parnell. In time, his portrait—now hanging in the dimly lit second-floor hall at home—might be relegated to an eminent position at the National Gallery. Why not? And years and years from now, when people heard the name Harry Wingfield, they would be stirred.

Ahead of him, he perceived the gray ramparts of Dublin Castle, and beyond, at the end of Dame Street, the tower of Christ Church. If he had had the time, he would have liked to offer a prayer to God for the success of his mission, but if he did, he would have to retrace his steps back to the Castle, and he saw that the sentry at the gate was watching him.

Boldly, Harry stepped up to the box. "I am Harry Wingfield, and I'm to see my cousin, Lord Wimborne," he said in his best Harrovian accent. "He is expecting me."

Without waiting for permission, Harry began to walk through the gate. From experience, he knew that members of the lower class should never be given the opportunity to decline to serve members of the ruling class. It was their duty. One never asked; instead, one told.

And it had worked, for Harry, out of the corner of his eye, saw that the sentry did not leave his post to follow him.

There was a good deal of activity in the Castle Yard, but no one approached him as he made his way to the Viceroy's Apartments. A sentry stood at the entrance, and Harry repeated what he had said to the first, adding, "I am Sir Richard Wingfield's son."

Once again, he was allowed to pass. It seemed uncanny, almost as if he were expected.

Inside the door, a footman asked, "Your coat, sir?"

It hadn't occurred to Harry that it would appear odd for him to keep his coat on, as the day was mild. "It's quite all right," he answered. "I shall be staying only for a short while."

"As you wish, sir. If you'll follow me, please."

Harry followed the man up the broad staircase to the second floor. He could feel the rifle knocking gently against his hip, his hand gripping its stock through a slit he had made in his pocket.

By the time he reached the hall, he was gulping for air. His legs felt like iron, and his mouth was dry from fear.

At a door midway down the hall, the footman stopped, knocked twice, then said, "Your guest has arrived, sir."

A voice from within the room answered, "You may show him in."

The footman held open the door as Harry entered. He blinked his eyes in an effort to see. The curtains had been drawn, and the room was in shadows. As the door behind him closed, he heard the clicking of its lock.

Harry squinted in the darkness and made out Lord Wimborne seated at a desk directly opposite him. He was surprised that the Viceroy didn't stand. It was most unlike him.

Then Harry saw what Lord Wimborne held in his hand, and he began to tremble.

It was a pistol.

"So it's you, you bastard," Lord Wimborne said.

Harry fought for breath. He felt faint and was unable to make his tongue form words.

Wimborne rose from his desk, the pistol trained on his guest. "Drop your weapon, Harry, and slowly put your hands in the air."

Harry breathed as if he had just run a race, and when he spoke, he could scarcely recognize his own voice.

"This is a social call, sir," he said.

"You're a damn liar, Harry. Now do as I say, or I shall shoot you dead. Ease your weapon to the floor."

Slowly, Harry lifted the rifle barrel from the hem of his coat and let it drop gently to the floor.

"Now put your hands in the air."

Harry did as he was told, then watched as Lord Wimborne kicked the rifle across the room.

"You're even more of an ass than your father is, Harry," he said. "We received a warning from a young woman no more than ten minutes ago that an attempt would be made on my life, but I never thought it would be from a member of my own family."

Kitty O'Neill! That Celtic cunt! She must have hurried to the Castle by taxi to inform the authorities.

"You're a disgrace to your class," Wimborne continued. Harry's eyes filled with tears.

"Stop that sniveling at once! Be a man. The next thing, you'll be wetting your trousers. Now sit down here and tell me what in God's name made you do this idiotic thing!"

Harry flung himself into the chair that Lord Wimborne held for him, then buried his face in his hands and began to sob.

"I shall give you twenty seconds to collect yourself," Wimborne declared. "Time is of the essence. First we received information from a young lady who refused to identify herself, and now you appear with a Mauser, if I'm not mistaken. What does it mean, Harry?"

He would be the laughingstock of Ireland, despised more than ever by his father, held in ridicule by Lucy Caverly. Harry sobbed uncontrollably.

"I warn you, Harry, if you do not cooperate, I shall summon the guards at once and have you arrested for treason." Lord Wimborne waited. "If you tell me everything you know, I shall put you on a train to Cork within the hour and you shall receive no more punishment than what your father chooses to give you. He will probably thrash you, which is what you deserve. But you will survive it. Under no circumstances will you survive a firing squad."

Harry removed his wet hands from his tear-streaked face. Why had Kitty O'Neill betrayed him? For having called her a shrew? Or to test his mettle? He was a dilettante, she had said; was she trying to make sure he would fail? To win an argument, was she willing to sacrifice a cause? By God, she was no more fit for revolution than he.

"Dublin is to rise," he whispered.

Lord Wimborne narrowed his eyes. "Rise?" he asked.

"Sometime this morning, insurgents will seize the General Post Office, the Four Courts building, the Custom House"—Harry fought for breath—"Boland's Mill, Jacob's Biscuit Factory, and Stephen's Green. There may be more, but that's all I can remember."

"The Irish Volunteers?" Lord Wimborne asked incredulously.

Harry nodded his head in affirmation.

Lord Wimborne rushed to the door and pulled it open. He shouted for his adjutant, who came running down the hall.

"Dublin is in a state of insurgency!" he roared. "Advise all units throughout the country to be on the alert, effective immediately." He turned to Harry and spat out the words: "We shall meet those bastards with every bit of strength we have."

As Harry heard the sounds of bugles in the Castle Yard, tears washed down his cheeks.

10

At midmorning, Patrick left the cottage, telling his mother that he had an errand to run before his father and brothers awoke.

Earlier, before dawn, he had listened to them return home, one by one, from Doonmara House. Lambi was the first to crawl into the loft, singing softly to himself. Next came Eamon, who smelled of whiskey and vomit, and moaned as he mounted the steep ladder to his bed. The sun had already streaked the morning sky when John Mary entered the house and lifted himself into bed next to the hearth, mumbling his prayers in Gaelic.

Last came Thomas, whistling gaily as he walked down the hill. He was smiling as he lay down next to Patrick in the loft and whispered, "Today is the day, lad. We shall be free men before dark."

"If it please God," Patrick replied.

Patrick slept for another hour or two, then rose when he heard his mother rinsing the kettle outside the kitchen door. He left his straw mat and made his way down the ladder, then to the rear of the house, where he cupped his hands in cold water from the spring and bathed his face.

Silently, so as not to awake his tired father, he sat at the kitchen table with his mother and sipped tea and ate brown cake, which she had sliced for him and spread with butter. He explained to her that it was necessary for him to ride to Castle Caverly, but that he would be back before the sun was high in the sky.

He saddled the white mare and rode up the long hill toward the coast road, then turned westward, away from Skibbereen. At the roadside, he saw articles taken the night before from Doonmara House, but discarded either because of their weight or their impracticality. A huge armoire lay in a ditch surrounded by tall foxglove and blossoming blackberries. Beyond it lay a French chair with silk upholstery.

He wished that he could restore to the Wingfields what belonged to them, and he hoped that Harry wouldn't hate him too much when he returned from Dublin to find his ancestral house sacked by the people he professed to love. Of all the landlords the natives might have exacted their revenge upon, it was a cruelty—and a puzzlement—that they had chosen the Wingfields. Though Sir Richard was despotic, Harry was sweetness itself, and Lady Prudence had always been cordial.

In time, he could make out the many chimneys of Doonmara House in the distance, sitting in its great park at the sea's edge. He was relieved to find it still standing because during the night he had dreamed that the people in their rage had burned it to the ground. It *was* a beautiful house—there was no denying it—and it deserved to survive in order to remind future generations how people had once lived. Yet even now it was an anachronism. Such spacious houses warped the minds of those who lived in them and gave them perverted views of mankind. So great was their greed that compassion could never take root in their minds, and thus they invited still one more revolution.

In America, Patrick had been told, there were no palaces. All citizens, rich and poor alike, lived in wooden houses of modest size. And wasn't it true that a man born in a one-room log cabin could one day become President of the United States, as Abe Lincoln had? To Patrick, it was exhilarating. In Ireland, until recently, a Catholic could not even own land or vote or attend school. Far from aspiring to the presidency—if there had been one— an Irishman was not even permitted to own a horse worth more than five pounds.

Yet today, as Thomas had said, they would all be free men before dark.

As he rode along the rocky road, he perceived that the mare had thrown a shoe. He paused by a stone wall to look at her hoof, then walked beside her as she favored one leg. It would delay him somewhat. He considered turning back to Doonmara House in order to rouse a stableboy to reshoe the mare, but decided instead to push on to Castle Caverly. Perhaps he could borrow a mount from Lady Caverly.

How she would react to him, he had no way of knowing. Lucy, he was sure, would be sympathetic, but he was uncertain of Lady Caverly. As much addicted to Irish culture as she was, she was irrevocably English. It was possible, Patrick thought, that he would be turned away from the door.

As he rode up the long avenue to the house, he saw a horse and carriage waiting by the entrance. Even before he left his mount, Lucy rushed from the front door and down the steps to meet him.

"You're in great danger, Patrick," she cried. "You must leave for Queenstown at once. I have your papers."

He slipped down from the saddle and stood before her. "Ireland is rising today, within the hour."

"It will be too late," she replied. "British soldiers are due any minute from Cork City."

Patrick's heart fell.

"They have come for you and your family," she said. "I shall take you to Queenstown at once."

But Patrick would not permit her. He jumped up into the carriage, and as he did, Lucy Caverly sat beside him. He whipped the horse to a frenzy, and it flew down the avenue toward the coast road and the village.

Gulls swooped over the black currachs lying in the sand at the water's edge, yet no fisherman came to ease them into the sea. In front of the small cottages, roosters scratched the gravel vainly, and cattle bent their heads over ivied walls, peering at unopened doors. After their night of debauching, the people of the village were sleeping late.

Suddenly, from the top of the hill came the roar of motors, and in a minute a lorry appeared, followed by another, then another. As they thundered into the village, the gulls circled higher in the sky, darkening the sun, and the roosters flew blindly against the walls.

93

In a great cloud of dust, the lorries halted, and soldiers leaped from them, rifles drawn.

A voice boomed out in the still morning air: *"John Cassidy!* In the name of His Majesty's Government, I command you to lay down your arms and surrender!"

All sound ceased. The wind from the sea died, and the leaves hung limply on the trees. Nothing stirred within the cottage.

"Give them a taste of British bullets!" the commander shouted.

A round of fire slammed against the plastered wall and shattered the windowpanes. Dust rose from pulverized stone and wood, and the smell of gunpowder was everywhere.

Slowly, the door was opened, and a black-shawled woman stood there, waiting, so that the soldiers could see that she was unarmed.

"Let the old hag through!" the commander ordered his men.

She lifted the edges of her long skirt, then hurried down the street and into another cottage.

When no one else appeared, the commander moved from behind a lorry to scan the windows. "John Cassidy!" he yelled. "I command you to surrender at once!"

Suddenly, orange fire burst from behind the broken glass as four rifles answered him. He grabbed an arm, then fell to the ground.

"Burn the savages out!" he screamed as he was dragged behind the lorry. "Show them no mercy!"

Thirty-six British rifles fired at the windows and the splintered door, and from the hill behind the house a soldier rose to throw a petrol-soaked rag onto the thatched roof. As flaming bullets struck it, the roof began to smoke, and soon scarlet fire broke out.

Inside, John Mary lay on the earthen floor, his face ashen, gore oozing from a huge wound at the side of his head. Thomas had seen a section of his skull flying through the air as he was struck. Even before Thomas reached him, his father's eyes were opened wide and sightless.

He had begged him not to resist and to strike a bargain

with the British troops, but John Mary would have none of it. Then Lambi had appeared with one of the rifles hidden in the loft, and in resignation Thomas had passed out the others. John Mary had said that all they need do was hold off the soldiers until help arrived. The Republic would come to their aid, he said.

Now that his father was dead, Thomas tried once more to persuade his brothers. "They'll not hurt us if we surrender," he told them.

Lambi replied, "They'll kill us either way, Tom."

"If I have to die," Eamon shouted, "I shall send an Englishman to Hell before I do."

Thomas knew that his brothers could not be reasoned with while John Mary's body lay lifeless before them. Smoke filled the room, and when Thomas looked overhead, he saw flames climbing the dry thatch of the roof toward the peak. Lambi dropped his rifle and raced to the pail of water kept by the hearth. Screaming, he flung it at the roof, and as he did, his body was silhouetted between the inferno and the windows. A torrent of bullets ripped into his flesh, and he slumped to the floor.

The slender rafters were soon torches, and as they began to creak and give way, the air was sucked from the room and Thomas fought for breath. He shouted at Eamon to save himself, then stood with his face against the wall as the roof collapsed. He felt a searing pain and cried out as a rafter struck the back of his head and his shoulder. His shirt was in flames. Blindly, he ripped at it until he had pulled it off in shreds, then hurled himself toward the door.

Eamon was standing behind it, struggling with the lock; then all at once he pulled it open. Rifle blazing, he fell into the street. A fusillade of bullets struck him with such force that he danced from side to side, his head flung back, before he fell.

In defeat, Thomas stood at the door, his hands high over his head.

From behind a lorry, a voice shouted, "Hold your fire!"

Slowly, Thomas began to walk from the burning cabin.

"Where are the others?" the voice demanded.

Thomas knew that Patrick had not been among them. Wherever he had gone, the British must not know that he had survived, so that he could carry on the struggle.

"They are all dead," he whispered, "where they are free men at last."

Soldiers swarmed from everywhere and bound his hands behind his back.

"We shall use this man as an example for the peasantry," the commander said. "March him to the top of the hill, where he will be seen for miles around."

Patrick watched gray smoke curl into the sky, like smoke from burning gorse, but darker and more menacing. Beyond it, on the road to Skibbereen, a cloud of dust followed in the wake of three lorries speeding away from the village.

They had done their mischief and gone. They had exacted retribution, as they had done for centuries, then left the Irish to salvage what was left of their lives. Patrick knew with certainty that it was his cabin that was burning, and it had not been the first time his family had been burned out by the British. Each time, they had rebuilt it and endured, just as Ireland itself had.

Suddenly, his hands went limp, the reins slackened, and the horse pulling Lucy's carriage slowed down, then stopped.

The bell in the church tower at the top of the hill knelled mournfully, and men and women of the village flung themselves on their knees in the dusty road in front of it. Patrick's skin grew icy cold.

He left the carriage and began to walk toward the huge tree in the churchyard, and as he did, he was mesmerized by what he saw. It did not seem possible, but his eyes could not lie. From one of the limbs of the tree a man hung, a noose around his neck. His back was bare, his ankles and hands were tied, and his face looked seaward, but Patrick knew at once who he was, and his lip began to tremble.

So this was how the dreams would end. Once more, his countrymen had struck for liberty, and once more they had met with British vengeance. There came a time when a defeated man could dream no more, for God must surely have abandoned Ireland.

When he reached the tree, he lifted Thomas gently upward so as to ease an agony already ended. On her knees, keening with the others, he saw his mother, but when he looked for John Mary and Eamon and Lambi, they were not there, and he knew at once that he should look no more.

A peace came over him, a sense of resignation. He would leave this dark and tormented land and never return. He would banish it from his mind. From this day onward, he would bury all that was Irish about him and seek out a new life in a country where hopes and aspirations were not met with a boot in the face, a bayonet in the entrails.

Suddenly, in the crowd, a bearded man cried out above the wailing, *"God save Ireland,"* but Patrick shook his head in denial. He had done all he could, and would do no more. He would leave the suffering and the pain behind him and live his life elsewhere. Far too much Cassidy blood had already turned Ireland's green grass crimson, and he would not spend his, too, on a nation that was lost.

He closed his eyes and prayed, and when he had finished, he begged for a knife to cut the rope that held his brother to the limb, and as he cut it, he severed himself, once and for all, from his beloved homeland.

"Nora, ye will write to us as soon as ye gets there, will ye?" the ancient woman in the black shawl said to her daughter as they waited under the shelter of the wide eaves of the railroad station in Skibbereen. Nora's father and younger brother stood silently next to them. Rain pelted against the stone pavement at their feet.

Nora was wearing a new dress she had bought for the long trip by steamer to New York. In a small wicker basket, she carried a second dress, a shawl, a change of underclothes, stockings, a bar of soap, and food for the voyage—oat cakes and bread—so that she would have to buy nothing on board ship but tea.

Nora promised that she would have someone write a

letter as soon as she found a place to live in New York. Her plans had been made in desperate haste. Only four days before, she had dictated a letter to be sent to Mary McNamara in New York, but she had no way of knowing if Mary Mack was in the city.

In her wicker basket she also carried a knotted linen handkerchief holding a small amount of earth taken from Thomas's grave, having no ring or photograph or any other reminder of him. Thomas and his father and two brothers had been buried just one week ago, the only fatalities of the Rising outside those in Dublin and three men who were drowned in Kerry. Nora's mother begged her to remain at home until her grieving was over, but Nora insisted on leaving at once.

Patrick had not dared stay for the funerals and had left on the day of the killings, after having said good-bye to his mother. In the village it was thought that Lucy Caverly had driven him to Queenstown, but no one could confirm it, as she never returned to Castle Caverly. Harry Wingfield would have known, but Nora had not dared ask him the last day she saw him at Doonmara House.

She had gone there to collect the wicker basket she kept under her bed on the third floor. He had been sitting in the drawing room, still wearing the rumpled clothes he had worn the day he returned from Dublin, and he was drinking. The room was a shambles, and he had dismissed the staff, who might have tried to put it in order. Even the dining-room table still contained rank food, remains of the interrupted Easter dinner.

"I am sorry, Master Harry," she had said to him.

He looked at her through glazed eyes. "And so am I, Nora. What will become of you now?"

"I am on my way to America."

He considered it a long time before replying, "Well, that is one solution, I suppose."

Shyly, she asked, "Will you be after staying here, Master Harry?"

The old smile returned to his face. "There isn't much left to stay in, Nora. My father is closing the house, he says. Even if he weren't, I doubt that he would want me around the place. We have had a falling out. He and my mother plan to live in England."

"But the Rising has failed. It's all over. The men in Dublin have been put in prison."

"Yes, it has failed." Sadly, he added, "And so have I. My father, I am sure, will want to settle scores with me. He is determined that I not set foot out of England again. He says Ireland is bad for me."

Nora felt a great pity for Harry Wingfield. He was the gentlest Englishman she had ever met.

"The young man who was hanged," he began. "That was the man you were to marry, wasn't it?"

Nora could not reply, but her eyes told him that he had spoken truly.

He rose from where he was seated and walked toward her. "Then it is my turn to apologize." He touched her hand sympathetically. "We do such unspeakable things to each other, we English and we Irish. We seem to exist only in order to torment the other. It's uncanny." He waited. "I wish you luck in America, Nora. You deserve it."

"And so do you, Master Harry," she had replied.

Now as she stood at the railroad station, in the distance she could hear the shrill cry of the train's whistle. She had promised herself that she would not weep before her family. "I shall be all right," she said to them. "You mustn't worry over me."

The train pulled into the station, spewing dark smoke into the rain-washed air. She embraced her family once more and as she did, her mother opened Nora's fist and placed something in it. It was the rosary that had belonged to Nora's grandmother, the one she had clasped and prayed over through famine and disease.

"Take it with ye," her mother said. "When times do ye bad, ye will have your faith, if nothing else."

Her father lifted her basket up to the third-class coach, and Nora climbed in after it. As the train began to move slowly from the station, she stood by the window and waved. Long after they were lost in rain and mist, she still looked back to where they had stood, fixing it in her memory forever.

SUNSHINE
AND SHADOWS

11

"Watch where you're walkin', miss," a rude voice bellowed as Nora stepped from the streetcar into the terrible heat and blinding sun of Lower Broadway. "You're not livin' in the bogs anymore."

Nora had not meant to collide with him, but ever since she had arrived in New York, three days ago, she had marveled at everything she saw, and sometimes dawdled on the sidewalk. If it wasn't the tall buildings, it was the traffic in the streets. And if it wasn't the traffic, it was the dizzying collection of faces she passed. No one had prepared her for American faces. In Ireland, all faces, whether Norman or Danish or Celtic, were merely varieties of a single face, while in New York each face was entirely different from the next. Some were dark and brooding, some were light and golden-haired, some were black, some were olive, some were yellow.

And the tongues they spoke were every bit as exotic as their features. At times, Nora thought that she was the only one in the city who spoke English. She listened to people who had been born thousands of miles away in snowy countries, in deserts, on mountaintops or plains, who still used the language of their fathers. Nora had already learned never to ask directions of them, as the jabber that came from their mouths was incomprehensible, and, moreover, they seemed to be as lost as she was.

Providentially, it was an Irish policeman who instructed her where to board the streetcar, and an Irish conductor who told her where to disembark. When she heard their sweet voices, she purred with relief. It was grand altogether that the Yanks used Irish lads in positions of authority in order to make it easier for greenhorns like

103

Nora, though it seemed to her that they would be of little help to Russian Jews or Italians or Germans. She pitied those newcomers who could not speak English. If just venturing into the streets was a terror for her, she wondered what it must be for those who understood nothing of what they heard.

She looked up now at the numerals on the buildings, then compared what she saw with what had been written on the back of the envelope she carried. The woman at whose rooming house on Tenth Avenue and Thirty-first Street she was staying had recommended an employment agency that specialized in domestics, and for the time being, Nora could hope for nothing more exalted. Mary McNamara would be of no help at all, as Nora had gone to the house where she worked and been told by the maid next door that the family who owned the house were in Newport, Rhode Island, for the warm months.

Nora looked about her for a sign that would indicate where the employment agency was and saw a large board on which the names of many firms were listed. Painstakingly, she compared the letters on the envelope—they spelled out "Gotham Agency for Household Help"—until she found one that matched them on the board, and the numeral 3 following it. She made her way to the staircase and began to climb.

Never in her life, except when she was ill with fever, had she been so excruciatingly hot. It was well over ninety degrees, the Irish policeman had told her, which accounted for her discomfort, and the heavy dress she wore only made it worse. The Yanks, she perceived, wore white dresses and light suits and seemed not to suffer from the heat quite so much.

When she reached the third floor, she looked around and again attempted to match the letters on the envelope with those printed on doors. If was more difficult this time, as they seemed to be written at a slant, but at last a door opened and a young lady emerged, dressed in the long black dress of an immigrant, and Nora deduced that she, too, was seeking employment.

"Could you tell me if this is the employment agency?" Nora asked.

The girl looked at her in bewilderment. She shrugged her shoulders. "No—*spreche Inglisch*," she said, then hurried down the stairs.

Nora opened the door and entered. A woman sat at a desk, and a second woman sat in an inner office. The latter was interviewing someone who occupied a chair in front of her.

"Yes, may I help you?" the first woman asked.

Nora swallowed with fear, then spoke hesitantly. "I'm after being told I could find employment here."

The woman's smile disappeared. "You're Irish?"

"I am, ma'am."

The woman bit her lip. "I'm not sure that we're interviewing any more girls today. Let me check." She rose from her chair. "What do you do?"

"I've worked as a cook's helper, ma'am."

"A scullery maid?"

"No, ma'am. I've helped prepare meals."

The woman handed Nora a piece of paper and a pen. "I'll see if we have anything. Could you fill this out for us, please?"

Nora stared at the form she had been asked to complete. She looked at the pen and wished that she could make it create words, but nothing came. She could not even write her name. Her face turned crimson.

"Mrs. Watrous will see you in a few moments," the woman said when she returned, looking down at the incompleted form. She lifted it from Nora's hand. "Don't be embarrassed, honey. If you're hired, you'll be hired as a cook's helper, not as a poet, so it really doesn't matter that much." She smiled. "Where you from, anyway, dearie?"

Nora told her that she was from Ireland.

"You're kidding," the woman replied, laughing. "You coulda fooled me. I meant, *where* in Ireland?"

"County Cork."

"My mother came from Louth, if you've ever heard of that, but I don't know the first thing about the place. Where approximately is County Cork?"

"It's in the south, ma'am. At the very tip."

"What's your name?"

"Nora Shannon," she answered.

The woman studied the prim and frightened girl. "Well, Nora, the first thing you'll want to do is learn how to read and write. Not that it will make you a better cook's helper, but in this country if you don't know how to read, you'll be cheated blind by those people who do." She smiled again. "I think Mrs. Watrous is ready now."

Nora waited until the other young lady left the office, then walked in. The woman at the desk finished writing something, and as she did, she looked up at Nora.

"You're a *beauty*," she said, almost rhapsodically.

Nora didn't know how to respond, so she said nothing at all.

"The most beautiful skin, the most beautiful eyes I've ever seen. I envy you. Sit down, won't you?"

Nora was not accustomed to flattery and scarcely knew what to make of it, particularly when it came from a stranger.

"Your name is Nora Shannon, and you're a cook's helper, you say. It's a pity to hide you in a kitchen. You wouldn't—be interested in doing housework instead?"

After all the compliments, Nora had expected more than this. It was a decided disappointment. She hated to think that she was worthy of nothing other than dusting and scrubbing.

"I've had three years' experience working in the kitchen of a great manor house in Ireland, ma'am. I had hoped that I could use my skills over here."

The woman arched her eyebrows. "Have you references, Nora?"

How could Nora explain? What would a foreigner think of it? "I would have, ma'am, except as how my lady left Ireland suddenly—because of the—the Rising." She had very nearly not been able to say the word.

"Oh, yes, I think I read something about that." She waited, scrutinizing Nora as she did. "Irish girls are not all that popular in New York kitchens, Nora—as cooks, at any rate. There is a certain—how to say it?—prejudice against them. It's felt"—it was now her turn to stumble over words—"that sometimes you people aren't—as *clean* as Americans like their kitchen staffs to be."

106

Nora could feel the anger rise in her. Her heart began to beat wildly, but she held her tongue.

"But you look clean, Nora," the woman resumed. "As I say, New Yorkers would prefer a German or a Swede in the kitchen, but—who knows?—someone might be adventuresome enough to take you on. What exactly can you cook, Nora?"

Nora's mind was rattled. There was almost nothing she couldn't cook. She had helped Hannah with everything.

"My last employers preferred French food," she answered.

"*French* food?" Mrs. Watrous replied skeptically. "Can you prepare *suprêmes de volaille aux champignons? Or tournédos sauté chasseur?*" As she watched confusion overwhelm Nora's face, she pressed on. "*Gigot de chevreuil* or *tarte au citron?*"

Embarrassed, Nora declared, "We never called them by such elegant names, so I would not know. But I can do a nice roast duck in an orange sauce—

"*Caneton à l'orange!*" Mrs. Watrous interrupted.

"—and a much admired veal stew with onions and mushrooms."

"*Blanquette de veau à l'ancienne!*" the woman exclaimed rapturously.

"And for dessert," Nora continued, "the Wingfields were very fond of the little pancakes I made for them with an orange and almond butter. Redmond McCarthy would put a drop of cognac, it was called, over them, then touch a flame to it, and it was a sight to behold."

"*Crêpes fourrées et flambées!*" the woman exclaimed, clapping her hands. "But how marvelous, Nora! I think we might have something for you, after all." She consulted an index file on her desk. "Mrs. Austin Griswold is particularly desirous of finding someone who is familiar with French cuisine. She has asked for a Frenchwoman, but they're exceedingly difficult to run to ground. I suppose it's lethargy or something that prevents them from leaving France."

She removed a sheet of paper from a desk drawer and hastily began to write a note. "Mrs. Griswold has had a

107

bit of bad luck with Irish girls in the past and considers them temperamentally unsuited for her household, but I'm sure that you will win her over, Nora, once you recite your repertoire of French dishes. I'm writing a note of introduction for you now. You'll be expected, of course, to pay the agency a modest fee for our service, but we shall take care of that for you, deducting it from your salary."

"A fee?" Nora asked in surprise.

"A very modest ten percent of your first three months' wages. And I must remind you, Nora dear, that we are very firm and do not allow for delinquency. You understand, of course. We will not be able to help other poor and destitute girls like yourself, newcomers to our great city, unless our fees are paid promptly."

It was a lovely way to make a living, Nora thought. For writing a few words on a sheet of paper, the woman was to be paid for the next three months. For her three minutes' work, Nora would have to turn over part of her salary to her. Americans were very cunning indeed.

Mrs. Watrous stood and handed her the letter of introduction. "Here we are, my dear. I know how grateful you must feel. It is one of the keenest pleasures of life for me to watch the gratitude of young, friendless girls, adrift in a strange and often perilous land, who find friendship and refuge at the Gotham agency, established by my loving father over fifty-five years ago. And since then, Nora dear, we have dealt with clients from the very minute they step off the boat until the day they die in service. I humbly hope that we can have a long and mutually satisfactory association with you, as well."

Nora did not even ask the secretary in the outer office how to reach the address on East Sixty-seventh Street, for fear that she would be charged another ten percent of her salary for the favor. Instead, she walked along the teeming sidewalk—a babble of strange voices all around her—until she spied a policeman whose ginger hair and freckled face were guarantees that he would answer her question readily and without presenting her a bill, and perhaps even gab for a minute or two about

Clare or Mayo or wherever he was from, and Nora would derive comfort from his sweet, lilting talk.

Most of the houses she passed on the street that led off Fifth Avenue were of an unsavory brown shade of stone. A more revolting color she had never seen. Ornate wrought-iron railings at their stoops, however, tended to relieve some of the gloom, and gay geraniums and climbing wisteria added warmth and color. From time to time in the block, she saw white stone houses that looked very much like miniature versions of the palaces she remembered in the Italian and French prints the Wingfields had hanging on their walls, and it was in such a house that the Griswolds lived.

A man in a black suit and wearing a green apron was polishing the brass at the huge front door.

"I beg your pardon," Nora said, "but am I at the residence of the Austin Griswold family?"

He looked at her suspiciously. "If you are one of those lunatic evangelists, Madame has asked that you not call on her."

"I have been sent by Mrs. Watrous at the employment agency," she declared. "I am a cook."

The man stood up from his work and studied her. "Mr. Griswold is a most fastidious eater. Our last cook was French."

Once again, Nora explained that her previous employers had kept a French kitchen.

"The Griswolds are also exceedingly Christian," he continued, "as I am myself. The last Irish girl we had proved to be a drinker and was let go."

"I don't drink."

He picked up his polishing gear. "Then come with me. I shall ask Madame if she would care to see you. She is napping, I believe. Madame is sometimes afflicted with headaches."

Nora was shown into an opulent hall. A crystal chandelier hung from the ceiling, and red damask covered the walls. The furniture was of black horsehair upholstery from an earlier era and appeared never to have been sat upon. Potted plants—huge ferns and palms—filled the corners, and there was an odor of dust and decline about the place. Except for a long mahogany clock against the wall that ticked the seconds, there wasn't a sound.

In a minute, the butler reappeared. "Madame will see you."

Nora had expected to be led to a sitting room, but was instead invited to follow the butler up the stairs. At a door, he knocked, then opened it.

"You may sit down," a voice said to her from across the room.

A very young lady—she couldn't have been more than thirty—reclined on a chaise longue in a bedroom, fanning herself with what appeared to be a large paper leaf. Her hair was severely held at the back of her head by a bun, and she wore a dress that would have been more suitable for an elderly woman. Her face was pallid, and her eyes were hard and lusterless from fatigue or pain.

"I don't as a rule receive people in my bedroom," she began, "but I have one of my migraine headaches, and I find it helps to stay out of the bright light." The shutters in the room were half-drawn, and the windows looked northward onto a cool and leafy garden.

"It says here that you know something about French cuisine," she continued, holding up the letter. "My husband is very partial to it. He spent much of his youth in Paris, and has returned to New York only within the last four years."

"I am able to cook in the French style, ma'am."

A half-smile crossed the woman's face. "You're just a child."

"I'm almost eighteen, ma'am."

"And how, might I ask, have you learned to prepare French cuisine at such a young age?"

"I entered service when I was ten, ma'am. For three years I worked as a parlormaid, and when a vacancy occurred in the kitchen, I asked to be transferred. The Wingfields—my last employers—kept a French table."

"I see," she answered. "I'm afraid that I'm in no position to hire you, as my husband must do that, but perhaps you could prepare a meal for him so that he can judge your talents. I eat very little myself. Would you be able to do that this evening, do you think?" The woman consulted a lapel watch that hung from her bodice. "It's almost three o'clock. We generally dine at seven."

Nora knew that it would be a terrible challenge. At Doonmara House, she and Hannah had often spent the entire day preparing the single main meal. "I know nothing about obtaining provisions, ma'am," she replied truthfully.

"You could make a list of things you need, and Jack— he's the butler—will do the shopping for you. It needn't be an elaborate dinner. My husband would simply like something other than"—she paused, then grimaced— "*steak*. He says New Yorkers eat nothing but beefsteak."

"Then he will not have beefsteak tonight, ma'am."

"You're willing to try?"

"You've given me very little time, but I shall do something so that he won't go to bed hungry this evening."

"Very well," Mrs. Griswold answered, then leaned over to ring a bell. "If we do take you on, I might mention that we are resolute Christians and, apart from my husband's fondness for French food, we lead very simple lives. My husband insists on just two things: that we set a good table, and that profligacy will forever be a stranger to this house."

Profligacy? Nora could only guess what it meant. Sinfulness, she supposed. She was willing to concede that some people would consider her sinful for carrying a baby since she was unmarried. But to Nora, it seemed that an even greater sin would occur if she could not give the baby life and care for it, neither of which she could do unless she found employment.

"I am a Catholic, ma'am," she said, leaving it at that.

"We are not opposed to Papists, so long as you maintain a degree of self-control. My husband prides himself on his. I mention it now only because I would hate for us to have a misunderstanding later on, in the event that my husband finds your cooking to his satisfaction."

"I hope I don't disappoint you, ma'am."

The butler knocked, then entered the room. As he did, Mrs. Griswold said, "Jack, this young Irish girl will prepare a meal for us this evening. Will you be good enough to show her the kitchen and do the shopping for her? I've told her that we sit down to table at seven."

"Yes, Madame. Will that be all?"

As Nora rose to leave, the woman squinted at the pale light through the window shutters. "Will you close the shutters all the way, Jack. I am going to try to sleep for an hour or two. I got no sleep at all last night."

"Very good, Madame." He brought the shutters together, then adjusted them. "I shall ask the maid to be quiet."

To Nora, it seemed almost impossible for a house to be quieter than the Griswolds' as it was at the moment. It was very nearly sepulchral.

As he led her down the dark mahogany staircase, the butler turned to her and whispered, "Madame has had a tragedy. We all hope that your cooking proves satisfactory to Monsieur, as dining is his solitary pleasure in life now, apart from his religion."

Nora followed him into the gloomy kitchen.

Within the hour, Jack returned, laden with bags, and accompanied by a butcher's boy, who entered on the run, carrying the meats and the fish. Jack explained that henceforth, if she remained in the house, she would do her own shopping in the morning and her provisions would be delivered in the early afternoon. The neighborhood to the north of them, he said, was inhabited by German-Americans, and it was commonly thought that they were the best butchers and grocers in New York.

"They're all puffed out with pride now," he continued, "seeing as how the Kaiser is about to become emperor of the world, but my advice to you is never to listen to a German talk politics. Sausage and pastry and beer and a *guten Tag* from time to time—I'd limit my conversation to that."

They certainly acquitted themselves very well in the fowl department. She had never seen a finer, plumper chicken. In Ireland, the chickens were often tough and scrawny, having spent most of their lives digging around the muck heaps next to the stables, but these Yankee chickens looked as if they had dined on buttered toast and fresh cream. And the livers she had asked for in order to make a pâté were big enough to play golf with, yet tender to the touch. Only the fish disappointed her. She had asked for a sole, and what Jack produced didn't quite look like one, though he said that the butcher had told him it tasted about the same. A flounder, he called it.

As an appetizer, Nora decided to serve the pâté—it was one of the few French words she knew, and pronounced by Hannah as "potty"—because Lady Wingfield had always liked it before the fish course. The American sole she would do in a white wine with a cream and egg-yolk sauce. The beautiful chicken she would roast in red wine and mushrooms, and with it she would serve asparagus—they were gorgeous; she marveled at their beauty—and buttered rice. For dessert, she would create both lemon tarts and a strawberry soufflé, and the Griswolds could choose one or the other.

She set to work with a frenzy, and the very first thing she did was open the windows, which appeared not to have been disturbed in twenty years. Next, with the aid of Jack, she made a wood fire in the enormous stove, Jack explaining that Mr. Griswold would not tolerate the use of any other fuel, as it spoiled the flavor of food, he maintained.

She did the desserts first, as she knew that they could be cooling while the rest of the meal was prepared. She removed her heavy woolen jacket and worked in her shirt sleeves, but still found that she was wringing wet by the time she had them ready for the oven. She made herself a cup of tea to fortify herself, then set herself to the task of grinding the pâté. There would be no soup course, as was customary in Ireland, because the weather was too hot, and the chilled pâté on thin slices of toast would awaken and enliven the appetite far better.

Jack had asked her what kind of wine she would need for the fish and chicken, and Nora had to confess that she didn't know. Hannah had always chosen the wines for cooking.

"Madame and Monsieur do not imbibe," Jack said,

"as it is against their religion. But they permit wine to be used in their cooking, because its alcoholic content is rendered out of it during the process."

Nora applauded their reasoning, then suggested that Jack make the choices himself.

When he returned, minutes later, with two bottles, he declared, "The wine cellar has not been touched since our last cook left the household. It shows you, Miss Shannon, that temperance is often a matter of racial disposition. Madame and Monsieur Griswold both derive from old New England families, and the baser human instincts have been bred out of them."

"I see," Nora replied, then began to ready the fish and the chicken. As she did, Jack told her a bit about the family. The house had belonged to Mr. Griswold's father, who had begun as a Boston merchant, but transferred his activities to New York. The younger Mr. Griswold—who preferred to be addressed as Monsieur—had gone to Paris after having graduated from Harvard, and had hoped to become an artist. Upon his father's death, however, he had returned home to look after the family business, a department store on Fifth Avenue. It was said that he had no great zeal for his work.

"And what of Mrs. Griswold?" Nora asked.

"He married her shortly after he returned to this country, and they had a beautiful little baby girl, but just last year"—he paused under the burden of emotion—"she was called to God."

"The poor creature."

"And now we are all hoping that Madame will have another child, but God has not granted one yet."

"What did their baby die of, Jack?"

He looked toward the door to see if anyone was listening, then bent over and whispered, "If you ask me, she died of neglect, but you can't tell that to the Griswolds. No doctor was called. You see, their faith does not permit it. Divine healing alone is allowed."

Nora was surprised to learn that there was such a branch of Christianity. Until now, in fact, she had thought that the world had only two religions, Catholic and Protestant, though she had heard that there were a few Jews

114

as well, who were sometimes irritants, but in an amiable sort of way.

"I am a Methodist," Jack said, "and Muriel, the maid, is a Baptist, so we do not share the Griswolds' views."

"Do the Methodists in America have wars against the Baptists?" she asked.

He looked outraged. "In this country, there are hundreds of religions. Though some are less fashionable than others, all are tolerated. We live together in harmony."

She looked up from her work. "You don't hate each other?"

"We don't always agree with each other, but we don't hate each other. You see, Miss Shannon—it is 'Miss,' isn't it?"

Nora faltered. "It's *Mrs.* My husband is dead."

"Ah," he said. "You have my pity, Mrs. Shannon. As I was saying, in this country, all men are equal and all religions are equal. You have left ignorance and despotism behind you. You are in a free land now."

Despite the heat in the kitchen from the roaring wood fire, and the fear that she might perhaps have disremembered one of Hannah's recipes, Nora felt at ease, as if she had stumbled upon a sanctuary. In time, when her pregnancy became obvious, she would have to appeal to the Griswolds' Christianity. And if they believed that God could will deaths, as in the case of their baby girl, it seemed to Nora that they might also believe that God was capable of willing life, as in the case of Nora's own child. Certainly there was something almost miraculous about a baby who lived inside her, even now drawing sustenance from her, while Thomas lay sleeping in his dark grave.

Yes, Nora considered herself very fortunate to have found the Griswolds. As she prepared the evening meal, she worked with a passion, praying that they would like her sufficiently well to take her on.

At seven o'clock, when Nora handed the pâté and toast to Jack to be carried into the dining room, her hands were trembling. The air was aromatic with herbs, spices, and wines, and she had watched heads poke out of windows across the courtyard to determine its source, yet Nora was nonetheless apprehensive. The neighbors were perhaps less discriminating than Monsieur Griswold.

She waited until Jack returned the empty plates—the pâté was consumed, though some toast wedges remained —before she lifted the fish from its pan and onto the platter. Nothing was more ruinous to good food than having it served cold.

"What do they be saying, Jack?" she asked as she poured the rich sauce over the fish.

"Nothing," he replied. "I warn you, these New Englanders are not very demonstrative. They've got a firm grip on their emotions, Mrs. Shannon."

"Not a word about the potty?"

"Not a word."

After Jack had brought the fish to the table and served it, Nora left the chicken momentarily to peek through the crack between the door and the frame. At one end of the table sat Mrs. Griswold, who had changed into a somewhat less severe dress for dinner. Listlessly, she brought her fork to her mouth, then rested it on her plate. Her attention did not seem to be on her food, but on her husband, who sat at the other end of the table in a dark business suit. He was addressing himself entirely to his meal and did not speak to, or even look at, his wife. Apart from the fact that his hair was thinning—he would be bald in a number of years—he was a handsome man of forty or so, Nora would say, older than his wife. Nora could not read his face at all; whether he was enjoying his food or not, she was unable to tell.

Almost with desperation, she now finished the sauce for the chicken and that for the asparagus, which would be served with it. By the time Jack returned the used dishes, she was ready with the next course.

"Did they say anything yet?" she asked.

He shook his head sadly.

When Jack left with the platter, she did not this time follow him to look through the crack of the door. She sat down in a chair by an opened window and watched a small portion of the sky not hidden by buildings and yearned for the huge, cloud-strewn skies of Ireland.

She hoped at least that they would give her something

116

for her day's work, and carfare home. By the time she had cleaned up—though Jack had told her that he would help—it would be after nine, and she still had to get back to her room on Tenth Avenue. Hell's Kitchen, her landlady had called it, and Nora had been surprised to hear such an unflattering description of a neighborhood. It was the summer heat and the people screaming and yelling at each other through opened windows that led to its name, she supposed. The little room she had found was quite tidy. Nora had told the woman at the rooming house that she would probably not be staying beyond a week, as she expected to be living in the house where she worked. What she didn't tell the woman was that she couldn't afford to stay there beyond a week. She had to find a job at once.

Tomorrow, she would simply have to go back to Mrs. Watrous at the employment agency and ask if any vacancies existed for Irish housemaids. If she had to scrub floors in order to survive, she would do it. She had done it before.

When Jack carried the dirty dishes into the kitchen, she didn't ask him what their comments had been. Instead, she pointed to the two desserts waiting on the kitchen table.

"They look very good to me, Mrs. Shannon," he said optimistically.

Nora smiled weakly but did not reply. After he had brought the lemon tarts and the strawberry soufflé into the dining room, she began to scrape the dishes and prepare to wash them.

She did not even hear Jack enter the kitchen and set the plates near the sink.

"Which dessert did they eat, Jack?"

"Both."

Both? God in Heaven, they ate two lemon tarts and a whole strawberry soufflé!

"And what did they say, Jack?"

"Nothing. I told you, Mrs. Shannon, they're New Englanders."

In another minute, Jack answered the bell that was controlled by a button on the floor next to Mr. Griswold's

117

feet. When he returned to the kitchen, he announced, "Monsieur would like to see you."

Nora removed the apron she had tied around her long black skirt, smoothed back her hair, then entered the dining room. She stood before Mr. Griswold.

"You called, sir?"

He peered at her through metal-rimmed spectacles. "Yes," he replied. "Tomorrow, we shall have you fitted for uniforms, one for the morning and one for evening. Before I leave for work, I shall discuss the supper menu with you. You will live with us and will be expected to work every day but Sunday. Your salary will be four dollars a week, and for Christmas you will receive a four-dollar bonus. I think that is all. You may go now. Good-night."

Nora curtsied, then hurried from the room. These rich Yanks certainly rationed their enthusiasm. Except for small portions she had kept aside for Jack and herself, the Griswolds had eaten everything in sight, yet hadn't paid her a single compliment. Perhaps New Englanders considered animation a sign of inferior breeding.

As for the salary, it wasn't much, but it would do. She would have her meals and a free room, and apart from buying a dress for Sundays, she would have virtually nothing in the way of expenses. Most of what she earned could be sent to her family in Ireland, where four dollars a week was considered a fortune.

Late that night when she returned to her rooming house, she informed her landlady that she would be leaving the following day. She had a small favor to ask of her, however. Could she be permitted to have her mail sent to her at the rooming house? She had already provided her parents with the address, she said, and she did not want to confuse them.

It was a bit unusual, the landlady replied, but she had no objection.

If that was the case, Nora would call once a week, each Sunday, in order to collect what mail she might receive.

"Very good, Miss Shannon," the woman said.

Though Nora hated deception, she saw no alternative. Under no circumstances could her family—or anyone else in Ireland—learn of her condition. She had told the Griswolds that she was married, but her letters from home would be addressed to Miss Nora Shannon. Besides, Patrick was somewhere in the New World, and it was quite possible that he would attempt to trace her.

Long after she had gone to bed, Nora lay with the rosary still in her hands, drawing strength from it just as her mother had said she would. Though she had sinned in the eyes of the Church, her faith alone would see her through the ordeal ahead. Her faith and her beloved Thomas. For if, because of her fall from grace, God was no longer watching her, she knew with certainty that Thomas was, and he would intercede on her behalf.

In spite... ...

Nearly four blocks away from the city two-and-a-half inhabitants—nearly a million had arrived the year before—... looked ... their ... Then ... blood and sorrow ...

12

Only four blocks away in a city awash with immigrants —nearly a million had arrived the year before— Patrick looked down onto Ninth Avenue near Thirty-fourth Street and wondered how anyone could sleep in such heat and such deafening noise. An elevated train roared up the avenue only inches away from him—he could lean out the window and almost touch it—shaking the floor beneath his feet and rattling the windowpanes. The huge black steel skeleton on which it sped occupied everything on the street but the sidewalks, and was even uglier in daylight than at night.

God knows, he would never have chosen the place to live had he not met an Irish porter the minute he stepped off the ferryboat from Ellis Island. At the Battery, the man greeted him with great conviviality, as if he'd known him all his life, then grabbed his few belongings and walked him toward a taxi. He represented a rooming house, he explained, where Hibernians were especially welcome, which was something of a novelty in New York City. It was most convenient to public transportation, he added, neglecting to mention that the el passed only a few feet from the windows.

When Patrick saw the room, however, he was sure he would have done far better on his own, but by that time he was aware that the porter made his living enticing newly arrived immigrants to the squalid rooming house; if Patrick turned down the room, the poor man might lose his job. Out of pity more than anything, he decided to remain.

The next morning, the first thing he did was make his way on foot to Gramercy Park in search of Mary Mc-

Namara. Not only was she Patrick's solitary connection in New York, but Nora's as well, and he was sure that Nora had set out from Ireland shortly after he did. When he located the redbrick house, it appeared to be unlived in; the curtains were drawn and no one answered the door. He left, vowing to return several days later.

This evening, he had called again at the house on Gramercy Park, and this time a young maid in a starched white uniform spoke to him from the steps of the house next door.

"If it's the Pincus family you're calling on, they are in Newport, Rhode Island, for the summer," she told him.

Patrick explained that it was Mary McNamara who was the object of his visit.

"Sure and you're the second greenhorn within the week who's come looking for her."

"And who was the first, may I ask?"

"A young colleen who looked as if she just got off the boat. She was still carrying her satchel, and her eyes were as big as saucers."

"Did she say where she was staying?"

"That she didn't. I told her what I've just told yourself, then she left, quick as a mouse."

Patrick supplied her with his address in the event that Nora should reappear, though it seemed to him doubtful. As soon as he returned to his room, he wrote a letter to Nora's mother and father—they could not read, but someone could perform the service for them—asking for Nora's whereabouts in the New World.

He was very apprehensive about her, for if the city was frightening and intimidating to Patrick, he could imagine how poor Nora must be reacting to it. And he had not forgotten the pledge he had made to Thomas to look after her if anything happened to him.

It was well after midnight now, and Patrick was tired from having spent the day searching for work in the merciless heat. His feet, unused to sidewalks, were badly blistered, and his ankles ached. Tomorrow he would have to begin again. He could have been hired a dozen times had he been willing to wield a pick and shovel or serve as hod carrier, but he hoped for something that offered brighter prospects. An office job of some sort, perhaps, where he could use his mind. Or a modest managerial position. But whenever he applied for such jobs, he was reminded that he had no experience and no references.

He left the window and returned to his bed. He was naked, but even the sheets were hot. Huge gnats—mosquitoes, the Yanks called them—swarmed against the screens, and vermin scurried over the bare floor. The room was airless and smelled of dirt and decay. In the distance, another train began its thunderous approach.

He closed his eyes and thought of Lucy Caverly.

It was she who had spirited him away from West Cork and out of the country. In his rage, Patrick would have gone in pursuit of the constabulary, had it not been for her. But she had persuaded him that he must leave for Queenstown immediately or forfeit his life: "It is the age-old pattern, Patrick. An outrage is committed, and there is need of a reprisal. Then there is another outrage that results in still another reprisal. If you don't leave Ireland now, you're a dead man. Please, for my sake, go."

He had had time only for a hasty farewell to his grieving mother before they set out for the Cove of Cork. Lucy drove at dizzying speed, and he sat next to her, his head flung back, dazed and remote.

At the steamship office, she took charge of everything in her brisk, efficient way. He was to travel under the name John Caverly in the event that the constabulary had been alerted and attempted to prevent him from boarding the ship. She supplied him with fifty pounds, asking him to return what he didn't use, as she had need of it as well. If someday he could pay it back, she would be thankful; if not, she would understand.

"Why are you doing this for me?" he asked at last.

"Because I like you," she replied. "If our families weren't so different and our religions so opposed, I think that I should love you."

Patrick, too, had felt an emotion not unlike love, and he had also dismissed it. He was a peasant, if perhaps cleverer than most. Lucy was a very grand lady, if perhaps less grand than some.

"What will happen between you and Harry Wingfield?" he asked.

"I hope nothing," she answered. "No matter what else has been accomplished—the Rising, the death and destruction—I know that my life can never be the same, and I doubt that Harry's will be, either. I'm not going to marry him, I know that now. I never wanted to. I was just trying to oblige my mother. The best thing for me to do now is to go to England and throw myself at the mercy of my cousins. They'll help me, I'm sure."

"Then you're leaving Ireland, too?"

"I am leaving Ireland, too," she said sadly. "We are like the Wild Geese of old, Patrick—scattered and homeless and dispossessed."

"I shall never forget you, Lucy," he declared, "and what you've done for me."

"Nor shall I ever forget you, Patrick."

Quickly, she kissed him, then turned and ran.

He had not heard a word of her since.

Now, in another country and after an almost sleepless night, Patrick stood in front of a short, balding man with dolorous brown eyes. His skin looked jaundiced, and his hands trembled as he relit a black cigar.

"If you're a friend of that *schlemiel* I just kicked out of here," he said, "you're wasting my time, gentleman."

Patrick explained how he had come to inquire about the vacancy. He had scoured lower Manhattan all morning long looking for work, but had found nothing open for Irish immigrants other than the most menial of jobs. At a newspaper stand around the corner, he had overheard a young girl complain that she had been fired from her job only minutes before, and that Mr. Ginsburg, her supervisor, had been discharged at the same time. Ten minutes later, Patrick was applying for the latter's position at the Diamond Shirtwaist Company on Greene Street.

"The bastard was dallying with my girls," Mr. Weiss, the manager, said to him from behind his cluttered desk. "What a man does on his own time is his business, but what he does on company time is my business and Mr.

Balaban's business. I caught him trying to bang a girl in the shipping room, so I fired both of 'em."

Patrick confessed that he would have no need for such adventures, as he was a good Catholic and firmly resisted carnal temptation.

The man's sad eyes lit up. "When I was your age, I wore out all the women. But no more because my prostate is shot to hell. Enjoy yourself while you can. But I'll tell you one thing"—he shook his black cigar at Patrick—"if you do it on company time, you're finished at Diamond Shirtwaist."

Patrick wondered if all New Yorkers were as earthy as Mr. Weiss, or if such candor was peculiar to managers of shirtwaist factories. Yet the man was not without charm. There was a warmth and openness about him.

"Listen, Mick," he continued, using the name that New Yorkers often applied to male Hibernians, "someone has to help me look after those animals out there." He waved his arm toward a window that separated his office from the factory where women sat at sewing machines. "I hate them, I won't foolya. They're my enemies and they're Mr. Balaban's enemies, but I have to live with them or I go out of business. They lie and they cheat and they steal. Most of all, they steal. If I don't stand by the door at quitting time every day, there isn't a woman in the place who wouldn't try to stuff one of my shirtwaists in her pocketbook and sell it once she gets to the street. I tell you, I wish I'd never heard of this damn business."

Mr. Weiss held his head in his hands.

"Don't get me wrong," he resumed. "I don't own the place. Mr. Balaban does, my wife's uncle. But if it don't show a profit, I'm the one who gets kicked in the ass. I've got a bad heart. I can't take much more of this. Life is hard enough without them animals out there stealing from me. How can Diamond Shirtwaist show a profit if those bohunks take Mr. Balaban's shirtwaists and hawk them around the corner on Washington Square? It's a problem. Do you agree, gentleman?"

Patrick agreed, then asked Mr. Weiss to describe the duties of a piecework supervisor.

"I got two kindsa employees, gentleman. I got cutters

125

and I got seamstresses. My cutters are men, and my seamstresses are animals. I keep a strict inventory of material that my cutters deliver to the women who sew it. I know exactly how many shirtwaists I can get out of a bolt of cloth. It goes from one side of the floor to the other; I see it leave, I see it arrive. I watch my seamstresses sew it together. Still, the bastards rob me blind. I don't know how. That's why I need a smart piecework supervisor who don't spend his time banging my girls in the shipping room. He has to make sure my product ain't stole. You follow me, gentleman? Can you read and write? Let me see you write something. Here."

He handed Patrick a sheet of paper and what appeared to be an order for shirtwaists. He then dipped a pen into an inkwell and placed it in Patrick's fist. *"Write!"* he commanded.

Slowly and with great care, Patrick began to copy it. His handwriting was neat and almost feminine in its grace, having been patterned after that of Lady Caverly.

"It ain't bad," Mr. Weiss said when Patrick had finished. "Do you know how to add and subtract? So tell me what nine plus seven is."

Without hesitation, Patrick replied, "Sixteen, sir."

"One hundred divided by three."

"Thirty-three and a third, sir."

"You're not so dumb," Mr. Weiss concluded. "Tellya what. If you promise not to bang my girls on company time, the job is yours. Okay, Cassidy? I'll get one of my supervisors to show you around." He rose from his desk and waddled to the door. Over the din of the sewing machines, he shouted, *"Kaganoff!"*

In a minute, a young man not much older than Patrick appeared. His face was gaunt, and his eyes were hard and glacial. He looked Christlike, or at least like those fanciful renditions Patrick had seen, though perhaps his hair was darker and he was more emaciated. As he approached, his eyes did not leave Patrick's for a second, and Patrick saw something like enmity or distrust in them.

"This Mick here will be doing Ginsburg's work from now on," Mr. Weiss said to him. "I want you to break him in. Show him what he has to do."

He than turned to Patrick. "As for you, Cassidy, just remember: no fraternizing with these bohunks here. I want a good day's work out of 'em. I don't want to hear of their complaints. There's no room here for troublemakers. If you find a troublemaker, you let me know, and out she goes on her butt. You understand? Okay. Kaganoff will tell you what you have to do. By tomorrow, I want you working like you been here for ten years, because tomorrow's Thursday, and that's the day that Mr. Balaban visits. It don't do to make him unhappy, Cassidy. If he's unhappy, my wife's unhappy, I'm unhappy, and you'll be unhappy, too. So what are you standing there for? Get going!"

Sheepishly, Patrick followed the dark-haired young man into the huge loft where four hundred women were bent, elbow to elbow, over sewing machines. In the stifling heat, sweat poured down their faces. A few appeared to be Irish, but most of them looked Eastern European or Mediterranean: Russian, Polish, or Italian. They still wore the peasant dresses of their native lands, and some, to protect their hair from flying lint, wore babushkas over their heads.

At last, Kaganoff stopped. "You will be responsible for the girls in the first twenty rows. As they complete a garment, you will examine it for imperfections and enter it in our inventory. Then you will provide them with cutwork for another blouse. Many of them do not understand English, and they will be terrified of you. Despite what Mr. Weiss has told you, it would be a kindness if you didn't tyrannize them. I can speak only for the Russian Jews; we have had more than our share of tyranny."

He spoke with an accent that was quite different from that of Mr. Weiss. "Then you are a Russian?" Patrick asked.

"I was," he replied. "I will soon be an American."

"And is Mr. Weiss also a Russian?"

Kaganoff snorted derisively. "He is also a Jew, but he is a German Jew. We have very little in common. I am sure that I can tell you what he called the women who work here. He called them animals, didn't he?" He waited, then continued, "To Mr. Balaban, his brother-in-law, he will say that *I* am an animal and you are, too."

He led Patrick down an aisle between two rows of machines, then stopped behind a woman who had just completed a shirtwaist. He examined it for imperfections, drawing his finger over the seams. "They must meet smoothly," he explained. "If they do not, Mr. Weiss will not pay for them. Most of the women are very accomplished seamstresses and know that if they are sloppy, their pay envelope on Saturday will reflect it. Mr. Weiss does not like them to relax between jobs, so you will have to anticipate when they are about to finish a blouse and provide them with cutwork for a new one. If it becomes necessary for them to use the toilet, they must ask your permission. If someone is gone for more than five minutes, you are to bring it to the attention of Mr. Weiss. We work ten hours a day, six days a week. As hard as it is, the girls would work a seventh day, too, because they need the money so desperately. As it is, they don't make enough to live on."

Patrick hadn't dared ask Mr. Weiss what his salary would be. He now put the question to Kaganoff.

"You will make nine dollars a week," he replied. "If the girls are fast and nimble, they are lucky to make seven."

But that was impossible! Patrick's rent for his room in Hell's Kitchen was five dollars a week. If he made what the seamstresses made, it would allow him only two dollars a week for food.

"For the love of God," Patrick exclaimed, "how do they stay alive?"

"Many of them don't. Almost a third of the girls you see here will be dead before they're twenty-five."

Patrick could not conceal his consternation. "But you say that some of them are Jews!"

"Sixty percent of them."

"And Mr. Weiss, the manager, is a Jew?"

"Yes, and Mr. Balaban, the owner, is also a Jew."

Patrick shook his head. "Then I don't understand."

"What don't you understand, Irishman?" Kaganoff asked. "Did you think that in this world only the British persecute the Irish? I assure you that the condition is universal. People *prey* upon other people. It is as human as drawing breath."

Patrick looked into Kaganoff's eyes and saw that the distrust that had been there only minutes ago had now disappeared.

"My name is Saul," Kaganoff said, holding out his hand.

"Cassidy. Patrick Cassidy. Is it all right to shake hands on company time?"

A grin lifted Saul Kaganoff's lips. "If Mr. Weiss sees us, he will probably dock our salaries."

"Isn't there any way we can open the windows and let some air in here?"

Saul turned to see if Mr. Weiss was within earshot. "The management is afraid that the girls will steal shirtwaists and throw them to their friends on the sidewalk."

"What about the doors in the back? Can't they be opened?"

Bitterly, Saul replied, "They are kept locked to prevent union organizers from entering the shop. They are not opened until closing time, when Mr. Weiss stands by the door and searches the girls as they leave."

Saul's eyes plumbed Patrick's face. When he was certain he had found what he hoped for, he said, "Welcome to America, Irishman."

During the course of the long afternoon, Patrick began to associate personalities with the faces that looked up at him as he collected their work. In almost all of them he detected fear.

Some were no older than fourteen, he thought, while others were as old as seventy. At least one was seventy-four.

A woman with gnarled fingers and a weather-beaten face pointed at herself and said proudly, "Sef-en-tee-four year olt. Is goot, no?"

Patrick admitted that it was very good indeed to be working ten hours a day, six days a week, at such an age, though he privately regretted that it was necessary.

129

He tapped his breast with a finger. "Eighteen," he told her.

"Is goot, eighteen," she answered.

"Is very good."

She smiled wildly. "I am Sophie," she said painstakingly, "Bernstein."

"Hello, Sophie. I am Patrick Cassidy."

She shook her head in confusion, objecting to the foreign name. "Kess—?" she began.

"*Cass*idy."

"No! You are Mr. Eighteen. Is more easy."

As he went from Singer machine to machine, from Wilcox and Gibbs stitcher to stitcher, he began to commit the names of the girls to memory. There were Yettas, Claras, Josephines, Celias, Roses, Idas, Julias, and Delias. Their last names sometimes defied pronunciation. Their features were unlike any he had ever seen before. Some had eyes set far apart, some had prominent noses, some had narrow foreheads, and almost all had dark skin and black hair. The Italian girls were more shy than frightened when he stood next to them, yet the minute he walked away they began to chatter in their own tongue, then laugh. Though he was not sure, he supposed that they were talking about him. The Russians and the Poles were less merry and more apprehensive, as if they were accustomed to cruel authority and had learned that silence was less likely to provoke antagonism than a word or a facial expression.

A few of the young girls were astonishingly pretty. One —Sonia Lipsky, as the name next to her machine number in his ledger read—was beautiful. She sat in the last of the rows that Patrick was expected to oversee, and he was not surprised when Saul Kaganoff gently touched her shoulder as he passed behind her.

"You are a friend of Saul's?" he asked the next time he stopped at her machine.

"We are both from Russia," she replied.

Patrick smiled. "This is my first job in America."

"*Mazel tov.*"

"*Mazel tov?*"

"Congratulations."

From time to time, as he ran out of cut material to be distributed, he had to fetch it from the cutters' tables at the very end of the room. The men who labored there wore black beards and tiny skull-caps. They worked with incredible haste, arranging layer after layer of the light material before them—*lawn,* one of them told him it was called—then placing their paper pattern over it and cutting through it with a short knife. Some worked on collars, some on arms, some on fronts and backs, and some on cuffs. They seldom spoke to one another as they worked, and when they did, it was in a foreign tongue.

One girl—Esther Hochfield was the name entered in the ledger next to her machine number—worked more slowly than the others, and twice during the afternoon she asked Patrick for permission to go to the toilet. The first time, immediately upon returning, he saw that she was offering him a completed shirtwaist, and he was surprised that it was finished, as it hadn't been when she left. The second time, he watched as a completed shirtwaist was passed down the long row of machines, from girl to girl, until it reached her empty seat, then Esther's just-begun shirtwaist traveled down the row in the opposite direction. It happened a third time, then a fourth, and on each occasion a different girl substituted a finished blouse for the unsewn cutwork material.

Patrick was mystified but said nothing and decided not to bring it to the attention of Mr. Weiss.

At the end of the day a shrill bell clanged, and almost at once the power for the sewing machines was cut. The girls tidied up, then rose to make their way to the dressing room for their wraps and their pocketbooks. As they left the factory, Mr. Weiss stood by the door that led to the staircase, and as each girl passed, she held out her opened pocketbook for him to inspect.

Patrick stood in line with the others, watching in fascination. One after another, the girls offered their pocketbooks to him. If something obstructed his view, his fist dug to the bottom, rifling the contents.

As Patrick stood in front of him, he half expected to be frisked, but without a word Mr. Weiss waved him through.

Waiting outside on the curb were Saul Kaganoff and Sonia Lipsky. As Patrick sailed from the building, Saul asked, "Did the Cossack make you bend over and drop your pants so he could look up your cheeks?"

Sonia laughed at the ribaldry and so did Patrick. "Why do you call him a Cossack?" he asked.

Sonia answered, "He's like the Cossack soldiers in Russia who drove us from our homes."

"I'm surprised that such people have been allowed to enter America."

"You've got a lot to learn, Irishman," Saul declared. "Everyone who comes to this country thinks that he's left his hated landlord behind him in Europe, but it doesn't happen that way. What happens, Cassidy, is that our landlords arrive on the next boat, except that they come first class. But we shall survive. We always do. How did your day go, Pat?"

Patrick replied that it had gone well. The job was less taxing on the intellect than on his feet. "There's only one thing," he added. "One girl doesn't seem to be working as hard as the others."

"You mean Esther?" Sonia replied. "She is ill."

"She has TB, and the Cossack would fire her if he knew that she isn't producing as much as the other girls. They all help her out, as they know her family needs the money."

"Ginsburg always overlooked it," Sonia said.

"Ginsburg? That's the fellow who was let go because he was bothering one of the girls?"

Saul looked at Sonia to see her reaction. "I told you the Cossack would tell a story like that." He turned to Patrick. "What exactly did he say?"

Patrick tried to recall. The word Mr. Weiss had used was "bang," which apparently was an Americanism. Patrick preferred to put it differently. "He said that Ginsburg was—taking liberties with a girl in the shipping room."

"Like hell he was," Sonia interrupted.

"Then what was it if it wasn't that?"

Saul waited, perhaps debating with himself, then decided that Patrick could be entrusted with the truth. "The Cossacks found out that Ginsburg was a union organizer, and they always fire such people. They keep an open shop, they say—which means that it's open for them, but for no one else. I'm sure he asked you to be alert for troublemakers."

Patrick confessed that he had. "But I didn't know what he meant."

Sonia smiled. "Now you do."

"By now, you should also know why Mr. Weiss hired you. He was sure you wouldn't be a troublemaker."

Patrick was stunned by the character evaluation. So Mr. Weiss had seen the resignation on his face, had he? Well, tragedy had placed it there, and Patrick no longer had an appetite for trouble. If something was less than perfect at the Diamond Shirtwaist Company, it was for others to correct, not him.

As his new friends turned to walk south toward Pike Slip, where they lived, Patrick stepped off the curb and, deep in thought, began to make his way west toward Ninth Avenue.

13

For fear that Monsieur Griswold would reconsider, Nora stood on the stoop of his handsome town house at shortly after dawn, a satchel in one arm, a shawl in the other: everything she owned in the world. It wasn't even six o'clock, and she was reluctant to ring the bell. At last, after the milkman arrived and made a fearful commotion, she saw a form move down the stairs and into the hall. She tapped softly on the windowpane.

A face—opalescent and spectral—peered out at her. At first, Nora did not recognize its owner, nor did Madame Griswold appear to understand the reason for Nora's being there. Revelation came to both more or less simultaneously. Madame Griswold opened the door.

"I've had a most awful night," she said to Nora, "but perhaps I shall be able to sleep an hour or two this morning."

"I shall fix some hot milk for you, Madame."

"Oh, that would be a kindness."

In the kitchen, Mrs. Griswold flung herself into a chair. She wore a long, flowing nightgown, and her hair was loose in back. Her fingers played nervously with it as she watched Nora make a fire in the stove and set a pan of milk over it. Nora asked her new employer if she had long been troubled by sleeplessness.

"I never sleep," Madame replied, "except in the mornings. For most of the night, I am at prayer." Mrs. Griswold's hands trembled as Nora set the warm milk before her.

"Sleep is a reward for an active life, Madame," Nora declared. "If you are busy during the day, I wager that you will be able to sleep at night. Do you have many activities?"

"Nothing other than my church," she replied. "My husband doesn't like me to leave the house without him. There is so much evil in New York, he says."

There was evil everywhere, Nora admitted. The fact that it existed in New York did not make the partaking of it compulsory. "I shall be doing my shopping late in the mornings," she began, "and Jack has volunteered to come with me. Once I am familiar with the neighborhood and the shops, perhaps you would like to come instead."

Mrs. Griswold shook her head. "My husband would never permit me, I'm sure."

"There would be no harm in asking, Madame."

As the woman sipped at her milk, she studied Nora. "You are very pretty, and walking down the street must be exhilarating. I'm very plain. I know that people laugh at me."

"But you have a very handsome face, Madame!"

"Handsome? Being handsome is not the same as being pretty. I take after my father. I have his features. It is the curse of New England girls that we look more like our fathers than our mothers."

Nora didn't know how to begin to commiserate, so said nothing at all. Instead, she busied herself by searching through the cupboards. She would like to make something special for Monsieur Griswold's breakfast, but she had very little time and the provisions left something to be desired.

"Would Monsieur care for hot scones for breakfast, Madame?" she asked.

"Monsieur Griswold never takes anything for breakfast other than coffee and his health tonic, which is a glass of vinegar containing a spoonful of honey."

Nora felt her lips pucker at the very mention of it. To begin a day with that in one's throat seemed to her the worst kind of punishment. "Is that a New England custom?" she asked. "Vinegar for breakfast?"

"We are very sturdy people," Madame replied.

You would have to be, Nora said to herself. She mixed the batter for the scones, anyway.

At eight o'clock—exactly midway through the tolling of the eighth hour on the long-case cherrywood clock—Monsieur Griswold sat down at the dining-room table, at which his breakfast plate had been set. His wife had already returned to bed. He opened the morning newspaper, then looked up at Nora, who stood near the door. While Nora pinched her fingers together, he swallowed without pause the pestilential-looking vinegar and honey she had provided him.

"I have prepared the supper menu for you," he said when he had finished, then handed her a sheet of business stationery on which it was written.

"I shall read it as soon as I have served your breakfast, sir."

"I have dispensed with the French," he continued, "as Madame informs me that you have no knowledge of that language."

It wasn't all that Nora lacked a knowledge of, but she thought it wise not to bring it to his attention. "That is true, sir," she said.

"You might have a look at it now."

Nora scrutinized the sheet of paper. She stroked her chin with her fingers and from time to time sighed. "Ah, yes," she said, tracing a line of Monsieur's script, "that will be lovely." Then again, "A nice touch. I'm particularly fond of this." And finally, "I'm sure we will have no trouble at all, Monsieur Griswold."

"Very well. You may serve coffee now," he concluded. "Mine alone, as Madame, who has had a catastrophic night, is still trying to get some sleep. I take nothing for breakfast but my vinegar tonic and coffee."

"Then you will not want scones, Monsieur?"

He pondered it. "It's doubtful, but you might send one or two in."

In the end, Nora supplied him with a plate of four, along with butter and marmalade, and he consumed every one. As he ate, Nora showed the supper menu to Jack.

"What do you think of it, Jack?" she asked.

He read it item by item. "I've always liked a leg of lamb in garlic sauce."

137

She clapped her hands together. "Sure and I do myself," she said with animation. "And I suppose with the lamb, Monsieur would like some nice roast potatoes?"

Jack squinted his eyes at her, then once again consulted the menu. "It's exactly what he has asked for."

"And a salad, I suppose?"

Jack cocked his head in bafflement. "You're having difficulty in reading his handwriting, I'd say."

"I'm not used to an American hand, Jack," she replied. "All these—curlicues. The English and the Irish never write this way."

He plucked the menu from her and reread it. It was the most Spartan, unadorned, businesslike hand he had ever read.

"You can't read a word, can you?" he said, confronting her.

"No," she answered truthfully. "Will you tell Monsieur?"

"Why should I tell him? I can read the damn things for you. Madame has asked me to help you with the shopping, anyway, until you find your way around."

"That's very good of you, Jack. I appreciate it."

He smiled. "Just save me a scone or two. That will be sufficient."

"Thank you, Jack."

Nora already felt at ease. Not only did she have a job, but she had also acquired a friend.

"Tonight after supper," he began, "I shall take you to a school where you can learn to read and write."

"But I would be ashamed to go there with all the children."

"*Hah!*" he exclaimed. "They're all greenhorns. You'll be one of the youngest ones there, I'd say. Many of them are grandmothers and grandfathers."

Nora was awed by the prospect. "Sure and it's amazing that in America grown people are encouraged to leave their ignorance behind them."

Jack smiled, then mimicked her lilting Irish speech. "Sure and it's even more amazin', darlin', that in the rest of the world, people are encouraged to remain ignorant."

They both had a good laugh, then began to plot their shopping expedition for the day.

One after another, down the long row, the heads of the girls at the sewing machines bent to their left, like bowling pins struck by a huge ball, and at the very end, near where Patrick stood, he heard the dread words they whispered: "The *Cossack!*"

Through the dirty windows facing Greene Street, Patrick saw a motorcar glistening in the early-morning sun. A uniformed chauffeur stood by the opened rear door, waiting for the Lord Chief Cossack, Mr. Balaban the owner.

When he emerged, Patrick was surprised at his smallness. He was short and bandy-legged and not the least bit menacing-looking from a distance. Despite the heat, he was dressed in a dark suit and wore a gray fedora on his head. He strutted on his short legs to the door of the building.

In the loft, the air was electric with fear. Esther, the girl with tuberculosis, stopped her work to hold a cupped hand over her mouth as she began to cough. The others worked with a frenzy, as if their very lives depended on it.

Mr. Balaban entered the floor and stood at the doorway gazing across the room. In a minute, he turned to make his way into the office, and was followed by Mr. Weiss, who solicitously began to place ledgers before him at the desk. From time to time, Mr. Weiss's mouth opened as he proferred an observation, yet Mr. Balaban did not appear to respond, so engrossed was he in his reading.

Patrick was obliged to continue his own work and did not see Mr. Balaban close the books, then leave the office and walk up the first row of girls at their sewing machines, then down the second row, and up the third. Patrick felt him before he saw him. His hair roots began to tingle, and when he looked up, Mr. Balaban was advancing toward him, the manager at his heels.

At their approach, Esther began to cough spasmodically and could be heard even above the rasping of the machines. Mr. Balaban stopped behind her and watched her quaking shoulders. His eyes narrowed to slits with displeasure, and as Esther turned and saw him there, her face became ashen; then suddenly there was a splashing sound as a puddle of urine formed beneath her chair. Mr. Balaban watched as she crouched lower and lower in her seat and drew her shoulders inward with shame. At last, without a word, he continued down the row.

The girl was too mortified to move. She held her hands in her lap and closed her eyes. At last, Sonia Lipsky rushed from her seat and helped her to the toilet room.

During the remainder of the owner's inspection, Patrick was unable to see him. Twenty minutes later, he stood once more at the doorway and looked across the enormous loft. Almost for the first time since he had arrived, his lips moved. Then he turned and left. In another minute, Patrick heard the motorcar start, and watched through the windows as it moved majestically down the street.

Esther returned to her machine, looking wretched, and found four completed shirtwaists there. Dutifully, Patrick entered them in the ledger beside Esther's name.

When the bell sounded for lunch, Mr. Weiss called his two piece-work supervisors into his office. "Business is slack just now," he said to them, "until the fall orders start coming in. Mr. Balaban has decided to let forty girls go for a month or so. These are their names. Wait until the end of the day to tell them, as Mr. Balaban does not want their last day's work impaired." He reignited his dead cigar. "You may inform them that they're free to come back when business improves. Do not distribute the pink slips until five minutes before the quitting-time bell, as we want to prevent any emotional demonstration. It sets a bad example, gentlemen."

Patrick read the list of names he had been provided. Other than that of Sophie Bernstein, the old woman, he could not associate any of the names with faces. He would have to locate them by their sewing-machine numbers.

"One other matter," Mr. Weiss resumed. "You are to fire that *schwein* who dirtied the floor." He tapped his cigar ash onto the desk. "And Mr. Balaban has also asked that we discharge the young lady who left her machine without permission to go to her aid."

Patrick and Saul retreated from the office and made their way to the dressing room, where they collected the lunches they had brought to work with them that morning. Neither said anything until they began to hurry down the stairwell to the street.

"The shitheels," Saul said at last.

"What can we say to the girls?"

"Nothing till closing time. Or we'll lose our own jobs, too."

The shirtwaist makers stood on the sidewalk in the shade of the building eating their meager lunches—more often than not, buttered bread—and as the two piecework supervisors left the building, all eyes looked up.

"You see," Saul began, "they're afraid of us, too. We're their enemies just like Balaban and Weiss. And that suits Diamond Shirtwaist fine because they know that the girls will never come to us for help and they're too weak to fight back by themselves."

Sonia left a group of friends she had been talking with and walked toward the two young men. "I made Esther go home," she said.

"That's where she belongs," Saul replied.

"Balaban *knew* that she was frightened. That's why he stood behind her. He wanted it to happen."

"Well, it's all over now."

"She's been fired, hasn't she?" Sonia asked. She waited for her Russian friend to nod his head. "The bastards," she said bitterly. "What happens to her now?"

Before he answered, Saul's eyes searched hers. "The same thing that will happen to you, Sonia. You survive and try to find another job."

She understood at once. "He's fired me as well?"

"And forty others have been let go for a month. But we are not to tell them till quitting time."

"And who is to tell them that they are to go without eating for a month? Will you answer that, Saul? Who tells them that for one month they have to suspend their lives just because Mr. Balaban won't need them? Is he God, Saul? I thought there was a God!"

Saul closed his eyes. "I'm sorry, Sonia. But what can I do? You know what would happen if we tried to resist them. I would be fired, too."

She turned to Patrick, fury in her eyes. "And what about you? Don't you have anything to say?"

What was she asking? A man as poor as he was could not risk what little he had for those who had even less.

"There's nothing I can do," he said.

A few minutes before quitting time, Patrick and Saul were asked to distribute the final pay envelopes to the forty girls who were being let go. Inside each was a pink slip, notifying them that their services would no longer be required, and though most of them could not read, they at once understood the color.

Some of the women became hysterical and implored Patrick to help them. They begged in Russian, Yiddish, Polish, Italian, German, and English, and grabbed his sleeves in supplication. Their eyes were filled with horror. For many of them, there was no other means of support for their families. They wailed and carried on so that Patrick had to run to the dressing room to get away from them.

Sonia Lipsky was there, her pay envelope with its pink slip still in her hand. "You make a good henchman," she said.

"I'm sorry, but I had nothing to do with it."

Her face was white with rage. "I'm going to talk to the people on Clinton Street and see if they can't help us."

"Who are they, and what can they do?"

"They're the union people. Maybe they won't be able to do anything, but at least they should know what's happening here."

She turned to leave the room, and as she did, Saul entered. "Will you wait for me outside?" he asked.

"No," she replied. "I'm going down to Clinton Street."

"You'll only make matters worse. The Cossacks will fire all of us."

"It's a chance I have to take. I also want to see Esther. She should be in a hospital."

Sonia left them to join the women waiting in line by

142

the door, their pocketbooks opened for inspection. One by one, they passed in front of Mr. Weiss, whose fingers tore into their purses in search of stolen shirtwaists. When Sonia reached him, she stood defiantly, arms crossed in front of her breasts, her closed pocketbook locked close to her body.

"You're forgetting something, miss," the manager said sternly.

"I'm forgetting *nothing*, mister," she answered.

"I want to see what's in your purse."

"It's empty. The only money I have is a dollar bill, and that's pinned to my bloomers. Do you want to see that, too, you bastard?" She pushed him out of the way, then hurried down the steps.

Mr. Weiss shouted after her, "You're a troublemaker, Lipsky! You'll never get another job in the garment industry, I'll see to that!"

By the time Patrick reached the street, Sonia had already gone.

14

As soon as the Griswolds' dinner was finished, Jack walked Nora down the street until they reached a redbrick building on Second Avenue. It was an elementary school, yet in most of the windows lights still burned.

Classes began late, Nora learned, because many of the students were domestics whose working day did not end until nine o'clock. A class had formed just the week before, but Nora was invited to join it if, between now and the next day, she could learn the English alphabet.

"God save us," she said, "I am not sure I am up to it, Jack."

Jack, however, convinced her that it was simplicity itself. And on the way home, he demonstrated just how simple. With a stone he picked up from the gutter, he drew a large *A* on the sidewalk.

"That is an *A*," he declared.

"An *A*? It do be very comely, Jack. Do it always look so comely?"

Jack realized that he had already made an error in instructing her. "That is a capital *A*," he said by way of correction. "There is a little *a*, too, that looks like this." He drew the letter.

"Sure and it isn't half as nice," she said. "And when do you use the big one, and when the little one?"

Jack hadn't expected to be grilled in this way. "Now let me see," he began. "You use the big one for a word that begins a sentence. And also for someone's name. And when it is an important thing you're talking about. Like America. That begins with an *A*."

With the stone, Nora scratched the two letters on the

145

sidewalk. "Might we not be arrested, Jack, for defacing the sidewalk?"

"The first rain will carry our scribblings away. If we can find a shop open, we'll buy you a notebook and a pencil. But until then, this will have to do. Now, are you ready for a *B*?"

"I am, Jack."

He created two *B*'s, one capital, one small, and Nora duplicated them. "Your *B* is better than mine, Nora," he said magnanimously.

"It is?"

"Much better. And now we shall push on to a *C*. This is a capital *C*—and this is a little *c*."

"Sure and they're the same article, expect that this little feller is a bit smaller."

It had never occurred to Jack before.

"Are there others like that," she asked, "which are alike, both the big and small?"

Jack searched his intellect, which was by no means vast. "A few," he replied. "An *S* and an *O* for sure, and perhaps others as well."

Nora was impressed. "It's grand altogether, the alphabet," she said. "And where did you acquire the knowledge, might I ask?"

Jack had gone through the sixth grade, and would have gone through the twelfth but for the fact that his father died. "You see, I was the oldest in the family. I had three sisters and two brothers. My mother took a job in a bakery, but still there wasn't enough money to feed us all, so I quit school and became a delivery boy. Then I went into domestic service a few years later. I have been with the Griswolds now for three years."

"They seem like nice people," Nora volunteered.

"Appearances are sometimes deceptive," he replied ominously.

She looked up in surprise. "Then you don't like them, do you, Jack?"

"Between the two of us," he whispered, "I am saving my money until I have enough to buy a spread of land somewhere out West. Wyoming or Montana. Let me warn you, Nora. New York City is no place to get ahead.

146

If you are born here in a slum and stay in the city, you will die in a slum. You must go West to prosper."

Nora didn't know much about the country just yet. And she had no money at all, so any travel plans would have to be deferred for some time. "Still," she concluded, "we could do worse than work for the Griswolds while we are waiting to move on, Jack."

"Quite possibly," he replied. "Just don't get too close to them, Nora. Do your work and save your money. I have been in service now for almost eight years, and one thing I have learned is that the rich do not consider us people. I have seen too many servants burn themselves out, working for families, thinking that they were loved. But when they were no longer of use, they were turned out like mangy dogs. Don't forget that, Nora."

Nora promised that she wouldn't. One of the reasons, in fact, that she wanted to learn to read and write was to improve her station in life. "There are so many things I should like to know, Jack. Books I should like to read from cover to cover. Sometimes I pick one up and I think, Oh, how wonderful it would be if I could read about someone else's life. It would be a great wisdom, I'm thinking, to know how other people live."

Jack smiled. "Well, you have made a beginning. You have learned the first three letters of the alphabet!"

She blushed. "Now you do be codding me, Jack. I shall be ignorant for a very long time, I'm thinking."

"Nonsense," he said. "I bet you can read already. Look up there at that sign. Read it for me, Nora."

"Oh, I *never* could, Jack."

"Go ahead. Give it a try."

She looked beyond the end of his pointing finger, and what she saw suspended over the sidewalk left her dazzled. She sucked in her breath with emotion. In all her life, she had never thought that reading could be so easy. It was such a beautiful sign: golden letters on a black background. She had seen signs before in Dublin and in Cork City, but none glittered with such promise as this one did.

"Oh, *Jack!*" she said.

"Didn't I tell you? Now read it, Nora."

147

Nora didn't know if she should laugh or cry. She felt almost as if she could do both. She looked at the sign with awe and reverence. It was the loveliest thing she had ever seen, far lovelier than the flowers in the fields or sunsets or high mountains. It touched a chord within her that had never been touched before.

ABC, the sign read over the three brass balls. She would remember it for the rest of her life, for when she discovered it, the enslaved creature living in her mind broke from its bondage and rushed to freedom.

Suddenly she felt giddy, almost drunk. It was all Jack could do to persuade her to leave the sign for the ABC Pawnshop and make her way home.

On the way, he bought her the promised notebook and pencil set, then sat on the curb and copied the alphabet for her on the first page. He was wonderfully swift and adroit, Nora thought.

The minute she reached her room on the third floor of the Griswolds' house, she began to commit Jack's letters to memory. It was no more difficult, after all, than learning to distinguish between the new chicks behind her father's house in Ireland; and when, after copying the letters four or five times, from beginning to end, frequently consulting Jack's models, she was at last able to recreate the entire alphabet, it was like calling all the little chicks to the back door and recognizing each one of them as they tumbled out of the gorse.

She did it again and again until she was satisfied that what she had learned would not disappear by morning. It was almost midnight by the time she finished and wearily began to prepare for bed. She removed her clothes and carefully hung them in the wardrobe. Before she slipped into her nightgown, she stood before the long, walnut-framed mirror in the corner and saw herself in all her nakedness. With her hands, she touched her belly, comforting the baby she alone knew was growing inside her. Beneath her fingers, she could feel the roundness that had only just begun to form. With luck, she would be able to conceal her pregnancy until almost the end of her term, beneath the full skirt and the apron she wore.

Thomas was like a presence in the room. His hands seemed to stroke her and his lips found hers. In something like a swoon, she closed her eyes, overwhelmed by memory.

A minute later, she opened them with a start. She had heard a noise outside the door like footsteps moving away. Yet when she rushed to it and flung it open, covering her nakedness with her hands, the hallway was empty.

Below Delancey Street, Patrick looked about him and found that he was no longer in New York City at all but in a Russian *shtetl*.

The streets and the sidewalks were teeming with peddlers and pushcarts, and the air reeked of fish and used clothes, secondhand shoes and human sweat. White-bearded, black-hatted patriarchal-looking fellows held up pots and pans that were strung from ropes around their necks, and dark-eyed ladies dug their arms into pickle barrels, pulling out plump specimens, waving them in front of him as he passed. Men in skullcaps offered him worn shoes without laces and heels, or fit foul-smelling, ancient frock coats against his shoulders. Women with scarves around their heads held fish by their tails or chickens by their scrawny necks and called out to him to stop and consider them.

The noise was tremendous. How such gaunt-faced, hollow-eyed people—most of them looked half-starved—could generate such sound baffled Patrick. They screamed and whined; they threatened and cajoled. Several times when he asked for directions, they bellowed and carried on so much that he thought they would bludgeon him with their fish, their lifeless roosters, or their pathetic shoes that looked as if they had walked all the way across Europe, as perhaps they had. They could not be bothered with such civilities as providing counsel for strangers, even if they knew where Clinton Street was, which was doubtful, as most of them were strangers there themselves.

The congestion on the street level was repeated at all the windows of the tenements and even on the fire escapes. There, people did not offer wares, but instead created them. They sewed or embroidered or made lace.

Behind the windows, they cut or pressed. Children no more than six or seven were bent over sewing, just as aged women were. And in contrast to the noise in the street, they worked silently, joylessly, holding their work close to their eyes in the pale light.

Patrick pushed his way through the mass of humanity and made his way southward, down Orchard to Hester, east to Essex, and south again. The closer he got to his destination, the more cordial were the responses to his request for directions. Finally, when he reached East Broadway, a scholarly-looking gentleman replied in a cultured voice, "I wouldn't be surprised if it is Clinton Hall you're looking for. Is that correct?" He said it almost with veneration, as if Patrick had asked how to reach the temple.

He recognized Clinton Hall, the union headquarters, at once. Apart from the fact that a sign identified it as the headquarters of Local 25, it was the only building on the street that wasn't a tenement. It seemed deserted, however, perhaps closed for the night. No one was in the lobby or on the first floor. He mounted the stairs to the second, and as he reached the top, he heard voices in the distance. One was Sonia's.

The door was ajar, and Patrick looked into a large, sparsely furnished room. A man and a woman sat at a table across from Sonia, whose back was toward the door. The woman looked Celtic; her hair was reddish-brown, and there were freckles on her nose. The man was huge. Six feet two, Patrick guessed, with the chest of a wrestler. His hair was dark and his skin pocked here and there. When he spoke, it was with a slight accent, very much like Saul's and Sonia's.

"We have tried before to organize the girls at Diamond Shirtwaist," the woman was saying to Sonia, "but without success. They're too afraid. They know that the owners will fire them if they're caught talking to union organizers."

"Yes, but they're very angry now," Sonia replied. "This time, Weiss and Balaban have gone too far. It wasn't just letting the forty girls go, putting them out on the streets because business was slow. It was—it was Esther."

The pockmarked man looked up with interest. "You say that they fired a girl for no reason at all? But that happens all the time."

Sonia struggled to explain. "But this was different. You see, everyone *helped* Esther. We all knew that she was ill, so we helped her with her work. Her father is a cantor and a *maskil*." She paused, then searched the face of the woman across from her. "Do you know what that means, Miss Flanagan?"

The woman looked perplexed until the swarthy fellow turned to her and said, "A wise man, Elizabeth. He is well known here on the Lower East Side."

"Yes," Sonia concurred. "A wise man. Everyone goes to him for advice, and Esther is his only child. All the girls in the shop know him, so when we saw that Esther couldn't do her work, we helped her out."

The woman named Elizabeth Flanagan nodded her head. "You say all the girls did? Or just some?"

Sonia sighed, then replied, "The Jewish girls."

"The Italians girls didn't help?"

"We didn't ask them."

The man appeared to consider this significant. "Why not?" he demanded.

Sonia was momentarily confused. "Because we didn't have to. We had enough of the Jewish girls who were willing to help."

"But that is why we can't organize Diamond Shirtwaist," Elizabeth Flanagan said with irritation. "Oh, yes, we can get every Jewish girl to cooperate, even the ones who are starving. They're willing to go on strike. But the Italian girls are too suspicious. They're suspicious of the owners, and they're also suspicious of the union. They won't listen to us."

There was silence; then the man pushed back his chair and walked to the window. He looked out onto the street. Pushcarts were being rolled off the sidewalks for the night, and peddlers were going home to their tenement dwellings. Rotten vegetables and animal droppings filled the gutters. Ragpickers and beggars poked through ankle-deep litter in front of the shops.

"You see," the man began, "we are dealing here with

cultural differences. We Jews are born dissenters. In Paradise itself, we shall find fault. We have always been outsiders, so we have nothing to lose if we offend the sensibilities of those in authority The Italian girls are different, Sonia. They have been taught to respect authority. For them to join in a strike against Mr. Balaban is like challenging the Church or God Himself."

Angrily, Sonia pounded her fist against the tabletop. "Then why can't we strike without them? There are more Jewish girls than Italians."

Elizabeth Flanagan appeared to consider it. "It might work," she declared. "If you went on strike, I doubt that the Italian girls would cross the picket line."

"They wouldn't at first," the man resumed, "but they would as soon as Balaban brought in scabs to break the strike."

"Scabs wouldn't dare cross our picket lines!"

"Yes, they would. Don't you know what the bosses are doing now? They're bringing in *swartzah* as strikebreakers."

"Swartzah?" Elizabeth Flanagan asked.

"The Negroes," he answered. "They're even worse off than the Jews. Poorer and more desperate. Sometimes the only way they can get jobs is to serve as strikebreakers."

"Then what are you saying?" Sonia demanded. "That we do nothing at all? That we just accept all this as if Mr. Balaban is doing us a favor? Do you think I came to America to be a slave?"

Sonia's face was filled with defeat. She was fighting back tears.

"Someone must work with the Italian girls," the man said in the silence that followed.

Elizabeth Flanagan shrugged her shoulders. "It's easier said than done. Most of them don't speak English. And they distrust union organizers. You just admitted that yourself."

"I know," the man agreed. "It will be difficult, but that is the only solution. If we can get the Italian girls to join the Jewish girls in a strike, we shall have Mr. Balaban on his knees." He reached out and touched Sonia's hand.

"Come back, Sonia, but wait until you are ready. Win the Italian girls to our side, then come back."

Sonia looked up and smiled weakly. "That's like asking me to walk on water."

"It's been done before, I hear."

"But not yet by a Jewish girl."

They all laughed; then Sonia rose and left the room. She frowned disapprovingly when she saw Patrick leaning against the wall outside the door, paused momentarily, then, without speaking, made her way to the stairs. Patrick hurried after her.

Halfway down the stairs, she finally said, "So what are you doing here?"

"I just wanted to see how things would go."

"Well, now you see, so you can go home."

"You *could* be a little more polite."

She turned to him at last as they reached the first floor. "Why be polite? Where does being polite get you? I'll tell you. It gets you nowhere. It gets you a kick in the behind."

Patrick couldn't resist grinning. "I don't think I've ever met anyone who's as angry as you are."

"So now you have. Congratulations." She turned away, dismissing him.

"I'm sorry," he began. "I just thought I could walk you home."

"You wouldn't like where I live."

"How will I know unless you let me take you there?"

"Okay, so come on. Did you have supper?" When he shook his head negatively, she added, "There's always something on the stove. Saul will probably be there."

"Saul? Does Saul live with you?"

"Does he live with me? Hell, he sleeps with me." She studied his face for his reaction.

"He sleeps with you?" he asked.

"*I* sleep in the bed. He sleeps on the floor—with the other boarders."

"You must have a big apartment."

"No. We have a small apartment, but a lot of boarders." She walked very swiftly, and it was all Patrick could do to keep up. "Listen, *goy,* if you have any anti-

153

Semitic tendencies, they'll all come out after you see the pack of Jews who are living with us."

"Your mother and father must be very kind."

She threw her head back and roared. "Kind, hell! They're poor. Kindness is a luxury poor people can't afford."

"But you just invited me over for supper."

"One way or another, you'll pay for it, Cassidy."

"My name is Patrick."

"I like Cassidy better. Come on. Let's see if kosher food will kill you."

She was right about her railroad flat on Pike Slip. It was small and also very congested. There were three rooms. The largest one, which had a fireplace, a stove, and two windows, served as the kitchen and working room. Opening off this, one after the other, were two small, windowless rooms that were used as sleeping quarters. The toilet was in the hall and shared by the occupants of three other flats.

As Patrick entered, he saw that some of the boarders had already retired for the night and were sprawled on the floor of one of the bedrooms. Others, including Sonia's mother and father, were still working in the kitchen. Some were sewing at foot-powered sewing machines, and some were pressing. The younger ones— brothers and sisters, Sonia said—were making artificial flowers. An immense man, dressed in his trousers, the top of his woolen underwear, and with his suspenders down, lay sleeping on a table, a black hat on his chest. He was snoring loudly.

Apart from Saul, who stood up when Patrick entered, no one paid any attention to him. Neither Sonia's mother nor her father spoke English, and both merely nodded when she explained who he was, then returned to their work.

"Hello, Irishman," Saul said brightly. "I had a feeling that you might go to Clinton Hall after work today." Then he asked Sonia, "What did they say?"

"They said the union can do nothing for us until the Italian girls are on our side."

"Impossible."

"That's what I told them."

"Who did you talk to?"

"Flanagan and Sarasohn."

She ladled a thick soup from a steaming pot on the stove, then handed the bowl to Patrick. It was dark and smelled good, but he had no idea what it was. There was an earthy, rooty aroma rising from it.

A single naked bulb on the ceiling provided the only light; Patrick was surprised that any sewing could be done in the room. The floor was littered with remnants, and a huge pail of glowing ashes sat next to the coal stove. Behind it, a ravaged wall and charred woodwork indicated a recent fire.

Patrick guessed that as many as fifteen people lived and worked in the three tiny rooms. Many of them were coughing—the rasping, drowning cough that came from diseased lungs. Across the room he saw Esther, her face pale and feverish. She should have been in a hospital; yet her hands were nimbly twisting wire for artificial flowers. Sonia sat next to him on the floor, holding her bowl of soup in her lap.

"We need an Italian organizer," Saul began, "but Weiss and Balaban would never let him in the shop."

"What would a union do for the workers?" Patrick asked innocently.

Sonia replied, "You saw for yourself that the girls are too afraid to speak up to the bosses."

"Even if they did," Saul interrupted, "the bosses wouldn't listen. They are all hard of hearing; it is a universal weakness among bosses. But if we were organized, the union would talk loud for us, and our bosses would have no choice but to listen. Our complaints would be heard. Mr. Weiss would hear, and even Mr. Balaban, far away in his town house on Washington Square." He paused to collect his thoughts. "We workers are not opposed to capitalism and free enterprise so much as we're opposed to exploitation. There is no difference between the Romanovs in Russia and the Balabans here in America. Do you follow me, Irishman? Either way, it's exploitation, and that's why we need unions to protect us."

Hesitantly, Patrick suggested, "I've read that many union leaders are Communists."

It was all that Sonia could do to contain her temper. "Anyone who objects to people being hungry or dying unnecessarily from disease while the rich stuff themselves and are waited on hand and foot by servants is a Communist. That's what management says. But it's a lie. Saul and I don't want to overthrow the rich. All we want is a fair shake. Otto Kahn, the financier, has a house on Long Island that's looked after by a hundred and twenty-five servants. *I* don't want a hundred and twenty-five servants. All I want is to put Esther in a sanitarium in Liberty, New York, so that she doesn't have to die in this tenement."

Patrick looked across the room and saw death on Esther's face. Yet she was working over her wretched artificial flowers as if her life were everlasting.

"Most people don't see it this way," Saul began heatedly, "but Sonia and I think that the real issue is the survival of a democratic society. Without unions, there will never be a middle class in America. There will be a ruling class and a peasant class, as there is in Europe. The only way that the working class can break out of its chains is through the unions. If we are successful, we will have contributed more to America than the Founding Fathers did."

Patrick was clearly sobered by what Saul had told him. Whether his Russian friend was right or wrong, he couldn't say. Maybe the unions could accomplish what revolutions could not. But Patrick wasn't in a position to find out. He had his own job to keep. He couldn't come to the aid of starving and abused Jewish and Italian shirtwaist workers.

He stayed for another hour in the stifling tenement room until the stink from the boarders as they removed their shoes for the night became too great. Sonia saw him to the street, and before he left, he asked her what she would do until she found another job. She would live, she answered. She was not lucky enough to die.

"Maybe I'll be able to see you from time to time," he suggested.

"Maybe," she answered, almost inaudibly, then turned and rushed up the stairs.

During the long walk home, he relived the evening, particularly the problem of the Italian girls.

At the corner of Chrystie Street, he spied a pushcart filled with used books, and though he knew that there were far better ways for him to spend his money, he began to poke around until he found what he was looking for.

It was a slender volume, paperbound, well-worn and spotted. He held it up to the whiskered old man who stood across from him. "How much for this?" he asked.

"Ten cents," the man replied.

"I'll give you five."

"Nine cents."

"Six!"

"I'm a poor man. I can't take less than seven," the old man shouted, and the bargain was struck. Patrick paid, then continued walking north, and as he did, he opened the pages and in the flickering light from the streetlamps, he began to read.

The following morning, he stood at the end of an aisle at the Diamond Shirtwaist Company, and to every second or third girl—the ones who looked Mediterranean—he welcomed them by saying, *"Buon giorno."*

They looked up first with suspicion, then with something like gratitude, and repeated the words to him. As they filed their way to their sewing machines, they talked excitedly among themselves. At last, one of them returned to where he was still standing and said shyly, as if until then she had been living in a world of silence, *"Grazie, signore."*

15

Before her, like a giant wing about to take flight, it loomed in all its majesty, full of promise and beauty, the most modern thing Nora had ever seen. All around her in Madison Square, people stood gaping at the slender tower of the Flatiron Building. Its sharp triangular edge was like the bow of a ship, and from where Nora stood, its twenty stories seemed to stretch infinitely into the sky.

She listened raptly as a youth in a white cap explained that more than seventeen hundred office workers entered the building every morning and left every night, and the mere thought of the crush and congestion left her breathless. The view from the roof, he continued, was better than that from the Matterhorn, and far more inspiring, the most celestial prospect they would see in their lifetimes.

The young man in the cap urged his listeners to join him on an expedition to the summit. "Yer takin' yer life into yer own hands, doin' it by yerself," he warned them, "but I'll getcha to the top without peril, and only for a nickel. If there are those who are afeard of elevators, I'll escort yez up on foot."

Nora would have loved to see the panorama from the roof, but she did not want to spend five cents for the pleasure. Today was Sunday, her day off, and among the wonders of the city she still hadn't experienced, and hoped to before the day was over, was a ride on the "slam-bang," as New Yorkers called the elevated, and that also cost a nickel. If she had to choose between climbing into the air in a dark box—she would not venture onto an elevator even at gunpoint, thank you—and riding at furious speed, suspended over Sixth Avenue, she preferred the latter, as she could always leap from it if necessary.

The square was mobbed with people who had come to look at the famous building, the most daring in New York. Jack was the one who had suggested that it would not be out of her way, after she told him that she would be calling on her former landlady in Hell's Kitchen. All she had to do was walk south, then east, he had said. "But keep your eyes open," he added, "because you'll be passing through a part of the Tenderloin."

When she had engaged her tiny room on Tenth Avenue, she had not known that it was near the center of vice in the city, but there was no mistaking it today. Girls in gaudy dresses stood in doorways, cigarettes in their hands, their faces pale and their cheeks brightly rouged. Nora knew at once what their vocation was, and she pitied them. She cast her eyes downward as she hurried along the sidewalk.

A letter was waiting for her at her former rooming house, and she asked the landlady to read it to her. It was from her mother and father in Ireland, but must have been written by one of the villagers who had been taught how to write by Lady Caverly.

A Chara Nora,

It is lovely to hear that ye have found a place with such fine people, and we are thankful for the three dollars ye sent in the envelope. It must be beautiful altogether in New York. We wonder what kind of weather have ye over there.

Father Daley has brought a letter from Pat Cassidy to his mother. He do be making great progress, he says, and is anxious to see ye as soon as he can. We have sent word to him where ye are living so that he can call.

We have had a Mass said for John Mary, Thomas, Lambi, and Eamon, and we thinks of them every day and the precious lives they have lost.

160

That is all the news for now. We hope ye are in good health and not lonely. God bless ye, Nora.

For a long time after the woman had finished reading it, Nora looked at the words that she could not fathom, then asked her former landlady to perform a favor for her. "It is possible that Patrick Cassidy may come here inquiring after me, but it is important that I don't see him. You are to tell him that my employment has taken me out of the city and that you are holding my mail for me."

The woman's tongue stroked a gold tooth in her head and her hardened eyes studied Nora, but she did not refuse her the favor, nor did she ask for an explanation when Nora dropped a dime into the palm of her hand.

As much as she wanted to see Patrick, she knew that she would be ashamed once he discovered that she was pregnant. No matter how kind and gentle Patrick was, he possessed an Irish conscience and would judge her accordingly, she thought. Worse, there was always the possibility that if he learned of her pregnancy, he might mention it in a letter to his mother in the village, and soon Nora's own family would know of it and sadness would be brought into their lives.

She would not tell anyone—not Patrick, not her family, not even the Griswolds—until it became impossible for her to conceal her pregnancy beneath her full skirts. Then she would ask Monsieur and Madame for help. They were Christians and would not treat her unmercifully.

Nora made room now as a newcomer sat next to her. She looked up to find that it was the youth in the white cap who had been trying to entice the Sunday strollers to the top of the Flatiron Building.

"What a lot of chintzy bastards," he said to her. One of his shoes was without laces, and he wore no socks.

"Weren't you able to attract any customers?" she asked.

"The bohunks don't have no money, and on windy days like today, all the Yanks want to do is watch the

161

girls' skirts fly up in the air." He pointed across the street to the knife-edged building. As women approached it, their hands fought to keep their skirts down, but the wind buffeted them upward, sometimes exposing their bloomers. "This here's the windiest corner in New York, they say."

"It's a gorgeous building."

"Ye must be a greenhorn." He bent over to look at her face beneath the new hat she had purchased with her first wages. She was wearing a white shirtwaist and skirt that Mrs. Griswold had bought for her at the same time she was fitted for uniforms.

"I am."

"I can tell by the way you look, ye must be Irish. Me old lady was Irish, and so was me old man. They're both dead now."

"And who do you live with?"

"With meself," he answered proudly. "Been on me own since I was ten."

"And how old are you now?"

"Fifteen," he replied. "Least, that's what I told me boss. Otherwise, he wouldn't have hired me. I'm thirteen. Me name's Timmy Callaghan." He grinned at her.

"My name is Nora. There are Callaghans in County Cork. Is that where your parents were from?"

"Never asked them, and they never told me. All's I know is that they were from Ireland. That's an island somewhere, ain't it?"

Nora was shocked. "Yes, it's an island somewhere," she answered sadly.

He readjusted the cap on his ginger-colored hair. "Well, I gotta go round up some more suckers now, if I can. If I don't, I don't eat. It's been nice talkin', ma'am." He stood up, then walked away. Even before he was five feet from her, he had begun to extol the virtues of the view of New York from the roof of the Flatiron, and quickly gathered a crowd.

He had been on his own, he said, since he was ten years old, and he was still strong and still alive. Nora drew strength from having talked to him. If he could survive, so could she and the baby she would soon give birth to.

Yet he knew nothing about the land of his father and mother except that it was an island somewhere. He would never be stirred the way Nora was when someone mentioned its magical name or told of its sorrows and glories.

Nora vowed that her own child would receive an education quite different from his. Her son or daughter would learn about the country its father had died for, and the manner of his death. As long as she lived, she would never let it be forgotten.

She continued to sit on the park bench even as twilight fell. She was reluctant to go home to the Griswold house. Jack was visiting his mother in Chelsea on his day off, and the Griswolds had motored up the Hudson to see some friends. It would be dark before they returned, they had told her, and Nora did not want to venture into the empty house by herself.

The crowd in the park had begun to thin out. The organ grinder and his marvelous pet monkey had left, as had the pushcart owners selling roasted chestnuts and sweets. The Yankees—conspicuous not only by their clothes but by the imperious way they commanded the paths—had retired to their brownstones and redbrick houses in the neighborhood, and left the park to the immigrants, who were not quite ready to return to their railroad flats. The new Americans were immediately recognizable because of their heavy clothing and the graceless way they walked in their unaccustomed shoes. Like Nora herself, most of them had never tread on a paved sidewalk before they came to the New World.

Nora was looking at the stubbly, sun-scorched grass in the park; yet all she could see was the mountain meadow behind her father's house in Cork. As she listened to the babble of foreign voices about her, she could hear the crashing of waves against the rocks below her father's house, and the cry of the gulls. She closed her eyes and dreamed.

She must have dozed off because it was dark by the

time she looked up. The lamps were lit in the park, and most of the benches had been emptied. Quickly, she gathered her purse and a bag of sweets she had purchased and began to make her way toward the street.

Suddenly, a voice said to her. "What's your hurry? Wouldn't you like to have a drink with me, girlie?"

Nora turned to find a man only a few feet behind her. He tipped his derby hat, removed a cigar from his mouth, smiled, and said, "I've got three bucks in my pocket says we can have a good time."

In a panic, Nora looked about for assistance, but no one was near. She began to run toward an exit, and as she did, the man grabbed her arm.

"Please, someone help me!" she cried.

At the entrance to the park, a gentleman in a dark suit had been standing, looking across the almost deserted street at the building as the first rays of moonlight struck it. When he heard Nora's cry, he turned and saw her running down the path, pursued by a man.

"I say," he shouted, "leave that girl alone!" He hurried toward her. As he did, Nora tripped and fell onto the path.

The man who had been chasing her turned heel and began to run in the opposite direction, followed now by the gentleman who had come to her aid. Nora sat up, fighting for breath. She had hurt her ankle. A sharp pain worked up her leg.

In a minute, the gentleman who had helped her was kneeling at her side. "He got away, the scoundrel," he said, breathing heavily from the effort of running. "Did he hurt you?"

When she spoke there was a tremor in her voice. "I've twisted my ankle, I think."

"Can you walk? We don't want to stay here."

"I'm sure I can."

Gently, he helped her to her feet, then wrapped an arm around her waist as she tested her ankle. "It's all right," she said. "I think I can manage now. Thank you so much."

"I can't leave you here. I'll see you home."

"You mustn't trouble yourself. I'm sure I've spoiled your evening as it is."

"The park is no place for a young girl after dark. New York is filled with rogues."

"I didn't know," she replied. "I came to see the Flatiron Building, and I must have forgotten the time."

"Do you live nearby?"

"Miles away. You would be helpful if you could direct me to the Sixth Avenue elevated."

"I'll do better than that. I'll take you home in a cab."

While she protested, he raised an arm and flagged down a taxi. For the first time, she was able to get a good look at him. He was dressed in a dark suit and wore a black mourning band around one of his sleeves. He was older than Nora, she thought. Perhaps in his thirties. He had strong features, black hair, and a black mustache.

He held the door of the taxi open while she entered.

"I have no money," she whispered in embarrassment, "except five cents."

"Then I shall pay the fare and you can pay me the five cents."

"I don't know how I can ever thank you."

He climbed into the cab after her. "You can thank me by staying out of the park after nightfall. Now—could you tell me Miss—? I don't even know your name."

"I'm Nora Shannon."

"All right, Nora Shannon. I am Charles Molloy. Now could you tell me where I am to deliver you so that I can get you home before you incite other men to misadventure?"

Nora told him, and he repeated the Griswolds' address to the driver. He leaned back in the cab and looked at her.

"And what did you think of the Flatiron Building, Miss Nora Shannon?"

Nora was nearly at a loss for words. It was more beautiful than a cathedral, she replied. Above all things, she hoped to find a picture postcard view of it so that she could send it to her family in Ireland.

He was certain that such articles existed. As for the

building, he did not quite share her enthusiasm. "It is flashily designed," he said, "and is dubiously functional. Granted, the sharp edge makes a pretty picture, viewed from the street, but the triangle is fundamentally an unnatural shape. We live in a world of circles, squares, and rectangles. I would have been far happier with the Flatiron had the tip of the property been used as a miniature park, and a more rectangular but higher building erected behind it." He turned to her and smiled. "I am in love with height."

"I know nothing about triangles and squares," she admitted, "but I do know when I am moved by something."

"Then you have it all over architects and engineers. Most of them work with figures rather than emotion. In one respect, you're quite right about the Flatiron. It *is* an emotional building. A functional failure, but an emotional success."

"You must be an architect, Mr. Molloy."

"A mere builder." He reached into his breast pocket and removed a calling card. He handed it to her, then watched the confusion on her face as she attempted to read it. He pointed through the window at the three-and four-story houses on Lexington Avenue they now passed. "One day, all of those will be gone and replaced by huge buildings, some of them even perhaps a mile high. You see, Manhattan is a very small island, and there is nowhere to go but up in the air. Just a few feet below the soil is hard rock, so there will be no limit to what can be erected. It will be very exciting, Miss Shannon, living here in New York during the next half-century."

"Then I have chosen the right place to live, haven't I?"

"You certainly have." He turned to her and smiled. "So long as you avoid Madison Square Park at night,"

During the trip north, he questioned her about her work and her plans in a most genial and relaxed way. Nora at once felt comfortable with him. She was intrigued by the mourning band on his sleeve, but as he made no reference to it, neither did she. She mentioned her employers' name. "They are merchants," Nora said, "and ever so grand."

In front of the Griswolds' house, he paid the cab and

alighted from it after Nora. "I shall take a bit of a walk before I go to bed tonight," he said.

Nora handed him her nickel.

"And what is this?" he asked.

"It is what I would have paid on the elevated, Mr. Molloy. If I had more, I would give you the full fare." She wouldn't permit him to return the coin.

As the taxi drew away from the curb, he stood before her on the sidewalk. "Well," he began, "I suppose I won't see you again."

"I am most thankful for your kind help, Mr. Molloy."

"Anyone would have done it."

"No, not anyone." She waited, then added, "Goodnight, Mr. Molloy."

"Goodnight."

He watched her make her way to the door. "Oh, Miss Shannon," he called.

She turned to face him. "Yes?"

He shrugged his shoulders awkwardly. "I just wanted —to remind you to be careful in our parks. I wouldn't want you to have a repetition of this evening's experience."

"I shall be very careful, Mr. Molloy. Goodnight."

"Goodnight, Miss Shannon."

Nora had forgotten her key and had to ring for Jack to let her in. As he did so, he saw the departing figure of Mr. Molloy.

"I see you have acquired a gentleman friend," he said good-naturedly.

Nora explained the circumstances that had led to their meeting in front of the Flatiron Building. She showed him the card he had given her.

Jack read the words aloud: "Charles A. Molloy and Company. Thirty-two Beaver Street. General Contractors."

"He is a builder or a mason, I believe."

Jack bent over the card. "And you met him in front of the Flatiron Building, did you say?"

"Yes. He was exceedingly critical of it, too."

"That's most peculiar," Jack replied. "Do you know who that was? That was the famous Charles Molloy, who

167

builds bridges and subways and high buildings, and even, if I'm not mistaken, helped build the Flatiron Building itself. My God, Nora, you sure know how to pick 'em!"

She clapped her hands in front of her open mouth. And to think that she had paid Mr. Molloy a nickel to take her home!

16

A bove the whir and rasp of three hundred and fifty
Singer sewing machines, Saul Kaganoff said to Patrick, "Sonia is across the street with Sarasohn, the union
leader. They want to see you after work."

Through the dirt-mottled windows overlooking Greene
Street, Patrick made out the slight figure of the Russian
girl, deep in conversation with Sarasohn. As she talked
excitedly, her hands knifed the air, and the man from
Clinton Hall listened intently. Slowly, he raised his eyes
until he saw Patrick at the window.

Patrick knew why they had come.

Not only had he been making progress with the Italian
workers, but he had stumbled upon one who spoke English. Every day for a week, he had said to a diffident and
slightly tremulous girl at the end of the row, "*Come sta,*
Annamarie?" And every day she had answered, "*Molto
bene, grazie,*" then resumed sewing.

But yesterday, something had made her say, "And how
are you, *signore?*"

Patrick was too flabbergasted to speak. Of all the girls at
the shirtwaist factory, the Italians clung most fiercely to
their language and customs. Moreover, they lived in an
area of the Lower East Side, on Mulberry and Mott
streets, where there was no need to speak any other language.

"You speak English, Annamarie?"

"Some, *signore.*"

He had noticed her before, not because she was overweight—which she was—and unpretty—her face was
very dark, her forehead narrow, and her cheeks swollen
and fleshy—but because one of her legs was shorter than

169

the other. Even walking down the aisle to the toilet room was a laborious process for her. She raced to keep up with her good leg, and at each plummeting step, her large body jerked and convulsed.

It occurred to Patrick that she might agree to serve as a translator for the other girls.

"Where did you learn to speak English, Annamarie?"

"From my father. He is a waiter at Delmonico's."

"You are a very good worker, Annamarie."

She blushed at the compliment. "Thank you, *signore.*"

The previous afternoon, Patrick had mentioned to Saul that one of the girls spoke English and might be invaluable to them. Now, Sonia and Sarasohn had come to question him.

"Tell me about *l'italiana*," Sarasohn said without preamble the minute he slid into the booth at a Bleecker Street saloon across from Patrick.

Next to the union leader sat Sonia, the dark patches under her eyes almost lavender. Her complexion had the blue-white luster of ice-cold milk. She was deferential to Sarasohn, and there was a kind of intimacy about it that suggested to Patrick that perhaps the two of them had slept together. Sonia was the sort of girl who could fall in love with a cause more readily, perhaps, than she could fall in love with a man. To win her carnally, a lover would first have to subdue her intellectually.

As for the union leader, had he been clear-skinned, he would have been an ugly man—his lips were gross, and his nose was cruelly misshapen—yet the acne craters that covered his face gave him almost an appearance of grandeur. His skin was like the soles of a Hindu ascetic who walks on nails or over burning coals, and revealed the same supremacy of mind over physical inconvenience. His eyes were still, like those of someone who has suffered a great deal and been ennobled by it.

In answer to Sarasohn's question, Patrick replied, "Her name is Annamarie. She was born on Ellis Island, and that makes her an American, so the other girls look up to her. If she didn't have a deformed leg, she wouldn't be working here as a seamstress. She's got a good head."

170

"What are her views?" Sarasohn asked.

"I'm not sure that she's been allowed to have too many. In Italian families, men are expected to make all the decisions."

Sarasohn tapped his fingers on the tabletop. "If she has no views," he began, "you must plant them. You have to understand that all these workers are just waiting for someone to help them. They are too timid to protest by themselves. You must inflame her, and she will inflame the others."

Patrick shook his head doubtfully. "I don't think that they'll ever strike. Nothing in the world will induce them. Without their salaries, they'd starve."

It was Sonia who said, "We have a small strike fund."

"They have large families."

Sarasohn continued, "Our strike fund will keep them fed for a few weeks, and then we shall enlist the aid of sympathizers here in New York City."

Suddenly Patrick was skeptical. Could Sarasohn be so innocent as to believe that the rest of the world cared? The public had too often been inconvenienced by strikers. Every few weeks, there were pickets and parades and sometimes interruptions of vital services provided by car conductors, meat packers, or coal miners. Demonstrations had been held by citizens who attacked and maligned strikers, particularly the Wobblies. Why would this strike be any different?

"Because it will be the first one in history conducted almost entirely by women," Sarasohn answered. "Never before have women gone to the picket lines the way they will when they strike against the shirtwaist makers. And when the bosses send in their scabs and strikebreakers, their policemen and militia with rifles and clubs, it will be women who must fight back. The public's sympathy will be kindled, I assure you."

"Some of them could get hurt."

"Whenever people protest against injustice, Cassidy," Sonia answered, "someone is bound to get hurt. In the past, men have paid the price. Now it is our turn. We can fight, too, and suffer as well."

"I still don't think the women will strike," Patrick said.

171

Sarasohn's eyes met his and did not blink. "Yes, they will, and do you know why? Because Balaban will push them too far. The bosses always do."

"He is right," Sonia added. "All we want to do is to have the women ready when Balaban does it."

"And you and your Annamarie will help us."

It wasn't a request, but a command. After he had said it, perhaps Sarasohn saw resistance in Patrick's expression. When he resumed, his voice was gentler, even soothing.

"We Jews and you Irish have much in common, Cassidy. The world has tried again and again to eradicate us, yet we persist. Do you know that almost all the labor leaders in America are either Irish or Jewish? Don't you find that remarkable? We have both passed through horrifying experiences of near-extinction, and should know enough by now no longer to pick fights with our tormentors. But we do. I consider it my duty. I should hope that you would do the same."

Patrick did not reply.

There was gravity in Sarasohn's voice as he continued, "We are counting on you to bring *l'italiana* and her friends into the fold. There is a meeting this Friday at Clinton Hall. Eight-thirty. Make sure the Italians are there."

The following afternoon, during his lunch break, Patrick wolfed down his bread-and-butter sandwich, then hurried down the stairs to the sidewalk, to where Annamarie was standing in the shade of the building. When the Italian girls saw him approach, their chatter ceased. Annamarie was even more ill at ease than the rest when he finally stood next to her.

"How goes it, Annamarie?" he asked.

"As always, *signore*."

"It's very hot in the loft today. One of the Jewish girls fainted this morning."

"We Sicilians are used to heat."

Patrick chose his words with care and spoke slowly. "It doesn't seem fair that Mr. Balaban and Mr. Weiss won't let us open the windows on such a hot day, does it?"

She looked at him stoically. "In the winters, we are cold and work in our heavy coats. In the summers, we suffer from the heat. It is a part of our lives, *signore*. We do not complain."

He watched as she wiped her forehead with a large red handkerchief, then stuffed it into the bodice of her dress.

"You will never improve your lot, Annamarie, unless you complain." He waited for her response, but none came. "It isn't too much to ask that the loft be heated in the winter or that the windows be opened in the summer, is it?"

She cocked back her head and threw out her chin. "When we are dead, *signore*, we shall improve our lot."

"In America, you can improve your lot right now. In some parts of the country, workers have already won the right to work just eight hours a day."

She was unimpressed. "They are men, *signore*. We are women."

He continued, "You have seen Mr. Balaban arrive here every Thursday morning in a limousine, Annamarie. There are almost four hundred people working in the loft, but only two toilets for all of them. Don't you think Mr. Balaban could afford to install one or two more?"

"We learn to control our bladders, *signore*."

"The loft is a dangerous and unhealthy place to work. Every night, I cough because I've been breathing lint all day. Some of the girls have TB, but they work right up to the day they hemorrhage. Do you think Mr. Balaban cares?"

At last, something was stirred in Annamarie. He saw the flicker of interest in her eyes, but she remained silent.

"There could be a fire in the loft, Annamarie, and no one would ever get out alive. The fire escape in back is badly corroded. Even if it weren't, Mr. Weiss keeps the steel shutters closed all the time, and no one could reach it." He watched as her eyes shut at the thought of such horror. "The cutters throw all their remnants on the floor or under their tables, and sometimes they aren't collected for a week. A fire would race through the loft in five minutes, Annamarie, killing hundreds. It happened at the Triangle loft, and it could happen here."

"We pray to God that there will never be a fire, *signore*."

"You will never have anything unless you demand it, Annamarie."

"Demand?" she asked. "How can I demand?"

He exhaled his breath, then refilled his lungs. "If you were a union member—you and your friends—the union would help you gain your rights. I promise you."

First disappointment, then terror enveloped her face. *"Scusi, signore,"* she said urgently and began to move away. "I must get back to work."

The bell had not yet rung, summoning the girls to their machines, yet Annamarie quickly made her way to the door, dragging her short leg behind her. It wasn't until she reached the entrance that he caught up with her.

"The people at Clinton Hall can help you," he whispered. "No one else can. Tell your friends, Annamarie. There is a meeting this Friday at Clinton Hall. Eight-thirty."

Her eyelids fluttered like those of a frightened bird. *"Non capisco, signore."*

"You understand," he insisted.

"Non capisco," she repeated, then ran into the building.

Thursday morning, at slightly before ten, the black motorcar drew up in front of the loft on Greene Street, and even before the chauffeur had fully stopped it, the rear door was flung open and Mr. Balaban emerged.

He was clearly agitated, as was Mr. Weiss, who waited inside the ground-floor door. Their voices could be heard on the staircase as they hurried up the stairs. When they reached the loft, Mr. Balaban went directly to the office, while the manager hurried to the cutting room supervisors, then the piecework supervisors, making the same announcement to all:

"Mr. Balaban is waiting to see you in my office."

At the end of an aisle, Patrick met Saul. "Something is very wrong," Saul said. "He's always let Weiss do his talking. He's never talked to us directly before."

The supervisors entered the office and found the owner of the Diamond Shirtwaist Company seated at the desk, his hands folded in front of him. A pleasant aroma of eau

174

de cologne rose from him. He looked alert and shrewd, calm and self-controlled.

"Sit down," he said to his supervisory staff.

He started to speak slowly, enunciating each word carefully. Patrick had assumed that his English would be as coarse as his manager's, but it was patrician, entirely without accent. As he leaned back in the chair now, a Phi Beta Kappa key dangled from his watch fob.

"My father and grandfather are upset," he began. "They have heard a rumor that Local Twenty-five of the Ladies' Shirtwaist Makers Union will very soon try to unionize our shop."

Patrick found it difficult to swallow.

"I have been looking after the Diamond Shirtwaist Company ever since I left college, and I think that I understand the women who work here as well as anyone does. One thing I know with absolute certainty is that sometimes they don't know what's good for them. That will sound arrogant, but it's true. Only the owners are qualified to look after the interests of these people because the women themselves are illiterate and easily exploited." He paused, and when he next spoke, his voice was firmer. "That is why my family will not sit by idly and permit Communists to manipulate these women for their own evil purposes."

Saul could be heard clearing his throat, but otherwise there was total silence.

"When my grandfather came to this country, he didn't have a penny. He started with a pushcart, selling used clothes, and he built his business up until it became what it is today. We own mills in New Jersey and Massachusetts where woolen and silk material is made. We own factories here in New York, in Boston, and in Philadelphia where that fabric is converted into garments. And very soon we will enter direct retailing. In our society, every man has the opportunity to pull himself up from poverty, as my grandfather did. *He* didn't go to the Communists and say, *'Here! Help me steal from the bosses!'* Everything my family has, we have worked for, and we do not intend to throw it all away now. That is why we are going to keep

175

this an open shop and shall do that no matter what the cost may be."

Balaban looked from face to face, then settled on Patrick's, perhaps because it was the fairest. "To accommodate these people now," he continued, "is to invite revolution. So this is what I want you to do. Anyone out there in the shop who you have reason to believe might have had contact with union organizers must be given a pink slip at once. Today. And you are to remind the others that for every woman sitting at one of my sewing machines, there are twenty women at Castle Garden, just off the ferry from Ellis Island, waiting for that job."

Suddenly, he stood at the desk. "During this last quarter, our profits have declined for a number of reasons. For one, we have recently expended a great deal of money in acquiring a second mill in New Jersey. For some time now, my family and I have contemplated making a slight adjustment here at Diamond Shirtwaist in order that we may better weather the storm, however temporary it is. Prudence would suggest that at this unsettled time, perhaps we should defer any such decision, and we may very well do that. If, however, we choose not to, our choice will be known by Saturday." He waited before going on. "My grandfather is of the opinion that there is only one way to meet this threat, and that is head-on. My father and I are not yet certain. But I thought I should mention it now so that you won't be caught totally unprepared in the event that my grandfather persuades us to take his course of action."

He looked about him. "Are there any questions?"

There appeared to be none. Then Saul stepped forward. "You've asked us to give pink slips to any workers we think might be in communication with union organizers. What sort of proof should we have?"

Balaban pondered it. "Use your intuition. If you think someone might be undermining us, get rid of her at once. We don't have to give reasons. Tell her you don't like the way she's been doing her work or something." He waited. "Anything else?"

There were no further questions.

"Okay," Balaban said, using an authentic Yankee expression, "then that will be all. Thanks for coming in." As they began to leave, he said to his manager, "Mr. Weiss, I won't go over the ledgers just now. Could you have someone carry them down to the car? I'll drop them off in the morning."

Patrick had been the last to reach the door, so Weiss asked him to remain a minute while he collected the ledgers. He brought four large books from the corner and rested them in Patrick's hands.

During their descent to the first floor, the owner walked in front of Patrick. Balaban moved very quickly. For a man of his age—nearly fifty, Patrick guessed—he was in good physical condition.

He held the door for Patrick, then preceded him to the waiting car.

"Put them in the back seat," Balaban said to him.

It was necessary for Patrick to step into the car in order to lay the books on the seat without spilling them. As he did, a young woman seated in the corner watched him.

"Hello," she said, then smiled.

She was blond, and her hair was bobbed. Her eyes were the palest blue, and her skin was creamy white. If she was Balaban's daughter, she shared none of his features.

"Hello," he answered, backing out of the car.

As he left, he heard his employer say to her, "Where do you want me to drop you off, Eva?" The young girl said something, but the motor started and her words were lost.

Eva. Eva Balaban, Patrick said to himself as he climbed the stairs to the sixth floor. At the top of the stairs, the manager was waiting for him. "Did the car leave?" he asked.

"Just now."

"I had some correspondence I wanted Mr. Balaban to sign, but neglected to give it to him. Perhaps you could take a few minutes off at lunchtime to run it over to his house. It's just around the corner on Washington Square."

Patrick said that it would be no trouble at all. Before

177

he went back to work, he asked, "Was that Mr. Balaban's daughter?"

"No," Mr. Weiss replied, "that was his wife."

Now that management was aware of Local Twenty-five's activity, even Saul admitted that there was no chance in the world of unionizing the shop. All morning long, the women at their machines worked harder than ever, as if their very lives depended on what they did. They knew that Mr. Balaban had summoned his floor supervisors into the office, yet had not toured the loft as he customarily did, and they could only deduce that he was vexed. Shortly before the machines were turned off for the lunch break, Saul notified two of the women in his section that their services were being terminated, and as soon as he did, fear swept through the floor.

He justified the firings to Patrick by saying that unless a few women were discharged, as Balaban had requested, suspicion would fall on Patrick and himself. Saul explained to Mr. Weiss that the two women appeared to be leaders and agitators, and in order to preserve an open shop, it was best to let them go. Weiss agreed.

Saul's reasoning seemed brutal to Patrick, and he was too upset even to eat his meager lunch. Instead, he collected the correspondence from the office and set out for Washington Square.

As he walked through the elegant square, he admired the handsome Greek Revival houses that bordered it. It was no longer as fashionable as it once had been, he had been told, the very rich having moved north along Fifth Avenue during the last quarter century, but the younger rich and the daring rich had discovered the area. He could only assume that it had been Eva Balaban's choice, not her husband's. Now, at midday, as he made his way across the green, he saw professorial types from the nearby university, a student or two, nannies pushing perambulators.

At the address Mr. Weiss had supplied, Patrick mounted the stairs and lifted a brass knocker. He expected a parlormaid to answer, but instead it was the young woman herself. When she saw him, she was nearly as surprised as he.

At last, Patrick broke the silence. "Mr. Weiss sent me over with some letters for Mr. Balaban to sign."

"Are you to wait for them?"

"He didn't say."

Momentarily, she seemed undecided, as if she might ask him to step inside while her husband attended to the papers, but then thought better of it. "Please tell Mr. Weiss that we'll send someone over to the office with them."

He looked at her expectantly, wishing he didn't have to leave. "I shall do that, Mrs. Balaban. Good afternoon."

For the rest of the day, he could not get her out of his mind. Every time he conjured up her youthful face, he also saw her husband's, tired and lined, cold and ungenerous-looking.

After work, as he did every night, he crossed the park on his way to the West Side, and in the soft twilight he looked up at the house where he had been earlier in the day. So engrossed was he that he didn't at once notice the woman approaching him on the path, a tiny dog at her feet, tugging at its leash.

"Good evening, Mr. Cassidy," she said.

He was so flustered that she had passed before he could speak. "Oh, Mrs. Balaban! I almost didn't recognize you. That's a good-looking dog you have."

She smiled. "It's a monstrous dog sometimes, but good company."

"It's a lovely evening, isn't it?"

"Lovely, Mr. Cassidy."

And with that, she continued walking down the path away from him. It wasn't until he had left the park and was walking west on Washington Place that he realized she had called him by name, though he was sure he hadn't introduced himself. How had she known? Had she telephoned Mr. Weiss in order to ask? Or did her husband perhaps keep records of his employees somewhere at home?

Whichever way, it had required both curiosity and effort. Patrick was buoyed by it. She had taken note of him.

As he sailed down the narrow street, he began to whistle.

The next morning, as he walked through the square at a quarter to seven, he half expected to see her walking her dog, but she wasn't there and he was disappointed.

At lunchtime, he told Saul that he couldn't join him and the men from the cutting room, and instead hurried to the park, but once again Eva Balaban wasn't there. Dejected, he sat on a bench and opened the piece of newspaper in which his landlady had wrapped his sandwich. Even before he was halfway through, he could feel that someone was looking at him; when he turned, there she was, without the dog this time.

"You're dining *al fresco,* Mr. Cassidy," she said to him.

He stood at once. "I decided that I needed some fresh air."

"It must be horrid working in that loft."

"It sometimes is."

He knew that in another second she would rush away unless he prevented it. "Wouldn't you like to sit down for a minute, Mrs. Balaban? The world is really more interesting when you're seated. It's far easier to watch other people."

She smiled. "I think I might, just for a minute." She sat on the bench at a good distance from him. "Don't let me interfere with your lunch, Mr. Cassidy."

He felt ill at ease eating in front of her, but he was sure that he would feel even worse holding his uneaten sandwich in his hands. "I see you've left your monstrous dog at home."

"I'm about to spend the afternoon with a former classmate of mine from Bryn Mawr who lives on Bank Street and is not partial to dogs." She waited, then added, "Friday is always a holiday for me because my husband doesn't come home for his supper. He dines with his family."

It was a peculiar way to phrase it, as if she were not a part of his family.

Suddenly she turned to him. "Why are you working for my husband?"

He would have liked to ask why she was married to him. Instead, he replied, "Why not? It's a living."

She fixed her eyes on him. "You wouldn't be a union agitator?"

He laughed outright. "You flatter me, Mrs. Balaban. I'm an ignorant Irish peasant, newly arrived in America."

"Less ignorant than I," she said suspiciously. "You're far too clever to be doing what you are."

"And much too hungry not to be doing it."

"He pays you very little, doesn't he?"

"It suffices."

"When you came from Ireland, were you penniless?"

"Very nearly."

"And were you a patriot in Ireland during the Rising?"

He shrugged his shoulders. *"Before* the Rising, I was a patriot. Afterward, I no longer was. I stopped believing."

She studied his face. "In patriotism, Mr. Cassidy, or in everything?"

It was some time before he answered. "I'm not sure."

"I may have stopped believing, too," she volunteered. "I now believe in trinkets. Rings and bracelets, necklaces and brooches." She held up a hand, then a wrist. Precious stones and silver flashed in the sun's rays. "At Bryn Mawr, I read Nietzsche, but now I read the Tiffany catalog. My husband is very generous."

Did he dare say what was on his tongue? "Selectively generous, I'd say."

"Ah!" she exclaimed mirthfully. "I knew I'd rouse you. You *are* an agitator. Don't be afraid, Mr. Cassidy. My husband and I have very little in common."

"Except a fondness for trinkets on your part, and the ability to give them on his?"

She was pleased with the repartee. "It is great fun to talk to you, Mr. Cassidy. My husband is an educated man but does little more than grunt."

He bowed his head in acknowledgment. "It's a pleasure to sit next to you, Mrs. Balaban. I'm sure that not many bosses' wives would go to the trouble of being so cordial to a worker."

Her eyes held his and would not let go. "Not many workers would stroll through the park early in the morning and look up at my window for a sign of the boss's wife."

"You saw me?"

"I waited." When she spoke again, her voice had a different quality to it. "If I were a stronger woman, I might have run across the street to walk with you, but I'm weak, Mr. Cassidy. I am too fond of my trinkets."

"There are other gifts in the world, Mrs. Balaban."

He could feel her flesh tingle, her silken skin and thighs. She was lonely, by God, and half-starved for affection.

"Yes," she said, but whether to him or herself, he couldn't say.

Suddenly she collected herself, remembering who she was. "I really can't stay. My friend is expecting me."

"Then it would be wrong for me to detain you, wouldn't it?"

"Yes, it would."

"I hope you have a pleasant afternoon."

"I hope so, too, Mr. Cassidy."

Still, she didn't leave. Patrick could see the indecision on her face. As hazardous as it might be, he was going to take the chance. He blurted out the words: "Would it be possible for me to see you again, Mrs. Balaban?"

She seemed to draw back. "I'm sorry if I've misled you," she answered, rising from the bench. "I must be going now."

In confusion, he stood up and watched as she hurried away. She hadn't misled him; he was convinced of it.

Late in the afternoon, when Patrick saw the manager leave the loft and disappear down the stairs, he made his way into the empty office. In the slender directory beneath the wall telephone, he found the listing he was looking for: J. Wilson Balaban, 8 Washington Square North. He picked up the telephone and gave the operator the number.

The telephone rang four times, then a fifth. When at last it was picked up, Eva Balaban answered sleepily, "Hello?"

. She must have been taking a nap. He closed his eyes and saw her naked.

"I have to see you," he said.

She didn't reply; nor did she hang up. He could hear her breathing.

"I must ask you not to call again," she said almost inaudibly.

Patrick looked through the glass wall of the office for Mr. Weiss, knowing that he would have to hang up the minute he came into view. "But you want to see me, I know you do. You're unhappy. I can tell you are."

"Whether I'm unhappy or not is not the issue. The issue is that it's quite impossible for me to do anything about it."

The connection was broken. Disconsolately, Patrick placed the receiver back on its cradle, then returned to his work.

The afternoon seemed endless. When Saul reminded him that there would be a meeting at eight-thirty that night at Clinton Hall, he said that he would be there, but he wasn't looking forward to it. He knew for a fact that the Italians wouldn't appear.

At quitting time, there was a mad rush to the dressing room, and today Patrick was among the first to get there. Once more, he would walk through the park on his way home to see if she had changed her mind. He had just reached the top of the stairs when the manager stopped him.

"There's a telegram for you in the office," he said. "It came five minutes ago."

His heart thumped wildly as he made his way to the office and picked up the small envelope on Mr. Weiss's desk. He tore it open.

Sunday at three o'clock, the Brevoort Hotel. We must end this.

It was unsigned, but he knew that Eva would be waiting for him there when he arrived.

By eight-thirty Friday night, the gloom in the main

meeting room at Clinton Hall was palpable. Seated at the table were Sarasohn, Elizabeth Flanagan, Sonia, Patrick, and Saul, who was even more dejected than the others. Benches and straight-backed chairs had been neatly arranged in front of them, but none was occupied.

They sat looking into space, wondering why they had failed. For the first half hour, Sarasohn had talked with animation, trying to cheer the others up. The Jewish girls, he said, must be observing the Sabbath. He could not otherwise account for their being absent. It was beyond reason.

Sonia provided the explanation no one wanted to listen to. "They got scared," she declared. "They were with us, but then Balaban scared them yesterday, and now they're as meek as the Italian girls."

Sarasohn looked hurt to the point of annihilation. He took it as a personal blow. They were rejecting him as much as they were rejecting the union.

"So what do we do now?" Saul asked.

"Nothing," Elizabeth Flanagan replied. "Tread water. Go underground. If you show your hand now, Weiss or Balaban will know who our organizers are, and they'll have you out of there so fast you won't know what's happened."

It was all right with Patrick. He was not sure that he wanted a confrontation with Balaban just now, anyway.

Suddenly, Sarasohn reached over and touched the nape of Sonia's neck. "We might as well go home. Let the bastards suffer if they want to. I just don't understand. It's like the Old Country. You try to help them, but they're afraid they might have to lose what they already have before they get anything more." Softly, he kneaded the back of her neck.

Sonia wiped her frizzy hair out of her eyes. The dark circles under them were enormous, as if something fatal were eating at her entrails and she were drowning in poison. She looked tired. "It's like Russia all over again. The Cossacks always win. The poor people always lose. Maybe we deserve to lose if we're too cowardly to fight."

She pushed her chair back and stood at the table. As

she did, there was a timid knock on the frame of the door, and all eyes turned to look.

"It is here, *nichtwahr?*" Sophie Bernstein asked.

Behind her stood three other women, and behind them, three more. And that was all. They were among the forty who had been laid off and who had been unable to find other work. They looked old and beaten.

Patrick didn't know if he should laugh or cry. They had called a meeting of workers at the Diamond Shirtwaist Company, and not one of them had shown up. Instead, seven ancient women had appeared, and they were no longer even employed there, so they could not very well strike against the company.

A sob escaped from Sonia's throat; then she ran across the room to welcome the women. The others followed, escorting them to their chairs, where the ladies sat primly, their pocketbooks in their laps, and looked through their spectacles at the young people seated at the table.

At last, Sarasohn rose and tapped a gavel against the tabletop.

"This meeting of Local Twenty-five of the Ladies' Shirtwaist Makers Union will now come to order," he began, his voice almost breaking.

As he spoke, he looked at the worn and leathery faces in front of him.

"Tonight, ladies," he said softly, "we have learned an important lesson. Everyone at this table should have known it by now, but we forgot it at some point during our journey from the Old World to the New." He searched the tired eyes beneath their white or steel-gray hair. "What we have learned tonight is that people will not fight back until everything has been taken away from them. Until then, they will be meek and hopeful, and above all, patient. But once the bosses have taken everything, even the meek will lose their timidity and the hopeful will lose their patience and, by God, they will fight like soldiers in the fields!"

He pounded his fist against the table. It was doubtful that the ladies understood his message, as they were German, Latvian, Russian, and Italian, but they listened

185

raptly. And as the table shook under his anger, they stood and clapped their hands loudly.

On Saturday morning, rain pelted the shirtwaist workers as they hurried along the sidewalks of the Lower East Side toward the loft on Greene Street. They pulled their babushkas tightly around their heads and kept close to the shelter of the tenements, yet were soaked to the skin even before they had reached Delancey Street.

They walked with a lively step, partly in a vain attempt to outrun the rain, and partly because only twelve hours separated them from a blissful rest that would not be interrupted until Monday morning. Tonight was payday, and tomorrow was theirs, the one day of the week that did not belong to the bosses. They would sleep late in the morning, have a decent midday meal, and in the afternoon perhaps walk across the Williamsburg Bridge.

Much of their salaries was already spoken for, but that did not matter. A quarter, perhaps, was due the tailor, a dollar the butcher, fifty cents for the cobbler, but the great bulk of it went to their landlords to pay for their lodgings. Only a few had surplus dimes and quarters to deposit to their new accounts at the immigrant banks. Yet for all that, who did not feel like a millionaire with a dollar or two in her pocketbook even for just a day?

Their pay envelopes were distributed at quitting time, and the women knew, down to the last penny, what was owed them. During the week as the piecework supervisors recorded their work in their ledgers, the women also kept track, though in a less sophisticated way. Sometimes a sunflower seed or a raisin would be transferred from one pocket to the next, and at the end of the week, they would be counted for the total number of shirtwaists produced. Though most could not read or write, many understood numbers and had learned simple arithmetic in order to avoid being cheated by merchants, and they multiplied their total output by the piecework rate. Those who lacked the skill had friends do it for them. From Thursday through Saturday, they talked of little else than what their pay envelopes would contain and how it would be spent.

But now, at a quarter to seven, as they scurried up

Greene Street in the pouring rain, all that lay ahead of them. They rushed up the stairs to the dressing room, where they removed their wet outer clothing and combed their hair. It would be noon, at least, before their dresses and shoes were dry, and by then the loft would reek of wet clothing and perspiration.

At seven o'clock, when the power was turned on, they bent over and began their day's work.

It had been almost midnight when Patrick had returned to his room in Hell's Kitchen, and even so, he had not been able to go to sleep. He could think of nothing but Eva and the coming events at the shirtwaist factory. Sarasohn was convinced, as Saul was, too, that the owners were going to lay off another forty or fifty women. And if another forty were without work, Sarasohn reasoned, perhaps another seven or eight of them might become union members. If eighty women were discharged, the remaining three hundred or so might begin to weaken. And fourteen union members made a formidable picket line.

Yet every time Sarasohn cursed Balaban, the owner, something was triggered in Patrick's head, and he saw instead the owner's wife.

Tonight, after work, he would scrub himself beneath a shower at the public baths on Allen Street, and in the morning would venture down to Orchard Street and spend a precious dollar for a new shirt—the two he owned were sadly frayed and faded—and perhaps a new cravat. He would spot-clean his single suit as best he could so that he would not look too much like a peasant as he entered the Hotel Brevoort, and he would polish his worn shoes to within an inch of their lives. Sartorially, he would be no match for Mr. Balaban, but beneath his clothes, Patrick hoped that Eva would find a much more interesting man.

All day long as he worked, he hungered for her. By quitting time, when the electric power was shut off, he was drenched with sweat.

Unlike other days, there was no mad scramble to the dressing room. The women continued to sit at their machines, waiting for Mr. Weiss to deliver the pay envelopes to his supervisors, who in turn would distribute them.

187

Without a word, the manager handed his share to Patrick, who immediately began to pass them out. They were arranged by chair number, so he began at one end of the aisle and worked toward the other. As he presented each woman with her envelope, she quickly opened it and began to count her pay.

He was almost at the end of the first row when he became aware of voices behind him. When he turned, he saw women standing at their machines, incredulity on their faces, counting their money again and again. Then they began to shout words that he could not understand.

Suddenly Annamarie was hobbling down the aisle, pulling her crippled foot after her.

"It is not enough, *signore!*" she cried.

Into the palm of his hand, she counted the bills and the change from her pay envelope. "It is six dollars and a half, *signore!* I am owed seven dollars and eighty-five cents!"

Everywhere around him, women waved their pay envelopes in the air and shouted complaints in half a dozen languages. They were angry and looked betrayed.

"*Ist nicht genucht!*" a woman yelled. "*Ist* short. Our pay *ist* short!"

Patrick was baffled. The accounting was done in the office, he attempted to explain. An error must have been made.

Over the din, he heard a whoop and a howl, and Saul began to run down the aisle toward him. His face was incandescent with joy.

"Balaban *did* it! The son of a bitch did it!" Behind him came workers from other aisles, all waving their pay envelopes and shouting with rage.

"The women say their pay is short," Patrick yelled.

"You're damned right it is!" Saul screamed into his ear. "Balaban reduced the piecework rate by ten percent. Weiss just told me."

The women began to converge on the office, but the manager was no longer there. He had locked the door and run down the stairs when he saw the effect the wage reduction had created. The workers pounded on the closed door and yelled into the empty room through the huge glass window. The words they were saying Patrick could not comprehend.

But as they turned and made their way toward the stairs, he heard them clearly now. They began as a whisper, but soon they were roars. "Clinton Hall!" the voices shouted. *"Clinton Hall!"*

17

The note had been delivered late Friday afternoon by a uniformed chauffeur, and as Monsieur Griswold had just stepped into the house, he had taken it from the man, assuming it was for him.

"It is for Miss Shannon," the driver had explained.

Even in an egalitarian society, it is something of a novelty for a domestic servant to receive hand-delivered correspondence from a young black man dressed in livery. In a Christian household, like the Griswolds', it was nothing less than alarming. After Monsieur gave the note to Jack with instructions to pass it on to the cook, he made his way to the second floor. Madame Griswold was just rising from her late-afternoon nap.

"I'm afraid we're going to have trouble with that Shannon woman," Monsieur said. "I should have known that something like this would happen when we agreed to hire a member of the Irish race."

Quite understandably, Madame was concerned. What was the nature of the trouble they were about to have?

"She has met a colored man, and he was brazen enough to deliver a letter to her, arranging an assignation, no doubt."

Madame advised caution. "You know how difficult it was to find her," she began. "And the poor thing needs some amusement. One might have hoped that her head hadn't been turned by a black man, but as you say, the Irish are often morally unfit."

"I will not have a woman of loose morals in my house," he objected, "no matter how well she cooks."

Madame agreed entirely. She would have a chat with Nora that very evening.

As for Nora, she was busy in the kitchen preparing the Griswolds' supper when Jack carried the letter to her.

"Your grand friend has sent you a message," he said, and Nora knew at once whom he meant.

She had certainly thought of Charles Molloy on more than one occasion since the preceding Sunday, yet each time she had, she had been ashamed of herself for having done so.

Though she was progressing well with her lessons at night school, Nora was unable to read the note, and Jack performed the duty for her.

> *My Dear Miss Shannon,*
>
> *I should be most honored if you would permit me to see you this Sunday afternoon. You are probably very busy and have a great many young friends, so I shall not take more than a few hours of your time. If it should prove satisfactory to you, I shall be waiting in front of the main entrance to the Zoological Gardens in Central Park at two o'clock.*
>
> > *Cordially,*
> > *Charles A. Molloy*

After it was read to her, Nora was silent. How could she possibly allow herself to see Mr. Molloy when she was carrying another man's child? It would be unfair to him.

"You will meet him, of course," Jack urged. "He would be a great catch, Nora."

In embarrassment, she cried, "Mr. Molloy would never think of me that way. He came to my aid the evening I was given the terrible fright in the park, and I am sure he is now inquiring after the state of my health. That is all."

Jack protested, "You are a very beautiful woman, Nora, and you deserve the best. You don't want to spend the rest of your life working in someone else's kitchen, do you? The Molloys are members of the Brooklyn aristocracy. They have a huge house on Saint Mark's Avenue."

Nora knew nothing about the aristocracy except that they made very demanding employers.

"He is a widower, too, I believe," Jack added, "and would appreciate a good, sound girl like you."

Nora's face flushed scarlet. She would not listen to another word. A dinner had to be served that required her full attention.

She could not possibly meet Charles Molloy, a man who had made such a great noise for himself in the world. At most, he pitied her for being a greenhorn, but she was sure that his pity would turn to scorn if he knew that another life existed within her. Under no circumstances could she be anywhere near the Zoological Gardens on Sunday.

After supper, while Nora was putting the leftover food in the icebox, Madame Griswold made an unexpected call to the kitchen.

"Monsieur was particularly pleased with your *coquilles St. Jacques*. He sends his compliments."

If he did, it was the first time. Nora thanked her, though she preferred to think that Madame had invented the compliment from her laconic husband as an excuse to chat with her.

"Come sit down a minute, Nora," she said.

Nora waited for Madame to seat herself, then occupied a chair opposite her at the kitchen table.

"We are very pleased with your services, Nora dear," she began.

Once again, Nora replied, "Thank you, ma'am."

"It has been a great pleasure having you in the house. I listen to your merry singing in the kitchen, and I also feel merry. My husband does as well, I'm sure."

Nora did not know what to say, so said nothing.

"That is why we are concerned about you, my dear. New York is filled with temptations, and many an Irish girl has been ruined here. We would not want this to happen to you."

"Nor would I, ma'am."

"It is part of our religion, Nora, to be scrupulously clean and upright. We cannot tolerate scandalous conduct among our help. Monsieur and I merely wanted to remind you that you are in a Christian household and that you must vigilantly fight evil, as we ourselves do. We have invited you often to join in our prayer sessions, and when you have declined, saying that you prefer your own Catholic religion, we have not pressed. But one thing we must be insistent on, and that is your conduct, both outside and inside our house. It must be impeccable, Nora."

What was she getting at? Whatever it was, Nora felt her face smarting under the criticism.

"We hope that we will not have to mention it again, Nora. But *do* be careful in choosing your friends. For anything you might do to discredit yourself will also discredit Monsieur. You must remember that, Nora."

Breathlessly, Nora replied, "Yes, I shall. Thank you, ma'am."

All day Saturday, whenever Nora thought of Charles Molloy and his invitation to join him at the Zoological Gardens the following day, a panic swept over her. Finally she dismissed him from her mind. On Sunday she would call at her old rooming house on Tenth Avenue for whatever mail might have arrived from Ireland, after which she might walk down to Altman's or the Siegel-Cooper Company on Sixth Avenue and look at their marvelous windows.

Under no circumstances would she keep the appointment with Mr. Molloy.

On Sunday morning, when she went to early Mass, she again told herself that she would not be able to see him. Nothing could come of it other than sadness and ultimate heartbreak. No matter how well she might get on with him, in time, the rounder her belly grew and the more imminent her confinement, she would have to discontinue seeing him. So why see him at all?

There were no guests at the midday meal and Nora had done most of the baking the day before, so it was concluded and the kitchen was in reasonable order by one o'clock. She went to her room on the third floor to prepare herself for her afternoon off.

She removed her clothes, then sponged herself at the sink in the corner. Gently, she dabbed cologne over her body, knowing that she would perspire in the desperate heat. As she did, she caught sight of her ungirdled body in the long mirror, and the curvature of her stomach was now unmistakable.

Something made her turn. It was not a noise but a presence. Once again, she had the feeling that she was being watched.

Quickly she pulled on a robe that Madame Griswold had given her and dashed to the door. She opened it and stepped into the hall.

"Is someone out here?" she asked.

Jack had told her that he would be visiting his mother in Chelsea as soon as he had helped serve the Sunday dinner, but she had not seen him leave the house. He was a bachelor, she knew, and mother-dominated, and perhaps the loneliness had warped his mind, though she hated to think so. She hurried down the hall to his room. The door was open, as it always was when he wasn't there, and the room was empty. She retraced her steps to her own room. At one side of it was a storeroom where luggage and trunks and surplus furniture were kept. She tried the knob, but the door was locked.

She could not understand it. Perhaps it was her imagination.

Back in her room, she dressed hurriedly and arranged her hair. When she had finished, she rushed down the stairs and in the first-floor hall found Madame.

"Is Monsieur at home?" Nora asked.

"He left the house right after dinner for his constitutional. Why? Did you have something to say to him, Nora?"

It was unimportant, Nora replied. She would mention it some other time perhaps.

"Well, enjoy your Sunday off," Madame said.

Once she was on the sidewalk, Nora didn't quite know which way to go. To walk toward Fifth Avenue and take a bus south might expose her to Mr. Molloy, who would be going to the park. Instead, she walked toward Madison, then turned and stood at a corner, waiting for a trolley. As she did, she heard a clock toll two.

In no time at all, a trolley came clanging down the

avenue and Nora hopped on board. A great crowd of people were on it, and she was at first unable to find a seat, but one young man, then another, rose, doffed their hats, and offered her the seats they had occupied. She was too frightened by their show of generosity to thank them, but she smiled and accepted the closer seat.

Well, she had made the decision and now she was on her way to Thirty-fourth Street, where she would disembark and walk across town to Tenth Avenue. It was a terrible hike, but she would enjoy it, as it would enable her to see such a great variety of faces and costumes, store windows, and motorcars. As the trolley paused at Fifty-seventh Street, Nora realized that it was now too late to reconsider. It was almost two-fifteen. She peered at the private houses they passed, less elegant than those on Fifth, but substantial nonetheless. Gradually she found that she was no longer looking at them. She studied her hands on her lap, and they were shaking.

When the conductor announced Forty-second Street, Nora flew from the seat and made her way down the crowded aisle to the exit. She began to walk west on the broad avenue. The trolley had been stuffy, and she was in need of air. Once she reached Fifth, she could either board an open-topped bus, spending another precious nickel, or she could walk south on Fifth to Thirty-fourth Street, then west again. In either case, she would avoid running into Mr. Molloy, who would have entered the park in the Sixties.

Yet when she reached the avenue, she turned north, rather than south, scarcely knowing why she was doing it, as her mail—provided she had any—was waiting for her at Tenth and Thirty-first. She walked from Forty-second to Fifty-second to Sixty-second. Twenty blocks. And as she neared her destination, she was almost running.

In the distance, she saw the entrance to the zoo. An organ grinder and a monkey amused a small crowd on the sidewalk, and a balloon seller hawked his wares. Pigeons swooped through the air and landed in great multitudes on the shoulders and head of the peddler, and a cry went up among the children.

Nora's eyes searched the benches, but it was now almost three o'clock and Mr. Molloy had obviously left. Feeling both relief and disappointment, she sat down and began to fan her face with a handkerchief.

"Hello," a gentle voice said to her.

She looked up and there he was, a small bouquet of flowers in his hand. "Hello," she answered. "I'm most awfully late."

"I know. I've been following you in the car since the minute you left the house. You were certainly undecided, weren't you?"

Nora began to laugh, and so did he.

It was far too fine a day to peer at the creatures in their cages, Charles Molloy said. Would Nora perhaps care instead to take a short ride to Long Island, where it was bound to be cooler? "I generally drive out to Southampton on Sunday afternoons," he continued. "If you've never seen the ocean from *this* side of the Atlantic, it's well worth a visit."

Nora was not opposed to his suggestion. She had taken one whiff of the ammoniac smells rising from the zoo and decided that no matter how exotic the animals were, she would just as soon not spend an afternoon walking among their cages.

The car was waiting at the Fifth Avenue entrance to the zoo, and the driver stood at the rear door, holding it open for them. His black face glistened under a thin layer of sweat.

"We are going to Southampton, Jim," Charles Molloy said to the man, then sat back next to Nora as the car pulled into the traffic.

Not only had Nora never been in such an elegant motorcar before, she had never been in a car at all. Once, in Ireland, she had sat in the front seat of a lorry for a few minutes to see what it was like, but that was all.

"It is a gorgeous automobile, Mr. Molloy," she said. "I will never want to walk again."

"It's a convenience," he answered. "Jim worked for my father, and when my father died, we didn't want to let him go. He is like a member of the family."

As they left Manhattan, he told her a bit about the

197

Brooklyn Molloys. His grandfather was from Tipperary, he said, and his first job in the New World was as a hod carrier; then he became a bricklayer and finally opened a construction business of his own. His four sons, one of whom was Charles Molloy's father, eventually joined the business.

"We are responsible for many of the abominations we're now passing," Charles said as the car made its way down First Avenue toward the Queensboro Bridge. "My grandfather and father built hundreds of brownstones and thousands of tenements, and the buildings are sturdy. They will last for centuries unless people decide to pull them down. My father predicted that steel would replace wooden beams as buildings got higher, and he thought it would be a good idea for someone in the family to know a little bit about engineering. So he sent me to the Massachusetts Institute of Technology, thinking that I would be taught how to put up a building that would never fall down. Thus far, I have been lucky." He knocked on the frame of the divider between the front and rear seats. "We were using steel at a time when other builders were afraid to handle it, so we had a head start. From there, it was easy to go into building bridges and subways." He turned to her and smiled. "Now, have I bored the daylights out of you yet?"

"No, Mr. Molloy," she replied earnestly. "I find it most interesting. To build a building or a bridge that lasts for centuries is almost a link with eternity."

He nodded sadly. "It is all I have. I failed with the other." When it became obvious that Nora did not fathom his meaning, he added, "My wife died in childbirth."

"And the poor baby?"

"That, too."

For a time he was quiet; then he resumed. "So here I am, almost middle-aged, and on Sundays my only amusement is to ride to Southampton, Long Island."

"You don't look at all middle-aged," Nora said cheerfully.

"I bet I'm twice your age," he replied. "How old are you?"

"I'll be eighteen in November."

"Then I'm *more* than twice your age. I'm thirty-eight. I was thirty-six when I married." He waited. "They say in my family that it took me thirty-six years to propose to my first wife, and it will probably take me another thirty-six to propose to a second."

After he said it, he was embarrassed. He looked away as the color rose to his face.

"And do you live in Manhattan, Mr. Molloy?" she said to break the silence.

"In Brooklyn. We have not yet been tempted into Manhattan. We are still very Irish and uncomfortable in New York society, such as it is. My grandmother was a parlormaid, and the New York grandees will never let us forget that. And we are Catholic, of course, and generally despised because of it. In Brooklyn, we have our friends, our priests, our church." He turned to her and smiled. "Now you must tell me about yourself, Nora. May I call you Nora?"

Nora blushed uncontrollably. "I am just a cook, Mr. Molloy."

"Don't underestimate it. To be a good cook is as important as being a good doctor or a good lawyer or a good engineer. I love good food just as I love to listen to Beethoven. A woman who hates food and cooking also hates life."

"Do you think so, Mr. Molloy?"

He smiled. "Do you think so, *Charles*. Yes, I do, but tell me, what else do you like?"

"I am going to school at nights to improve my mind, and they say I am making progress. I have begun to read a little book by Mr. Washington Irving, and it is very lovely. I also like music. At home we had only the fiddle and the squeeze box, but here I have been to the Academy of Music on Fourteenth Street and heard an opera by Mr. Puccini. Jack took me, and I could not sleep all night long with all the singing in my head."

He smiled, then asked her to tell him more.

During the trip to Southampton, she described her family in Ireland, and Charles Molloy asked many questions. He had been to Russia, where his firm was building a railroad, and was about to leave for Argentina, where Molloy & Company was building a bridge across the Río de la Plata, but he had never been to Ireland.

"And you had no young man in County Cork?" he asked.

"Thomas Cassidy, the man I was to have married, was hanged by British soldiers."

For a very long time, Charles Molloy said nothing at all. Then, at last, he turned to look at her.

"Poor Nora," he said. "Poor seventeen-year-old Nora, setting out all by yourself from Ireland, leaving the man you loved behind you. You are very brave."

She turned from his gaze and looked through the car's window.

Nora had never seen such houses before. They were made of wood, not stone, and many of them—the closer they got to the shore—were shingled. Charles Molloy said of them, "They are not houses, properly speaking. They are cottages."

Cottages! They were immense. Some of them, Nora was sure, contained thirty or forty rooms. Most had huge porches in front and in the rear, and some had porches all around them, filled with wicker and wrought-iron furniture.

At last, at the end of a winding road, the car slowed down, and on the horizon Nora saw a house very much like the others, yet different. The same brown shingles covered it, the same chimneys rose from its gabled roof, and the same verandas looked both seaward and inland. Yet the windows had all been boarded up, and where lawn should have been were sand dunes, high weeds, rusting wheelbarrows, and random pieces of weathered lumber.

There was no driveway leading to the house, so the car stopped on the road, and Charles Molloy helped Nora out. They began to walk across the dunes.

"I built it for my wife," Charles Molloy said, "and our baby. We had hoped to use it during the summer months and close the house in Brooklyn. But when they died, I didn't have the heart to finish it. I told the men to stop what they were doing, and they did. I come out on Sundays to see if vandals have broken in, but so far, even they have found it inhospitable."

Nora stopped and looked at the huge cottage. In Ireland it would be called a mansion, though surely no one would know what to make of all the wood. It was a sad place, and yet it wasn't. It looked strong and sturdy and indomitable, capable of weathering any kind of storm. It would be a beautiful house if there were children playing on its broad verandas and happy voices coming through its open windows.

Charles Molloy showed it to her, room by room, all twelve bedrooms and six bathrooms. Sawhorses and carpenters' tools still sat in the hallways and on the landings. A kind of twilight seeped through the boarded windows, and two years of dust covered the floors.

It was a house of death when it was meant to be a house of life.

"I don't want to sell it," Charles Molloy said, "and yet I can't finish it. Isn't that peculiar, Nora?"

No, Nora did not find it peculiar. She found it appropriate. As they searched through the barren house, Nora was aware that Charles was trying to say something to her, and she was relieved when they heard raindrops striking against the roof and he said instead, "It's raining, Nora. We'll have to dash for it if we don't want to get wet."

On the trip back to the city, they were subdued, both of them. When, as they neared Manhattan, he asked if she would have supper with him, she lied and said that she was expected back at the Griswolds' by nine o'clock and they were very strict.

At her request, the car dropped her off not in front of the Griswolds' town house but at the corner.

"Could I see you tomorrow?" he asked.

Tell him, she said to herself. Yet she could not form the words.

"Just for a few minutes," he added. "I could meet you here at the corner at eight o'clock. Or eight-thirty, if you like."

Tell him, she commanded herself, but was unable to.

"All right," she replied. "Eight-thirty."

* * *

Except for a light in the second-floor hallway, the house was dark. Jack would not be home until late, he had said that morning, as he was spending his Sunday having his compulsory dinner with his mother in Chelsea —doing his penance, he described it—and the Griswolds were to have supper at the Claremont Inn overlooking the Hudson River. Nora went directly to the kitchen, where she put the kettle on for tea.

She sat at the kitchen table and waited for the water to begin to sigh and boil. It was a soothing sound. She could relax and think while listening to it. Decisions had to be made.

It would not be fair to lead Mr. Molloy on. What would his family in Brooklyn think if they knew he had spent the day with an unmarried woman who was about to have a baby? They would not understand, any more than Mr. Molloy himself would. They would see Nora as unfit and unworthy.

And that being the case, it was best to try to terminate the relationship before it became more complicated. There were but two ways she could do it, she thought. She could tell him that she was not the innocent young girl he assumed she was. Or she could lie and say that she was about to marry someone else. She would invent a name. Or she could use Jack's name.

To do the latter would not be a bad idea at all. Though he might be temporarily hurt by what she told him, in the end it would be a kindness, as a greater hurt, later on, could be avoided.

Yes, she would tell him that she had promised herself to Jack.

The water in the kettle was now boiling, and Nora rose to remove it from the stove. As she did, she heard someone behind her, and when she turned, she saw Monsieur Griswold. He and Madame must have finished supper earlier than they had planned.

His suit jacket had been removed, and the collar of his shirt had been loosened. His hair was disheveled, and his eyes looked wild.

202

"I have been watching you," he whispered. "Don't think I haven't, you whore of Babylon."

He began to walk toward her, and as he did, Nora became afraid. He walked like a drunken man, though she knew he did not drink. He looked crazed and possessed.

"You are ill, Monsieur," she said urgently. "I shall get Madame."

"I've given her a sedative. She will not wake until morning."

Nora backed up against the wall; he continued to come toward her.

He slurred his words as he spoke. "You are carrying someone's filth in your belly. I have watched it grow."

So it was Monsieur's eyes that she had felt watching her.

"You have been sent by the Devil," he resumed. "You are a messenger from Hell, lodging in our Christian home, tempting me with your round belly. And I have prayed for the strength to resist you, you whore of Babylon."

"Please, Monsieur, don't hurt me!"

"You whore of Babylon," he repeated, advancing toward her.

In horror, Nora watched as he unbuttoned his trousers and his white and wormlike manhood sprang into view. It quivered and grew, its huge veins pulsating, then stood erect.

"The Devil has sent you, but I shall vanquish both you and your master, you slut."

He rushed toward her and pulled at her dress from the neck, ripping it away. She struggled with all her might, but his hand clawed at her underclothes until he had pulled them down.

"No!" she cried, breaking away.

And as she did, she saw someone at the door, a wraithlike figure in a flowing white gown, her hair down to her shoulders. It was Madame.

"Please help me," Nora sobbed.

Monsieur did not see his wife, but once again made his way to where Nora stood cowering against the wall. Behind him, Madame ran in her bare feet across the floor to the stove and grabbed the steaming kettle.

He turned and met the boiling water as it splashed

against his opened trousers. He screamed out in pain, held his hands in front of his burning flesh, then rolled on the floor.

"Please go at once," Madame said to Nora. "The Devil has made him do this. Please go."

Madame sank to her knees, closed her eyes, directed her face heavenward, and began to pray.

The following evening, Charles Molloy stood on the corner waiting for Nora from ten minutes to eight until almost nine-thirty. When there was no sign of her, he walked down the block to the Griswold house and rang the bell.

"I was to have met Miss Shannon this evening," he said to Jack when the latter opened the door.

"Miss Shannon is no longer employed by the Griswolds," Jack answered.

When Charles Molloy's face registered confusion, Jack explained as best he could. "Monsieur has been taken ill and will be hospitalized for a month or so. During that time, Madame will be living with her parents in Massachusetts. She is closing the house here in New York."

Jack listened up the hall staircase, then stepped out to the stoop, closing the door behind him. In a low voice he said to Molloy, "There was a terrible row last night, and Monsieur has had a breakdown." He waited, then added, "He tried to attack Nora."

"Oh, my God," Charles Molloy said. "Where is she?"

Jack did not at once reply. "She asked that I tell no one."

"Not even me?"

"Especially you, Mr. Molloy."

Jack watched the hurt and disappointment on the man's face. Perhaps something about the barrenness of his own life, something about opportunities that he himself had thrown away, now compelled him to disobey Nora's request.

"She has told you, has she, about the young man in Ireland she was to have married?" he said at last.

"Thomas Cassidy," Molloy replied. "I know all about that."

204

"Not all, Mr. Molloy."

"He was executed by the British after the Rising."

Jack nodded. "And Nora is carrying his child. That is why she has chosen not to see you, Mr. Molloy, and why she asked me not to reveal her whereabouts."

In the darkness it was difficult for Jack to read Charles Molloy's face. At first there was something like surprise, followed by something like understanding. If there was anger or disgust, Jack was not able to perceive it.

"You must tell me where she is," Molloy insisted.

Jack did not reply.

"I must talk to her," Molloy continued. "Afterward, if she doesn't want to see me again, that will be her decision. But I must talk to her."

Jack relented.

When she heard the knock, Nora thought it was on the door across the hall, and did not leave the chair by the window to answer it. The knocking continued, and she was halfway across the room when the knob turned and Charles Molloy entered.

Wordlessly, they confronted each other.

"Today is Monday," Molloy began at last. "With your permission, we shall be married on Friday. On Saturday, at noon, we shall board a ship bound for Buenos Aires, where business will keep me for a year or more."

He waited for her to speak, but Nora remained silent.

"We shall name the first child, if it is a boy, Thomas Cassidy Molloy. And if it is a girl, we shall name her Nora Cassidy Molloy. And that child will enrich our lives, Nora, just as you will enrich mine."

Nora's voice was tremulous. "Then you know?"

"I know. And we need never speak of it again. If you marry me, your child will become my child, and I shall raise it with the same degree of love Thomas Cassidy would have given it. I will cherish it as my own."

He wrapped his arms around her until her trembling stopped. "Will you marry me, Nora?" he asked.

"I will," she heard herself say.

18

As Patrick made his way into the lobby of the Brevoort shortly before three on Sunday afternoon, a page boy was repeating his name.

Inside the envelope he was handed was a single sheet of hotel stationery, and in a firm, businesslike hand, without frills or embellishment, was written *Room 34*, and nothing else, not even a signature.

It was a peculiar way for Eva to announce her whereabouts, Patrick thought, but he supposed that she had decided it would be imprudent to meet him in one of the public rooms at Greenwich Village's most famous hotel. After all, her home was just around the corner on Washington Square and someone from the neighborhood was bound to recognize her.

When he knocked on the door to the room, her voice said, "It's open," and he entered what appeared to be a small suite. Eva was standing at a window looking down onto the street and didn't turn to welcome him.

When he saw who was sitting on a sofa, he understood why. It was her husband.

"Come sit down," Balaban said, indicating a chair across from him. "Don't look so tragic. My wife and I have a very modern relationship, and she told me that she was seeing a young Irishman who works for me. My wife is a very beautiful woman, Mr. Cassidy, and sometimes when she meets men, she gives rise—how shall I say it?—to unwarranted expectations." He smiled. "I am always interested in the young men my wife attracts. You are the first Gentile, I believe. Eva herself is a *meshumed*—a convert to Christianity—but as a rule feels more comfortable with rich old Jews like me." He peered over his shoulder in the direction of his wife, but she did not acknowledge what he had said.

Patrick had not yet taken the chair offered him, and now Balaban suddenly rose from the sofa. "I have a business proposition for you," he said.

When Patrick did not respond, he bit off the tip of a cigar, then prepared to light it. "You are a union organizer, aren't you?" he asked, blowing clouds of smoke into the air.

Patrick met his eyes but didn't answer.

"One of our informers among the women has told us that you have been agitating the Italian workers. I just learned yesterday and was prepared to give you a pink slip on Monday, but now that my wife has arranged this meeting so fortuitously, perhaps we can offer you something else." He stopped, and when he spoke again, his tone had changed. "Would you like to better yourself, Mr. Cassidy?"

Patrick had hoped to better himself in bed with Eva Balaban. He was not prepared to commit himself to any other form of self-improvement.

"My family is in need of someone who is close to Clinton Hall in order that we can be one step ahead of the union leaders. For such a contact, Mr. Cassidy, we are willing to reward you handsomely. You are now making nine dollars a week, I understand. We could be persuaded, I think, to triple that."

Almost thirty dollars a week. It was a fantastic salary. Mr. Weiss, the manager, could not make more.

When Balaban saw the indecision on Patrick's face, he pressed on. "America is a land of opportunity, Patrick." He used the first name adroitly, soothingly. "It is no place for the timid and the backward. What do you want out of life, anyway? A nice place to live? A little money in the bank so that you don't have to worry about how you're going to pay for tomorrow's food? Nice clothes? Nice friends? In time, you will want to marry and raise a family. You cannot always covet other men's wives." He returned to the sofa. "I am offering you security. Most men would jump at the chance. What do you say, Patrick?"

At last, Eva Balaban turned to look at him, but he could not fathom what she was thinking.

"My life wouldn't be worth much," he replied, "if the union found out that I was talking to you. What good is thirty dollars a week to me if I'm floating in the East River?"

Balaban agreed that he had a point. "As soon as our crisis is over at Diamond Shirtwaist, I shall see to it that you are transferred to one of my family's mills in New Jersey or Massachusetts. No harm will come to you. You will be given a supervisory job and paid thirty dollars a week."

Eva held her chin in her hand and watched Patrick, waiting for his answer.

"And what would you like to know?" he asked at last.

"I want to know in advance when your meetings will be held so that I can stop them."

"Stop them? But does the Constitution give you such a right?"

Balaban's eyes darkened, and his face became grim. "The Constitution does not give the right to foreign rabble-rousers to preach their Communistic doctrines. I shall get a court order to prevent them."

As if Balaban anticipated the question on Patrick's lips, he confided, "I have many friends who share my point of view, Mr. Cassidy, and some of them sit in courts of law. Others occupy important positions in the police department. I assure you that they will not hesitate to perform a favor for me." He waited. "Now will you tell me what the hooligans at Clinton Hall are up to?"

Patrick turned toward Eva, hoping that she would give him a clue as to how he should answer, but her face was unreadable.

If Balaban already had an informer among the workers, he would learn of the scheduled meeting anyhow. Why not let him think Patrick was on his side? If he felt in charge of the situation, he might relax and be less of a threat.

Quietly, Patrick began, "A meeting is planned for eight o'clock tonight. A strike vote will be taken."

He watched Eva's lips move as if she were about to say something, but she remained silent.

Excitedly, Balaban jumped from his chair. "Where is it being held?"

"By the Arch in Washington Square."

The owner consulted his pocket watch. "It's almost three-thirty. Where the hell is Judge Davis on Sunday afternoon? Tuxedo Park! I must get him back to Manhattan at once to issue the court order. This damn strike will be stopped before it starts!"

He hurried to the telephone at the other end of the room. As he waited for his call to be completed, he said to Patrick, "I am a man of my word. I shall look after you, Cassidy, I promise you I will. Keep in close touch and tell me whatever the union leaders are plotting, and I shall reward you."

As he began to speak into the telephone, Patrick drifted into the hall. He pressed the button for the elevator.

Eva was standing next to him. "You are very easily bought," she said.

"I suppose the same could be said about you."

"I didn't sell myself for thirty dollars a week."

"For what, then? Fifty? One hundred?" Patrick listened to the cables humming in the elevator shaft. "Why did you tell him that you were meeting me?"

She lifted the sleeve of her dress to reveal a dark bruise high on her arm. "He forced me."

"Why don't you leave him?" he whispered.

Sadly she said, "But you've already answered that for me, Mr. Cassidy. I'm as easily bought as you are.

The elevator arrived, and as the attendant pulled the door open, Eva Balaban disappeared into the room.

By seven-thirty that evening, when the first women began to assemble by the arch in Washington Square, they were met by mounted policemen, one hundred or more of them. They had not expected so many blue-uniformed men, and the fact that they were mounted, as the dreaded Cossacks had been, caused some to turn back.

But others remained and more arrived, so that by

eight o'clock, a great crowd had gathered beneath the Arch. And when, at last, their union leaders could be seen approaching from Waverly Place, cries of encouragement could be heard in many different languages.

Sarasohn led the group, and behind him came Elizabeth Flanagan, Sonia Lipsky, Saul Kaganoff, and Patrick Cassidy. They looked intent and purposeful, and when they perceived the policemen on horseback, they paused only momentarily, then continued toward the Arch.

Saul was carrying a wooden crate, and as they arrived at their destination, he placed it on the cobblestones so that Sarasohn could stand on it and be seen by the crowd.

On the steps of the Balabans' handsome town house, the owner of the Diamond Shirtwaist Company was in deep conversation with an elderly man and a gentleman dressed in the uniform of an assistant chief of police. They watched the proceedings as they talked, and did not appear to be unduly alarmed.

As Sarasohn stepped onto the wooden crate, and even before he spoke, a uniformed deputy said to him, "If this meeting is not disbanded at once, I shall have to arrest you, sir."

Sarasohn stepped off the crate. "On what grounds?" he asked.

"We have a court order, sir, forbidding this assembly." He handed the order to Sarasohn, who silently began to read it. The women were quiet now, awaiting their fate. Only the nervous shifting of the horses' hooves against the cobblestones could be heard.

From where he stood, Patrick could see Eva Balaban at a window of the town house.

"I shall have to make an announcement informing them of this," Sarasohn said placidly to the server of the court order.

Once again, he stepped onto the wooden crate. "Ladies," he began, "we have been enjoined by court order from holding our meeting tonight in the borough of Manhattan."

As his words were translated into Yiddish, Russian,

211

and Italian, sharp cries of disappointment could be heard.

But Sarasohn had not finished. "And that is why, ladies," he resumed, and there was defiance in his voice, "we shall march as free citizens in a democratic society from the borough of Manhattan"—he clenched his fist and held it high—"to the borough of *Brooklyn!*"

The roar from the crowd was tremendous. Quickly, Sarasohn's four assistants spread out among the women to organize the march before the mounted policemen could react. Even while Balaban was shouting, "Stop them! *Stop* them!" the first marchers had already begun to leave the park.

"That damn Cassidy doublecrossed me!" Balaban cried as he ran across the street toward the Arch. "Stop them!" he implored the policemen. "I command you to stop them!" But the men on horseback shrugged their shoulders, knowing that they lacked authority. The court order prevented the assembly in Manhattan; it did not prevent a peaceful march to Brooklyn.

"Anyone who strikes is fired!" Balaban screamed after the marchers. "Do you hear me? If you vote to strike, you are all *fired!*"

Arms joined, the workers marched east to University Place, and as they did, students and professors who had watched the confrontation broke into applause and urged them on. Many marched with them, crowding the street and the sidewalks, and some began to sing, and finally "Solidarity Forever" could be heard loud and clear, even though most of the workers could only mimic the English words. And as they made their way toward Houston Street, heads poked out of tenement windows, and people marveled at the women's courage and shouted praise and reassurance.

At the broad approaches to the Williamsburg Bridge, torches were passed out, and as the marchers climbed the ramp onto the bridge, they looked like phantoms against the night sky. When the first of them reached the dark water of the East River, they yelled for joy, leaving Manhattan behind them.

Midway across, Sarasohn held up his hand to halt

them. "We are now in the free and independent borough of Brooklyn, ladies!" he announced, and the roar that met his words could be heard all the way to the Battery.

Once again, Saul placed the wooden crate on the pavement and Sarasohn climbed up on it. He held out both arms for silence, and when it came, save for the passing tugboats, he declared, "Ladies! Tonight we have left serfdom behind us!"

Those who stood in the crowd felt the bridge sway under their stomping feet as his remarks were quickly translated into Yiddish and Italian, Russian and Polish.

"But let me warn you," he continued. "In the days ahead, our mettle will be sorely tested. We will be called Bolsheviks and enemies of America. We will be hated and vilified. The police will treat us as common criminals, and many of us will be jailed. Some of us will be hurt. Scabs and strikebreakers will try to take our jobs. We will be hungry, living on the pittance the union can give us. But do not despair! Do not weaken! Because in the end, we shall triumph!"

Patrick stood near Annamarie, who translated Sarasohn's words with the same ardor he used in speaking them. Her face was drenched with sweat, her hair was wild, and her voice was hoarse from shouting.

"On Monday," Sarasohn told the workers, "we shall meet with the bosses and present our demands. Even the beasts who toil in the fields are allowed rest, and that will be our first demand." He waited. "No more *ten*-hour days! No more *twelve*-hour days! . . . But an *eight*-hour day with no reduction in wages!"

A huge cry went up, and tears rolled down the women's cheeks.

"We want job security," Sarasohn began again when they were silent. "We now have no more rights than slaves do. We are fired without reason and our wages are reduced at the boss's whim. But let us remind our employers: *they* do not make *us* rich men. *We* make *them* rich men, and without us, they are nothing. We *demand* to be treated like men and women, not like animals!"

It was a long time before there was sufficient quiet for Sarasohn to resume.

"And finally, ladies," he concluded, "we demand recognition of our union, because without it, we are voiceless people with little hope, doomed to lives of poverty and despair. The bosses look at us in our strange clothing and listen to our peculiar accents, and they say: Why should we help these people who are foreigners on our shores, uninvited and unwanted? And *we* shall say to them that this Promised Land is as much *ours* as it is theirs. We have left our homelands in order to begin new lives, not to feel the boot of the oppressor once again. We have come to this sweet and bountiful land for our share of America, and if the bosses will not willingly give it, then—so help us God!—we shall seize it!"

He looked from face to face, and when he spoke again, he did so almost gently. "We shall now take a vote. All those in favor of striking against the Diamond Shirtwaist Company, please respond by saying aye."

There was a sudden calm as nearly four hundred breaths were held, then a great wave of sound shook the bridge.

"AYE! AYE! AYE!"

It was after midnight when Patrick climbed the steep stairs to his room on Tenth Avenue. He was spent, emotionally and physically, yet knew that he would not get much sleep. He had promised to be at the factory no later than six in the morning to help set up the picket line, and he would have to leave his room by five.

He opened the door and turned on the ceiling light.

Eva Balaban rose from the only chair in the room. She wore a broad-rimmed hat with a dark veil, and there were diamonds at her neck.

"And did your husband come with you this time, too?" Patrick asked.

"I had no choice this afternoon. I told you. He forced me."

He eased the door shut behind him, then stood and contemplated his guest. "Where is your husband now?"

"He is spending the night with his father and grand-

214

father, planning strategy. There will be a strike, won't there?"

Patrick nodded. "Why is it so important to them? It's just a small factory. They own others much larger."

"They think if one is unionized, all will be."

"And would that be so terrible?"

"From their point of view, it would be."

He stepped toward her. "And from yours?"

Her voice was almost inaudible. "Would I be here if I agreed with them?"

"Why *are* you here?"

"Because I was once as poor as you are," she replied, "and I sold myself too cheaply." She waited, then added, "I've brought a gift for you."

He watched as she raised her slender fingers to unclasp a large brooch on her dress. She handed it to him.

It dazzled as it caught the light from the single bulb: in a field of blue-white diamonds, an emerald glowed like the eye of a crazed animal.

"Please give it to the strike fund."

He caught his breath. "You amaze me, Mrs. Balaban."

She lifted her veil and removed her hat. "I amaze myself." Once again, her hands sought out her neck. "I have another gift," she began.

Slowly, her fingers worked at the buttons of her dress. "You said to me that there are finer gifts in the world than trinkets, and I was so corrupted I'd very nearly forgotten." She let the top of her dress fall from her shoulders, then lowered the straps of her chemise. Her breasts sprang loose.

To convert her husband's jewelry into food for his striking workers was not defiance enough. She would do more than that. If she had sold her body to Balaban, she would give it away to his enemy.

"Will you have me?" she asked.

From the minute he'd seen her for the first time, so aloof and inaccessible in the back seat of the huge motorcar, he'd wanted to reach out and touch her, but hadn't dared.

He did so now. In spite of the summer's heat, she was shivering. When his hands met her naked shoulders, a

215

tremor passed over her and she cried out, *"Oh, God!"* Even as she said it, he covered her mouth with his.

The first elevated train of the new day shrieked as it flew by the open window, and Patrick stirred. Eva's scent was everywhere in the room, but she had gone, having given what she had come to give. Or taken what she was compelled to take.

What now? Where could they go from there? For the life of him, he could not see the future, for no matter how swiftly class distinctions disappeared in bed, elsewhere they remained. Eva may once have been poor, but she was accustomed to the comforts Balaban provided her. The only comfort Patrick had to offer was flesh.

Early-morning light seeped through the window, and somewhere a clock tolled five times. He watched the sky lighten, and with a start he knew that he had lived this dawn once before. Where was it?

In Ireland in prison on Easter morning, while he waited for his father and his brothers, he had felt the same apprehension he felt now. His skin was clammy and his entrails knotted. When he came to America, he had pledged to advance himself and let noble causes be damned. He had vowed to fight his own battles and no one else's. So what was he doing? All he wanted from his new life was a few dollars in the bank, yet in an hour's time he would be confronting Balaban just as his brothers and father had confronted British soldiers. *Why?*

God knows, a man has to live with himself, has to take stands, and sometimes has to help those who are weaker than he. The women at the factory had shamed him. They wanted so little, yet Balaban was unwilling to give them even that. Some were crippled, some were old, most were half-starved, but they were about to take to the streets to demand their rights. Patrick had no choice but to join them. If he hadn't, he would have been no son of John Mary, no brother to Thomas, Lambi, and Eamon.

At the side of his bed, he knelt and prayed in the language of his fathers, inviting God to watch over the women on Greene Street this day. Finished, he crossed himself, then rose and washed at the cold-water tap. He dressed quickly and placed his tweed cap on his head. Only as he was about to leave the room did he remember Eva's other gift. On the table next to the bed he found the glittering pin and stuffed it into his pocket, covering it with his hand for fear that he would lose it. He would give it to Sarasohn without revealing its source.

He walked to work to save the carfare and to give himself courage.

By the time he turned onto Greene Street, it was nearly six. A group of women already waited in front of the building, and not until he was almost on top of them did he recognize who they were.

"Come va, signore?" Annamarie asked.

"Va bene," he said, smiling. Even Sarasohn hadn't arrived yet, yet Annamarie and the Italian women with her stood waiting impatiently. Patrick was very proud of her. Only a few weeks before, she had been suspicious of the union, and now she was its champion.

"You're very early, Annamarie," he said to her.

"Who can sleep late on so important a day, *signore?*"

Sarasohn soon appeared with almost one hundred Yiddish- and Russian-speaking women, and he immediately took charge. They were not to respond to provocations. They were to picket peacefully on the sidewalk in front of the building, and no rowdiness would be tolerated. People entering the building to work on any of the other five floors would be allowed through the line.

"Balaban will try to bring in scabs," Sarasohn told them, "but they will be countrymen of yours. He's probably down at Castle Garden right now recruiting them. They will not understand what is happening here. *Appeal* to them, ladies. Speak to them. But do not do anything that will antagonize the police."

Sonia and Saul arrived, carrying the signs they were to distribute.

Still more women came, until by six-thirty there were almost three hundred. Others had promised to come in at noon to relieve those who picketed in the morning. The signs were in three languages, English, Yiddish, and Italian, and all said fundamentally the same thing: *We want*

217

an Eight-Hour Day! We Want a Union Shop! We Want Job Security! And most of all: *Keep the Scabs Out!*

By a quarter to seven, all the lights in the building were on except those on the sixth floor. The windows of the Diamond Shirtwaist Company were dark, and there was no sign of Weiss or Balaban as the pickets now took their stations on the sidewalk. They began to move silently back and forth in front of the building.

Patrick saw Sarasohn standing at the corner next to Saul. He reached into his pocket for the diamond brooch and handed it to the union leader. "It's from a sympathizer," he explained.

Sarasohn inspected it and whistled softly. "It's real."

"Whatever you get for it goes to the strike fund," Patrick continued.

Sarasohn replied, "Tell our sympathizer many thanks."

"It's nice to know we have someone rich on our side," Saul said.

Patrick waited, then asked Sarasohn, "Where are the scabs?"

"They will be here. Balaban is collecting them now. I just hope that he gets them at Castle Garden."

"Where else would he find them?" Patrick inquired.

"I'm too afraid even to say it out loud," Sarasohn answered. He held up his finger. "Listen!"

In the distance, horses' hooves could be heard against the cobblestones, and as Patrick turned to look, he saw a platoon of mounted policemen round the corner in tight formation. They proceeded slowly up the street until a command was given for them to halt directly across from the building. They created a line that stretched the length of the sidewalk where the pickets marched. Apart from the officer who had halted them, they remained mounted, facing the women. They looked at the moving picket line, their eyes emotionless.

Patrick found a place in the line behind Annamarie.

"What will they do now, *signore?*" she asked.

"They are here to keep order, Annamarie," he said reassuringly, "in case Balaban tries to send his scabs through the line. You remember what Sarasohn told you to do if there is trouble?"

"We are not to anger the *polizia, signore,* and they will not hurt us."

Patrick smiled encouragingly. "How are the girls?"

"It is hard on the fat ones. They are complaining."

"Tell them that they will lose weight and be more beautiful when the strike is over."

"Some, like me, would be ugly even if we were not fat, *signore.*"

"You have a very beautiful heart, Annamarie, and that is all that matters."

She blushed. "Thank you, *signore.* I have prayed this morning for the success of our strike." She waited. "First in English, then in Italian."

"And I in Gaelic, Annamarie. Sarasohn told me he prayed in Yiddish."

"Then I think God will understand this time, *signore.*"

It was not until almost nine o'clock that a shout went up: "Here they come!"

As Patrick looked, two flat trucks turned the corner, one after the other, then paused as Balaban's limousine eased past them on the narrow street and parked. Balaban remained in the back seat while Weiss leaped out and spoke to the truck drivers.

"In front of the entrance," he instructed them. "Park right in front of the entrance."

Across the street, the horses sniffed the air nervously and lifted their hooves while the mounted policemen looked about them.

The open trucks moved slowly down the street carrying women in black dresses and aprons. On their laps were wicker baskets and boxes tied with rope. Around the necks of some were still cards that had been tied there when they had passed through Ellis Island the day before.

"Officers," Weiss yelled to the mounted policemen, "I want you to open this picket line for my new workers."

Suddenly Sonia's voice called out, *"No scabs!"* and a stream of Yiddish invective was directed at the women on the trucks, who answered it at once.

"No scabs!" Annamarie repeated, grabbing the hand of a woman on the nearest truck. *"Amica,* I am from Palermo. These are Sicilians and Neapolitans with me,

219

and we are striking against our bosses." In rapid Italian, she began to explain.

It was immediately apparent that the women hired at Castle Garden had not been told that they were to be used as strikebreakers.

"Come along," Weiss said coaxingly, but they did not budge from the trucks. "Don't listen to these Communists."

Still, the women did not move. They shook their heads, declining to leave the truck.

"Officers!" Weiss said to the policemen, "please help me get these damn women off the trucks."

A ruddy-faced Irishman replied, "If they want to, they will do it themselves. We cannot force them."

Weiss hurried toward the motorcar where Balaban was sitting, and they conferred momentarily. When he returned, the manager announced, "I have wasted my precious time. These women are no good to me. Order them off the trucks and I shall find replacements."

The Irishman looked down from where he sat on his horse. "I am afraid we cannot do that, nor do we want these people wandering the streets of the city. You will be expected to return them to Castle Garden where you got them."

Weiss's reply was lost in the great cheer that rose from the women on the picket line. He shook his fist at them, said a few words to the truck drivers, then hurried toward Balaban's car.

"We have won the first round," Sarasohn declared as the procession moved away. "But they will be back. Balaban will pass out more money to the police, and then you will see whose side they are on."

Still, the longer they could prevent the scabs from taking their jobs, the greater was their chance of victory.

"Well done," Patrick commended Annamarie after it was all over.

"I was frightened, *signore*."

"You have no reason to be frightened, Annamarie. You're among friends now. We'll take care of you."

She smiled appreciatively. "I thank God every day, *signore*, that I am now among friends."

220

By noon, Balaban and his manager had not returned. At twelve-thirty, the mounted policemen rode away, and the strikers were sure that they had left for the day.

"Balaban won't be back today," Saul said hopefully.

"He'll be back," Sarasohn insisted.

"Even if he can find scabs who are willing to cross our line, why would he bother for just a half day of work?"

"Because if he does it today, he won't have to do it tomorrow."

"There isn't a woman in New York who would pass through our pickets."

"You're wrong," Sarasohn answered. "There are plenty of them. I just hope Balaban isn't smart enough to find them."

At one-thirty, the mounted policemen reappeared, and this time they were doubled in number. As before, they took their positions in the street and watched from a distance as the women resumed their picketing.

By two o'clock, nothing had happened, and then by three. Yet the policemen did not leave, and those on the line were uncomfortable under the watchful eyes of the men who carried long, thick clubs and wore pistols at their waists.

Few even noticed the fire engine when it turned the corner. Those who saw it were perplexed when it stopped by the hydrant across the street.

"Is there a fire, *signore?*" Annamarie asked, peering up at the building. "I see no smoke, do you?"

Word passed quickly among the women that there was a fire in one of the lofts, yet after the firemen had attached their hose to the hydrant, they remained by their truck, staring at the women on the sidewalk, their hands in their pockets.

"I do not understand, *signore*," Annamarie said.

Suddenly Sarasohn was running down the walk, warning everyone. "They are going to try again, and this time they may use the hoses, but don't be afraid. Water won't hurt you."

Balaban's elegant motorcar appeared and parked at the curb. Both Balaban and Weiss left the car and stood by its hood, looking up the street toward the corner.

The women in the picket line stopped and watched as the first truck turned onto the street.

Patrick squinted but could not make out the passengers in the rear.

"*Swartzah*," Sarasohn said in resignation. "The bastard is using *swartzah*."

Both trucks were now in full view, and Patrick could make out the faces of the women Balaban was paying to cross the picket line. They were Negroes. As the truck stopped, the passengers looked with apprehension at the women on the sidewalk.

There was terror on Annamarie's face. She asked Patrick, "What should we do, *signore?*"

Patrick was at a loss for words. Of all the strike-breakers Balaban could have found, he had come upon the only ones who owed nothing to the women on the picket line. If anything, the Negroes were even worse off than the Europeans. If the Europeans lived on seven dollars a week, they lived on five dollars—when they could find jobs, and very often they couldn't because Yankee employers preferred to hire the new immigrants.

The scabs had no reason in the world to love the immigrants. Now that they had been offered jobs, they were going to accept them.

The black women stood by the trucks, waiting for a signal to proceed.

"Don't let them through the line!" Sonia screamed. "Keep the scabs out!"

Suddenly Balaban raised his hand, and as he did, a torrent of water shot from the firehose into the women on the line. Many were knocked by its force onto the pavement.

Patrick had been swept off his feet and hurled against the building. Momentarily, he was blinded. When he was able to see once more, he could not find Annamarie.

Sonia was enraged. "Don't let them through the line!" she shouted to the women as they reformed. "Hold them back!"

Dazed and half-drowned, the women joined hands on the sidewalk, and though the fury of the hose passed over them once more, they were able to stay on their feet.

"Keep the scabs out!" Sonia urged them. "Don't let them through!"

The black women stepped forward, and as they did, they met a wall of bodies. In their fury, some of the women on the line began to strike out at the scabs, who quickly pulled back.

"May God punish you, Mr. Shirtwaist Maker!" Sonia cried to Balaban.

Balaban's face darkened with rage. He snapped his fingers as a signal to the police, and the huge police horses charged the line. From their mounts, the men swung their billy clubs wildly. As wood met bone, there were agonizing cries.

A club struck Patrick in the shoulder, and he sank to his knees on the sidewalk. Everywhere there were rearing horses and swinging clubs and terrified women trying to escape them.

Far away, Patrick could hear Sonia screaming, "Help me! Someone help me!" But she was nowhere to be seen. He looked frantically for Annamarie, but she had disappeared.

Suddenly a shrill whistle pierced the air, and the mounted policemen withdrew. Their attack had lasted no more than a few minutes, yet women lay scattered all over the sidewalk, moaning.

At last, Patrick saw Sonia. She was sitting up, and one side of her face looked pulverized. It was raw, like fresh meat, the result of a kick from a horse's hoof. She held her hands to her bloodied eyes and sobbed, "I can't see! I can't see!"

Patrick knelt next to her, and in a minute Sarasohn was bending over them. His shirtfront was scarlet from a head wound.

"My God," he said when he saw her face, "what have they done to you?"

Sonia reached out and clung to his hand. "Did we keep the scabs out?" she asked.

There were tears on Sarasohn's face.

Saul rushed up to them, eyes wide with horror. "One was crushed," he exclaimed.

Sarasohn asked, "Is she badly hurt?"

Saul spoke not to the union leader but to Patrick. "It's *l'italiana*. She is dead."

They made their way to the curb, where Annamarie lay face down, hideously twisted, blood darkening the pavement beneath her. In her haste to run from the horses, she had lost a shoe, but whether it was from her deformed leg or the other was impossible to tell.

Patrick couldn't breathe.

"*Mi spiace*," he said. "Forgive me. *Mi spiace*."

The following morning at a quarter to seven, the women of the Diamond Shirtwaist Company silently made their way up the six flights of stairs to the loft, where they sat at the chairs before their sewing machines. At seven, Weiss turned the power on, and their machines began to whir.

The strike was broken. The great majority of the women had returned. The union organizers had been discharged and replaced by men who had promised to keep an open shop.

At seven-thirty, a taxi drew up in front of the town house at 8 Washington Square North. Eva Balaban left it to enter the house, but the taxi remained at the curb, its motor running.

Her husband was waiting in the hall. "I've been worried sick," he said. "No one knew what happened to you."

"I'm in a great rush," Eva replied, then hurried up the stairs to her bedroom.

Her husband followed her and watched in astonishment as she pulled down two suitcases from a closet shelf and began to fill them with clothes.

"I know you're angry," Balaban said, "but I had to break the strike. I couldn't let the Communists destroy everything I've worked so hard to build, could I?"

Eva did not reply. She pulled open dresser drawers and took great fistfuls of clothes and stuffed them in the suitcases.

At last, she turned to face him. "I'm leaving you."

Balaban shook his head incredulously. "I don't understand."

"What is there to understand? I'm *leaving* you."

Balaban's jaw trembled. "Just because a few women got hurt? Or have you found yourself a new man? Is it the Irishman at the factory? Don't be a fool, Eva."

When she didn't answer, he shook her by the shoulders. "If you leave me, you will not take one penny of my money with you."

"I don't want your money. It's bloodstained. I'm taking nothing but my clothes."

She pulled away from him and snapped her suitcases shut.

"You'll be sorry for this," he shouted as she left the room.

He ran after her down the mahogany staircase. "Please don't leave me," he begged.

She flung open the front door and quickly made her way down the steps. Across the street, strollers on Washington Square looked up.

Balaban stood at the opened door and called after her, "Don't leave me, Eva." He watched as the Irishman helped her into the taxi and slid into the seat next to her. "*Please*, Eva," he implored, but the cab moved away from the curb.

GOLDEN GIRLS AND GOLDEN BOYS

19

On Friday morning, the telephone rang in the study that separated Tom Molloy's bedroom from his roommate's at Lowell House, and in a minute John Phipps poked his head into the room and said, "It's for you."

Tom had been reading on the bed, although he had been warned almost all his life—first by his mother, then by scolding priests at Portsmouth Priory—that doing so was bad for the eyesight and the spine. He lifted himself gently to the floor and walked in stockinged feet to the next room.

Like all the Molloy children—at last count, a. phenomenal nine—Thomas Molloy was strikingly good-looking. Even at Harvard, where he was a senior and where homely boys were rarities, he was generally thought to be the handsomest member of the class of 1938. Socially, however, his distinction was considerably less because he was an Irish Catholic and the son of a New Yorker, not, as he himself put it, "descended from lunatic Puritans or cowards who bought their way out of service during the Civil War." His roommate, John Phipps, who *was*, and also an alumnus of the Groton School, where no Irish Catholic dared venture except to sweep up the floors, once described Tom as being Lace Curtain, but an exceptionally fine quality of lace.

He had his mother's looks, except for her coloring. He was much lighter, and he was the only one in the family who was flaxen-haired, though it was a common joke that Nora Molloy was bound to produce another before her breeding days were over if only she kept trying. As she was now thirty-nine, even Tom had been a bit embarrassed to announce the birth of his youngest sister the year before. ("Is she claw-footed and huge-headed or does she have all her faculties?" he was asked in the Lowell House dining hall), and he hoped that his mother and father would soon begin to practice abstinence.

He fell into a chair by the littered desk and picked up the phone. He was expecting a call from Peggy Sweeney, a girl he had met in North Cambridge the spring before but had told no one about, not even his roommate.

"Is that you, Peggy?" he said into the telephone.

The hesitation was sufficiently long for him to deduce that it wasn't, but he wasn't prepared for the voice that spoke to him.

"It's your mother, Thomas," Nora Molloy answered with a bright cheerfulness. He knew with certainty that she had filed away somewhere in her head the name *Peggy*, and the next time he was home, he would have to account for it.

"I wasn't expecting a call from you," he stammered. "It's the middle of the day."

"I'm aware of that, Thomas dear, but you said a week ago that you would telephone us last night to let us know if you'd be coming home this weekend, and you never did."

"I'm sorry. It completely slipped my mind."

"I was sure it had," Nora resumed, "and your father asked this morning, so I thought I'd better get in touch."

"I'm supposed to be driving down to New York this afternoon with Phipps," he replied without enthusiasm.

Nora Molloy perceived the ambiguity at once. "You are *supposed* to, you say. Does that mean that you intend to, Thomas, or not?"

It was, in fact, what he had been trying to decide. A few days ago, he had promised his roommate that he would attend a party at the Phipps's house in Glen Cove on Saturday night—in honor of John's sister, Laura, who was at Vassar—but Peggy Sweeney was expecting him to spend the weekend with her in North Cambridge. Obviously, he couldn't do both. The question was: Which did he prefer to do? To pass four or five hours with Laura Phipps's snappy friends on Long Island? Or to lie with his arms around Peggy Sweeney in her furnished apartment?

Superficially, anyway, that was the question. Yet for Tom Molloy, there was an additional one because he was the son of Nora and Charles Molloy, which meant that he had certain social *duties*. If anything, his parents were even sterner taskmasters than the priests. He had promised Phipps's sister that he would attend her party, and for a Molloy to break a promise was unthinkable.

"I'll know by two o'clock if I can leave or not," he said to his mother.

"What is so important in Boston that it requires your presence over the weekend?"

"I'm trying to finish a paper for my class in government," he replied, knowing that he would have to mention the falsehood during his next confession. He was in his senior year and the work load was sometimes stupendous, but the fact of the matter was that he had already turned in his paper.

"Just don't wait too late before you start; otherwise, it will be the middle of the night when you arrive. Will you be stopping at the house in New York for anything?"

In addition to their Southampton cottage, the Molloys maintained a house on East Seventy-first Street. As a rule, the cottage was used during the summer and early fall months and the city house during the winter, but they often spent winter weekends on Long Island, and the East Side house was kept open all summer long because the family was so immense that someone was always popping up to use it.

"I don't think so, unless Phipps has to stop."

His friend's family lived on Park Avenue in the Sixties, though when he was in the city, John spent most of his time at the Molloys' house. The very first time John had visited it, four years before, he had taken one look at all the children in the hall and said, "Oh, I'll come back some other time when you don't have company," and Tom had had to explain that they were members of the clan and lived there permanently. Phipps himself had only one sister.

"I think that they're all out here on the Island," Nora

231

Molloy volunteered. "I heard that they're having a big party for their daughter tomorrow night."

Such was the complexity of New York society that while Tom and John were the best of friends, the Molloys never saw the Phippses socially and belonged to none of the same clubs. The real difference between the families, John Phipps once said, was that every time the Molloys added a new room to their vast Southampton cottage, they brought a priest out to sprinkle holy water and to bless it, while every time the Phippses added a room, they gave a cocktail party.

"I know," Tom said to his mother. "I'm invited to the party."

As soon as he had said it, there was no doubt about where he would be spending the weekend.

"Thomas dear," his mother began with firmness in her voice, "if you have accepted an invitation, you must attend." She waited for a response, but none came. "If you leave by two or two-thirty, you should be here by nine. I shall have Annie save supper for you. Drive carefully, Thomas."

Tom made arrangements to meet Phipps on the steps of Widener Library after his one o'clock class, then hurried to Massachusetts Avenue to board a train into Boston. He had told Peggy that he would meet her at noon on Copley Square, near which she worked, and he hoped that he could patch up the quarrel they'd had two days before.

Their relationship was peculiar; even Tom had to admit it. In bed, they were infinitely compatible; out of bed, there were problems. Just two days before, she had accused him of never having introduced her to any of his friends in Cambridge, and he had not known what to say. What she considered an omission, he considered a kindness. She was so *different* from any of his friends. That was why he hadn't brought her to Harvard.

Peggy had left home as soon as she finished high school, and had found a secretarial position at an insurance agency in Boston. She was a pretty girl with auburn hair and bright blue eyes, but shy and easily overwhelmed. When Tom first met her, she was recovering from an affair with a married man at the office where she worked. Tom was a virgin; she was not. Peggy seduced him.

There is no gratitude in all the world like that of a young man toward the woman who has led him out of innocence. Until he met her, all his sexual energies had been spilled on the football field. He had been co-captain and quarterback of the Portsmouth Priory eleven, had played with a fury and savagery that at least some of his teammates had ascribed to the fact that he was the only one of the lot who didn't masturbate. Or if he did, he didn't talk about it. Or if he talked about it, it was only to a priest.

Tom was uncommonly religious. He had been an altar boy at the Church of St. Vincent Ferrer in New York, and at one time or another during the performance of his duties, he had even felt something like ecstasy. But the minute that Peggy unbuttoned her blouse and placed his hand on her bare breast, he was lost. He might as well have been a pagan.

Yet afterward, because at heart all Irishmen, no matter what their age, remain altar boys forever, there was guilt and self-reproach. And for Tom, there was even more than that. He was terrified that his mother and father might discover what he had done. To offend them was almost as bad as offending God.

"Hi," Peggy said as she walked up to him on the corner of Boylston Street. She kissed him lightly on the cheek. "Am I late?"

"I just got here, Peg. I can't stay. I have to be back for a one o'clock class." He studied the face that he had seen so often beneath him in bed. There was a tiny pimple on one side of her cheek that she had tried to cover with powder but had succeeded only in making more conspicuous.

"Do you want any lunch?" he asked.

No, she was trying to lose five pounds. The women in her family tended to be overweight, and from time to

233

time she would fast when she thought that her face was getting puffy.

"Look," he began, "I have to go home this weekend. My mother called this morning."

She was clearly disappointed. "But you said you were going to take me to the movies."

"We can go to the movies anytime, Peg. I'm expected home for the weekend, so I have to be there, that's all there is to it."

She began to walk away from him down the sidewalk, and he hurried to catch up. "Now you're mad again," he said.

"If you're going to New York," she began petulantly, "why can't you take me with you? I've never even met your mother and father."

"We can do that some other time, Peggy," he answered.

She walked quickly toward Trinity Church, and did not turn to look at him as she spoke. "Your mother and father were up here last spring, and your father was here only a month ago. You always tell me that you're going to introduce me, but you never do."

Tom closed his eyes and sighed. "My father came up on business. I only saw him for about an hour."

"So that's long enough to introduce me to him." At last, she stopped, and he could see that her lip was trembling. "Do you know what someone at the office told me? She told me never to date a Harvard man because all they do is *use* you, then throw you out like you're a piece of garbage when they don't want you anymore."

Tom felt genuinely contrite. He had known that sooner or later she would no longer put up with the arrangement, but he had hoped that her tolerance might last for the rest of the year.

"I've never even seen where you live at college. My friend asked me where you live, and I had to tell her I don't know. I've never even been in your room."

"Girls aren't allowed," he said ineffectually.

"My friend asked me if Lowell House is in Harvard Yard, and I said I wasn't sure but I thought it was on the river." There were tears in her eyes. "How do you think

234

it makes me feel that you've never once introduced me to any of your swell friends?"

He exhaled all his breath, then sucked in a lungful of air. "Okay, okay, as soon as I get back from New York, I'll introduce you to my swell friends. So what will you talk about? You want to talk about the Spanish Civil War? You want to talk about T. S. Eliot? You want to talk about transcendentalism?" He waited. "I thought you said you felt uncomfortable with most college guys, and one reason you liked me is that I never talk about those stuffy things."

"Listen!" she said angrily. "If I go out to Harvard, do I have to talk about trans-sil—whatever it is? Can't you simply say, 'This is Miss Peggy Sweeney. This is Mr. So-and-So.' And I can say, 'How do you do?' And he can say, 'Fine.' I mean, is it a *law* at Harvard that you have to talk about the Spanish Civil War or tran-sil—whatever it is?"

In view of her gravity, Tom shouldn't have laughed, but he couldn't help it. For a second, she didn't know how to react; then, at last, she smiled.

"Oh, dammit," she said, "I don't know why we fight, Tom. I love you, you *know* that. I wish I didn't have to work this afternoon. I wish I could go back to the apartment with you, right now."

Tom wished it, too. His groin ached, just being next to her.

"I can see you on Monday, Peggy. I'll meet you after work. We can have dinner, and then. . . ."

Even thinking about it was dizzying. She wore the wrong makeup, she never read books, and sometimes she even said *he don't,* but he owed her so much. With her, he felt a peace and comfort he experienced with no one else in the world. She spoke a kind of Boston ghetto English, she chewed gum, she smoked cigarettes on the street, and virtually the only meal she knew how to prepare on her two-burner stove was meat patties and mashed potatoes. She was an impossible housekeeper; there was an undisturbed layer of dust over everything, it seemed. In the more than two and a half years she had lived there, she had not once taken the trouble to wash the windows, and every day the view of the street became more and more diffused, like looking at the world through waxed paper.

But she offered her flesh with an abandon that made everything else seem trivial. When he lay in bed with her, she drove everything out of his head: the priests who had kept his mind in a stranglehold since he was a child, his mother and father, his friends, his schoolwork, his career. She worked like opium on his senses, and when he was deprived of her, his nerve ends were raw, his mouth was parched, and his entrails ached.

"And will you show me where you live at the college when you come back?" she asked.

"When I come back, Peggy. Okay?"

"Okay, Tommy. Have a good time. I'll dream about you tonight, and tomorrow night, and Sunday night, too. When I go to bed and when I wake up again, I'll touch myself—you know where—and wish you were inside me."

Oh, God! How could he bear to spend the weekend away from her!

It was Thomas Cassidy Carlos Molloy, the second of his middle names commemorating his birth in Argentina, where his father was known by the Spanish form of the name. In addition to Tom, the Molloy children were Liam, twenty; Caitlin, eighteen; Robert, sixteen; Paul, fourteen; Mary, twelve; Deirdre, ten; Edward, eight— then a long respite during which time Nora Molloy was ill and thought to be dying, and finally, at her resurrection: Megan, one.

Their home in Southampton was no longer the unfinished place Charles Molloy had shown Nora back in the year 1916—that house was now being used by a nephew of his—but a new one, built just before the Crash of 1929. Unlike most of the large wooden houses in the area, it was a huge gray granite French château, more in the style of Newport than Southampton. Other Molloy houses of varying sizes were nearby, because by that time Charles Molloy and his brothers, and his brothers' children, owned more than three hundred waterfront acres, and as they were Catholics living in an area populated by Protestants, they tended to build within earshot of each other, as much for security as for conviviality.

It was said by some in Southampton that it was impossible to get within a mile of the Molloy compound without first reciting three Hail Marys to a guard at the end of the road.

Like so many tales told about them, however, it was an exaggeration. For one thing, there was no guard, and for another, the Molloys would have welcomed Protestant visitors, but few came—few of the elder Molloys' generation, in any event.

Their children's friends were around the house all the time, much preferring the easy, relaxed Irish ways they found there to the strained atmosphere at their own homes. John Phipps, for example, whose family had a vast house in Glen Cove, kept at least half of his clothes in Tom Molloy's bedroom at Southampton. His mother and father were slightly annoyed that he should consider Nora and Charles Molloy more interesting than his own parents, and they asked questions. After their initial curiosity ("Do the Molloys really have pictures of the Virgin Mary on all the walls?" To which he had replied, "No, but they have a Dürer and a Constable too"), they had paid little attention to "that Irish pack," as they called them.

Virtually nothing was known about Nora Molloy except that she loved children and kept one of the best tables in New York or Long Island. Those who were lucky enough to dine with the family, as John Phipps was, long remembered what they had been served ("Corned beef and cabbage?" his mother had asked. "Not on your life," he had answered blissfully. "I think she must have studied Cordon Bleu cooking in Paris"). It was thought that Mrs. Molloy might have California connections, though others said that she came from a rich Irish-Argentinian family. In either case, and whatever her background, she seemed consummately well-bred. She had about her a grace and repose that was the envy of everyone who met her. Moreover, and unlike many women in her station of life, she had opinions. In almost

accentless speech—some perceived a haunting lilt to it—
she could outargue most men. It was she, for example,
who insisted that her son Thomas go to Harvard, not
Georgetown, which was his father's preference. She expected great things from her children, more perhaps from
Tom than from any of the others, and it was her view
that his faith was strong enough to defy the temptations
of Cambridge, Massachusetts.

If Nora Molloy saw the family's social destiny, it was
Charles who made certain that all the bills could be paid.
Upon the birth of each one of his children, he took the
precaution of buying stock for them. When Tom was
born, twenty-two years before, he had invested heavily in
public utilities; at Liam's birth, he had gone into rail-
roads; at Caitlin's, into tin; at Robert's, into corn oil
products; at Paul's, into shipping; at Mary's, steel; Deirdre, natural gas; Edward, diamonds; and Megan, automobile manufacturing. It was Nora who plotted her
children's lives and careers; Charles saw to it that they
would be comfortable.

Tom was most special of all. Even his brothers and
sisters considered him to be that, yet were in no way
jealous that he was more wildly good-looking than they,
and a hero first at his prep school and now at Harvard.
Nora did not want him to enter his father's construction
business—the other boys could do that, she said—but to
attend law school and perhaps then devote his life to
public service. To her, it seemed that the rich had an
obligation to those who were less fortunate, and if they
were clever and attractive, as Tom was, then it was to be
hoped that they would serve God best by helping people
in greater need than they themselves.

She had often talked to Tom about it. He would never
have to worry about money, so instead he could worry
about such important matters as social injustice, poverty,
and disease. Tom agreed. It was also what he wanted to
do.

Every now and then, however, Nora saw signs of weakness in her oldest son. Once, at his prep school in Rhode
Island, he had disappeared for two days and two nights
after having been sacked from the football team for

punching a teammate in the locker room. Not only had Nora successfully implored the priests to readmit him, but she had also persuaded them not to record the episode on his official transcript, which might otherwise have kept him out of Harvard. Once, during his freshman year at Harvard, he and several of his classmates had been arrested in Scollay Square for public drunkenness, which was bad enough, but also for creating a disturbance with a prostitute who charged that the boys had enjoyed her favors in the rear seat of a car without having paid the price agreed upon. It was Nora who went to Boston to make certain that the police records would not be released to the press, and also that the Harvard authorities would treat it as an undergraduate lark and forget that it had ever occurred.

Nora would not permit her oldest son to squander his tremendous gifts. Few people, she thought, were endowed with such magical charm and intellect, and most who were lacked the financial resources to use their talents in order to serve mankind. To those who knew both of them, it seemed almost as if Nora were making of her son an instrument either to correct an old wrong or to advance the family in a way that only Nora herself could divine. If Tom was sometimes uncertain about his abilities, his mother never was. He *would* succeed. She would give him no alternative.

It was dusk when John Phipps nosed his blue Packard convertible up the long avenue that led to the house in Southampton. In the pale light the entire Molloy family was playing croquet on the immense lawn. As soon as the children saw the car, they let out a whoop and flung their mallets to the ground, then raced across the grass to greet their brother.

Caitlin got there first and was hugging him when the others arrived. "Is John staying here tonight?" she whispered anxiously.

"Not till tomorrow night."

"I was so hoping," she said, disappointed.

Nora Molloy handed year-old Megan to the nurse and took Tom in her arms. "We're so glad you could get

239

home," she said. "We've been so worried. All week long, there's been nothing except talk of war, but thank God, Chamberlain has got that madman to pledge peace."

The meeting in Munich between Hitler, Mussolini, Daladier, and Chamberlain had been the talk of Cambridge for the past two days.

Charles Molloy shook his hand, then John's. "The terms are ghastly," he said. "Czechoslovakia has been given away by the British and French. The Czechs weren't even invited to the conference table."

"We heard the report on the radio this morning, and I must say some of us were unhappy," Tom observed. "Hitler will not be satisfied with Czechoslovakia. He'll want more.

"I just hope that Britain realizes that America won't come to her aid after this mistake they've made," his father said.

"John," Nora Molloy interrupted, "will you stay and have supper? I asked Annie to set aside enough for two."

John Phipps said that he was expected home. He would be back in the morning, however, to help the young Molloys navigate their 210 International. "I wouldn't stay around my own house tomorrow for anything in the world," he said. "There'll be florists and caterers all over the place, and my mother will be roaring orders at everyone."

His sister was making her debut this year, and the party the following night was one of what he called an endless series of tedious affairs designed to make homely girls more attractive to suitors. It was an unfair description of his sister, Laura, who was tall and skinny, to be sure, but quite pretty.

"I'll see you in the morning," he said, turning to enter his car. He reached over and tugged at the end of Caitlin's hair, and she squealed. Then he slid into the front seat, turned the engine over, and backed out of the long drive.

"He's such a dream," Caitlin sighed as the car disappeared.

"And you're being very tiresome," her mother told her. "Get the children to collect the croquet gear, will you,

Caitlin? Otherwise, it gets lost in the grass and the gardener runs over it with the mower. Come on in, Tom. I'm sure Annie put your supper in the stove the minute she saw the car."

As his brothers and sisters ran through the grass to pick up lost croquet balls, Tom began to walk toward the house, his father at one side of him, his mother at the other, her arm around his waist.

When Caitlin was out of earshot, Nora said to her oldest son, "Caitlin had so hoped that John would ask her to the party tomorrow."

"He's going with a girl named Thayer from Boston."

"I must say," Charles Molloy volunteered, "Caitlin behaved herself today with him, though she usually does everything in the world to make a nuisance of herself. No wonder he doesn't ask her to dances!"

They all laughed. Tom turned to his mother and asked, "Did you ever make a nuisance of yourself when he was courting you?"

"I wouldn't have dared."

"But she almost stood me up once," his father said. "I'd invited her to look at the savage animals in the Central Park Zoo, and she very nearly didn't come. Do you remember that, Nora?"

"I'll never forget it."

"And are you glad you didn't break the date?" Tom inquired.

"If I hadn't gone," she replied, "I wouldn't have married your father, and I wouldn't now be the happiest woman in the world."

"Listen to her!" Charles Molloy said in embarrassment. "If that isn't blarney, there never was such a thing."

Tom opened the front door for his mother and father, and as he did, he saw that Nora Molloy's eyes were glistening. He knew for a fact that she was telling the truth. And because his mother was the happiest woman in the world, his family was the best in the world. He wouldn't change places with anyone he knew.

"Are you hungry, Tom?" his mother asked when they entered the hall of the house.

"Starved. I haven't had a decent meal since I went back to school."

"Lovely. I'll go see how Annie is coming along. You'll probably want to go up and wash."

Tom agreed that it was a good idea. As his mother hurried toward the kitchen, he started up the stairs.

From the bottom, his father said to him, "I'm worried about what's happening in Europe, Tom."

Tom stopped and looked down the steps at his father. "Then you think that there's going to be a war?"

"I think there already *is* a war. It started at one o'clock this morning in Munich when Germany was handed Czechoslovakia, lock, stock, and barrel."

"I think so, too." He waited, then asked, "How will it affect the business?"

"Molloy and Company? We're ready for it. We've been talking to people in Washington all week long. If there's mobilization here, the government will need thousands of places to house soldiers. We've developed a prefabricating system. We'll build the units at factories, then ship them out to be assembled at the sites. We're also advising them on roadbuilding and landing fields. Oh, no, Tom, a war won't hurt our business. Wars seldom do. That's not what I'm worried about."

It was difficult for him to proceed. "I just want you to know that in the event there's a war, the firm should be able to get an exemption for you. You'll be very helpful to the company." He stopped. "I don't want you to do anything rash."

"Why would I do anything rash?"

"Because you're young," his father replied, "and you know a bit less about the world than your mother and I do. Heroes are very easily forgotten, Tom."

He said it sadly and with a significance that Tom saw as personal but could not quite fathom.

"No one could be prouder of a son than I am of you," his father continued. "I respect your judgment in almost everything. Yet sometimes I see a headstrong quality that will serve you badly unless you can tame it. That's why I've asked you to promise me not to do anything rash in case there's a war. Like joining up with the British or Canadian forces. Will you promise?"

In fact, there had been a good deal of talk in Cambridge about doing just that in the event that America remained neutral during a European war. Until now, Tom had not given it much thought. "Why would I ever do anything like that?" he answered at last. "After all, it's not my war."

"And who is Peggy?" his mother asked the minute he had finished his supper at the kitchen table.

"A girl I know," he answered, draining his glass of milk.

"I assumed *that,* Thomas. But how do you know her?"

Tom stuffed a second piece of cake into his mouth to buy some time. When he finished chewing, he said. "Uhmmm, this is good. Did you make it or did Annie?"

"I did," Nora said, "but you didn't answer my question."

Thomas watched his mother smile and could not resist doing the same. In so many ways, they were conspirators. As far back as he could remember, whenever he'd done something that wasn't entirely exemplary, his mother had first asked for an explanation, then analyzed what he had done, and finally said, "All right, Thomas, this is between the two of us. We shall not tell your father, as he has too many other things to occupy his mind. But I do not want it ever to happen again."

Astonishingly, the more his mother expected perfection from him, the more likely he was to deliver. In time, he found himself doing things that would bring pleasure to her, and to his surprise, they also brought pleasure to him. They agreed on almost everything.

The exception, of course, was the choice of a girl friend. Tom was convinced that Nora Molloy couldn't judge his needs fairly because she was not a man.

"Her name is Peggy Sweeney," he answered at last. "She's a secretary for an insurance company. Her father's dead. Her mother works in Worcester."

"How old is she?"

"Eighteen."

243

"Is it serious, do you think?"

He shrugged his shoulders. "I like her a lot."

"Then you must bring her home so that your father and I can meet her," she said brightly. "If you give me her address, I shall write her a note inviting her down next weekend."

Sweat poured down his arms into his shirt. He pushed back his chair and carried his empty glass to the sink, where he rinsed it, then filled it with water and brought it to his lips. As he did, he stood with his back to her and looked across the dark lawn to the moonlit waters of the Atlantic.

He turned to face her. "I don't want you to do that."

She rose from her chair, walked to him, and rested her hands on his shoulders. "You're afraid that your father and I would disapprove of her."

He closed his eyes and pulled away. All his life it had been this way. He had not once been able to do anything without his mother's knowing more about it than he did. He resented it, as it made him feel childlike and inept.

"She's Irish," he said by way of defense. "She's a Catholic. And she's nice." He paused. "Her family's poor, and she's not—well, she didn't go to college or anything, but she's nice."

"Neither did I go to college. And *I* was poor. Thomas, you have no idea how poor my family was. I certainly wouldn't hold that against her."

He would have to get it off his chest. If he didn't, they would talk around the matter for the next two hours.

"You always—" he faltered, then stopped. "For as long as I can remember, you have said you wanted me to marry someone—who could help my career." From the effort of saying the few words, he was almost breathless. "You always said—I should aim for the best. And that was why I went to Harvard, not Georgetown. You always said"—he could feel the perspiration break out on his forehead—"one of the most important decisions a man ever makes is choosing the girl he marries. Well, you made it sound so—methodical and impossible to attain. Peggy is just—well, she's just a nice girl."

"Then I shall like her, Thomas. And so will your father."

How could he begin to explain what it was about Peggy that he loved, and what it was that he was ashamed of?

"I won't press, Thomas," she told him. "If you're serious about the girl, I should like to meet her. But if you don't want me to do that just now, I shall defer to your wishes."

For the thousandth time, he was overwhelmed by his mother's wisdom and compassion. "Thanks," he said.

"And in the meantime—"

"—we-shall-keep-it-from-your-father," he interrupted, using the words he had so often heard.

On Saturday, a glorious day of wind-whipped waves and scudding clouds and sunshine, Tom and Caitlin Molloy and John Phipps set out on the Molloy sailboat, the *Noreen III*. Caitlin was coming down with a cold but wouldn't consider being left home. She had privately vowed to throw herself overboard if John wasn't civil to her.

They sailed halfway around the Island to Sag Harbor, where John suggested that they telephone his sister and tell her that the mast had broken and they would not be able to attend her damned party. He'd almost persuaded himself but at the last minute lacked the courage. Laura would be hopping mad if any of her Vassar friends lacked boys to dance with.

"There is nothing more terrible in all the world than a scorned Vassar girl," John observed.

It was late afternoon before they began the return trip to Southampton, and the wind was against them. By the time they eased the boat into its jetty, they were tired, sunburned, and running late. It was almost six, and they were due at the sit-down dinner by seven-thirty.

John would be sleeping overnight at the Molloys', as his own room would be occupied by Laura's friends, and he had brought his white dinner jacket and black trousers with him. As the two young men took turns showering, they discussed what they would do if the party took a turn for the worse.

"I've got a bottle of Scotch hidden in my room," John shouted from behind the shower curtain while Tom shaved at the basin, "so if Mother's punch is too weak, we can always get pissed."

"What do you know about the girls?" Tom asked.

"It's the usual crowd—Boston, New York, and Chicago. Philadelphia, too, because one of Laura's roommates is a Biddle. Do you know Emily Thayer?"

"I met her once."

"I forgot that you had. She's my dinner partner."

"Who's mine?"

"Can't remember. I told Mother that unless she gave you someone interesting to talk to, you'd be in a rage."

John turned off the spray, pulled back the curtain, and stepped out onto the bathmat in a cloud of steam. "Emily's such a stick-in-the-mud. If I kiss her more than two or three times, you'd think that I'd raped her." He rubbed himself vigorously with a huge terry-cloth towel. "Between you and me, Tom, the solution is to do what the old man does. He has Mother around to look after the house, but he keeps a mistress, too."

Tom was astonished. Lamont Phipps seemed so proper. He had his own brokerage house, and his photograph frequently appeared in the financial news. Hardly a playboy type.

"I saw her myself," John continued. "She's a showgirl or something. She was dressed in a mink coat the time I ran into her outside the Plaza, and I'd bet anything that the old man's money paid for it." He rubbed his scalp, drying his hair. "He introduced her as a client, but I think it was the other way around."

"I wonder if *my* father has a mistress," Tom mused.

"Shouldn't think so. He has your mother for carnal pleasures and the priests for spiritual ones. What more could he ask?" He pulled on his trousers, then stuffed his arms into a starched shirt. "We'd better hurry. We wouldn't want your date to eat without you."

"I bet you anything that she's awful."

"She may very well be. There are a lot of awful girls in our set. If she is, just remember where I keep the Scotch: bottom drawer of my dresser. It helps. After the

246

second or third drink, it's surprising how nice an awful girl can look."

The Phippses lived in a grandiose Tudor-style mansion in Glen Cove, built, as John explained it, by his grandfather the robber baron at a time when income taxes were minimal and he was able to indulge his fancies, which were not particularly refined. Inside, it was a dark, morose place filled with antique oak paneling, shipped piece by piece from England and painstakingly reassembled on Long Island.

A member of the household staff had been assigned to park the cars as they arrived, and the minute John pulled up in front of the entrance, the man said to him, "Good evening, Mr. John. Your sister was just out inquiring after you. They are about to sit down for supper."

Tom was always embarrassed when he met the Irish servants of his friends; he never knew how to react.

The two-storied front hall was filled with young people, all dressed in dinner jackets or long gowns, waiting for the signal to proceed into the dining room. When Laura spied her brother and Tom, she hurried toward them, looking somewhat exasperated.

"Really, Tom," she complained, "you've held us up for almost ten minutes. And poor Emily has been all by herself."

"Then I shall go over and apologize to poor Emily right now." Phipps disappeared among the crowd, searching for his date.

"Tom," Laura began, "I hope you like Nancy. She's a great favorite of mine. She lives down the hall from me at school. There she is over there. Come on."

Laura pulled him toward a girl who just at that moment looked up. Thank God, she was pretty, he thought. Not overwhelmingly pretty, but very adequately pretty. She looked wholesome and well-scrubbed, her face almost without makeup. Her hair was light blond and cropped raffishly short, as if she couldn't be bothered with it. She was dressed in a simple white organza gown that was not nearly so spectacular as many Tom could see, but above it was a resplendent necklace in an old-fashioned setting.

247

Somehow the necklace seemed too elaborate for the girl. She looked as though something simpler would be more to her taste.

"Will you please introduce yourselves while I try to get this herd of people seated before my mother has a nervous breakdown?" Laura said and then hurried away.

Tom complied with a smile. "Hello. I'm Tom Molloy."

"I'm Nancy Delano," his dinner date replied.

The name rang an emphatic bell. "I suppose you wouldn't be one of those Delanos connected with the Roosevelts."

"Just cousins," she said dryly.

Tom was convinced that Laura had matched them because Mrs. Phipps would never have attempted anything so daring. The contrast between their lineages was breathtaking. The Delanos derived from seventeenth-century French and Dutch settlers and owned vast holdings in the Hudson River Valley. They had married Roosevelts and Van Rensselaers and Schermerhorns and lived very quiet lives, not outside society so much as above it. Except when one of their more aggressive members went into public life, the family preferred to keep its name out of the newspapers. They seldom left the pastoral settings of their immense baronies. They both predated the Boston aristocrats and looked down on them because, unlike the Bostonians, they were not businessmen and never had been. They were landowners and grandees.

Yet despite that, the minute they sat down to dinner, Nancy Delano said to him, "I've heard such astonishing things about your family," as if the Molloys were far more interesting. "Laura says that you have scads of brothers and sisters. Fifteen or twenty or some such mad figure."

Tom laughed. "Just eight."

"You're so lucky. I don't have any at all."

To be raised as an only child guaranteed either permanent childishness or premature adulthood. Nancy seemed older and less giddy than most of the girls Tom knew.

"I've always yearned for brothers and sisters," she said wistfully.

248

"I'll be happy to share mine. In order to survive, all you have to do is yell louder than they do."

In answer to his probing, she told him that her parents had not permitted her to attend school until she was almost fourteen. "My mother was forever hiring Ph.D. candidates from Columbia to come up and tutor me for a year. Then after one of them developed a crush on me, I was sent to Virginia to school. I spent the next four years on horseback. I love horses. I didn't want to go to Vassar, but my father insisted. He said otherwise I'd be ignorant." She waited. "I didn't want to come to this party, either. I detest parties. But my mother made me."

"Then we have something in common because my mother made me come, too."

Tom was amused. She was incontestably feminine, yet her interests were those of a tomboy. She confessed that she loved to hunt and that she had fired her first rifle when she was just six years old.

"For the love of God," he replied, "it must have thrown you off your feet."

"I landed on my fanny, but I shot the rabbit."

"My brother Liam and I were in Wyoming for three months last summer. We lived in a two-room cabin and hunted almost every day. When we didn't hunt, we fished."

"*I* love to fish."

"Do you like sports?" he asked.

"Swimming and skiing and sailing, mostly."

"Good God! Those are my favorite sports, too!"

Tom was almost embarrassed. He hoped that she wouldn't misunderstand and think that he was trying to ingratiate himself with her. With a name like hers and the fact that she was an only child, he was sure that she didn't lack admirers.

After they had finished talking about horses and boats, there was a lull in the conversation, then Tom asked, "There's something I've always wanted to ask someone like you. I mean, you have such famous cousins and your name is so well-known. Has it been an asset?"

She placed her fork on the edge of her plate. "A liability, I think."

"How?"

"People always expect me to be something different from what I am."

"And what exactly are you?"

She looked up at him skeptically. "Do you really want to know, or are you just asking that to make conversation?"

He wasn't offended by her directness. "Let's put it this way," he began. "I've been drawing some conclusions about you, and it would be fun to see if they're correct or not."

"Okay," she replied. "I'm not especially interested in politics, though everyone thinks I should be. I love dogs and horses, and I've always been a little uncomfortable with people. Especially when I have to dress up for them."

Tom threw back his head and laughed. "I figured someone made you wear that enormous bauble around your neck, and you would have been happier without it."

"My mother was angry because I didn't stop at Bonwit's for a new dress. She said I'd probably look a little less appalling if I wore the necklace. It was my grandmother's."

He looked at her seriously. "You said that you're uncomfortable with people. But if you were, I'd feel it, and I don't."

She waited. "Then I suppose that means I don't feel uncomfortable with you, doesn't it?"

"I'd say that, Nancy."

She smiled amiably. "Then I would say that, too."

After dinner, the hall and the living room were thrown open to form a large dance floor, and a band began to play popular songs. Nancy was a competent but somewhat self-conscious dancer, as if she had learned the steps at dancing class and had no spontaneity. He could feel the tension in her hands and her shoulders.

At last, after three dances, he said, "You don't really like to dance all that much, do you?"

"No, but I hadn't meant it to show."

"What about a walk down the beach?"

"I was hoping you'd suggest it."

They drifted through the long French windows to the terrace, then made their way across the lawn to the sand. There, they kicked off their shoes and walked ankle-deep in the water, Nancy clutching the edge of her dress to avoid getting it wet.

"This is infinitely better, Tom. I'm sorry, though, for spoiling your fun."

"Who said you were? I bet everyone back there wishes they could be doing this," he grinned.

They ran through the wet sand, and inevitably Tom tripped on a half-buried log. Before he could get up, Nancy was flinging sand at him. He reached for a fistful and pitched it at her dress, and she howled with laughter. In a few minutes, both were dirty and gritty. Tom raced to the water and belly-flopped into it, fully clothed. When he surfaced, spouting water, he saw Nancy Delano bob up next to him, her white dress clinging to her body, her fabulous necklace glittering in the moonlight.

"This is perfectly mad," she exclaimed. "What will they say back at the house?"

"Who cares what they say?"

Hip-deep in water, Tom reached out and brought her into his arms. Water streamed down her face as he kissed it.

Then suddenly it was all over. The minute his lips pressed against hers, he could once again feel the tenseness in her body. She pulled away.

"We'd better go back," she said. "They'll be worrying about us."

Tom remained in the water as she made her way to shore. He saw Nancy step onto the sand, her dress glued to her small, tidy behind, and he wished that she were Peggy Sweeney. Peggy didn't hold herself back, wasn't ashamed of her body.

"Are you coming?" she asked.

Her shoulders curved inward as she held her arms over her breasts. She was shivering, even though the night was warm.

Their wet clothes earned them a good deal of teasing from Laura's friends, and raised eyebrows from her

251

mother, though Mrs. Phipps had the good manners not to ask what had happened. Nancy sat in a bathrobe in one of the bedrooms while a fan circulated air over her formal until it was dry. Tom occupied himself at the bar, dripping water on the floor, and in answer to questions said that he had just swum the Hellespont.

It was after two in the morning when the party finally began to break up. Many of the girls were being driven to houses on the South Shore, and some had to be returned to New York City. Even those who were staying overnight at the Phippses' were due back at their campuses Monday morning and would have to leave Long Island Sunday afternoon.

In the gaslight outside the door, Nancy said, "I've enjoyed myself a lot, Tom."

"Me, too." Awkwardly, he added, "I hope you get back to Poughkeepsie all right tomorrow."

"I'll sleep on the train."

Dutifully, he kissed her on the cheek, and once again he felt a sudden coldness. He could not understand it.

"Maybe you could come up some weekend for a football game," he suggested without enthusiasm.

"Oh, I'd love that! And you must come down to Poughkeepsie."

The horn of the Packard convertible was honking, and Tom turned to find his friend waiting for him. "I have to go now. Goodnight, Nancy."

"Goodnight, Tom. I've never had such a good time in my life."

In puzzlement, Tom sprinted toward the car. If she meant that, why hadn't she let him touch her? Didn't she trust him? He didn't want to ravish her, just kiss her.

He entered the car, and almost at once, the wheels spun in the white gravel as Phipps steered it toward the road.

"What did you think of Nancy Delano?" Phipps asked.

"She's okay, I guess."

"I was watching her at dinner, and if you ask me, pal, she looked like she was falling for you." His fist reached out and smacked Tom's knee. "Lucky dog!"

Lucky dog? Tom wasn't so sure. Maybe he had been

spoiled by the Irish girls he had known. Even those who were convent-trained and mumbled their prayers like nuns were stirred the minute they were caressed, and they had always let Tom kiss them to his heart's desire. Peggy Sweeney had done much more than that. But Nancy Delano? He could not figure her out.

"She seems like a cold fish," Tom said at last.

"If she is, she's got company. So is Emily Thayer." He yawned. "Jesus, I'm tired."

Tom leaned his head back on the seat. "Is it okay if we head back to school early tomorrow? I've got some reading to do in government."

Phipps was surprised but accommodating. "Sure," he replied. "No trouble. We can leave a little after noon."

That would be fine. Perfect. That way, Tom would arrive in Cambridge by early evening, time enough for him to bury himself in Peggy's compliant body.

The following day, it rained buckets. The boys slept late, recovering from their night of debauching, such as it was, and the Molloy children tiptoed as they passed the closed bedroom door. It was nearly eleven when they awoke, and when they came downstairs in pajamas and robes, they were groggy and uncommunicative.

Nora was disappointed that they wouldn't be staying for Sunday dinner, but she agreed that breakfast at eleven-thirty and dinner an hour later was not an ideal arrangement. She would make a picnic hamper for them, she said, and they could pull off the road somewhere during their trip north.

They left in a cloudburst, and every Molloy in the house was under an umbrella in the driveway to see them off. Each time her oldest son left the house, Nora hated to see him go. Yet she was pleased that he was strong and self-sufficient and not so emotionally bound to his mother as some Irish boys were. He did not seem to have a fear in the world. Thomas Cassidy would have been proud of his American son, just as Charles Molloy was.

After they left, the family was about to sit down to Sunday dinner when the doorbell rang, and because the

253

staff was busy in the kitchen preparing to serve the meal, Caitlin answered the door.

In a minute, she returned carrying a yellow envelope. "It was a Western Union boy," she announced. "He pedaled all the way out from town on a bicycle, poor thing." She handed the wire to her mother.

"It's for Tom," Nora declared. "Who could be sending him wires?"

"You'd better open it, Nora," Charles urged her. "If it's important, we can call him the minute he arrives in Cambridge."

Nora tore open the envelope and read its contents:

> DEAR TOM THANK YOU AGAIN FOR MARVELOUS TIME LAST NIGHT STOP I'M SO LOOKING FORWARD TO SEEING YOU AGAIN STOP I HOPE YOU MEANT IT WHEN YOU SAID I COULD COME UP FOR FOOTBALL GAME STOP I'LL EVEN ROOT FOR OLD HARVARD
>
> LOVE
> NANCY DELANO

How very peculiar. Nora had asked Tom if he'd enjoyed himself the evening before, and he had replied that he'd had a pretty good time. The girl seemed a lot more enthusiastic than that.

"I think Tom has turned a girl's head," she said almost breathlessly.

"Read it out loud," her oldest daughter commanded.

"Not for anything in the world. It's far too private." She waited, then asked, "Who would Nancy Delano be, do you think?"

Charles Molloy arched his eyebrows. "If she's a Delano, she's related to that White House crowd, I bet."

"The family's very nobby," Caitlin observed. "She lives in Dutchess County and goes to Vassar."

Nora repeated the name to herself. Delano. Of course. She knew it now. Few American names were more distinguished. It ornamented history books and society pages alike.

"Delano," she repeated aloud. "It's strange that Tom didn't mention her. I wonder what she's like."

With the exception of the youngest, everyone at the table interpreted her statement as a declaration of intent. If Nora Molloy wondered what someone was like, she would make it her business to find out.

A Delano indeed.

Tom couldn't possibly do better. What troubled Nora, however, was that he had rushed back to Cambridge without having said a word about her. And what was it that had caused him to return so urgently to school? Did it have something to do with the girl named Peggy Sweeney? The girl he was afraid to introduce to his parents?

20

An advance member of State Senator Robert Conroy's party hurried up the dingy staircase next to the hiring hall on San Francisco's waterfront and pushed open the door at the top.

Inside the small office, the young man looked about him and was baffled. Not only was it empty, but it gave every appearance of having been burned out. The paint was blistered and the woodwork charred. Three desks showed evidence of fire and water damage and the locks were broken on one wall of wooden cabinets. The room was desolate.

The young man consulted a sheet of paper in his hand. "This can't be the right goddam place," he said aloud.

From behind him, footsteps mounted the stairs, and through the opened door he saw a broad-shouldered, craggy-faced man making his way toward him. His hair was gray above the ears, but his face had the everlastingly boyish quality of the Irish. He wore a tweed suit badly in need of a pressing and a white shirt with a shamrock-studded tie. He was holding a coffee mug.

"I take it that you are one of Conroy's henchmen," the Irishman remarked to his visitor. "I'm sorry I kept you waiting. Won't you sit down?"

"Yes, I'm Emmett Doyle."

The young man searched for a chair that was not occupied by folders and ledgers, then waited for one to be cleared for him.

"What the hell happened here?" he asked. "It looks like someone set a bonfire in the middle of the floor."

Patrick Cassidy relocated a huge pile of files, then pushed a chair toward his guest.

"It dates from 1934," he replied. "A vigilante group dropped by unexpectedly one night and rearranged the place a bit."

"Now I remember. That was during the big general strike, wasn't it?"

Cassidy nodded. "The shipowners thought that if they couldn't beat us honorably, then they'd burn us out, and that's what they did." He sat down behind his desk and placed his coffee mug before him. "The vigilantes wrecked the office and set it on fire, but we were never used to comforts, anyway, so we survived." He paused. "When does Conroy arrive?"

"That's what I came to tell you. About noon. Will you be able to have a good crowd for us?"

"No trouble at all. That's lunchtime. We'll have a big turnout."

"The senator is a great admirer of yours, Mr. Cassidy, and he'd like to talk to you for a few minutes in private after he speaks to the longshoremen. Will that be possible?"

"What's he doing for lunch?"

The young man consulted his schedule. "Nothing, I think. He was just going to grab a sandwich somewhere."

"Worst thing in the world. If he's not careful, he'll end up with a politician's stomach. Tell you what. I'll call my wife and ask her to set another place. She'd like to meet him, anyway."

The young man rose from his chair. "I'm sure that Senator Conroy would enjoy that. Why don't we plan on it? He'll talk to your men from twelve to twelve-thirty—"

Cassidy interrupted, "Make that twelve to twelve-fifteen. If he talks too much, my men won't like him."

"Good enough. From twelve to twelve-fifteen. Then he'll have lunch with you and your wife. Thank you, sir. I'm very honored to have met the famous Patrick Cassidy."

"Well, don't be too honored, because next week I might be in jail."

"I heard about that, sir. I certainly hope it doesn't happen again."

"You and me both. And, I might add, Senator Conroy,

258

too. Because if I'm in jail, no one is going to bring my men out to the polling booths to vote for him."

The senator's aide looked grave. "I understand, sir."

"Good," Cassidy said, picking up his coffee mug. "If the senator and I understand each other right from the start, we'll be able to cut the bullshit. I am a very great enemy of bullshit."

"Yes, *sir!*" the young man replied, then rushed down the stairs.

After he had left, Patrick continued to sit at the desk, pleased that he had been able to put the fear of God into a member of a state senator's staff.

It proved once again that power was almost as negotiable as money. It was a good thing, too, because Pat had very little of the latter. He was more than two months overdue in paying rent on his house, and even the paperboy who delivered the *Chronicle* had threatened to discontinue service until the account was settled. The Cassidys' credit was always stretched to the utmost, and grocers and butchers and utility companies were forever sending them haranguing letters.

Yet for all that, Pat Cassidy was known all over California, and in Washington and New York as well. His face often appeared in the newsreels, and his name could be found in editorials and in the news columns. He was loved and venerated by some and hated with a passion by others.

No, he didn't have money, but he had come a long way since he and Eva had left New York City in 1916 and gone clear across the country. He had followed the advice of a countryman, Michael Barrett, when he chose San Francisco, and because he and Eva desperately needed money, he had taken the first job his friend could find for him. He had become a stevedore.

It had been damned hard work. He would never forget it. Every morning, Pat had reported to the hiring hall for the shape-up, hoping to be given work for that day, but not until Mike Barrett informed him that he was expected to show his appreciation to the gang bosses was he hired with any regularity.

"You have to give them a kickback," Mike advised him.

"And what if I don't?"

"If you don't pay them for giving you jobs, you won't get any."

"Then I'll complain to the union."

"The union is controlled by the shipowners, not the workers, and if you complain, you'll be blacklisted."

Pat was indignant but powerless. He had married Eva as soon as her divorce from Balaban became final. It was one thing to be a firebrand when he was responsible just for his own welfare, but he didn't dare risk his job when he had a wife to support.

So he went along with the system. By 1920, when his daughter was born, he was a member of what was called a star gang and received preferential treatment in hiring. He knew most of the gang bosses, and they were always the first to get their cuts from his salary. He despised paying them, but there was no one to complain to. The union was corrupt and ineffectual and more of a spokesman for the companies than the workers. The West Coast waterfront was desperately anxious for the right man to come along to awaken the longshoremen, but it couldn't be Pat. Two years after the birth of Mary—Mimi, as they called her—Eva was pregnant again. Pat swallowed his pride and accepted pay just barely adequate to keep his family alive.

His low wages were in no way related to the lack of business, because the ports were booming and the shipowners were making astronomical profits. In just ten years' time, four officers of one line whose ships Pat helped load and unload received almost fifteen million dollars in salaries and bonuses. During the same time, the average longshoreman, including Pat, made no more than twenty-five dollars a month.

Patrick had even thought of going back to Ireland because, as he said, things could not get worse in California. But worse they got. After the Stock Market Crash of 1929, thousands of longshoremen were thrown out of work altogether. Even with his connections, Pat sometimes had to wait three or four hours during the shape-up just for a half day's work. So when the International Longshoremen's Association was formed in 1933, Pat Cassidy became one of its first members. Three days later, he was blacklisted and unable to find work.

But by then, his two children were in school and Eva offered to pitch in and get a job in order to put food on the table. Far from being upset because he had thrown away what little he had, she was pleased. After all, what had made them cast their lot together was a shared feeling for principles and justice. So they lived on Eva's six dollars a week as a clerk in a department store.

It was during the great strike of 1934 that Pat Cassidy leaped from obscurity to fame. Now, four years later, he was still comparatively poor, but powerful enough to be courted by a state senator.

On the wall next to his desk, the telephone was ringing. It was Eva.

"Reverend Mother just telephoned me," she said.

"Is she dunning us for money again?"

It was a source of embarrassment that the Cassidys were unable to pay Mimi's tuition to her Order of the Sacred Heart school or Joe's to his Jesuit school the moment the bills were presented, but, as Patrick said, somehow they were always paid in the end, and wasn't patience an admirable virtue?

"It isn't that," Eva replied. "It's Mimi. She's in trouble of some sort, and Reverend Mother wants to talk to us."

Patrick closed his eyes in despair. "What kind of trouble?"

"She didn't say, but she sounded upset." She waited, then added, "I have a feeling that this time it might be serious."

Of their two children, Joe was pacificity itself—at the age of five, he'd already decided that he wanted to become a priest—but Mimi was volatile and unmanageable. They'd had problems with her before.

"When does she want to see us?"

"Right now. But could you see her alone? I always lose my temper."

Patrick looked at the clock on the wall. It was a little

261

after nine. The senator was due at twelve, and under no circumstances could he be kept waiting.

"Okay, I'll go out and talk to her. Look! I invited Robert Conroy over for lunch. We should be there by twelve-thirty or so."

"Robert who?"

"Conroy. He's doing some politicking here on the waterfront, and I told his aide that we could give him something more substantial than a sandwich."

"*Senator* Conroy! Really, Pat! The house is a mess."

"He's not coming over to buy the house—which we couldn't sell him, anyway, because it isn't ours—but to have something to eat."

"All I was going to have was what's left of the pot roast from yesterday."

"So peel another spud and put it in the pot."

Now that Eva no longer worked at the department store, the Cassidys generally ate their main meal of the day at noon. Pat was often busy in the evenings, and too many suppers had been delayed until ten at night for Eva to attempt seven o'clock dinners anymore.

"I wish I had time to do something special," she complained.

"Conroy probably eats something special every day he's in Sacramento. It'll do him good to have something plain."

"Okay, I'll do my best," Eva said, then added, "I'm worried about Mimi."

Patrick was worried, too, though God knows he should have been inured to her escapades. She had always defied convention, and had been a rebel since she'd first started walking.

As Pat Cassidy's old Ford—it was already six years old when he'd bought it two years before—mounted the crest of the hill, he saw the red-tiled roof of the campanile, then the low-lying terra-cotta-colored buildings on either side of it. It was Spanish-arched and ancient-looking, though he knew that like many things in California, it was only a facsimile of truth and, in fact, dated from the 1920s.

Still, he loved the peace and sanctity of the place. It awoke something in him that even Ireland no longer did, for as he became more American, Patrick held even more steadfastly to his faith. He could relinquish his Irishness, but never his religion, he'd said a thousand times.

Ireland could have been a universe away. He no longer even corresponded with anyone there since his mother's death in 1925. At that time, he had heard that Nora Shannon had married a Yankee named Molloy and was living in New York City, and he had planned to get in touch with her, remembering his pledge to his brother Thomas, but then thought better of it, as it would only reopen old wounds.

It was astonishing how easily one could renounce one nation for another. Patrick certainly *felt* American. His wife was American and so were his children. He did not mind all that much giving up his allegiance to his former country; what sorely vexed him was the possibility that his daughter might give up the faith of his fathers.

Even when she was younger, Mimi had always questioned her faith. His son, Joe, had believed everything implicitly—the more marvelous the miracles, the readier he was to give them credence—but Mimi was a profound doubter. Once she had even confessed to him that the sacrament of Communion seemed to her rather farfetched, and for months and months when she was ten years old she had refused to partake of it.

If Patrick had loved her less, perhaps he would not have been hurt so much, but his love was almost boundless, and Mimi knew it, too, and reciprocated. He admired Joe—the dogged scholar who never did anything wrong—but his dedication to Mimi was total. Joe was a soft and almost feminine creature and would in time make an ideal priest. Mimi was sometimes feisty and contentious, yet few girls possessed greater beauty and grace.

But she certainly had what the school authorities called disruptively high spirits. She had once freed all the white mice in her science class, and the school building had had to be closed for three days while the exterminator dealt with them. Whatever she had done this time, he would stick by her, as he always had in the past. If there was insurrection in her character, he knew where it came from.

He parked his car in the area reserved for visitors, then hurried toward the long steps that led to Reverend Mother's office. A sudden whiff of lemony flowers came from shrubberies planted at the convent's walls, and in the distance he could see two wrinkled and elderly nuns walking down a shaded walk, head bent in prayer.

Why was Mimi unable to see the beauty of it?

Outside Reverend Mother's door, he listened, then knocked and was instructed to enter. Mimi was kneeling in front of the desk, and Reverend Mother was standing over her with a ruler held in midair.

Involuntarily, Patrick clenched his fists. He hated corporal punishment of any type. It did nothing but breed resentment.

"What has she done?"

Reverend Mother placed her ruler on her desk, then turned to Mimi and said, "You may leave the room."

"No, I should like her to be here so that she can tell her side of the story."

Reverend Mother was displeased, but attempted not to show it. "As you like," she began, then reached for a sheet of paper on her desk blotter. She handed it to Patrick. "Sister Winifred intercepted this earlier this morning in chemistry class."

Patrick studied the drawing. It was a most unflattering caricature of Sister Winifred. Her face was even more witchlike than nature made it, and short gray whiskers were growing from her chin. Her eyes were maniacal. Though she was dressed in her nunnish habit, she was airborne and riding what was unmistakably a broom.

He didn't dare look at Mimi for fear that she would see him pinching his fingers together to hold back the laughter. He turned his back toward her until he was able to control himself, then placed the drawing on the desk in front of him.

"Is it yours?" he asked at last, facing his daughter.

Her eyes did not meet his. They were downcast. "Yes, Daddy."

"Why did you draw it?"

Mimi shrugged her shoulders. "I don't like chemistry. It's a terrible bore."

"It's good discipline for the mind."

"For some girls, maybe."

Reverend Mother interrupted, "Your daughter will be failing chemistry this year as a result of this."

Patrick was angry. "Because of that silly drawing?"

"Mr. Cassidy," Reverend Mother began patiently, "she has made a laughingstock of Sister Winifred. I cannot allow her back in class. She will have to wait until January when Sister Philomena's class is formed."

"Then I won't be able to graduate in June!" Mimi protested.

"You should have thought of that, young lady, when you were making this filthy drawing."

She clutched the sheet of paper and crumpled it in her fist, then thrust it in the wastebasket next to her desk.

"I'd like to talk to my daughter for a moment in private," Patrick requested.

"I shall be in the hall," Reverend Mother replied, scurrying across the room toward the door.

The second she left, Mimi ran to her father and threw herself into his arms. He felt her wet tears against the front of his shirt.

"It was a very funny picture, Mimi," he began, "but I have a feeling that Sister Winifred doesn't have a sense of humor. You should have *known* that."

She pulled back, drying her eyes with her fingers. "I know, Daddy. I'm sorry. I didn't mean to hurt her feelings."

"Then why did you do it, pigeon?"

Without hesitation, she replied, "Because I hate it here."

"And what do you hate about it?"

"The sisters are inhuman. They're so bitter and disappointed, Daddy, as if they hate life. We're almost never allowed to talk. We can't receive mail from anyone except our parents. We're not permitted to listen to the radio or even read magazines or newspapers. They let us take showers three times a week, then a nun stands outside the door, timing us, afraid that we'll do something *naughty*. They're just not human. Daddy, I'm sorry to disappoint you. I know that it's been a sacrifice for you to pay the fees and everything." She waited, then added, "The girls make fun of me because my tuition is never paid on time."

His face darkened. "They make fun of you?"

She nodded. "They all know who you are. They tease me because you've been in jail."

Patrick had to fight to control his rage. "I'm not ashamed to have been in jail. I was arrested during the strike of 1934 by deputies who were paid by the shipowners. But in the end, Mimi, the government said that I was right and the shipowners were wrong. We won the strike."

"I know, Daddy. I love you for it. The other girls have fathers who are lawyers or businessmen, and all they talk about is money. I'm proud that you've been in jail. It'll be in the history books. But I hate this place. Most of the other girls are such prudes and snobs."

That was it. With such an attitude, Patrick knew that nothing would be accomplished by keeping her in school.

"Then how would you like to come home and go back to a public school?"

"I'd like it, Daddy, I'd be much happier."

Patrick was sure that Reverend Mother would also be happier. He told Mimi to go to her room and get her things ready while he announced the decision.

He was disappointed, of course. Maybe it had been too much to ask that both of his children would be zealous Catholics. He would have to settle for one. Some people were just not born with a capacity to believe and conform, and Mimi was apparently one of them.

When he informed Reverend Mother of his decision, she replied, "I think it's for the best, Mr. Cassidy. I don't envy you and your wife, as I have the feeling that Mary will be a great deal of trouble before she grows up."

Patrick was willing to concede that she might be. But once she had grown up, as Reverend Mother called it, what a marvelous woman she would be!

After he had delivered Mimi to her mother, Patrick returned to the hiring hall on the waterfront to marshal as large an audience as possible for Robert Conroy's appearance. As always at this time of day, the hall was crowded with men seeking work. A huge influx of unemployed had drifted westward during the Depression and were still arriving by the carload. Those who could not find work in the fields as farmhands or fruitpickers invariably ended up on the docks.

Since the strike of 1934, hiring had been controlled by the union, and the shameful practice of buying jobs from gang bosses had almost disappeared. Moreover, Patrick had begun to discern a new spirit of cooperation, particularly on the part of the shipowners, who were less likely to consider their employees as enemies. Now that war was imminent and it was essential that labor concord be maintained, the owners had given in to most of the union's demands without contesting them.

Patrick made the rounds to determine which ships were in port, which were in the process of being loaded, and the number of longshoremen needed and already at work. The hall was buzzing with activity because the port was busy. It seemed that every businessman in the world— from manufacturers in America stockpiling latex, to Far Easterners dumping their merchandise—was trying to beat the war.

Ahead of him was the huge board that showed where stevedores were being used. Mario Aglietti, who was keeping the entries current, erased a number with a large rag, then wrote another. As he saw Pat approach, he spoke out of the corner of his mouth: "Hey, you hear what that asshole Chamberlain said over the radio? Peace with honor, he said. He's fulla crap. He gave away Czechoslovakia. Is that honor?"

"It's a wonder he didn't offer them the United States while he was at it."

"You're Irish. I bet you hate the Limeys, don't you?"

Did he? Patrick wasn't sure. At breakfast, when he had listened to the rebroadcast of Chamberlain's address to Parliament, he had felt his heart thumping wildly in his chest and sweat break out on his forehead. Chamberlain's speech was delivered in aristocratic English, not unlike

267

that of Sir Richard Wingfield, who had ordered the seizure and execution of Patrick's family. Yet Chamberlain earnestly hoped for peace. Germany lusted for war. Ireland, Pat was sure, would give its allegiance to neither. It was dizzying, all right. England, the persecutor, was about to become the victim; and Ireland, fallen and almost lifeless, could now dance at England's funeral. But would she?

"There are good men and wicked men. Whether they are English or Irish or German or Japanese is beside the point. I hate them for their wickedness, but for nothing else," he answered.

"Yeah," Aglietti said, "I guess you're right. We're all the same. We got the same set of nuts or the same crack between our legs. It don't matter if you're a Wop or a Jap or a Mick." He stuffed a cigar into his mouth. "You better check on the *Comstock Orient*. The guys who were loading it stopped work about a half hour ago."

"Has Flynn been giving them a hard time again?"

Peter Flynn was the owner of the ship and Pat had had dealings with him before. In the past, they had been able to settle their difficulties without work stoppages.

"Don't know, but the *Comstock* is due to sail at four, and unless it's loaded, it don't go nowhere."

As Pat made his way down the docks toward the *Comstock Orient*, he was greeted amiably by longshoremen he passed. It was a damn sight different from what it was like back in 1933 when the union was first being organized. Back then, he was as often hated as admired. Not until the men realized that they had no future at all unless they unionized did they finally accept him as a friend.

They were a peculiar hodgepodge, tough as new steel and as mean, some of them, as wild dogs. Yet he had seen them cry on Bloody Thursday, 1934, when the police had opened fire on the picket lines and killed two men and wounded over one hundred. Pat would never forget that day. It was the Fourth of July. If until then his commitment to the union movement had been uncertain, afterward it was firm and irrevocable.

Of course, the charge had been made that some of

the strikers were Reds, but Pat could not see that even that was justification for killing them. The Depression had made Reds of a good many Americans who thought that the system had failed, and Pat counted among his personal friends more than one avowed member of the party. The burghers of San Francisco, however, saw the whole lot of them as a menace to their way of life. They associated communism with godlessness, while the Red agitators Pat knew wanted only three square meals a day. If that was a threat to the democratic system, it was nothing to what the police had done when they fired on the strikers with live ammunition.

The Fourth of July. The birthdate of the Republic, and Pat's, too. Not because it really was, but for lack of any other. When Pat had taken out his first papers for citizenship, it had been necessary for him to write to the county council's office in Cork City to ascertain his date of birth, and he was astounded to learn that it had never been recorded. Nor had the priest who baptized him taken the trouble to make note of the fact, and as a consequence, there was no legal record of his birth. As the fisherfolk of western Ireland, lacking calendars, seldom observed birthdays, and he had never done so, he had the entire year to choose from. What better choice than the fourth of July? He would celebrate his own newfound emancipation on the same day that his adopted country did.

Yet the police rifles on that Bloody Thursday in July had taught him that democracy was subject to interpretation, and that not everyone saw the function of the Republic as he did. Pat vowed never to forget that day; it would live in his memory along with the massacre of his family and the death of Annamarie in New York City. And he marveled at the mystery of human nature. How men of roughly similar intelligence and sensibilities could react to the same set of circumstances in entirely different ways, he found everlastingly baffling.

He'd had time enough to contemplate it, because after the union office had been raided by members of the Citizens' Law and Order Association, he had been thrown in jail. And because the police and the judicial system were both sympathetic to the shippers, he remained in jail for almost two weeks.

The day he was at last released, he was asked by a reporter, "What were the charges, Mr. Cassidy?"

"I was suspected of being a Red."

"And why did you not stand trial?"

Without pausing, he replied, "It's suspected that the charges were dismissed."

The reporter was not at all amused. "Are you or are you not a Red?"

"I understand that some of my best friends are."

"That is no answer, sir."

Patrick turned away. "That is no question, sir."

Whether he believed in Thomas Jefferson, Karl Marx, or Peter Pan was no one's business but his own. He believed firmly in a democratic society—of that he was certain—but only if freedom and democracy were available to all citizens, not just a favored few. He was not prepared to admit that such a belief made him a Communist. Far from it. Those who did not share his views, in fact, and hoped to ration out freedom in a selective sort of way were bloody damn close to being Fascists.

As he approached the bow of the *Comstock Orient*, riding high in the water, he saw the stevedores standing sullenly by the unloaded crates on the dock. On the ship itself was Peter Flynn, its owner, looking down on the idle workers.

To Pat, it semed like a tableau. The feudal lord and his vassals once again in confrontation, but this time in San Francisco in the year 1938. It was his duty as a union leader to persuade them that their goals were essentially the same: the owners sought profits that would enable them to lead comfortable lives, and the workers wanted salaries to accomplish the same purpose. It was so utterly simple. There was no need for them to be at each others' throats.

He saw that half the ship had been loaded. A container being lifted into the hold had broken open on the deck, spilling its contents. In the pale San Francisco sunlight, it looked like junk.

In fact, that's what it was.

Angelo Candela, a section leader, hurried up to Pat. Tattoos covered his arms, and curly black hair broke over the top of his blue shirt. "I thought we'd already settled this shit with Flynn," he said angrily.

"He's still shipping scrap iron?"

"He tried to sneak it out. He's put the goddam stuff in boxes."

There was nothing particularly novel about sending scrap iron to Japan. It had been going on for the past ten years. Euphemistically, it was known as "raw material" destined for steel mills, and until just two years before it had been shipped openly. Even Reds—Candela was one and not the least bit ashamed of it—had considered it little more than junk from America. If the Japs wanted it, they were welcome to it.

But when Japanese troops had swept into mainland China in July 1937, many of them carrying arms made from American scrap iron, some of the union members, particularly the Reds, had begun to object. Then, in December, Japanese planes had bombed the U.S. Navy gunboat *Panay* as it lay at anchor in the Yangtze River, and two American sailors had been killed.

Pat Cassidy's men had refused to handle any more scrap iron bound for Japan. The shipowners, among them Peter Flynn, had agreed to end their shipments. But now it was obvious that Flynn was simply placing all the scrap metal in huge wooden containers before it reached the waterfront.

"Okay, I'll see what Flynn has to say about it. You guys take a rest."

By the time Pat reached the top of the gangplank, Flynn was no longer there. A deckhand told him that the shipowner could be found in the captain's cabin.

He smiled at the stratagem. Flynn would be seated and comfortable when Pat arrived, and Pat would at once be placed on the defensive.

Yet when he stood before the opened door leading to the captain's quarters, he saw that Flynn had an additional surprise for him. Another man was seated in the room.

271

"Mr. Cassidy," Flynn said with a grand flourish, "Mr. Ishikawa."

The Oriental stood and shook hands in Western fashion. Then from the small Japanese came faultless English.

"I have read about you, Mr. Cassidy," he began. "You were the subject of a great deal of controversy when I was at U.C.L.A."

"Mr. Ishikawa has a law degree from the University of California," Flynn interrupted.

"That's more than I have," Pat replied, more belligerently than he had intended.

"My family has always had close ties to California, Mr. Cassidy," Ishikawa continued.

"At the moment, you are straining those ties, Mr. Ishikawa."

"Look!" Flynn said heatedly, "I won't be a bit surprised if Roosevelt places an embargo on all scrap metal shipments to Japan before the year is over. This may be one of our last shipments, Mr. Cassidy."

"No," Pat protested, "your *last* shipment was your last shipment. This one is not going to leave the docks. Didn't we agree on that four months ago?"

"Yes, but that was a concession to the goddam Reds in your union. Their bitch was that we were sending loose scrap metal. It troubled their consciences. So we boxed it, Mr. Cassidy. This way, they don't have to look at it and their consciences won't hurt when they load it."

"Even in boxes, it hurts *my* conscience, Mr. Flynn."

Not only was the scrap metal converted into armaments, but the Japanese warlords had within the last year signed a treaty with Germany and Italy. That alone was sufficient to give Mr. Ishikawa a bad odor.

"You misunderstand, I think," Ishikawa began in a soft, patient voice. "It is in the best interests of America for there to be peace in the Pacific, and only a strong Japan can provide that."

"By marching into China?"

Ishikawa shook his head in disagreement. "By preventing the Bolsheviks from marching into China. You see, Mr. Cassidy," Ishikawa continued, "you Westerners do not always comprehend events that take place in the

Orient. We Japanese will be able to give the Pacific stability, without which American businessmen will not be able to operate there. The scrap metal that so offends your longshoremen will be converted to useful items: to refrigerators, to steel beams for new factories, to tractors for our farmers, and to plows and farm machinery—"

"And shells and tanks and cannon," Pat concluded for him. "The answer is no, Mr. Ishikawa. Mr. Flynn is aware of how we feel on this issue. My men will not load any more scrap metal, and that's all there is to it."

Ishikawa looked at Flynn's face searchingly, then indicated with a nod of his head that the shipowner might now proceed in a slightly different direction.

"Patrick," Flynn said with surprising cordiality, "listen! So maybe we made a slight error in judgment on this. We thought we could get the goddam crates through without creating a stink. We were wrong. But don't punish us. Tell you what. Ask your men to finish loading the ship and they have my word that it will never happen again."

Ishikawa now stepped forward, a gentle smile on his face. "My family will lose a great deal of money, Mr. Cassidy, if we are unable to utilize this shipment of metal. We are quite prepared—I don't know how to say this—to make it easier for you to make a decision."

Flynn now took over. "You have two children, Patrick. What Mr. Ishikawa is suggesting is that—Jesus Christ, man!—why not make life a little easier for them? His family is prepared to set up"—Flynn paused until he found the right words—"a trust fund of some sort for your kids."

"How much?" Pat asked.

It was Ishikawa who replied. "Perhaps ten thousand for each?"

"Dollars or yen?"

"Dollars, of course."

Pat's union salary was under two thousand a year, and that was more than any of his men made.

Pat nodded his head. "I'd prefer it in yen."

"Yen?" Ishikawa asked. "I suppose that could be arranged."

"In small denominations," Pat continued. "In fact, in coins. With *sharp* edges." He waited, then added, "That way, you'll feel them more when I tell you that you can stuff them."

He turned to leave the room. "You sail at four with what you have in the hold. But the crates on the dock will still be here. There isn't a longshoreman in a West Coast port that would load them, Mr. Ishikawa."

As he left, he could see his men on the dock looking up at him anxiously. When he was halfway down the gangplank, Candela hurried up to meet him. "So what do we do? Do we load it or not?"

Patrick looked at the faces on the dock. If he had offered to share the twenty thousand with them, would they have accepted it despite their scruples? It was hard to say, but he had a feeling that most of them would have done just what he had.

How wonderful it would be to live without having to worry about money! Still, it was astonishing how well you could adapt to poverty if your principles remained intact. Once before, in New York City, he had been offered a bribe, and he had turned that down, too. Had he accepted it, he might now be the manager of one of Balaban's mills. And he would hate himself.

He yelled at the assembled men, "We don't load. Go back to the hall and we'll reassign you for the rest of the day."

A roar of approval met his words. It was better than money.

"Who's the broad he's with?" someone asked Pat the minute Robert Conroy stepped from his Ford roadster outside the hiring hall where the longshoremen had gathered. "Christ Almighty, that looks like Joan Magnuson," another volunteered.

Indeed it was. As a rule, she was described as the legendary Joan Magnuson, Hollywood star a bit past her prime, leading lady to such luminaries as Tyrone Power, Gary Cooper, and Clark Gable, both on the screen and off. She was the subject of endless movie magazine articles and the object of adoration of fans all around the world.

Joan Magnuson.

Pat had read somewhere during the past year that she was active in politics, but he had not known that she had thrown her support behind the young state senator. Granted, Conroy was one of those storybook-handsome Irishmen, but certainly he would be considered minor league in the company she kept. As he watched the two of them make their way through the crowd of men, the actress receiving far more attention than the politician, it occurred to Pat that perhaps the power-that-be were priming Conroy for greater things. People like Joan Magnuson did not waste their time on men who were content with remaining in the statehouse.

"Good afternoon, Mr. Conroy," Pat said, holding out his hand. "I'm Pat Cassidy. It's always a pleasure to meet another Irishman."

Up close, Conroy was a bigger man than Pat had imagined. He was at least six feet tall and his chest and arm muscles were those of an athlete. His face was bronzed from the sun.

Grinning, the senator replied, "I'm only half Irish. I've been led to believe that being all Irish is sometimes fatal."

Pat had the feeling that he wasn't expected to produce a riposte, but he offered one, anyway. "I hate to disappoint you, Senator, but being half Irish is like being half black. It's dominant and submerges everything else."

Conroy laughed robustly, grabbing Pat's upper arm affectionately. "Look, do you know Joan Magnuson?"

"Hello," she said. "I hope I'm not spoiling things."

Her platinum blonde hair hung to the top of a silver fox coat resting over her shoulders. Her eyebrows had been plucked and rearranged, and her teeth were so perfect that they had to be capped. Yet under her eyes, giving her a welcome humanity, were small crow's feet, and she looked tired.

"Not at all, Miss Magnuson," he answered. "In fact, the men would be delighted if you could stay."

"I stopped at Joan's house in Carmel," the senator

explained, "and when she found that I was coming up here, she asked if she could come along."

Pat wondered if Conroy had stopped at the house in Carmel the evening before or earlier that morning. Probably the former, he thought. It was very daring for a politician to do such a thing. Politicians could sleep with their wives, if they had them; or by themselves, if they didn't. Sleeping with actresses was generally frowned upon. Yet Pat could see why the senator had been tempted. Joan Magnuson was no longer a young girl—her late thirties, he thought—but she was very beautiful indeed.

The noon whistle sounded, and men swarmed to the front of the hiring hall where the senator was to speak from the back of a truck. Although Miss Magnuson at first protested, Conroy insisted that she occupy one of the three chairs behind the makeshift podium.

At a few minutes after twelve, when the crowd had assembled, Pat rose and asked for quiet.

His voice was deep and resonant and carried surprisingly well even without the use of a microphone. "We're fortunate today to have not one but two distinguished guests here on the waterfront," he began. "You all know Miss Magnuson, I'm sure."

As he turned to acknowledge the actress, the crowd squealed and yelped, then howled its approval. She stood by her chair, waving and smiling. It was some time before the whistling subsided.

"As for our other guest," he resumed, "it has been said that the most dangerous man in the world is the poor man who rises in life and is elected to public office, because after years of penury he is tempted to seize what is not rightfully his. Our guest today was born to wealth and has rejected it, preferring instead to serve the poor and the needful. Truly, he is a servant of the public and, I assure you, a friend of labor and the working class. During the strike of 1934, while other legislators encouraged the vigilantes, he was here on the waterfront marching with longshoremen. He has fought side by side with migrant workers in the Imperial Valley and grape pickers in the Napa Valley. He speaks their language, as he also speaks yours and mine. The officers of the

ILA endorse him one hundred percent, and we urge you to listen carefully as he speaks to you now. I give you Robert Conroy."

Even before the applause had died down, Conroy was launched on his speech: "This world is on the brink of war and is crying out for help from America, but we have turned our backs on the poor and suffering people of Europe!"

Patrick was stunned, and it was clear that the long-shoremen also were. The senator was about to deliver an anti-isolationist speech. California was teeming with America First members who advocated isolation, but few legislators had dared to speak out against them.

"During the few minutes I'll be with you today," he continued, "I shall not talk about the coming election. Instead, I shall talk about the coming war and the greatest challenge this country has faced since its founding." Conroy waited, searching the faces before him, savoring the silence. "Each and every one of us here today has ties that stretch back to the Old World, the great majority of them so recent as to be only a few years old. That world which our fathers left is about to be thrown into a war more devastating than any that history has ever known, yet there are those among us who say that it is none of our business!"

Once again, he paused, his words ringing in the air. "Last week in Munich, the appeasers of Adolf Hitler tried to buy peace. By treaty, France was obliged to go to the aid of Czechoslovakia, and England was obliged to aid France. Yet both chose the coward's way out and flung the bleeding carcass of that once-proud nation at Hitler's feet, hoping that it would satisfy his bloodlust. They are wrong.

"In Germany today, there is no labor movement, and labor leaders have been imprisoned. The common man has lost what rights he once had, and many Germans, Jews most of all, have been flung back into the terror and darkness of the Middle Ages. All over Germany, there are signs that read 'Jews Not Admitted,' and as a result, German Jews are unable to buy the necessities of life, and are even forbidden to sleep in hotel beds for fear

277

that they will contaminate members of the so-called master race.

"Hitler has vowed to create a thousand-year Reich, and all Europe has trembled in fear. The appeasers are about to surrender an entire continent, yet there are those among us who say that it is none of our business. I tell you, gentlemen, it is!"

Pat was bewildered. Why was Conroy expressing views that had little relevance to his job as state senator in Sacramento? Pat could only conclude that he was already barnstorming for the 1940 elections, two years ahead. But what was he after? The governorship or a seat in the U.S. Senate? In either case, he was banking on the longshoremen's ability to remember the warning he was now giving them.

"To us on the West Coast," Conroy went on, "what is happening in Europe sometimes seems very remote. What difference does it make, after all, if Europe goes up in flames? And I answer you that we have an obligation to history and civilization. Our families fled Europe, most of them in order to survive, and now it is our duty to reach out to Europeans in their anguish. The isolationists among us insist that we have no such responsibility, but they are wrong. Not only have they forgotten their origins but their sanity as well, for if we do not come to the aid of Europe during its hour of crisis, then we ourselves will become the next victims."

His voice became softer. "This coming war will be won on the oceans and in the air as much as on the battlefields, and you men will play strategic roles. The great majority of you are new Americans who have arrived in this country since the turn of the century, and now you have a unique opportunity to teach those *old* Americans in their snug white houses and their pretty little towns a thing or two about liberty. I urge you all, in the name of humanity, to speak out and let yourselves be heard before it is too late." He waited, then added, "Thank you, gentlemen, for your time."

The applause was deafening.

A magnetic and magical man, Pat concluded. And

principled as well, which made him a rarity among politicians. He would bear watching, to be sure.

Eva Cassidy opened the front door and was waiting on the stoop as Pat and Robert Conroy made their way from the parked car to the house. Age had been kind to her. In twenty years, she had put on ten pounds, which had merely enhanced her beauty, rounding out the sharp edges of youth. Her skin was as fair and unlined as ever, which she ascribed publicly to San Francisco's mild climate and privately to the fact that her husband loved her as much now as he had when they were first married.

Graciously, she extended her hand to Robert Conroy, not even waiting for Pat's introduction. "Hello, Senator," she said, smiling, "I'm Eva Cassidy."

Conroy was charmed, and said as much.

"We've had a little crisis this morning, so we're even more disordered than we usually are," she revealed. "I hope you'll understand."

By way of explanation, Pat said, half laughing, "My irascible daughter has been disinvited from her convent school. We've decided that she is most certainly not cut out to be a nun."

"I spent two years at a Jesuit seminary before I found —or before *they* found—that I had no future there," the senator responded.

"Then you'll have something in common," Eva said, turning toward the doorway. "Mary? Our guest has arrived."

Robert Conroy was unprepared for what he saw. He had expected an unruly child, but the creature who now stood in the doorway was a beautiful young woman. She had changed from her hideous school uniform into a smart dress the shade of heather. With her long black hair, dark eyes, and opalescent skin, she made a breathtaking appearance.

When he regained his composure, he said to her, "I hear that you're a noncomformist, Miss Cassidy."

She offered him her hand with a grace that no convent school had ever taught her and said, "I try to be, Mr. Conroy."

During lunch, they got along famously, all four of them. Mimi was accepted as an adult, which she very nearly was. On several occasions, Conroy found himself addressing her rather than her parents. Mimi was animated by the attention. She found herself listening carefully to the discussion of his future.

When her father asked, "What are your plans for 1940? I have a feeling that the statehouse can't hold you much longer," Conroy agreed.

"I'm thinking of running for governor," he said. "In fact, in two or three weeks I'll be setting up an office here in San Francisco with that in mind."

The Cassidys were pleased, Pat because it would be useful to have such a link to the governor's mansion, and Eva and Mimi because of the excitement involved in knowing someone who aspired to such an office. Pat at once pledged his support, and so did Eva, who had already worked for Democratic party candidates. She would be happy to spend two or three days a week at his office.

"That's wonderful," Conroy said. "I need all the help I can get."

Pat raised his glass of California zinfandel. "Here's to a very bright future, Senator," he said by way of a toast.

As Mimi joined in the toast, her eyes met Robert Conroy's, and suddenly she saw something disturbing in his gaze. A nakedness, almost. He, too, must have been aware of it because at the same instant that she turned away, he did as well.

"Perhaps Mimi could be of some help, too," Eva volunteered innocently. "She could type and address envelopes. It would be a good experience for her. Would you like that, Mimi?"

Mimi looked to her father for a clue to her response, but as always, he was allowing her to make her own decision. Next, she searched Robert Conroy's face, but saw fear there.

Yet she heard herself say aloud, "Yes, I think I should like that very much."

21

"The way I figure it," Nelson Wyman was saying in the Lowell House dining room, "we will be at war by Christmas at the latest. Roosevelt is just itching to get us in this war because it's the only way he'll have a secure place for himself in history. It's obvious that his New Deal has failed." He wiped the remnants of egg yolk from his breakfast plate with a blueberry muffin, then stuffed it in his mouth. "What's really immoral about Roosevelt," Wyman continued, "is that he's allowing the Fascists to win in Spain. And do you know why? Because he's afraid to intervene for fear that he'll offend the hugely influential American Catholic community. He's no more than a puppet of the Catholic Church."

Next to Tom, John Phipps snickered. "Did you hear that, Tom? Do you think that F.D.R. is a puppet of the Catholic Church?"

"Yes," Tom replied without cracking a smile. "We intend to make him the next pope."

Phipps roared with laughter. "And what about Eleanor?"

"No plans as yet. We'd make her a cardinal, but red isn't her color."

Tom had a fragile relationship with Nelson Wyman, whose family was a very prominent one in Maryland. Wyman was a member of the Porcellian Club, generally considered the best on campus, and he had once confessed to Tom that he had never *known* any Catholics until he met Tom.

"I wouldn't half mind going to Spain as a member of the International Brigade," Steve Hopkins spoke up, "but my parents would never hear of it."

"The Fascists are going to win because of Roosevelt—" Wyman began.

"—and the American Catholics," Tom interrupted.

"Yes!" Wyman agreed. "They're going to win because of Roosevelt and the Catholics, so why would you want to go over there to be on the losing side? Anyway, Franco isn't so bad. The Spaniards could do worse."

"I'd rather do what Cy Chisholm is going to do," Phipps said. "He says that he's going to join the R.A.F. the minute England enters the war."

"Of course, he's Anglo-American," Hopkins explained. "He went to Winchester."

"I give England about two weeks in a war with Germany," Wyman declared. "The *Luftwaffe* will destroy London in the first three or four days because the English have no air defenses. You've got to give it to the Germans. They've built a marvelous air force out of nothing and created an incredible country out of the ashes of the First World War. I was at the games in Berlin in 1936, and I was most impressed."

"You mean as far as you're concerned, Hitler isn't so bad. The English could do worse?" Tom asked sarcastically.

Wyman lifted his napkin to his lips, then said, "You know, Molloy, sometimes you give me a pain in the ass."

"I understood that you were getting stuffed every night by your roommate, so how could you tell?"

The fact of the matter was that rather unsavory stories had been circulated about Wyman and his roommate. Tom was pretty certain that they weren't true, but he could not allow Wyman's defense of the Third Reich to go unchallenged.

"You have a nasty tongue," Wyman said.

"You have a nasty mind."

Wyman left in a huff, vowing never again to eat at the same table as a Catholic.

"You won't dare say that after we make Roosevelt the next pope," Tom called after him.

Every morning, it was the same thing. No matter what table he found himself at, the conversation invariably turned to the impending war. Tom would feel his stomach muscles tighten.

"Listen," Phipps said as they, too, left the table, "we'd better hurry or we'll be late for class. I'll run ahead and get the mail."

As Phipps sprinted to the mailboxes, Tom searched the floor of the hall for the books he had dropped. Phipps came back and handed him a letter. Tom glanced at the envelope. His mother's handwriting was beautiful. Spencerian, almost. As he tore open the envelope, something fluttered to the ground, and he stooped to retrieve it. It was a telegram.

From Nancy Delano.

He read it once, then a second time. In a funny sort of way, he was elated that she'd taken the trouble to send such a pleasant wire. It wasn't the sort of thing her kind of girl generally did, and it must have cost her a good bit of pride.

"What does your mother say?" Phipps asked as they sailed out of Lowell House.

"I haven't read it yet," Tom replied, then handed his friend the telegram.

In a minute, Phipps returned it. "I told you she liked you. Are you going to do anything about it?"

Tom didn't answer immediately. But, yes, he was sure that he wanted to see Nancy Delano again. It was wrong of him to dismiss her just because she had rebuffed him sexually. It didn't matter that much now, anyway. He had just had two nights with Peggy.

"Maybe," he answered.

"I've invited Emily Thayer up for the Princeton game this Saturday. Why don't you ask Nancy?"

Tom considered it. It would certainly be a decent gesture. For one thing, he had promised her that he would. Yet it would mean the second weekend in a row away from Peggy.

"You could telephone her. She's just down the hall from Laura. Here, I'll write down the number."

Phipps tore a piece of paper from his notebook, then rested the notebook against Tom's back as he noted the

283

telephone number. He handed it to his friend, who accepted it without a word, stuffing it into his wallet.

As they resumed their walk toward classes, Phipps said, "Something's wrong, isn't it, Tom?"

Tom had to confide in someone. Almost with relief he began, "I've been seeing this girl who lives in North Cambridge. I don't know, but I think I'm in love with her."

Then he found himself telling his roommate all about Peggy Sweeney.

An immense black Duesenberg drew up to the curb in front of the priory of St. Vincent Ferrer at Lexington Avenue and Sixty-sixth Street, and in a minute a woman in a heavy veil left it and made her way up the sidewalk to the door.

The woman was expected. Even before she reached the door, it opened.

"Good afternoon, Father," Nora Molloy said to the priest who welcomed her.

"It is always a pleasure to see you, Mrs. Molloy. Won't you come in?"

She followed him down a hall to a comfortable room, where she showed her to a chair, then occupied a seat behind a desk. Except for a prie-dieu, well-worn and in need of reupholstery, and a huge crucifix on the wall, it might have been a lawyer's office.

Nora opened her purse and withdrew a check, which she placed on the desk before her. "I have brought along a little something for the archdiocese," she said.

As he glanced at it, his eyebrows rose ever so slightly. "As always, you are most generous, Mrs. Molloy. The archbishop will be grateful."

Nora snapped her purse shut. "I have a favor to ask of you, Father."

He smiled gently. "The offices of the archdiocese are at your service, Mrs. Molloy."

Nora did not quite know how to begin. She and her husband were not socially active in New York City, partly because they preferred to spend their time at home. And when they did socialize, it was invariably with Catholic business associates of Charles Molloy.

"I wonder if it might be possible, Father," she said, "for you or the archbishop to arrange a meeting between my husband and me and a family whose name I shall give you."

"The archbishop's acquaintance is extensive, I assure you."

She paused. "They are not of our faith. They are Protestants. Their name is Delano. Benjamin Delano and his wife. They live in Dutchess County near Millbrook."

"That is rather far afield, Mrs. Molloy," the priest replied at last. "It is estate country, I understand. They ride to hounds up there."

"Yes, I believe they do."

Thoughtfully, he tapped a finger on his desktop. "Could I perhaps have someone bring you tea, Mrs. Molloy, while I make a few telephone calls?"

"That would be lovely."

After he left, Nora continued to sit in the chair, her veil pulled back from her face. She had not told Charles that she was consulting her spiritual adviser today. She didn't know what he would think of her plan. He had so many decisions of his own to make that she preferred not to burden him with one more until she had something positive to report.

Apart from a ticking clock, the small office was noiseless, and Nora was startled when a nun carried in a tray with tea things, then departed.

She was sure that had she told the priest the true reason she desired to meet the Delanos, he would have tried to dissuade her.

"We are in great luck, Mrs. Molloy," he said as he treaded softly across the carpet into the room. "You know the Morrisseys, of course."

Who didn't know the Morrisseys? They were one of America's greatest Irish Catholic families, ranking second only to the Carrolls of Carrollton, with whom they had intermarried.

"I know Kate Morrissey," Nora volunteered.

The matriarch of the Morrissey family was even more

devoutly Catholic than Nora, if that was possible. Every year, she visited Lourdes, sometimes accompanied by children, grandchildren, or cousins with one infirmity or another, real or imagined, and every year she reported one more miraculous cure. She had been made a Dame of Malta and was permitted to use the title of duchess, but rarely did. At her huge apartment on Fifth Avenue, she had a private chapel constructed in which she spent a great deal of time.

"Mrs. Morrissey herself leads a very secluded life," the priest revealed, "but a daughter of hers married a Boyle. The Boyles are very smart and fashionable and have a house, I understand, at Millbrook, where they are friends of the Delanos."

Why, of course! Nina Boyle. What a fool Nora had been not to think of her in the first place. She would be the very person to arrange it.

"Thank you, Father," Nora said gratefully. "I knew that you would be able to help me."

His cherubic face was wreathed in smiles. "I am available at all times, Mrs. Molloy," he replied as she stood next to her chair. "Before you leave, would you have a minute to join me in prayers?"

"By all means, Father," Nora answered, sinking to the prie-dieu and bowing her head.

Yet as they began their prayers, her mind was already on the telephone call she would make the minute she returned home. "Kate, my dear," she imagined herself saying to Mrs. Morrissey, "I wonder if you and Nina might perhaps do me a small favor."

In the darkness, Peggy Sweeney's fingers enclosed Tom's limp penis. She held it gently, the heel of her hand buried in his pubic hair. His head lay against her naked breast and his eyes were closed, but she knew he wasn't sleeping.

As always, they had made love almost as soon as they had walked through the door. They were not in the bed, which remained rumpled and unmade from the night before, but on the living-room carpet. Their clothes

286

were scattered everywhere, and the grocery bag Peggy had been carrying still sat on the sofa.

"Tommy," she whispered at last, "we should fix supper."

Tom sighed. There was time enough for that. It was only a little after eight, and as a rule he did not head back to campus until eleven or so. With his tongue, he slowly licked the side of her breast, tasting the saltiness of her skin.

"That was real good, Tom," she said. "Didn't you think it was good?"

For Tom, there had never been a time when it wasn't good. From the night when they had made love for the very first time—only three hours after they'd met!—it had always been rare and fine.

That evening in May, he'd gone to a concert of the Boston Symphony and was returning to campus on the trolley. When he took his seat, he didn't even notice the pretty girl sitting next to him. He happened to see that she was holding a program that matched his own, and when their eyes met, he asked, "What did you think of the performance?"

It had been the first time Peggy had ever been to a concert, and she had gone by herself. She told him that she had particularly liked *Till*—She looked at her program, but couldn't pronounce it.

"*Eulenspiegel,*" he completed for her. "I'm very fond of Strauss myself. Richard, that is. I don't much care for the fellow who wrote the waltzes."

"Do you mean there was more than one?"

There was, indeed, he replied, then proceeded to explain how Johann was different from Richard.

"Isn't that the funniest thing?" she said. "I had no idea there were two. You know a lot about music. Do you go to Harvard?"

He was a junior, he replied, but he asked her not to hold it against him.

"I know someone who goes to Boston University, but you're about the first Harvard man I've ever met."

He smiled. "There comes a time in every girl's life

when she should meet a Harvard man," he said, then introduced himself.

"Hi! I'm Margaret Sweeney. Except everyone calls me Peggy."

She was a secretary, she told him, and lived alone because she didn't like Worcester, where her mother had moved after the death of her father.

"I like Boston," she said. "I mean, there are things to do here. I like to go to the movies and sometimes to cocktail lounges. This man I used to know, he used to take me. This is the first concert I ever been to. A woman in the office give me her ticket because she was coming down with a cold. Wasn't that nice-a her?"

When she explained that she lived in North Cambridge, well beyond his stop, he proposed that he see her home and perhaps buy her a hot chocolate or something when they got off the trolley. He had nothing else in mind.

When they left the streetcar, all the diners were closed, so Peggy volunteered to make hot chocolate for him at her apartment. On the way, he didn't even hold her hand. The minute they entered her living room, however, she kicked off her high heels, and suddenly she was much shorter and more vulnerable-looking. She turned her face up toward his.

"I been so lonely," she said.

He took her in his arms and kissed her, and right away he knew that it was different from the kisses he'd given to half a hundred other girls. She wouldn't take her lips away from his, and her tongue darted into his mouth. Her hands stroked his body and caressed his buttocks, and soon his hands were doing the same to hers. When he felt his erection grow, he moved away in embarrassment, but she pressed closer. Then before he knew what was happening, her hand was resting on top of it, kneading it.

He was half-crazed.

He tore at her clothes, then at his own, and in seconds they were naked. He fell onto the floor, covering her, and his hand stroked the furry mound between her legs.

"I don't have a rubber or anything," he whispered breathlessly when she eased him into her warm flesh."

"It don't matter. I got a diaphragm on."

Afterward, he realized that she must have been wearing it even while she sat listening to the Boston Symphony, hoping that she might meet someone who would ease her loneliness. But Tom didn't mind. All that mattered was that he was inside her, and it had never happened to him before.

"*Ah!*" he cried as she thrust her hips upward into his. "Tom! Tom! *Tom!*"

Now, months later, they were once again on the floor, once again naked, their supper still sitting in its grocery bag on the sofa. They must have slept momentarily because in the distance Tom heard bells toll the half hour. It was eight-thirty.

"You want a cigarette, Tommy?"

He shook his head, but through habit reached up to the end table next to him until his hand felt a pack of Lucky Strikes. He withdrew one, lit it, then placed it in her mouth.

"I can't stay too late," he began.

"How come?"

The usual reason. He had to study. Already he was falling behind in his schoolwork, and unless things improved dramatically by mid-term exams, he would be receiving C's in at least two courses. The admissions office of the law school wouldn't care for that.

"How long will you be in law school, anyway?" she asked.

"Three years, I guess."

She sucked at her cigarette, then exhaled a cloud of smoke. "What do you mean, you guess?"

"The war and everything, I mean."

She turned on her side, leaning on her elbow, and looked into his face. "Will you have to go if there's a war, Tommy?"

"My father says he thinks he could get me a deferment if they start drafting people."

289

"I couldn't bear it if you went into the army. How can your father get you a deferment?"

Tom couldn't tell her that his father would probably get in touch directly with a friend in Washington. He had contributed generously to President Roosevelt's reelection campaign in 1936 and knew many people in the administration on a first-name basis.

Instead he said, "He would tell the government that he needs me to work for him."

"What does he do?"

Tom searched for the right words. "He's sort of in the construction business."

"You mean he builds houses and things?"

"Something like that."

"Well, I hope you get a deferment. If I was a boy, I'd do anything to stay outa the army. There's this guy at the office, he says he's gonna tell the army he's a queer. I don't blame 'im."

Tom smiled. "I don't think they'd believe me if I tried that."

"I hope there's no draft."

"Me, too."

She punched out her cigarette in an ashtray, then once more encircled his penis with her hand. It throbbed, and suddenly it was huge.

"Oh, dear God!" he heard himself say as she sat on top of him and drew him into her.

He was half-starved. He'd had nothing to eat since lunchtime, and his belly growled for lack of food.

Even as she rose and fell over him, he reminded himself that he would have to grab a sandwich on the way home or else he would wake up at three in the morning with hunger pains.

It was almost ten o'clock by the time they were sated and ready to put their clothes on, and by then it was too late to start supper. Tom helped himself to a handful of graham crackers and stuffed them into his mouth.

"Look," he said while he tied his shoes, "you want to come out to the college tomorrow and meet some of the guys I know?"

Peggy was almost speechless. "You mean you're gonna show me where you live at Harvard and everything?"

That was exactly what he meant. After work, she could take the train as far as Harvard Square and he would meet her there at six o'clock. Maybe a friend of his would have dinner with them. John Phipps, his name was. Afterward, they could walk down to the river and he could show her where he lived.

Peggy said that it would be wonderful. She would wear something very special to the office.

"Don't"—he didn't know how to say it—"get too dressed up, Peg. I mean, just be—the way you always are."

He hurried down the stairs, then raced into the street. Tomorrow would be an ordeal.

The Molloys' town house in New York City was furnished with a mixture of elegance and informality. The elegance derived from costly furniture, paintings, and Oriental carpets, chosen partly by Nora Molloy and partly by handsome young decorators whose taste was impeccable, and the amiable informality came from dogs —the family always had two or three—from a multitude of children whose toy fire engines rode the tops of antique French tables and whose dolls lay buried between the cushions of sofas, and from the constant stream of visitors.

This morning, Nora herself had a caller.

Standing in front of the Molloys' Italianate doorway was a man with a beefy red face, wearing a black suit —shinier at the seat of the pants than elsewhere—and a soiled shirt from which a button had popped. As the maid opened the door, the first thing he asked her was for a drink of water, if it would not be too much trouble, as he had dashed all the way from Grand Central Station in terrible haste and his heart was all aflutter.

"Sit down, Mr. Lunney," Nora said to him when he was shown into the study. "I hadn't expected such a prompt response to my request."

Sinking into a chair, he sighed, "I have not slept in

the last forty-eight hours, Mrs. Molloy, as I was sure you was anxious to have this here info."

"How very kind of you." She knew nothing at all about the man except that he came highly recommended by her chauffeur, who described him as a former member of the Boston Police Department.

"You have been discreet, have you, Mr. Lunney?" she asked.

"I have been the very model of discretion, Mrs. Molloy. I posed as an agent representing a credit-reporting firm, and I must say that I did it very neatly. I let it be known that we was running a simple credit check on Subject Sweeney." He pulled a handerchief from his hip pocket and wiped his brow.

"And what have you learned?"

He slid his spectacles down the bridge of his nose, then looked over them in order to read from a small notebook on his lap. "I have learned the following, ma'am: Subject Sweeney is a female Caucasian, aged eighteen, five foot five, blue eyes, reddish-brown hair, weight approximately one hundred and twenty, and with no distinguishing scars other than a small crescent-shaped one on her left kneecap."

Nora's mouth fell open.

"Subject has lived at her present address for the past two and one-half years and has never been delinquent with her rent, with two exceptions. At Xmas 1936 and again at Xmas 1937, her rent was one month late, due, I am inclined to believe, to her having been carried away by the Xmas spirit and overspending, as we all sometimes do, Mrs. Molloy."

He had pronounced the word *Xmas,* and it wasn't until his third mention of it that Nora was able to fathom its meaning.

"Subject Sweeney maintains a savings account at the First National Bank of Boston, and her balance as of three P.M. October the eighth, 1938, was sixty-one dollars and twenty-five cents. At the same bank, she maintains a checking account, and her balance as of three-oh-five P.M., October the eighth, was thirty-six dollars and fifty-nine cents. She has never been overdrawn."

Mr. Lunney's voice had become raspy. "I wonder, Mrs. Molloy, if I could be so bold as to request another glass of water."

"By all means, Mr. Lunney." She indicated the water pitcher and the glass that the parlormaid had left on the desk, and watched as her visitor filled a glass and gulped it down.

"Thank you, Mrs. Molloy. I was perishing of thirst." He wiped the back of his hand across his mouth. "Now I shall proceed: Subject Sweeney is employed as a clerk-typiest in the annuity premium department of the John Hancock Insurance Company in Boston, and has been with said firm for two years and seven months. She is a sturdy little worker, I have learned, and keeps to herself. Since she was hired, she has been absent from work only three times, which I find most commendable, Mrs. Molloy."

Nora nodded in agreement. "And her personal life, Mr. Lunney?"

He leafed through several pages of his notebook until he found what he needed. "I have interviewed two of Subject Sweeney's neighbors in North Cambridge: one Bridie Fitzgerald, who lives in the apartment below, and one Stanislaus Purcell, who lives next door. Of the two, Bridie Fitzgerald, a charming and vivacious widow" —Lunney stopped in order to savor the memory— "was far more cooperative. I asked her if Subject ever had visitors at her apartment, and I am now prepared to tell you her answer, Mrs. Molloy. I sincerely hope that I will not offend your delicate sensibilities."

"Please go on."

"As you wish, Mrs. Molloy," he replied, tossing his head, then holding up his notebook. "Until late spring, Mrs. Fitzgerald reports that Subject had a gentleman caller whose habit it was to arrive early in the evening and to leave at one or two in the morning. He drove a green Terraplane, Mrs. Fitzgerald observed, and sometimes carried gifts: flowers and candy, I should imagine. On several occasions, while walking her dog at night, Mrs. Fitzgerald was able to see children's toys in the back seat of the parked auto, and she deduced that Subject's visitor was a married man and a father. She described him as being in his mid-thirties, perhaps." He paused. "When I asked the helpful Mrs. Fitzgerald if she thought that they had been— I don't know if I should go on, dear Mrs. Molloy."

"Do."

"—if they had been intimate, Bridie Fitzgerald replied positively. There was no doubt in her mind. She was scandalized, she said, and made several complaints to the landlord about the loose moral character of Subject Sweeney, but to no avail."

"You say that until last spring, the Sweeney girl was seeing a married man? She no longer does, is that it?"

"That is correct, ma'am."

Nora saw that she would have to extract information painfully from Lunney. "And does she now see someone else?"

"Yes, she does, Mrs. Molloy."

Almost bitterly, she asked, "And did Mrs. Fitzgerald give you a description?"

"She did, Mrs. Molloy," he began. "He is a student at Harvard. He often arrives carrying books and wearing an athletic sweater. He is a golden-haired youth, she says, good-looking and well-mannered. His first name is Tom, as she has often heard Subject Sweeney repeat it."

He bit his lip.

"And does Mrs. Fitzgerald have any opinion about the degree of their intimacy?"

"It is very deep, she says. He often spends the weekends there, and two or three nights a week."

Mrs. Fitzgerald was a tiresome fool, Nora told herself, but still it was doubtful that she would lie about such a matter. Yet Nora didn't want to be too hasty in her judgment, merely on the basis of a neighbor's conclusions. There might be far more to Peggy Sweeney than the facts seemed to suggest. After all, had Bridie Fitzgerald been in a position to judge Nora herself before her marriage to Charles Molloy, it's quite possible that Nora, too, would have been called a girl of loose moral character.

Nora was not the least bit proud of herself for having

employed a professional snoop to ferret out information, but she consoled herself that had Tom agreed to introduce the girl to his parents, it wouldn't have been necessary. Why had he chosen not to? That was all Nora wanted to learn. Lunney had revealed that they were sleeping together, but that was no reason to hide the girl. The knowledge that Peggy Sweeney had had a previous affair with a married man was a good deal more unsettling, but Nora would still not condemn the girl now so long as she and Tom loved each other.

Love! Perhaps that was it. Could Tom be sleeping with her—needing her, even being enriched by her—without being one hundred percent sure that he loved her?

Was he ashamed of the girl? Or of himself?

She thanked her informant, reminding him once again that what they had discussed was of the utmost confidentiality.

"Of course, Mrs. Molloy."

"And would you send the bill for your services directly to me at this address, not to my husband's business office?"

"I quite understand, Mrs. Molloy," he replied, still unable to think why a mother of a Harvard student should be concerned about the sowing of a young man's oats.

"The maid will see you out," she said to Lunney as a white-capped girl appeared at the door.

He backed out of the room, tipping his hat.

Peggy was almost twenty minutes late, and John Phipps and Tom stood under an umbrella in pouring rain on Harvard Square as trolley after trolley discharged passengers in the subterranean depths beneath their feet. John confessed without humor that he was wet up to the scrotum.

When at last Peggy walked up the steps to the square, it was obvious that she had been caught in the downpour as she rushed to the trolley in Boston. Her hair, generally in a soft pompadour, was glued to her head, and rain had soaked through the shoulders of her old raincoat onto her light-blue dress. She was nearly in tears.

"Margaret Sweeney," Tom said with desperate cheer, "John Phipps."

Peggy was ill at ease. She might have been meeting the president of Harvard instead of Tom's roommate. "How do you do," she uttered formally and without warmth.

"I've heard a lot about you, Peggy."

It was the wrong thing for Phipps to say because Peggy immediately assumed that Tom had told him about their sex life. As she looked from the one to the other, a pout formed on her face.

"Well, we can't see much until the rain lets up," Tom began, "so why don't we go over to the Georgian Cafeteria for some coffee or something?"

The minute they entered the place, Tom realized that he'd made the wrong decision. The restaurant was crowded and steamy. Peggy was one of two girls in the room, and every eye was on her hips as she made her way to the line.

"It's early, but we might as well have supper," Phipps suggested.

"I'm not very hungry," Peggy replied, "but you two go ahead and get something. I'll just have some pie and some coffee."

"Then that's all I'll have," Phipps said.

"Oh, no, go ahead. Don't mind me. I eat like a bird, anyway."

After they had gone through the serving line, Peggy took off her coat without assistance, though Tom had hurriedly dropped his tray on the table in order to help her. She sat down and pulled her chair to the table while Tom was still fumbling with the back of it. It occurred to him with a start that he had never bothered with such small acts of civility before—after all, they spent most of their time in her apartment—and she didn't know how to react.

Peggy spent ten minutes talking about the insurance business in answer to simple questions about her work. Phipps was asking only because he wanted her to feel comfortable; she didn't need to reply at such tiresome length.

It was all such a bore—Tom had *never* heard her talk about the dreary work she did or the colorless people she worked with—but at the end of her near-monologue, she said, "The insurance business is very fascinating."

"Yes, I'm sure it is," Phipps said, and Tom almost choked.

But if the conversation was awkward, the silence that followed was even worse.

"Shit," Tom said suddenly.

"What did you say?" Phipps asked.

"I said, we sure as hell picked a lousy day to show Peggy around Cambridge." He leaned across the table and covered her free hand with his own. My God, she was shaking, and he hadn't even noticed. She was so damned nervous that she was trembling. "Poor Peg, your pretty dress is all wet."

He had never seen the dress before, and now he was sure that she had bought it just to wear to Cambridge. "It's new, isn't it?"

"It was on sale at Filene's," she answered.

"It becomes you very well," Phipps complimented her.

She brushed one of her shoulders with her napkin. "I hope it don't make a stain, where the rain is, I mean."

Tom watched his roommate lock his lips in a tight and patronizing grin.

While the two boys tried to finish their meal, Peggy asked if there was a ladies' room she could use. As she stood, both Phipps and Tom sprang out of their chairs, and she looked at them as if they were about to accompany her to the rest room.

"We'll wait for you, Peggy," Tom said lamely.

"Okay. Sure. I'll be right back."

After she'd left, Tom didn't dare meet Phipps's eyes. He stared at the messy plate in front of him.

"I don't know why I got chicken croquettes," Phipps said to break the silence. "They always give me a belly-ache. I think what it is is that the machine they use to grind it just isn't kept hygienically clean, and so it's inevitable that—"

"Shit," Tom repeated.

Phipps stopped, then rested his knife and fork across

297

the upper-right-hand corner of his plate. "I'm sorry, Tom," he began. "I know it was important to you for me to like her."

At last, Tom looked up, "And you don't?"

Phipps exhaled, closed his eyes, then reopened them. "There are girls a man sleeps with, Tom, but doesn't consider marrying."

Tom felt as if icy water had been thrown in his face. He could feel his heart pumping blood wildly.

"I'm sorry, Tom. You asked me as a friend, and I'm telling you."

Tom had to fight to control his temper. "And on what do you base your exalted opinion? The fact that her grammar isn't as good as a Radcliffe girl's? That's goddam unfair."

"It isn't that," Phipps answered solemnly. "It's just— well, I guess she's a little cheap."

If his roommate had set out to hurt him, he couldn't have accomplished it more perfectly. Of course there were things about Peggy that needed correcting, but they were small and superficial. She was natural and easygoing. Uncontrived and without airs. Was that cheap? If she'd kept her mouth shut, like the languorous girls in the debutante set, John wouldn't have come to such harsh conclusions.

"You don't understand," he heard himself stammer.

Tom looked up as Peggy made her way through the crowded cafeteria toward them. She had fixed her face and combed her hair and looked pretty once again. He stared hard at her. She looked so defenseless. Was she cheap because she had cut her slice of apple pie into little pieces before eating it? Was she cheap because she stabbed the air with her fork while she was talking?

"You're a snob," he said to his roommate.

"And you're a fool."

The rain hadn't let up, so the minute that Peggy sat down again, Phipps said that they would simply have to consider it a bad show. Perhaps she could come back some other time. He had a lot of studying to do, anyway. As he spoke, there were signs of strain in his voice.

"It was very nice meeting you, John," Peggy said when he stood to leave.

"I'm sure we'll see each other again."

After he had left, Peggy said, "Gee, he was nice. He had class. You could tell right away."

Tom nodded almost sadly. John had class—and Peggy did not, and never would.

"I didn't tell you what happened to my scarf," she began.

If there was a transition, Tom had missed it. He looked up in surprise.

"My scarf," she said. "I got it at Filene's, and it cost two dollars. Well, while I was sitting on the potty, I don't know how, but it must have came—"

"Must have *come*," he said angrily, though he had never corrected her before.

"—must have come off because somehow the end of it fell in the toilet bowl. It was all wet, so I just flushed it. I hope it don't mess up the plumbing or anything."

It was a long time before he could reply, and when he did, it was almost a whisper. "I'm sure it won't, Peggy."

"It was a nice scarf, too."

He heard himself say, "I'll buy you another one."

When they got tired of sitting in the cafeteria, he showed her a bit of the Yard, but it was still pouring and neither enjoyed it. Without thinking, Phipps had taken the umbrella with him, and Peggy was worried about the rain soaking through the shoulders of her raincoat onto her dress. In fact, she was more concerned about that than she was about the glories of Harvard Yard, so after he had shown her Wigglesworth Hall, where he and Phipps had roomed as freshmen, he decided to call it quits.

"I think I'm coming down with the flu or something, anyway," he said as they returned to Massachusetts Avenue. "It's all over campus."

"You seemed sorta funny when we was eating, Tom. I thought maybe something like that was the matter."

In the end, it was decided that Peggy could get home by herself, as any further exposure to the rain would only contribute to Tom's illness.

When the train came roaring to a stop, she brought her face up to be kissed.

"Better not, Peg," he cautioned her. "I'll only give you the bug."

"Poor Tommy," she said.

She waved to him through the steamy windows, and he waved back, watching as she disappeared.

Instead of going directly home to Lowell House, Tom walked the deserted sidewalks of Cambridge in the torrential rain, head bowed, water streaming down his face. Again and again, he went over in his mind what had happened that evening.

It was wrong to have introduced her to his roommate. John had been so self-righteous and unyielding, and Peggy had been so damned oblivious to what was going on. Had he kept her to himself, apart from everyone else, he wouldn't now feel humiliated. Had they stayed at home in the apartment, he wouldn't have had to lie to her and this very minute they would be making love.

For another hour, Tom walked through the downpour. At last, he ventured into a drugstore and made his way to the rear, where the telephone booths were. It was after nine o'clock, and he at first thought that the switchboard he wanted to reach had closed, but his call went through. He stayed in the booth for five minutes or so, then left and turned toward the river.

When he entered their suite of rooms at Lowell House, Phipps was bent over his desk. He looked up, contrite and apologetic.

Tom peeled off his raincoat and removed his wet shoes and socks.

"It's getting cold," Phipps said. "The heat just came on."

Tom stepped out of his soaking corduroys and hung them over a closet door, then wrapped a tartan robe around him that he'd worn since his first year at Portsmouth Priory. In his bare feet, he walked toward the bathroom.

"I just called Nancy Delano and invited her up for the weekend," he said, then hurried toward the shower.

22

Dense patches of fog blew off the Pacific and left Patrick's face damp and salty as he walked along the wharves of the Embarcadero. In the distance mournful foghorns blew and whistles shrieked as freighters and scows felt their way slowly through the gray waters of the bay.

Nearer to him on the piers, yardarms dipped into the holds of ships just in from the Orient or the South Seas, raising cargo and piling it on the wharves. Spices and tea, hardwoods and copra, silks and coconuts. Dimestore china, cheap cotton goods, handpainted vases. No sooner had the huge boxes come to rest than stevedores struggled with them, loading them onto trucks. As they worked, they screamed friendly obscenities at one another to help pass the time of day. Even on this cool San Francisco morning, sweat drenched their faces, and the armpits of their blue workshirts were stained a deeper hue from the travail of lifting.

Yet when they saw Pat Cassidy, they called, "Hiya, Pat! Howya doin'!" faces enveloped in smiles.

Or "Hey, Paddy! What's new? You gettin' much? Don't give me no bushwa."

He liked to see them work. More times than he cared to recall, he had seen them hungry and dispirited, begging for jobs that didn't exist. The world was a different place if you had a job. As Pat often said, all it took was a few square meals and every damned anarchist in America would become an honest, law-abiding citizen.

Every morning, he made a quick tour of the wharves to watch his men unloading the huge freighters and also to collect complaints, inquire about the health of the ail-

301

ing, congratulate on the birth of children, or commiserate on the death of elderly parents. In short, to remind his men that he was their friend and concerned about their welfare. In return, he knew that they would stick with him through hell and high water. If he gave them work and a fair shake from the shipowners, they would give him steadfast allegiance.

But on this foggy morning in October, that allegiance was about to be tested.

Pat turned suddenly when he heard running footsteps behind him. It was one of the men he shared an office with.

"It's a telephone call, Pat," the young man said. "She said it's important."

"She? Do you mean Eva?"

His voice was reverential. "It's Joan Magnuson. You know who I mean?"

Pat did indeed. On his way back to the hiring hall, he tried to imagine why the hell she should be calling him.

In his office, he picked up the telephone and said, "Good morning, Miss Magnuson. What can I do for you?"

There was a slight pause before she spoke. Her voice was strained. "I've just heard some news that concerns you, and I thought you'd better know about it."

"News?"

Almost urgently, she asked, "Do you know someone named Craig Lee?"

"I don't think so. I meet a lot of people in the line of work I do, but that name doesn't ring a bell. I could check the office files if you like."

"He says he knows you."

Pat searched his memory. Craig Lee. A union member? A shipowner? A lawyer? Maybe someone in the neighborhood?

He worried his forehead. "I'm almost positive I don't know the fellow, but there's always an outside chance that I do." He waited. "Why? Is it important?"

"It's very, very important. Could I see you for a few minutes privately? I don't like to talk over the telephone."

Pat tried to think of the obligations he had during the day. He wasn't sure that he could take the time off to go all the way down to Carmel. He told her so.

"I'm here in the city," she declared. "On Russian Hill." She gave him an address on Chestnut Street. "You can come over here if you like. It will be easier to talk."

"Okay, I can do that. I just wish like hell I knew what's going on."

"On the way, try to remember if you know Craig Lee."

"Is he Chinese?" The surname was a very common one among Orientals on the West Coast.

"No, he is most certainly not Chinese. He lives in Beverly Hills—or maybe Brentwood—and that's where I met him. He's a movie producer."

"I sure as hell would have remembered it if I'd met a Hollywood producer. He must be thinking of someone else."

"I hope you're right."

There was the same chill to her voice. "Why is it so important to me, anyway, Miss Magnuson?"

"It's important," she began, "because Craig Lee is about to ruin your career. And if you're really unlucky, he might even get you deported."

What she'd said was too horrendous to comprehend.

"You'd better come right over," she urged. "I'll be waiting for you."

Russian Hill was dazzling in the sunlight, like a storied celestial city; below it, the bay and most of San Francisco were still buried in banks of fog. On the steep incline where the house sat, Pat turned the wheels of his car into the curb, then switched off the headlights and made his way toward the door.

It was a tall Victorian house with ornate cornices at its roof and gingerbread around its wide windows. A soft Mediterranean pink covered it, and red geraniums grew in wrought-iron containers on either side of the gleaming black door. There was a single bell, which indicated that it was a private house, but in the mailbox were yellowing papers and circulars, which suggested that the place was not presently in use.

In seconds, Joan Magnuson answered the bell. "Come on in, Patrick," she said. "I hope I haven't alarmed you too much."

"Let's just say that you've alarmed hell out of me, but I managed to get over here without running over anyone in the streets. What's it all about?"

"We can use the living room." She led him into a Victorian parlor of considerable charm, except that all the furniture had been covered with sheets. She removed one from a sofa, then sat at one end of it. "The house is for sale. I never use the damn thing, so I thought I might as well get rid of it. I bought it right after my last divorce, thinking that it would be a good idea to move to San Francisco and change my life." She smiled weakly. "So much for good ideas that fail."

He sat on a sheet-covered chair across from her. "You didn't call me up here to tell me that."

"No, I didn't. But what I'm about to tell you won't make any sense unless I furnish you with some background. Can I get you some coffee or something? I don't have any hard liquor around the house, or I'd offer you some. If I had it, I'd probably drink it." She held up both her hands and crossed her fingers. "I've been on the wagon now for almost a year. It's a great temptation to slide off."

"It's good to learn that people other than the Irish can't hold their booze."

"I hate to disappoint you, but I started out life as a Gillen. The name was changed when everything else was changed. My mother was French, though, so they should get part of the blame." She waited, then continued, "You said you don't think you've ever met anyone named Craig Lee?"

"I'm ninety-nine percent sure I haven't."

"All right. Have you ever heard of Oliver Struthers?"

"Who hasn't? He has something to do with the movies."

"Had," she said by way of correction. "He was killed in an automobile accident on Malibu Canyon Road about a year ago." She fumbled for a cigarette and lit it herself before Pat could rise to do it for her. "He was drunk. He also happens to have been my ex-husband."

"I'm sorry. I think now I remember something about that." It had been a grisly accident. Struthers's car had gone off the twisting canyon road and had burst into flame. He'd been incinerated.

"I married him in 1931, and it lasted for five years. They say that when people get married, they should have something in common, and what Oliver and I had in common was that we both liked to get drunk. That and—well, something else. Are you getting bored yet?"

Impatient, maybe, but not bored.

"When he wasn't drunk, he was a very smart man. I'm rather dumb myself. I mean, it was hard work for me to get through high school. Oliver had been to Yale Law before he decided that the law wasn't creative enough for him, so he came out here and began to direct. He'd known some of the liberal crowd in New Haven and New York, and a few of them wound up here on the Coast, too. He used to hang around with them. To make a long story short, he became a member of the Communist party sometime in the spring of 1930."

Pat was beginning to get the drift of it. He sat straight in his chair.

"A lot of people in Hollywood were party members back then, or they traveled with them. It was never done too openly, but it wasn't carried on with any great secrecy, either. I used to go along for the ride. Sometimes Oliver and I would go to bashes in Beverly Hills—I mean bashes with dancing and drinking—and a few nights later, we'd go to another bash, and a lot of the same people would be there. Except that they wouldn't be drinking so much and they never danced. It was Hollywood's idea of a Communist cell. We'd all sit around the swimming pool and worry about fascism. That's where I met Craig Lee."

Craig Lee. Every time she said the name, it sounded more and more familiar. He had a vague recollection of having seen "A Craig Lee Production" or "Produced by Craig Lee" either on the screen or in newspaper ads.

305

"What does he look like?" Pat asked.

She managed a small smile. "The last time I saw him, which was—let me see—probably at my husband's funeral, he had dark hair, a Beverly Hills suntan, a good-looking face, weighed maybe a hundred and eighty pounds, and was under six feet. I'll try to find a photograph when I get back to the house at Carmel."

"So you're saying that Craig Lee is also a Communist, is that it?"

"I assumed he was. Oliver never introduced his friends that way. But Craig Lee used to show up at both kinds of parties—the big ones with the booze, and the quiet ones around the swimming pools. All I know about him now is that he's an ex-Communist. He dropped out of the party during the great purges."

Patrick stood up and walked to the window. The fog had lifted from the bay, and he could see all the way to the hills of Marin County.

"I can almost feel it coming," he said aloud.

She nodded her head. "I don't see many of those people anymore. As I told you, I live in Carmel. I seldom even get down to Los Angeles, but from time to time, some of the old crowd drops by. A woman named Lily Carson did just yesterday. She used to be a girl friend of Craig Lee and also used to turn up sometimes at the swimming pool parties. She told me that Craig has been invited to Washington to appear before the Dies Committee."

Pat's eyes could no longer concentrate on the view. He turned to face her. "Martin Dies of Texas?" he asked. "The guy who's chairman of the House Un-American Activities Committee?"

"That's the man," Joan Magnuson replied. She stood up in order to meet his face. "And Craig Lee is going to testify that you are a Communist."

Pat felt himself sinking. Why was the man doing it? There had to be a reason. "Tell me more about him. Is he on the skids and hard up for money?"

She shook her head. "Lily Carson says he made a hundred and fifty thousand dollars last year."

Yet the man was a Communist. Or a former Com-

306

munist. It didn't make sense. All his life, Pat had fought for the working class, and had just barely made ends meet, but now he learned that a man who earned a hundred and fifty thousand dollars a year had been plotting a working-class revolution.

"He has a huge house," Joan Magnuson continued. "One of those places with about forty rooms and a staff of ten to look after it. He lives very well."

Yet he was going to try to wreck Pat's career and make it impossible for him even to pay his thirty-five-dollar-a-month rent.

If it were only his livelihood that was involved, Pat could probably weather the storm. But there was something far more threatening than that.

"You said something over the phone about"—he hated even to repeat the word—"deportation."

"Lily Carson was the one who mentioned it. I don't know where she got her information. I wasn't aware that you could deport citizens."

So that was it. It was more than Craig Lee—whoever he was—after all. Someone wanted him out of the longshoreman's union, and the way it was going to be done was by removing him from the country. A quick hearing, then a one-way ticket back to Ireland.

"I'm not a citizen," Pat replied with surprising composure. "I'm still an alien. I took out first papers for citizenship, but then I kept putting it off. I didn't think there was any reason to hurry."

When he married Eva, she was also an alien, having been born in Berlin and not brought to America until she was almost thirteen. She became an American citizen shortly after Mimi's birth, and Pat went to City Hall on Van Ness Avenue to witness the ceremony. But he himself held back. Perhaps he still had a peasant's suspicion of flags and banners. Perhaps he was too busy. What difference did a piece of paper make, anyway? Still, he promised Eva that he would attend to it as soon as he had time; yet he never did.

"You *are* in trouble."

"I guess I am."

"What could Craig Lee have against you?"

307

That was the most astonishing part of it. Was it possible that someone had discovered that he had left Ireland a wanted man and a member of the Irish Volunteers? Jesus Christ, that had happened in 1916 when Pat was just seventeen years old. Assuming that a twenty-two-year-old charge still existed on the books in some English court of law, what could it be? Insurrection against the Crown?

Was *that* grounds for deportation from the United States as an undesirable alien? Was insurrection against a foreign monarch considered a Communistic act? Or was Pat going to be charged because he tolerated Reds in the union? He had never attempted to weed them out because they weren't dangerous. In some cases, they acted as consciences for the other members. It was, after all, the Reds who complained about the shipment of scrap iron to Japan and arms to Italy.

"I don't understand any of this," he said at last.

"*Are* you a member of the party?"

"I'm a member of the human race—sometimes reluctantly—but that's about all. What else am I a member of? The Catholic Charities of San Francisco. Christ Almighty, they don't deport people for that, do they? The only Marx I know anything about is Groucho. I've always intended to read Karl Marx, just as I've always wanted to read *War and Peace,* but I've never got around to them."

"So if they ask you, all you have to do is tell them that."

There was a rage in his voice now. "If they ask me, I'll tell them to go to hell, is what I'll do!"

He had shouted the words at her. "I'm sorry," he said when he collected himself. "I don't know why I'm yelling at you. It's not your fault."

"I could try to help you."

"How?"

She outlined her plan. If he liked, she could drive him down to Los Angeles and there try to arrange a meeting between him and Craig Lee. At least he would know who his accuser was. It would have to be a spontaneous meeting, she said; otherwise, Lee would probably try to bolt. She wouldn't tell anyone that they were coming, not even Lily Carson. "If we leave by noon, we can be there by suppertime."

It seemed to Pat to be a sensible thing to do. If only he could have a look at Craig Lee, perhaps he would be able to understand what the man's motives were.

"Okay," he replied, "I have to go home for a few minutes. Then drop by the hiring hall. Could you meet me there?"

That would be fine. She could be there by eleven-thirty.

"I'm glad you warned me," he said. "A lot of people wouldn't have wanted to get involved in this kind of mess."

"It's partly selfish, partly political. Bob Conroy needs the support of your union, and if someone starts screaming that you're a Red, it'll cost him plenty."

"You said selfish."

She smiled wearily. "It gives me something to do so that I won't get into the booze. Because if I get into the booze, afterward I'll hate myself."

He touched her hand encouragingly. "Okay. I'll see you at eleven-thirty."

While he collected a clean shirt and a change of socks and underwear, he told Eva that he had union business in Los Angeles and would be gone overnight. Until he learned more about what was happening, he didn't want to burden her with what he'd learned from Joan Magnuson.

He was similarly circumspect at the union office. It was necessary for him to go to Los Angeles for personal reasons, he told his staff. He asked them to search the union files while he was gone to see if they could come up with any reference to a Craig Lee.

"Also get me Robert Conroy on the phone. His number in Sacramento is somewhere around here."

He wanted to confirm Craig Lee's appointment in Washington with Representative Martin Dies of Texas, and the only politician he knew well enough to ask was Senator Conroy.

"Conroy's not in Sacramento," Pat's assistant said in a minute, holding his hand over the phone. "His secretary says that he's out of town."

"Then leave a message. Ask him to call me sometime after noon tomorrow. Tell him that it's important."

"Will do, Paddy. Have a nice trip down to sunny L.A.

"I have a feeling I'm going to have a terrible trip."

"Who knows? Maybe they'll make a star out of you."

At the door, Pat said, "That's exactly what I'm afraid of."

It was nearly dusk when Pat steered Joan Magnuson's white Buick convertible off the Coast Highway onto Sunset Boulevard.

For the past half hour, she'd been sleeping. Every now and then, he took his eyes off the road long enough to look at her. Except for her suntan, she was all white: white slacks, white blouse, white cashmere sweater, white scarf over her head to keep her hair from flying, and white pearls around her neck. Only the sunglasses that covered her eyes were dark.

"We're almost there," he said to waken her. "You'll have to direct me."

She stirred in the seat and looked around. The road rose steeply from the water's edge, and on either side of it, beneath towering palms, were white palaces with red-tiled roofs. As they climbed, from time to time the road curved and they had a sweeping view of the coastline—blue sea, white-capped waves, sand, and green hills rising into the cloudless Southern California sky—and Pat had the distinct impression that he had seen it often in films.

"Nice," he said, not without truth.

"Hideous," Joan Magnuson replied.

"You have a funny way of looking at things."

"You would, too, if you'd lived here as long as I did. It looked nice to me, too, the first time I saw it. But it got ugly."

"*It* got ugly?"

She closed her eyes beneath her huge sunglasses. "Okay. I suppose I mean that my life got ugly."

"How did it happen?"

She leaned over to pound her just-lit cigarette into the ashtray. "I've been married four times, which may have contributed to it. First to a stunt man, then to an actor, then to a faggot, then to a director. The only one who didn't leave scars—literally; the others liked to knock me around—was the faggot." She reached for a fresh cigarette. "I've had three abortions and so many I-guess-you-would-call-them affairs, I couldn't count them if my life depended on it. After fifteen years of that, the flesh becomes tough and the mind becomes hardened. And Los Angeles, where it all happened, becomes hideous."

"No one made you get married four times."

"No one made me?" she repeated. "I wouldn't be so sure of that. I never knew who my father was. When I was nine years old, my mother abandoned me on a road in Indiana and drove off with a new boyfriend. I spent the next eight years of my life in institutions for unwanted children. Or in foster homes, which amounted to the same thing. I was seduced for the first time when I was eleven by a foster father; then his wife found out, and I was sent back to the home. In a while, I got a new set of foster parents and went to live with them. That time, my foster father didn't screw me, but the man next door did. So after another few months, I was shipped back to the home. That was the pattern." She took off her glasses to look at him, and her eyes were cold and lusterless. "No one made me get married four times? Hell, it's a wonder I wasn't married fourteen times." She reestablished the sunglasses on the bridge of her nose. "I always get the shakes when I'm in L.A. Promise me you won't let me drink tonight, because I'll die if I go off the wagon."

He promised to look after her. Where, exactly, were they headed?

"To Lily Carson's house. She's the screenwriter I was telling you about. One of Craig Lee's old girl friends. In L.A., if you have money and drive a nice car, you're

311

bound to have a lot of girl friends. If you like girls, that is. If you don't, you have a lot of boyfriends." She lit her twenty-second cigarette from the orange glow of the twenty-first. "He's married now, so maybe he's cut down on the girl friends, or maybe the old male member is wearing out." She pointed her cigarette toward the pavement in front of them. "It's one of these streets up there. I can never remember which."

"For someone who lived here for fifteen years, you don't know your way around very well."

"I told you, I was drunk most of the time. There it is now. Laurel Canyon. I hope Lily's home. You probably won't like her."

"Doesn't anyone in Hollywood like anyone else?"

"For a while, maybe, but it doesn't last."

The narrow road wound up a high hill, passing huge houses set in tropical splendor. Pat recognized eucalyptus trees, cypresses, pines, and pepper trees, and the air was heady with the scent of camellias.

"Does Lily Carson drink a lot?" he asked.

"Like a fish. Oliver always used to say that there was a great correlation between being a drunk and being a Red in Hollywood. A lot of the drunks became Communists in 1930 and 1931, I guess because they figured it was more exalting than joining the local Alcoholics Anonymous. There it is," she exclaimed as an ivied wall came into view. "Stop by the gate and I'll get out and open it. I know where the thingamajig is."

He pulled the car in front of a huge wrought-iron gate and watched as Joan left the car and fumbled in the ivy for the controls. In a minute, there was a humming noise, and the gates slowly parted. At the end of a driveway, behind a splashing fountain, was a white plazzo.

"Fantastic," he said.

"This is nothing. Wait till you see where Craig Lee lives."

"I don't mean the house."

What did he mean? It was the contradiction, he supposed. In these sumptuous houses were people who whispered the names Stalin or Trotsky as if they were their best friends. At cocktail parties, they talked about revolution, and on the following morning, they had breakfast in bed. While they plotted the overthrow of the government, hired gardeners mowed their lawns and watered their shrubs.

"If a revolution ever succeeded," he began, "I just wonder what in hell someone like Lily Carson would do in a Communistic state."

Joan's lips formed a tight smile. "She would want to be *queen.*"

There were lights on in the first story of the house, Scarlatti was being played on a phonograph somewhere in the distance, and a dog was barking thunderously on the other side of the door as Patrick knocked on it, but no one answered.

"Keep trying," Joan advised. "She's around somewhere." She cupped her hands on either side of her mouth. "Lily! Open the door. It's Joani."

In a minute, they heard the latch being moved, and the door began to open. Suddenly, what appeared to be a huge white pony bounded past them, almost knocking them over, and disappeared in the foliage.

"Now I'll never get the bastard back," Lily Carson said. In one hand, she held an old-fashioned glass and in the other, a cigarette in a long black holder. There were rings on all her fingers.

"What was it, anyway, darling?"

"A dog. I forget what you call them. Wolfhound. Never get one. He does that all the time. Now I'll never get the bastard back."

She directed her remarks exclusively to Joan, as if Patrick weren't there. Her face was mannish: square-jawed, bushy-eyebrowed, and thick-nosed. Her eyes were small and glacial. She was in her bare feet, but wearing an expensive dress wih a gem-studded pin on her bodice—the sort that's kept in hotel safes while traveling.

"You didn't say you were coming down here."

"We didn't know we were coming until almost noon." She touched Pat's arm. "This is Patrick Cassidy."

At last the woman's eyes took him in. Whether she was pleased or displeased was difficult to say. Her expression was as hard and stony as it had been when she'd opened the door.

"Come on in," she said to them, then opened the door all the way. "The house is a mess." She ushered them into a living room. "To be more precise, I didn't let the maid in this morning. I had a late night and wasn't up to listening to her push a goddam Hoover around. Sit down."

She remained standing while Joan and Pat occupied chairs. "You're not drinking, Joani," she said, "but can I fix *you* a drink?" she asked Patrick, omitting his name, although she had just been told it.

He explained that he wasn't drinking, either.

"Then I'll have to drink by myself, won't I?" She walked to a sideboard and poured a healthy dollop of bourbon into her glass.

On the table next to him, Pat saw two photographs, one of Lily Carson taken when she was younger, and one of Rex Hammil, who was, Joan had explained, also a writer, also a rummy, also a Red, and Lily Carson's lover of many years.

"I've told Joan everything I know, Mr. Cassidy," the woman said as she returned to where they sat. "I assume that you're here to talk about Craig Lee and not about moviemaking."

She assumed correctly. "Who told you that he intends to introduce my name at the Dies hearings?"

She looked into the air thoughtfully. "I think it was probably Rex. He's much more social than I am, drunk or sober, and he travels around a great deal from house to house. Someone no doubt mentioned it to him."

"How well do you know Craig Lee?"

She shrugged her formidable shoulders. "We used to go to the same fêtes. I worked on a film of his about four years ago, and though as a rule I'm not on speaking terms with producers, he and I always used to chat when we saw each other."

"I understand that he's no longer a member of the party."

Her eyes became slits. "Party, Mr. Cassidy?"

"The Communist party?"

"I wouldn't have the foggiest idea. I never talked about that with him."

"Okay," Pat replied, "it doesn't matter. What's bothering me is that someone I don't know is about to make an accusation against me, and I'm trying to determine why. What do you know about him?"

She watched his discomfort from over the rim of her glass, then sipped. "Let me see," she began. "I'm trying to think where I first ran into him, and what year it was." She waited. "Now I remember. I'd done a play on Broadway that was moderately successful in—oh, it must have been 1932, and Craig Lee almost optioned it. He wasn't yet the success that he is today. I had the feeling that he had trouble rounding up the money for the option, and in the meantime, someone else bought it. But he was a very —how to put it?—engaging fellow. He wanted desperately to get ahead."

"Was that in New York?"

"No, that was out here. I've always divided my time between Broadway and Hollywood."

"Patrick wants to have a look at him," Joan said. "Do you know where we can find him?"

"What for? How is that going to help?"

"If he's going to accuse me of being a Communist, I want to know what he looks like."

"You're sure you've never met him?"

"Not by that name, anyway."

With excitement, Joan said, "It's possible he's changed it. A lot of people do in Hollywood."

Of course. Pat hadn't even considered it. That was the answer.

"Then it's more important than ever for me to see what he looks like. Could you help?"

Lily appeared to weigh the advantages and disadvantages. She ran her fingertips over the rings on one hand, then said, "I could try. It might be interesting. I've always liked dramatic confrontations."

The Craig Lees were giving a party that night at their house in Brentwood, Lily informed them after having spent fifteen minutes on the telephone in her bedroom, and they could crash it without much difficulty.

They complained that they were not dressed for it, but Lily thought that what they were wearing would do fine. "Only the untalented and unsuccessful get dressed up," she said, but to be on the safe side, she offered Joan the use of a silver fox coat. It was just the right touch of glamour to add to her afternoon costume.

The screenwriter had a five-year-old Rolls-Royce, which she suggested they use, as it would be easier to get through Craig Lee's gates. "I feel more secure in the Rolls, anyway. I always feel beautiful when I'm behind the wheel."

Once again, Pat was dumbfounded. In the event of a revolution, what would become of all the Rolls-Royces? More important, what would become of the women who drove them? Was Lily Carson aware that in the Soviet Union, women were sent out in snowstorms with brooms in their hands to sweep up snow in the streets?

Softly, he began to laugh.

"What's wrong?" Joan asked, sitting next to him in the back seat.

"Nothing," he replied. "I guess it's just that everything seems so unreal."

As Lily drove the huge car down Sunset Boulevard, she said, "Apparently this is your first exposure to Hollywood, darling. Welcome to the Capital of the Unreal."

Two armed deputies stood at either side of the gate as Lily drew the Rolls to a stop.

"Could we have your invitations, please?" one of them asked.

"Darling, we never keep such things. You can phone the house if you like to tell them that Joan Magnuson and Lily Carson are here."

The policemen looked through the window and recognized the actress. "Good evening, Miss Magnuson. I'm sorry we've detained you." He stood back and waved them through.

Ahead of them was a huge Renaissance palace, floodlit from one end to the other, and through the opened windows came the sound of an orchestra. As Lily stopped the car in front of the colonnaded entrance, a moonlighting deputy sheriff prepared to enter it and park it for them.

"I think it used to belong to one of the Loews," Lily declared as they entered the two-story-high reception hall, crowded with guests.

Pat's eyes scanned the room, looking for his accuser. He saw actors and actresses, celebrities known all over the world, but the face he was looking for—the one that would engender instant understanding—was nowhere to be found.

"Is he here?" he asked Lily Carson urgently.

"I can't see him, but there's Belle, his wife. Come on. I'll introduce you."

Pat looked to the end of the room, where a woman stood chatting with guests as they passed onto the terrace where the band was playing. She was dark-haired and statuesque. Her eyes were violet-colored, and unlike most of the younger women in the room, her skin was not suntanned but creamy white. Her shoulders were bare, the better to display a stunning necklace, and she was talking with animation to one young man as a second one reached for her hand and kissed it.

"Do you recognize her?" Joan asked.

Pat didn't think so. Yet there was something about her that triggered a recollection of some sort. What was it?

"Belle darling," Lily was saying, "we were so bored, we decided to crash your little fête."

"But how delightful, Lily. And Joan! What a wonderful surprise. Craig told me that you've become a hermit."

"Every now and then I crawl out of my cave in Carmel and come down to see how lucky I am not to be living here anymore."

"Oh, darling," Craig Lee's wife cried, "you've become jaded."

Quickly, before others distracted her attention, Lily Carson said to her, "This is Patrick Cassidy."

If nothing else, she knew his name. Patrick saw instant recognition in her eyes. As suddenly as it appeared, it disappeared.

"How do you do," she said tonelessly.

"Do I know you from somewhere?" he asked.

317

"I can't imagine where," she answered tartly, "but any friend of Lily's is a friend of mine."

Quickly, Joan interrupted, "I haven't seen Craig anywhere."

"Oh, he's around somewhere. Now if you darlings will excuse me, I'll have to play the perfect hostess. Enjoy yourselves."

In another minute, she was being effusive to a group of new arrivals, and Pat and his two guides withdrew to the terrace. At one end was the bar and at the other the orchestra. Between them people were dancing. Tables had been placed on the lawn, and those who had partaken of the buffet sat at them while they ate. Others stood in small clusters, drinks in hand, talking.

Lily stopped in front of a willowy girl and her escort and asked, "Have you seen Craig, darling?"

"Oh, hello, Lily! He went flying by just a minute ago, in too much of a hurry even to be civil. He was going toward the garage."

"I think he's seen me," Pat said, then broke away from the women and began to run across the lawn toward the garage. It was a long, low structure, large enough to accommodate seven or eight automobiles, and the cobblestone pavement in front of it was crowded with guests' cars, while others had spilled over onto the grass.

As Patrick reached the pavement, a deputy drove a black open-topped Mercedes onto the lawn, directed by a young man in a tuxedo. He heard a roaring noise behind him, and a large car shot off in the other direction.

"I'm looking for Craig Lee," he shouted at the youth. "Has he been back here?"

The boy looked up. "That was Mr. Lee in the Hispano-Suizo."

Pat turned to see the taillights of the huge car disappear down the long drive toward the gate, then vanish in the darkness.

It was almost noon by the time he slid into his old Ford, parked in front of the hiring hall on the Embarcadero, and began to drive home. He was tired and defeated.

He had slept on and off during the night, or what was left of it by the time he had deposited Joan at her place in Carmel. He hadn't been able to rescue her at the party until she had got into the liquor, and by then she was in bad shape. She had cried most of the way north.

And when he attempted to leave her at three-thirty in the morning, she said she would die if she had to stay alone, so he sat next to her on the double chaise near the cliff behind her house and watched the sky lighten over the Pacific. Every now and then she whimpered in her sleep.

Craig Lee was just a pawn, Patrick was sure. For a reason he was unable to divine, Lee was being used by the shipowners to discredit him as a union leader. Their object was to bring deportation proceedings against him, and Lee was cooperating.

Would the congressmen on the Dies Committee require proof of Lee's accusations? Or would all the damage be done even before Patrick could testify on his own behalf? Most worrisome, how would the Department of Immigration and Naturalization react to the proceedings?

Patrick had been in nasty scrapes before, and had always survived through his wits, but this time he was convinced that only the system itself could save him.

When he drew up in front of his rented house, he knew at once that the trouble had begun. A car was parked at the curb, and in it sat a man in a gray fedora. Even before Pat had tured off the ignition, Eva was running down the sidewalk toward him.

"He's been here all morning," she cried. "He says he has to see you personally."

Emotionlessly, Pat replied, "I expect he does," then stepped from the car.

The man was waiting for him on the sidewalk. "Mr. Patrick Cassidy?" he asked, then watched as Pat nodded his head. "I am empowered to deliver a subpoena to you, sir, commanding you to appear before the House Un-American Activities Committee in Washington, D.C., the eighth day of December, 1938."

Patrick accepted it. "A pleasure," he replied.

23

Charles Molloy was a good deal more apprehensive riding with the Millrock Hunt than his wife was. As he explained it, Nora's figure had not been quite so ravaged by motherhood as his had by fatherhood, and because he had put on weight since his marriage, he always felt a certain resistance on the part of horses the minute he straddled them.

Nora, however, was insistent that they accept Nina Boyle's invitation to the hunt, which would be meeting at her house near Millbrook. Kate Morrissey had engineered the entire thing most diplomatically, suggesting to her daughter that she pass off the Molloys as prospective property owners in the area who wanted to meet some of the neighbors.

"And are we interested in buying a place up there?" Charles Molloy asked after he had gone to the trouble of having himself expensively outfitted in a new scarlet coat and jodphurs.

"Heavens, no," Nora replied, "but I want the Delanos to get to know us, and I couldn't think of any other way."

"You think it's that important, do you?"

"For Tom's sake, I do."

The Boyles had asked them to spend the night before the hunt at their house, so that they wouldn't have to dash up from the city early in the morning, but Charles would not hear of sleeping anywhere but in his own bed. If he had to discommode himself by spending the day on the back of a reluctant horse, the least Nora could allow him was a decent rest the night before. They could rise early and drive the Duesenberg up to Dutchess County.

"I don't think it will be acceptable," Nora said. "The Duesenberg, I mean."

"Why ever not?"

"Some people might find it flashy, Charles." In point of fact, the car was one of the last produced, and the Molloys or their chauffeur never drove it faster than twenty-five miles an hour. "I think the Chrysler would attract much less attention."

The Chrysler had been custom-made for them, partly because Charles was a friend of Walter Chrysler and had many business dealings with him. It was navy blue, very handsome, but not ostentatious.

"You're going to a lot of trouble to please those damned Delanos," he said. "I'll have you know that Benjamin Delano probably doesn't have half the money that I do."

"Charles," she began patiently, "that is exactly what you cannot make them feel. It's bad enough that we're Irish, but they'll resent us terribly if they discover that they're poorer than we are."

As always, he deferred to his wife's judgment on such matters. He merely hoped that it was their good breeding that was about to be tested, not his riding ability. As for Nora, he knew that she would cut a splendid figure on horseback. Until Southampton had become overpopulated, she kept a jumper there and would sometimes ride it up and down the beach without a saddle, hurdling over fences and boulders.

"And how do you want me to act in front of those damned Delanos?" he asked the night before the hunt.

"I wish you would stop calling them 'those damned Delanos,' Charles. They are related to two Presidents. As for how you should act, I don't want you to attract any attention at all. We simply want them to know that our name is Molloy and that we're friends of the Boyles."

"We're not friends of the Boyles. We would never have got an invitation if it weren't for that old harridan you know, that Morrissey woman."

"Kate Morrissey is a Dame of Malta."

"Is that better or worse than being related to two Presidents?"

"You're incorrigible, Charles."

"I just don't know why we have to be nice to those damned Delanos." He stopped. "I'm sorry, the *Delanos*."

But, of course, he did know. Nora was not seeking the Delanos' friendship so much as she was trying to prevent their possible enmity.

"One telegram from a girl, and you're already thinking about a wedding," he complained.

"They do not marry Catholics, Charles, not even French Catholics, who are thought to be several cuts above Irish Catholics. If Tom and Nancy should decide that they like each other, I don't want the Delanos to dismiss Tom just because they think we are a pack of savages."

"Then why are we dismissing the Sweeney girl?"

Charles had been furious when he learned that Nora had employed a private detective to snoop, but when he was told the results, he shared some of her apprehensions.

"We are not, Charles. That is not the issue. The issue is that Tom doesn't want us to meet the Sweeney girl, and I think he's trying to tell us something."

Nora and her womanly intuition! Yet it seldom failed her.

"I think he's trying to tell us," she continued, "that he *knows* it's wrong, but doesn't know how to stop it."

"So we shall do it for him," Charles said gruffly.

"No, we shall not. The decision has to be his own. We shall simply make it easier for him."

Charles would go along with that. Like Nora, he believed that Tom had a great future in law or politics, and on the basis of the description that the detective had provided them, the Sweeney girl seemed as if she might be a liability. Charles feared what his wife also feared: that Tom might throw away his career for the girl, not for love but for sexuality. A young man could easily become ensnared.

So Charles had agreed to the Millbrook trip, as much as he detested spending part of a day on horseback. If nothing else, Nancy Delano might distract Tom long enough for him to understand who he was and what he wanted to do with his life.

It was a crisp, bracing fall day when Nora and Charles Molloy drove up the long drive to the many-chimnied house and parked their car next to others on the white gravel. From a distance came the frenzied baying of hounds being assembled behind the barns.

A stand-up breakfast was being served inside the house. Men and women in riding habits stood before sunny bay windows and ate scrambled eggs and sausages, chatting among themselves as they did. They were all old friends, sharing a passion for horses, and they were relaxed and comfortable with one another.

"Nora!" Nina Morrissey Boyle exclaimed as she spied Nora and Charles Molloy enter the large living room. "I am so glad to see you. However did you get Charles away from his desk?"

"I'm not sure I did. He carries all his business affairs around in his head twenty-four hours a day," Nora replied, kissing the younger woman on the cheek.

"And how are the children?"

"I would have to give you an alphabetical account of them, one by one. Suffice it to say that they are all growing up, but in different ways. No two are alike."

Nora was embarrassed to ask Nina Boyle about her own children. She had been married for almost ten years now and should have had a new baby every year and a half, but hadn't. Kate Morrissey had even prayed for her daughter at Lourdes, but the fact of the matter was that the Boyles had no intention of having more than two children.

Nina and Andrew Boyle represented a new generation that was clever, good-looking, and innovative. Their crucifixes, if they had any at all, were installed not in the living room but in a dark corner of a bedroom. They had never journeyed to Ireland, and frankly lacked the desire. Their friends were all members of the smart set who wintered with them at Palm Beach, summered with them at Bar Harbor or Murray Bay, and autumned, so to speak, with them at Millbrook.

While their wealthy parents had chosen as country houses huge piles of stone or brick done in Gothic or Tudor style, they lived in a large Early American house of white clapboard and green shutters. Inside, it was easy and informal, furnished in chintz-covered chairs and sofas, and light and airy, as the Boyles themselves were. There were always one or two dogs, setters or pointers, lying in front of a blazing fire, and horses were often tethered next to the front door.

Charles Molloy was already deep in conversation with Andrew, whom he knew from the Street. Nora bent over to Nina and whispered, "I think that your mother may have mentioned the little favor we're asking your mother to perform for us. I hope we're not being a nuisance."

"Not at all. We're not really that close to the Delanos because they don't mix all that much, but they're very charming people. A bit inhibited, I'd say." She took Nora by the hand. "Here, let me introduce you to Constance. I don't see Benjamin anywhere at the moment. They live here year-round, while most of the rest of us are just weekenders. All this land used to belong to them, I believe." Suddenly she turned to look at Nora's face. "Nora, you are so *beautiful!* Mother was saying just the other day that you still look to be twenty-two. Of course, it's a great joke in New York that you're the only mother in town who plays football with her children."

"Just touch football," she replied, "and it's very good exercise for all of us."

Nina Boyle was leading her across the room toward two women who stood in the shadows away from the windows. One had close-cropped hair and wore metal-rimmed spectacles; she was squat and fattish. The other was tall, very thin, gray-haired, and Hellenic-faced. When she spoke, her lips barely moved.

"Constance," Nina said when she was abreast of the latter, "may I interrupt to introduce you to Nora Molloy? She and her husband are thinking of buying a house in the neighborhood, and I told her that you're an authority on almost everything."

Constance Delano did not deny it.

"Hello!" Nora cried, taking her hand. "It's so nice to meet you."

Adroitly, Nina helped the short-haired woman away by insisting that she refill her plate at the buffet table, and

Nora was left alone with Nancy Delano's mother. She looked patrician, to be sure, but also lonely and unhappy. Actually, she wasn't much older than Nora, but looked as though she were in her mid-fifties. Her eyes were tired, and there were deep wrinkles at her neck.

"The Satterlees' house is for sale," Constance Delano announced, "but perhaps it might be too large for you. How many are there in your family?"

"My husband and I have nine children."

Something like horror or disbelief crossed the woman's face. Her mouth opened ever so slightly.

"But the house needn't be that large," Nora continued. "We don't mind doubling up if necessary. Sometimes at our place in Southampton, we have as many as twenty-five sleeping in our bedrooms. My children are forever inviting their friends out."

There was something like criticism in Constance Delano's voice as she asked, "Then you live in Southampton?" It was newer and less chic than the North Shore.

"We like the beach during the summer, and my children are great sailors. My husband and I thought it would be nice to keep a few horses, but we don't have enough pasturage for them on Long Island. Nina's mother has been telling us about Millbrook. Perhaps you know her. Kate Morrissey?"

"No," Constance Delano answered, as if the possibility were too farfetched even to consider.

Nora waited for the woman to elaborate, but when nothing was forthcoming, she added, "Perhaps we could have a look at the Satterlee place before we leave."

"I expect that you would have to do it through the real-estate people."

"I see."

It wasn't, Nora decided, that the woman was uncordial. She was merely shy, and as Nina Boyle had said, inhibited.

"You really ought to have some breakfast," Constance Delano finally said. "We'll be out in the fields all morning."

326

"Yes, I think I might have something. Could I fill your plate while I'm at it?"

"Nothing, thank you. I have rather a fragile stomach, and I'm under medication."

"What a pity. Eating is one of the great pleasures of life."

For the second time, Constance Delano looked at her with incredulity.

"I'll be right back," Nora said as she hurried to the buffet and heaped food on her plate. But when she returned, Constance Delano had disappeared.

On the other side of the room, however, Charles Molloy was deep in conversation with Benjamin Delano, whose chief physical characteristic was a huge bald head, very pink and shiny. Unlike his wife, he was quite convivial and easy to talk to. Inevitably, they discussed business.

"I see that Delano Mining is moving into Chile," Charles began.

"In a small way. We're after the copper down there, but the problems are immense. For every dollar we invest to bring the mineral out of the soil, we spend two dollars bribing officials to permit us. Baksheesh is a way of life in South America as it is in the Middle East."

"I would say that it is definitely worth the effort. In the coming war, South American copper will soar in price."

Delano looked up with interest. "You really think so?"

"Absolutely. African copper will be almost unavailable because of U-boats in the South Atlantic, but it's doubtful that they'll venture to the Pacific coast to interfere with shipping there."

Thoughtfully, Delano observed, "You might have something. At the moment, we have options on an additional two thousand acres north of Santiago, and we've been thinking of letting them expire. I'm not sure that we should."

"You'll be losing money if you do." Charles waited, then went on, "I wouldn't be at all opposed to investing in the scheme if you'd permit me."

Benjamin Delano was too much of a businessman to

327

show unreserved enthusiasm. Guardedly, he said, "It might be worth talking about."

In the distance, the hunting horn was sounded, and people began to leave the house.

"Why don't we get together sometime next week for lunch?" Delano suggested.

"I think we ought to. Would Wednesday suit you?"

"Wednesday would be fine. About noon?"

"Racquet Club?"

"Is that your club? That's mine, too! Lovely." Benjamin Delano reached out and robustly shook Molloy's hand. "On Wednesday then, Charles."

As Delano left to join his wife, Charles looked around for Nora. In a minute, she appeared, riding crop in hand. She looked glum.

"I'm afraid it went badly," she said with obvious disappointment. "I doubt that we'll ever get to know them. She's rather unfriendly."

"He's not," Charles replied. "We're having lunch on Wednesday."

Nora squeezed his arm. "But how marvelous of you to get him to like you, Charles!"

"I don't think it was that. I'd heard that his mining company needed capital, so I volunteered to help him out."

Nora looked at him adoringly. They had reached the courtyard, where a groom was holding their borrowed mounts.

"All I want to know in return, Noreen," he said to her, "is that now that we've met those damned Delanos, would you be upset if we don't stay for the entire hunt?"

Nora began to laugh softly. "No, Charles dear. And thank you ever so much."

Peggy Sweeney sat across from Tom at the kitchen table, dressed in a quilted robe that was frayed at both sleeves. Her eyes were pinched from lack of sleep, and she used the edge of her hand to keep the morning sun from striking them.

Tom had waited until just a few minutes before to tell her that he wouldn't be able to spend the rest of the day with her, or Sunday, either. It was now a little after eight on Saturday morning, and he had promised Nancy Delano that he would meet her train at South Station at ten.

"I can't get out of it. It's sort of an obligation. This girl I met in New York—I have to take her to the game today and the dance tonight," he said.

He had been almost resigned to an explosive reaction, but he wasn't at all prepared for her silence. She looked at him with something like animosity.

"I spent last night here, didn't I? And I was here Monday night and Wednesday night. Jesus Christ, I have to have a life of my own, too. We're not *married*."

Suddenly, all her anxiety found expression. "You never intend to marry me, do you?"

For the past six months, Tom had been asking himself that same question, and he had not been able to arrive at a satisfactory answer.

"Why do we have to talk about marriage?" he demanded. "I'm not even out of college yet, and you're asking me to make a decision like that."

She was fighting back tears. "I've already been dumped on my fanny by one man who couldn't marry me. I don't know if I can stand it if it happens again."

He slammed his coffee cup on the tabletop. "That's neurotic."

When he'd first met her, she was still reeling from her affair with the married man at her office, and she'd confessed that sometimes she was too afraid to venture out on the streets by herself. She had sat at home in the dark and cried. The first time she had gone out in months was the evening she had attended the Boston Symphony, and she had almost turned back two or three times. Had she done so, she never would have met Tom.

"We're different," she said. "I've always had to fight for everything I've wanted, and half the time I never got it, anyway. My mother doesn't care if I'm dead or alive. All the time I was growing up, I was hungry or I dreamed about pretty dresses or about boyfriends, but I went without. So maybe I'm neurotic. There would be something wrong with me if I weren't neurotic. Anyway, I never heard you complaining when you were screwing me."

329

It was true. When he was between her legs, he was mindless.

"I've told you a hundred times, Peggy," he protested, "you wouldn't have any fun at a Lowell House dance. And you hate football, you know you do. So why all of a sudden do you want to see the Harvard-Princeton game?"

"And what about the girl you're taking?" she spat out. "What's so special about her that she can have fun at dances and I can't? I'd like to know what's so wrong with me that I can't go to dances or football games." She began to break down. "Why do I have to stay home all by myself when everyone else in the world is having fun?"

Sobbing, she buried her head in her arms on the table-top.

Why had Tom even mentioned the game and the dance? Why hadn't he pleaded the necessities of scholar-ship, as he had in the past? *Why?* Unless a part of him *wanted* to bring the matter to a head.

Suddenly he was angry. He jumped from the chair, knocking it against the table. When he spoke, he was shouting. "All right! I've got some complaints, too. I'd like to know why the hell everyone wants me to be something different. My mother wants one thing; my father wants another. You want one thing; Nancy Delano wants some-thing else. All I'd like to know is when you goddam peo-ple are going to let me be what I *am!*"

He was gasping for breath. He grabbed his wind-breaker and rushed from the room.

Unwashed, unshaven, hair matted, wearing the same clothes he'd worn the day before, he ran like a maniac down the station platform, pushing past people swarming toward the exit, but Nancy was nowhere in sight.

Then he could see her at the very end of the platform, standing by a suitcase, looking anxiously in his direction. She was dressed in a powder-blue cashmere sweater and a matching skirt and carried a tan polo coat over her arm. When she saw him, she stood on her toes and waved above the crowd.

330

"I'm so sorry," he said when he skidded to a stop in front of her. "How long have you been waiting?"

When she spoke, there was peace and repose in her voice. "Just a few minutes."

He didn't know what to say. "You look great, Nancy," he stammered at last. "I mean, you really do. I guess I must look like a mess." He wiped a hand across his unshaven chin.

"Your eyes are sort of red."

He yanked his handkerchief from a hip pocket and turned his head away while he blew his nose. Coming into Boston on the trolley, he had suddenly found himself crying. He hated it because it was unmanly, but he hadn't been able to stop it.

"I haven't showered or anything," he explained, then lied: "I overslept." He reached down to pick up her Mark Cross suitcase. "I made reservations for you at the Commander. It's near Harvard Square. Is that all right?"

She walked next to him toward the station. "I made one at the Copley, but I can always cancel it."

"Gee, no. I can take you to the Copley."

"I'd really rather stay in Cambridge, but I didn't know there was a hotel there."

"It's no great shakes."

"That's all right."

The Copley Plaza was certainly a far better hotel, and Tom regretted having chosen the Commander. It indicated a lack of concern for her comfort; he was sure of it. Already, he was being a boor.

"The game starts at one-thirty," he said, "so you'll have time to check in, then we can have lunch. There's a dance at Lowell tonight. I told you, didn't I?"

"I brought a formal and also just a dressy dress. You didn't tell me if it was formal or not."

Tom put the suitcase down and faced her, then said, "I've been so mixed up, Nancy."

Nancy looked at him and said quietly, "You've been crying, haven't you?"

He nodded his head.

"What's wrong, Tom?"

331

He let all the breath out of his lungs. "There's this girl I've been seeing, and I'm very confused."

To one side of them was a restaurant. "Why don't we go over there and talk about it?" she suggested.

"Oh, Jesus, Nancy! Could we?"

At last he would be able to unburden himself. He hadn't been able to confess it to a priest because it was so infinitely private, shameful, and mysterious. Yet he was about to reveal everything to a tender Vassar girl who probably knew nothing about life.

"I think what it is, is that I'm very base," he began as they made their way to the restaurant. "I'm an animal."

"But who isn't?" replied the cousin of two Presidents.

They spent most of the afternoon at the table, missing the football game entirely. At four o'clock, they were still there. They had consumed numberless cups of coffee, annoyed hell out of a waitress who wanted them to vacate the table, and were unconscious of everything that went on around them.

There was nothing he didn't tell her, and yet she didn't seem repelled by his story. She even supplied excuses for him.

When he said, "I thought I'd taught her self-confidence, but maybe all I taught her was to depend on me," Nancy's answer was, "That's the risk everyone takes. If that's the way she reacted, the deficiency's in her, not in you. I mean, there's no reason for you to feel so guilty."

"Then you don't hate me?"

She pondered it. "I like you even more for telling me. Most people are selfish and don't share their lives with anyone else, but I knew right away, the first time I met you, that you were different. You're so warm and outgoing. Maybe it's because you're Irish or something, but you're more *human* than anyone else I've ever met."

More fallible, too, Tom thought.

"You have feelings," she went on. "You have emotions. Just being next to you, I can feel all this electricity in you. Some people are dead, right at the center of themselves. They can't *feel*. My mother never does. Do you know that in all my life I've never seen my mother get upset or lose her temper or cry or even laugh very much? But you were so *moved* by what's happening to you that you cried. That's really very wonderful, Tom. It really is."

Tom was certainly willing to take her word for it. For the first time in weeks, he felt as if his mind had stopped racing and there was no more adrenaline left in his body. His hands weren't clenched, and he wasn't sitting on the edge of his chair.

"We missed the football game," he said apologetically.

"I didn't want to see it, anyway."

"I thought that's why you came up from Poughkeepsie."

"I came up to see you."

Tom felt spent, drained, blissfully exhausted. Even after he'd made love to Peggy, he had never felt so emptied of worries, so at peace with himself and the world.

"I'd better take you to the hotel now," he said, "or they'll give your room to someone else. Then I have to go back to the dorm to shower and everything." He ran his fingers through his uncombed hair. "I'm glad you came, Nancy." He paused to catch his breath. "You're really—I don't know what," he began, then faltered. With a sudden rush of words, he got it out: "I think you're about the nicest girl I've ever met."

Tom was euphoric by the time he burst into his room at Lowell House. One look at John Phipps, however, told him that his mood was to be short-lived.

"That girl friend of yours has been calling ever since I got back from the game," Phipps said from his leather armchair. He was wearing a stocking cap, a six-foot-long crimson and white muffler, and Jockey shorts. In his hand was an old-fashioned glass. "Do you want a drink? I think I'm going to get pissed tonight."

Emily Thayer had not come up for the weekend because she had the flu, and John hadn't been able to find another date. Tom had volunteered Caitlin, but Phipps had thrown his hands up in horror, saying that he was not a masochist. Caitlin was a child. A pleasant enough child, but a child nonetheless.

333

Tom began to pull off his clothes in order to shower. "What did she want?"

"I had the distinct impression that she wanted *you*."

Peggy was going to try to spoil everything, damn her. Well, it wasn't going to work. He wouldn't let it.

He was halfway into the bathroom when the telephone began to ring. "Please answer it and say I'm not here."

Phipps got up from his chair and walked to the desk. His hand hovered over the phone. "I've already said that I'd give you her message."

"Tell her that you still haven't seen me."

Phipps drank from his glass, then picked up the receiver. He listened as Peggy once again asked for Tom, then repeated what his roommate had told him.

"Will you be seeing him at the dance?" Peggy asked.

"I'm not going to the dance."

"Then there's no way I can get in touch with him?"

"I could try to leave a message downstairs before I go out. But there's no way of guaranteeing that he'll get it." He paused. "Why? Is something wrong, Miss Sweeney?"

No, nothing was wrong, she replied. It was just that she had to talk to Tom. It was important.

Once more, Phipps said that all he could do was leave another message.

"All right," Peggy answered. "Thank you."

Tom had closed his eyes as he listened to the conversation. He felt rotten about what he was doing, but Peggy was being unreasonable. She didn't own him. He had to regain *some* of his freedom.

"Listen," Phipps began with surprising sobriety, "don't take it so badly. That's what she wants."

"I guess you're right."

"I know I'm right."

Still, Tom worried. If his relationship with Peggy was about to end, he had to make the break as painless as possible. Whatever Nancy had said, he had a responsibility. Next week, he would start promoting the idea that Peggy begin seeing other boys. He'd tell her to get out and do things. It was just not healthy for her to sit in her apartment all day telephoning him at Lowell House.

As he scrubbed himself under the shower spray, he heard the telephone ring again. He knew that Phipps was still in the room—how far, after all, could he go dressed in nothing but his underwear and a six-foot-long muffler? —but when, several minutes later, he stepped out of the shower and asked his roommate who had called, Phipps replied that no one had.

There were probably too many pretty girls at the Lowell House dance—young ladies from Wellesley and Radcliffe and Smith—for Nancy Delano to be the center of attraction because of her appearance. Nancy's face was more interesting than it was beautiful. She looked clever, alert, and composed. Tom had told her, the minute he saw her walk from the elevator at the hotel, that she was positively gorgeous, but he meant the entire person: the mind, the body, the bearing.

But at some point during the course of the dance, it occurred to Tom that Nancy *was* the center of attraction, for reasons apart from her appearance.

"Hey, Molloy!" a friend said to him when Nancy had left for a minute. "Someone said that's a Roosevelt you're with."

"Someone gave you the wrong information. She's only a Delano."

"It's the same thing, isn't it?"

"I think she finds it quite different."

"*Lucky* guy! I bet you'll be having Thanksgiving dinner at the White House."

Tom felt himself stirred by the idea, then immediately ashamed of himself for having reacted that way. Was the fact that her family was so distinguished one of the reasons he liked Nancy? If so, wasn't that reprehensible?

He fretted about it.

Later, as they danced, he was aware that friends of his at Lowell were cutting in far more than they ought to. Some had been introduced to Nancy, and some had not, yet they cut in relentlessly. The first six or seven times, Tom was patient, but then he became annoyed.

"Look, Nancy," he said, "could we sit this one out?"

"I'd love to. You know how I feel about dancing, anyway."

So they adjourned to a corner of the house library and sat on a leather sofa.

What he had to say would not be easy. "There are a lot of things you still don't know about my family," he began.

She smiled. "I can think of one way to correct that."

"We're a Brooklyn family. I mean, the Molloys are. The house my dad was born in on Saint Mark's Avenue— well, it's like a hundred other houses in the neighborhood. We haven't always lived on East Seventy-first Street and in Southampton."

"Not many people have."

There was no way of breaking her down. He would have to approach it from another direction.

"My mother," he said, then paused. "Before she got married, she worked."

"She's very lucky. I envy women who work."

He would have to be more direct. "She started working when she was ten."

Nancy's eyes opened wide. "Ten years *old?*"

Yes, and a sister of his mother's had started working as a domestic when she was only nine. "It happened in Ireland," he explained. "You see, it was the only way they could stay alive. Where my mother lived, all the girls in the family had to go into service because they couldn't be fed at home."

"That's absolutely astonishing!"

"Not many people know it. I've never even told Phipps, and he's pretty understanding about most things."

She turned to him. "No, I mean it's astonishing because I never knew that anything like that ever happened. How wonderful that your mother has done what she's done since she came to America."

What he was about to say now was the most difficult at all. "A lot of people in New York have cut my mother because of it. Not that they know the whole story. But because she's more Irish than my father. And of course she's a Catholic, too, which doesn't help much in society."

"Some people are very ignorant, Tom. You mustn't pay any attention to them. They're trivial and unimportant."

She waited. "I would really like to meet your mother."

"I'd like you to meet her, too. She has—well, funny ideas about me. She says because I've been given advantages it's my duty to help those who don't have them. She calls it my destiny. I know it sounds silly."

It was a long time before Nancy replied. "I don't think it sounds silly."

"She wants me to do something special with my life. Go into politics or be a public servant because I won't have to worry about money the way other people do. She says it's my obligation."

"She's right, Tom. And you'd be very good, too."

He was relieved that he'd been able to carry the conversation as far as he had. "That's really what I wanted to talk about. I'm afraid—well, I'm afraid that people will think that I'm seeing you—just because of your famous cousin. And what you could do for my career."

Nancy looked at him. "Do you always examine your motives that way?"

"The Jesuits taught me. And once you've been taught, you can never unlearn it."

"Tom, a lot of people have—what's the word I want? —courted me because of the White House connections. But you didn't. In Southampton, remember, you walked away from me when we were on the beach. I was just a girl and you were just a boy."

"But I came back."

"Not because of anyone's famous cousin, did you?"

"I don't think so. But just to be on the safe side, would it be all right if we keep your famous cousin out of our lives?"

She waited for him to be more specific.

"Let's never talk about him," he suggested.

"All right."

He let out his breath. "Whew! I feel better now. Someone just came up to me and made a crack about the White House and F.D.R., and I felt—I don't know how I felt—like an opportunist, I think."

"Well, take it from me, you're not."

He reached out for her hand. "Okay, I'm not." He waited, then added, "There's another thing."

She looked up expectantly.

"How would you like to have Thanksgiving dinner with me and my family in New York?" he asked.

"I'd really like that, Tom."

It was after one in the morning when he walked her to her hotel. They made arrangements to meet at ten o'clock for a late breakfast. They would have most of Sunday to amuse themselves, as Nancy's train didn't leave until early evening. They could poke around Cambridge until they got tired, and then, if the day was fine, they could loll on the banks of the Charles River in the October sun.

When he kissed her goodnight, he felt her body trembling in his arms.

He whistled as he walked down Boylston Street toward the dorm, kicking at the fallen leaves on the sidewalk and marveling at the star-filled sky. For the first time, he could envisage a future that was not at war with the present.

Lowell House was deserted. The crepe paper that had been strung in the dining hall for the dance now lay curled in corners. When Tom entered his room and turned on the light, he found a sheet of paper on the floor. It was from Phipps.

Tom,

I'm sleeping in Steffenson's room tonight. That damn girl friend of yours has been calling every ten minutes since you left.

When are you going to come to your senses? It was a bad show right from the beginning. If you can't tell her it's all over, then, by God, I shall.

J.P.

Phipps was right, of course. If the relationship wasn't working out, it would have to be terminated. Peggy would have to be told.

Even as he read it, the telephone began to ring, and suddenly he was furious that she should behave in such a way, making him appear ridiculous in front of Phipps.

"Peggy, for the love of God, what are you *doing!*" he shouted into the receiver.

There was a slight hesitation, then a voice began, "Mr. Thomas Molloy?"

Tom's blood ran cold. "I'm Tom Molloy," he answered.

"I'm calling from Massachusetts General Hospital, Mr. Molloy," the voice continued. "We are trying to identify a young woman. Your name and address were on an envelope in her purse."

It was all Tom could do to form the words. "What's happened?"

"I'm afraid she has tried to kill herself. She jumped from India Wharf at shortly after eleven this evening, Mr. Molloy."

Blood pumped through his temples until he thought his head would burst. He let the receiver fall, then raced from the room.

Pale sunlight filtered through the windows and struck Tom's gaunt face as he waited in the hospital corridor. A wilted carnation lay limply on the lapel of his navy-blue Brooks Brothers suit, and his tie had been pulled away from his unbuttoned collar.

He had just come from the telephone, where, after having tried since two o'clock, he had finally been able to reach Peggy's mother in Worcester. Her speech had been slurred and less than coherent, so Tom could only deduce that she had helped close the bars. She had not been particularly alarmed by the news that Peggy was in Massachusetts General. "If she expects me to pay the bill, she's mistaken," Mrs. Sweeney had said. Tom had answered that the bills would be paid, then added, "She's tried to kill herself."

"It isn't the first time," Mrs. Sweeney had replied philosophically.

Tom had waited until sunrise to call Phipps to break the news. His roommate had been more angry than sympathetic. "Don't you see what she's trying to do, Tom?" he had said. "Don't let her suck you in that way.

I'll be down in a half hour or so. Hold on until then. Don't let her suck you in."

Peggy was in an intensive care unit. She had done more than attempt to drown herself. She had taken a half bottle of sleeping pills and had drunk most of a fifth of cheap red wine before jumping into the water.

A nurse approached, and Tom hurried to intercept her. "Is it possible for me to see Miss Sweeney?" he asked urgently.

She looked at him disapprovingly. The opulence and gaiety of his dress—the red carnation, the regimental striped tie, the Brooks Brothers suit—offended her, he was sure.

Crossly, she questioned him, "Are you a member of the family?"

For all practical purposes, he was. "Yes," he replied, lowering his eyes.

"You can go in for a few minutes. But she won't respond to you. She's in a deep, sound sleep and will be for some time. The poor girl almost died."

Slowly he entered the room and walked toward the bed until he stood next to where Peggy lay. Her lips were chapped and bloodless, and her nostrils were bruised, as if an instrument had been forced down them when her stomach was pumped. She had cut her forehead, and her hair was stringy and damp to the touch. She looked fevered, yet her face was gray.

Suddenly he sank his head onto her breast and covered her with his arms.

He was lost, he knew that now. A prisoner of his emotions. It was all his fault. He had provided her with a stability she had never known before, then had threatened to take it away. He had betrayed her, while she had shown him that her love was so boundless that she found life without him unthinkable.

"Oh, Peggy," he sobbed. *"I'll never leave you again!"*

From the doorway, John Phipps watched in silent sorrow.

24

It was a dark, wet day in November, and the trees in the Boston Common were black against the sky. At the curb near the State House a Duesenberg was parked, its driver waiting, its engine idling, while a woman walked back and forth on the sidewalk. Almost at the same second as the spired clocks of the city began to toll the hour, there was the sound of rushing feet and a young man hurried out of the autumn gloom.

"I hope I haven't kept you waiting, Mrs. Molloy," John Phipps said breathlessly.

"I've only just arrived, John. Now you must tell me at once what all this means."

While the elegant car waited, they walked in the Common, Nora's arm resting against the crook of John Phipps's elbow. As best he could, he began to describe what had happened during the past few weeks.

"I don't want Tom ever to know that I've talked to you, Mrs. Molloy. But he's throwing his life away. We have to save him."

Nora's knowledge of recent events was restricted to a call from Tom several nights before, revealing that he wouldn't be spending Thanksgiving with his family after all, but would instead remain in Cambridge. Then, last night, John Phipps had telephoned.

"She's not a bad sort," Phipps went on. "She's—elemental, I'd call her. Rather pretty, but not very smart. What she is is what my old man would call a mistress, except that her hold on Tom is so unbreakable, I'm afraid he might marry her."

That was precisely what Nora herself feared.

"You know what a tremendous sense of duty he

341

has, Mrs. Molloy. Well, he's decided that he can't leave Peggy Sweeney. He sent Nancy home the day after the suicide attempt and hasn't seen her since. And that's a month now."

"Do you think Peggy really loves him, John, or is it his money?"

Phipps wasn't entirely sure. "It's possible, of course, that she's found out about you people, but Tom told me that he's never said anything to her about his family."

"I must meet her," Nora said resolutely. "I must see her for myself. Can that be arranged?"

It could be done almost at once. Peggy worked on Copley Square and would be finished at five. It was now a little after four-thirty. Phipps could point her out; then Nora Molloy could approach her and identify herself.

"Tom isn't seeing her tonight. Since the suicide attempt, he's been with her every single night, and as a result is now failing two courses. Do you see what I mean? He's spinning out of control."

Nora agreed that immediate steps would have to be taken, though she didn't know what they could be, and wouldn't until she'd met the girl. If Peggy Sweeney were an opportunist, Nora hoped that she would be able to smoke her out.

"And if she is honestly in love with Tom, and Tom with her, then I must give them my blessing," she concluded.

They entered the Duesenberg and began the drive to Copley Square.

At ten minutes past five, John Phipps pointed to a frail young girl who had just spun out from a revolving door, and said, "There she is. Good luck, Mrs. Molloy."

After he had left the car, Nora instructed her driver to follow the girl for a block or so. While she was still unobserved and unknown, she wanted to have a look at Peggy Sweeney. Perhaps she could come to some conclusions just on the basis of her appearance.

She was certainly no ravishing beauty. Moreover, she walked with her shoulders bent inward, as if to protect her tiny breasts, and with her eyes directed at the sidewalk. The clothes she wore weren't gaudy or in bad taste, nor did they particularly become her. In short, she was the sort of girl who didn't offend, but didn't recommend herself, either.

As Peggy Sweeney waited at the corner for the light to change, Nora rolled down the window.

"Miss Sweeney?" she inquired. When the girl looked into the enormous car, Nora added, "I'm Tom's mother. Could I have a word with you, please?"

"I don't understand," Peggy said as she entered the car. "Tom never mentioned that you'd be in Boston."

"He doesn't know that I'm here," Nora replied. "I thought it would be best if we could have a chat, just the two of us." She held out her hand. "I'm Nora Molloy."

"Margaret Sweeney," the girl answered, "but almost everyone calls me Peggy." She looked around at the plush interior of the Duesenberg. "This is a beautiful car, Mrs. Molloy. I don't think I've ever seen such a beautiful car before."

"Then would you mind if we just rode around a bit while we get to know one another? We'd probably be more comfortable here than back at the Ritz. I'm staying only for the night, then returning to New York in the morning."

"I've never been inside the Ritz," she volunteered. "I've walked by it and looked in, but I've never been brave enough to open the door."

"Hasn't Tom ever taken you to nice places, Peggy?"

She turned to look at Nora Molloy. "He had me out to Harvard a few weeks ago and I met his roommate. It's a real pretty place. But mostly—well, we stay around the apartment. We listen to the radio and things. I really don't like to go out that much."

"Do you live with your mother and father?" Nora asked, though she knew the answer.

"My father's dead. He was gassed in the war and was in bad health a long time before he died. My mother —well, she drinks. We never got along too good. I don't live with her anymore. I live by myself."

"You're young to be on your own."

"I'm eighteen."

Nora Molloy leaned back against the upholstery and half closed her eyes. "When I was your age, I was also on my own. I was by myself in a strange country. The man I loved, the man I was going to marry, had been killed." She opened her eyes and faced the young girl next to her. "He was hanged by British soldiers for his part in the Easter Rising of 1916."

For a moment, Nora was unable to continue. When she began again, she spoke softly. "We were so very much in love, Thomas Cassidy and I. He had such grand and beautiful dreams. Like almost all of us where we grew up, he had no education to speak of, but he was clever and wanted desperately to come to America in order to improve himself. Yet he was not even nineteen when he died. It was such a waste, I thought. Such an injustice."

Peggy's mouth opened as if she were about to say something but then thought better of it.

"Charles Molloy saved my life," Nora resumed. "He brought me a love I thought I would never have again. And because he knew of Thomas Cassidy, he insisted we name our first child after him. On the day Tom was born, I made a pledge to his namesake that Tom would do what he himself had been unable to do. I promised him that Tom would serve mankind in some way. Of all my children, he alone has that destiny. And he knows it, too. It has always been our wish that he enter public life."

"Public life?" Peggy Sweeney asked.

"My husband, Charles Molloy, has been unusually fortunate in business, and as a result Tom will never have to work for a living. It is a luxury allowed very few, Peggy. With such freedom granted him, we have hoped that Tom would run for an elective office in New York State. As you have perhaps perceived, my son is a very charming and winning fellow. And he has a good mind." She waited until Peggy's eyes met hers. "There is nothing Tom cannot do if he tries hard enough. In New York or in Washington. His only enemy is himself. Sometimes—he loses sight of his goal."

344

In a small voice, Peggy asked, "Why are you telling me this?"

"I am telling you this, Peggy, because I know just how devoted he is to you. Yet I ask you in all frankness: would you want to be a governor's wife?"

Without hesitation, Peggy replied, "No."

"A senator's wife?"

Almost inaudibly, she answered, "No, Mrs. Molloy. I'm not that kind of girl. Tom knows that."

It was exactly what Nora had hoped she would say. "And knowing that, what would Tom do if he were married to you, Peggy?"

Tears formed in her eyes. "You don't want me to marry him, do you?"

"You have not answered my question, Peggy. What would Tom do if you were his wife and he knew that you did not want the kind of life his destiny would impose upon him?"

Softly, she answered, "He would give up his destiny."

"I know he would, for that is his weakness. Love could destroy him, Peggy. He would give up his dreams." Nora reached out and grasped the girl's hand. "We must not let him throw his life away. I beg you."

The huge car traveled slowly along the Fenway, and in the back seat, Nora and the young girl each looked through a window, lost in thought.

"The girl from New York," Peggy began. "You want Tom to marry her, don't you?"

"If he loves her, Peggy. They are suited to one another. But he will not marry her so long as he feels obligated to you. I know him too well."

"And you want me to let him go?" She looked toward the older woman for an answer, but before one came, she added, "I thought it was—customary to buy off girls who interfered with rich boys. You haven't offered me a penny."

"I know I haven't."

"And it's a damn good thing you didn't, because if you had, I wouldn't have given Tommy up for anything."

Nora nodded her head. "I was sure of that."

Peggy dried her cheeks with a handkerchief. "What do you want me to say, Mrs. Molloy? That I love him too much and I don't care about any of his dreams? Or am I supposed to say that yes, I'll gladly give him up because I don't want to ruin his life? Hell, Mrs. Molloy, I'm just a working-class girl. I know that. I'm not—very refined or anything. I knew all along that I needed Tommy more than he needed me. He's tried to break it up before, but I wouldn't let him."

She buttoned her raincoat. "I didn't know he wanted to be any of those things you just told me. To be a senator or governor. Maybe he does; maybe he doesn't. We're very close, Tommy and me, but not that way. We never talked about those things. We were too busy—I guess we were too busy just loving one another."

Once again, her eyes brimmed with tears. "I don't know what to say, Mrs. Molly. I really don't."

"Then don't say anything, Peggy. Just consider what I've told you. Whatever decision you reach, I'll honor."

"Could you let me off at the next corner? I can get a trolley from there."

"I'll drive you home, Peggy."

"No. I want to think, Mrs. Molloy. I can think on a trolley. I'm not used to cars like this."

As the Duesenberg pulled up to the curb, Nora reached over and held Peggy Sweeney in her arms. "You must hate me," she said.

"I don't hate you. Because I know you love Tom, too. But I can't guarantee anything. He's all I have. How can I give him up?" She opened the door of the car. "What do I know about destiny? All I know is that I love him. Isn't that destiny, too, Mrs. Molloy?"

"It may be, Peggy. The decision is yours. But just remember my story. There can be another love for you, too."

Peggy smiled weakly. She held out her hand. "Well, it was nice meeting you. Maybe I'll see you again. And maybe I won't." She was on the sidewalk now, looking at the black Duesenberg, glistening in the rain. "So long, Mrs. Molloy."

Nora watched as she walked away, bareheaded in the rain, head downward.

All morning long, the talk of Cambridge was of the Night of the Broken Glass. In residence halls, in classrooms, and in libraries, Harvard men discussed the newest threat to peace. By the thousands, S.S. troops had swarmed across Germany setting fire to synagogues and the houses and shops of Jews. The Boston newspapers reported that as many as twenty thousand Jews had been arrested.

It sent a chill across campus, though no one knew exactly what it meant. A temporary madness, most Harvard men supposed, and by way of apologizing for it, they were unusually solicitous to Jewish classmates.

Provided that they knew any.

Tom Molloy argued in his political science class that something a good deal stronger and more effective than a mere protest should be lodged against the Third Reich, but his view was in the minority. At all costs, America could not antagonize Nazi Germany, his classmates argued. A show of force now would immediately precipitate war, and America was unprepared.

Late in the afternoon, Tom had a conference with his philosophy instructor in Emerson Hall, and though he tried to direct the discussion toward the confrontation between members of the Master Race and members of the Chosen People, Professor Ambrose was far more concerned with Tom's scholarship. He pointed at a bluebook that Tom had filled with incomprehensible gibberish for his midterm. For his efforts, he had received a D.

"I shouldn't have given you a D, Mr. Molloy, except that I was rather enchanted that someone who hadn't read any of the source material could write so volubly about it."

"I'm afraid my mind hasn't been on my schoolwork recently."

"And what occupies your attention, Mr. Molloy? The fate of the world?"

"Yes, sir," Tom answered brightly. "And that of my-

347

self, too. It's a fevered age we're living in, sir. One scarcely knows what to do."

"My advice, Mr. Molloy, is to turn to scholarship. Let the world look after itself, as it will inevitably do, anyway. You have not completed any of the assigned readings in Kant or Schopenhauer. I shall give you one more opportunity in view of your past excellence in the department. If you can complete the readings by this time next week and drop in to chat with me about them, perhaps I will not have to fail you, Mr. Molloy."

"Yes, sir, I shall do that. Thanks for being understanding."

As he left the room, he looked up at the clock on Professor Ambrose's wall. Good Lord, it was almost six, and he had promised to meet Peggy at her apartment, then take her out to dinner at the Cock Horse on Brattle Street.

He rushed down the hall until he came to a public telephone booth in the lobby and called Peggy's apartment in order to let her know that he would be a few minutes late, but there was no answer. She had probably been delayed, too. He would simply have to hurry. He had made reservations at the Cock Horse for seven.

It was almost six-thirty by the time he ran up the stairs to Peggy's apartment and pounded on the door.

"She's not there," the woman next door said, opening her door a crack.

"Maybe she had to work late."

"No. She moved out today. The apartment's already been rented to someone else. I told the landlord I wouldn't live next to a single girl again. They're scandalous."

What was the old crone talking about? Peggy *couldn't* have moved out. Tom had spent the night with her and eaten breakfast at her kitchen table that very morning. How could she have moved out?

"Fella come in a taxi around noon," the woman continued, "and helped her with her suitcases. She never had much, I'll say that. Lived like a Gypsy."

"We're going out to dinner tonight. How can she have moved somewhere else?"

348

"I'm sorry, sonny-boy, but I wouldn't be a bit surprised but that she's walked out on you. If your name's Molloy, there's a letter she left for you downstairs on the table."

Tom bounded down the steps three at a time and tore at the envelope he found beneath the mirror. He unfolded the single sheet of stationery. On it was a childlike scrawl.

Dearest Tommy,

You met me at a time in my life when I was friendless and coming to pieces, and I will always be grateful for what you did for me. But my life is changing again and yours must change, too.

Do you remember the man I was seeing before I met you? Well, he has come back, but this time he has divorced his wife and asked me to marry him. I have told him yes, Tommy. He has a chance to buy into a small insurance agency in Florida, so we are going down there to begin a new life and live in all the sunshine.

You mustn't think too badly of me for wasting your time and promising things I could never deliver. I am what I am, Tommy, and you are what you are. I will always remember you, and I wish you all the luck in the world.

Love
Peggy

In agony, Tom read the letter again and again, then buried his face in his hands. She had deserted him. He had given her everything precious he had, including his future, and she had turned it down. He felt broken and abused and angry. Yet, liberated.

25

Robert Conroy propped his legs up on a coffee table, then opened a briefcase on his lap and spread papers on the sofa next to him.

"What do you know about Martin Dies?" he asked.

Before answering, Pat once again glanced at the headline in the morning *Chronicle:*

LONGSHOREMAN BOSS CALLED
RED, FACES DEPORTATION

"All I know about him," Pat answered, "is that he's dangerous as hell."

Conroy rattled some papers at his side until he found what he wanted. "Dies has been opposed to virtually every piece of social legislation since he entered Congress. He thinks that Americans derive their rights from Almighty God, not from government or society. The only trouble is that Dies is a Texan and it's his opinion that God also is. He sees Him as a kind of West Texas county sheriff."

"Is he nuts?"

"He's young, ambitious, and a Southerner, but I don't think that he's nuts. He's certainly beleaguered, which brings out the worst in all of us. He doesn't like any of that Roosevelt crowd in Washington and considers the New Deal to be a Communist conspiracy. He's pro-corporation and antiunion. Pro-American and antialien. He has an obsession about people who—to use his words—'care nothing about America,' but of course there is only one way to care, and that is the way he does. Like another distinguished Southerner, Congress-

351

man Taylor of Tennessee, he thinks that such people should be hunted down like rattlesnakes and kicked out of the country." Conroy paused. "That's a direct quote."

Patrick held his forehead in his hand. "What kind of chance do I have with someone like that?"

Conroy smiled. "If nothing else works, we'll keep you in America on zoological grounds. We'll tell him that there are no rattlesnakes in Ireland."

Robert Conroy was volunteering his legal services free of charge. He had thrown himself into the project because, as he explained, he was attracted to underdogs and detested Southern demagogues. Although what he was doing was politically hazardous, he was willing to take the chance because he believed that Patrick was innocent. If Patrick won, as Conroy was confident he would, then the rising politician who helped him would also be a winner.

"Will they be private or public?" he asked Conroy. "The hearings, I mean."

"The way it goes, Pat, is that witnesses are first interviewed in executive sessions. Just the seven members of the committee and their witnesses. Then, if there appears to be reason to warrant it, there's a public hearing."

"Are they all like the chairman?"

Conroy read from a piece of paper in front of him. "I can't honestly say that you'll be among friends. First, we have Joe Starnes from the enlightened state of Alabama. Next, we have Harold Mosier from Ohio. *His* constituents read the Bible almost every day and live in towns where it's impossible to buy a drink, even if you're dying." He wet his lips. "You'll also be facing J. Parnell Thomas of New Jersey and Noah Mason of Illinois. They're anti-New Deal. The one they'd really like to deport is Franklin D. Roosevelt, but since that is impossible, they'll settle for a union leader who votes the Democratic ticket."

With alarm, Pat asked, "Aren't there any Democrats on the committee?"

"Of course. Starnes and Mosier are Democrats, but they're more conservative than most Republicans. Same is true of Martin Dies himself. The last two members are also Democrats. There's Arthur Healey of Massachusetts—"

"I might get sympathy from him," Pat declared.

Conroy did not look particularly hopeful, "You might, if he attends the hearings, but he happens to think that they're a waste of time. He's often absent during crucial votes. Moreover, he's unpredictable. Sometimes he's conservative; sometimes he's liberal."

"And sometimes he's not even there," Pat concluded for him.

Conroy nodded his head. "Then we have John J. Dempsey of New Mexico."

Pat let out a whoop. "Thanks be to God! How the hell did an Irishman wind up in the deserts of New Mexico? It can only be a miracle. His name has to be John Joseph."

"I'm not sure," Conroy observed, "but he may be your salvation. He's the only one of the lot who could be called a New Deal Democrat. He also has an interesting frontier style when attacking congressmen from the Deep South. He shoots from the hip."

"Then he's our hope."

"Almost your only hope, Pat." He tapped his finger against his opened briefcase. "You are everything that the committee members hate. You are foreign-born, you are a union leader, and— Do you want to pour yourself a drink before you hear it?"

Pat turned to face him. "Go ahead."

Sadly, Conroy whispered, "You're married to a Jew."

In despair, Pat closed his eyes. "I don't believe it. This is America. This isn't Nazi Germany. Don't those bastards know that? Besides, she's not Jewish anymore. She converted. She's a Catholic."

Conroy shook his head. "The same standards are used by conservative congressmen in Washington as are used in Nuremberg. Eva was born a Jew, and she is still a Jew."

Pat very nearly roared, "What the hell difference does it make!"

"Don't you see, Pat? It proves their point. Communism is a far greater threat to America, they think, than Nazism. And—are you sure you don't want that drink?—the American Communist party is dominated by aliens and Jews, they say. You are, according to biographical material already supplied the committee, married to what someone has politely called a Semite. Ergo, because you're also an alien and a union leader, you must be a Communist, too."

Eva was standing at the doorway, looking into the room. "I suppose it's too late for me to become a Southern Baptist," she said. "Poor Patrick. I'm so sorry. I guess I'm more of a liability than I thought I was."

Pat was in a rage. "I'm not going to let those bastards get away with it! If they make even one crack about Eva, I'll throttle each and every one of them, so help me God!" He hurried to Eva and wrapped his arms around her protectively.

"I've been trying my damnedest," Conroy resumed, "to learn something more about Craig Lee. Almost no one who lives in Los Angeles has a history, but he has less than most. It's an absolute blank."

"But he does know me," Pat replied. "I'm sure of that. He high-tailed it the minute he saw me at his house."

"And you didn't see him at all?"

"Not even a glance. I met his wife, though. Something rang a bell there, but I don't know what."

"You mean you recognized her?"

"I wasn't sure. I may have met her at some time in my life, but I don't know."

Eva suggested, "Why don't you describe her?"

Pat walked across the room and flung himself into a chair. He rested his fists over his closed eyes. "She was in her mid-twenties, I'd say. Very pretty. Honey-blond hair. Nice skin. Interesting eyes. She looked foreign somehow, but for the life of me, I can't tell you how. I just saw her for a few seconds. She was wearing a white, sequined dress, bare at the shoulders, and an enormous diamond brooch on a white band at her neck. There were emeralds at the center, shaped like an eye, and in the middle of that was a ruby. You couldn't look away from it. It was haunting."

Eva rushed across the room to him. "Ten diamonds, eleven tiny emeralds, and a single ruby? Was that what it was? Twenty-two stones in all?"

Pat was mystified. "How would I know how many stones? All I know is it was shaped like an eye, more or less."

"A tiger's eye." She turned toward Conroy. *"Tiger, tiger, burning bright . . . in the forests of the night.* It was my favorite poem, and that's why the necklace was made for me."

"I don't understand," Conroy said.

"Twenty-two stones. I received it as a present on my twenty-second birthday from my former husband. I gave it to you, Pat. Do you remember? The night I went to your room in Hell's Kitchen? I told you that I no longer had any use for it and that you should—"

It all came back. "Give it to the strike fund," he completed for her. "The Diamond Shirtwaist Company strike fund. And I did. I gave it to—" He stopped, searching the dark past for a name. "Was it Sarasohn?" he asked himself tentatively. "Sarasohn. I gave it to Sarasohn. He was to sell it and use the money for the workers, but a few days later, the strike failed. Sarasohn. It was *Sarasohn!*"

"Then it appears that we have found our accuser," Conroy declared. "Your Sarasohn and our Craig Lee are one and the same."

He had locked it deep in the center of his memory, and now it came rushing out. A girl named Sonia. A young man named Kaganoff. The march across the Williamsburg Bridge in defiance of a court order. The mounted police charge against the strikers.

The death of Annamarie.

Sarasohn had been there, a part of it all.

"I can't believe it," Patrick said after he had told Conroy everything he could remember. "He loved the workers. They were his life. How is it possible that he could have betrayed them for a handful of jewels?"

355

Conroy had no ready explanation. He was as perplexed as Pat. "At least we have a real name to work with," he said. "We have four days before we're due in Washington. During that time, we'll try to find out everything we can about our Mr. Sarasohn. You say that you, a Russian girl named Sonia, someone named Kaganoff—"

"Saul," Pat interrupted. "That was his name. Saul Kaganoff."

"—and Sarasohn were all involved in organizing the shirtwaist workers. They were Communists. Is that it?"

Pat dredged his mind. "I always thought that Sarasohn might be. The other two—I don't know. We never talked about it, not even once. It was the first job I had in this country, and I knew nothing about any kind of politics. In Ireland, my family was opposed to British rule. That was the only politics an Irishman ever had. I sure as hell wasn't a Communist, either in Ireland or in New York. If Sarasohn is going to say that I was, he's a goddam liar."

Eva asked, "But why would he even want to make such an accusation?"

Conroy left the sofa and strode to where Patrick sat. He touched him reassuringly on the shoulder. "Between now and Friday, we'll try to figure out what Sarasohn's angle is so that we can be ready for him. We have four days. A lot can be learned in four days."

In the corner, the telephone began to ring.

"It might be for me," Conroy explained. "I told my office where I'd be."

It was, in fact. Eva Cassidy handed the receiver to the young state senator. As she did, she said to her husband, "It's Joan Magnuson."

Conroy listened intently to what the actress had to say. "Okay," he replied at last. "You've been very helpful. Except that now I find we've given you the wrong name."

"Wrong name?" Joan asked.

"We're not interested in Craig Lee anymore. We're interested in someone named Sarasohn." He cupped the

356

receiver with his hand and turned to Pat. "Does he have a first name?"

"If he does, I never heard it," Pat answered.

"S-a-r-a-s-o-h-n," Conroy spelled into the telephone. "At some time between 1916 and the late twenties, Sarasohn apparently became Craig Lee. We want you to ask your Hollywood friends if they ever knew him as Sarasohn."

"I have no Hollywood friends," she replied. "No one in Hollywood has friends."

"Okay, I won't argue. Then ask some of the crowd you used to hang around with."

"Rex Hammil's driving up this afternoon," she volunteered. "Do you want to talk to him?"

"Who's he?"

"Lily Carson's longtime roommate. Novelist, screenwriter, Communist, and drunk—not necessarily in that order of importance. If anyone would know anything about Sarasohn, he would."

Once again, Conroy turned to Pat. "Do you want to see a fellow name Rex Hammil? He'll be at Joan Magnuson's house in Carmel this afternoon. There's a good chance that he'll be able to tell us something about Sarasohn."

Pat didn't have to be persuaded.

Conroy pulled the car off the winding road into a driveway that led to a long, rambling, shake-roofed house. Roses and vines and hollyhocks were planted at its foundations, and huge daisies spilled from window boxes.

"Hammil is already here," he said, parking next to a pea-green Jaguar in front of a four-car garage.

Joan Magnuson was waiting for them inside the opened door. "He's in the bathroom now," she whispered.

She showed them into a sunken living room, at one end of which was an immense window overlooking the sea.

"Does he know why we're here?" Conroy asked.

"Vaguely. He's very upset himself because he's afraid

357

that Craig Lee might implicate him and Lily Carson."

"Have you asked him about Sarasohn's arrival in Los Angeles, before he became Craig Lee?"

"I thought I'd let you two do that."

There was a flushing sound in the distance, and in a minute a small, round-shouldered, red-faced man entered the room. He wore a blue blazer, a rumpled sport shirt, gray trousers, and a pair of white sneakers without socks. His eyes were shielded by dark sunglasses. If he hadn't existed, Hollywood would certainly have invented him.

Joan made the introductions, and when she had finished, Hammil announced that he really ought to be going.

"We've come down from San Francisco especially to talk to you," Pat declared.

"I've already told Joan everything I know about Craig Lee, which isn't much. I'm not particularly a fan of his and never have been. While I admire a man who follows his convictions, I don't think he should publicly malign his former comrades in the process."

Hammil remained standing, his car keys in his hands. Quite obviously, he didn't intend to stay in order to be grilled.

"How would you characterize Craig Lee?" Conroy asked.

"Characterize him?" the novelist-screenwriter repeated. "I'd say he's a fairly competent producer, but he takes terrible chances. He lacks judgment."

"Politically, I meant."

Hammil pondered it only momentarily. "Same thing. He's a bit of a gambler, literally and figuratively. For a time, it served his purposes to be a party member. Now it no longer does, so he's gambling on something else."

"You said literally," Pat reminded him.

"Yeah," Hammil replied. "So I did. He loves to play poker and blackjack. Sometimes he wins a lot; sometimes he loses a lot."

"I have reason to believe," Pat began, "that the man who calls himself Craig Lee is actually someone I knew more than twenty years ago by a different name. The name was Sarasohn."

Hammil's body went limp. "Sarasohn?" he said incredulously. "*You* knew Sarasohn?"

Briefly, Pat described the circumstances that had led him to Clinton Hall back in 1916. "'I never asked him if he was a party member. It seems to me now that he might very well have been. I was involved in the strike and nothing more."

"You knew Sarasohn!" Hammil repeated. "And now you think that through some magical Hollywood metamorphosis he's become Craig Lee. Well, I have news for you, Mr. Cassidy. You are wrong."

"Can you be certain?" Joan asked.

Vehemently, he answered, "You're damned right I can be certain. Sarasohn"—he paused when his voice nearly broke—"Sarasohn was one of the men who tried to organize the migrant workers in the Imperial Valley. He lived with the workers and marched with them. He went to jail for them. And you tell me you think he may be Craig Lee, that simpleminded, posturing old fool!"

Stranger things had happened, Conroy said. Sometimes, if necessary, men took on entirely new identities.

"Not Sarasohn," Hammil protested. "I don't think I ever saw him when he wasn't hungry or his clothes weren't frayed. If you offered him a dime, five cents of it went to someone who needed it more than he did. Sarasohn had almost nothing to do with the Hollywood Reds. He detested them. In his eyes, they were useless, parasitic dilettantes who joined the party because they were bored with their own lives. Of all the men I've met because of my political persuasions, only two stand out as heroes. One was John Reed, who was born a millionaire and gave it all up to serve the working class. And the other"—once again his voice began to break—"was Sarasohn, who lived for one thing alone: a world in which all men could stand up tall, off their knees. He died for his beliefs."

"*Died?*" Patrick asked.

"He was a member of the Abraham Lincoln Brigade in

Spain and was killed in the Valley of Jarama during the siege of Madrid."

He was *dead*. Sarasohn was dead. Even now, Pat remembered his sorrowful face. He should have known that the man behind that pocked and ravaged face would never compromise his ideals.

Yet Sarasohn had been given Eva's jewelry, and now it was being worn by Craig Lee's wife. What was the connection? Patrick put the question to Rex Hammil.

"He probably did just what you asked him to do," Hammil answered. "He sold the brooch and used the money to support the strikers in the Imperial Valley."

Conroy excitedly interrupted, "And when he sold it to Craig Lee in Hollywood, he also—quite understandably —happened to tell him how he came to be in possession of it. He mentioned your name, Pat."

That had to be the explanation. There could be no other.

"And now Craig Lee, whoever he is, is about to sell the story in Washington."

For the first time, Pat saw his enemy not as a man, recognizable and human, but as ignorance and fear. Would seven American congressmen, sitting on a duly convened committee of the House of Representatives, accept uncorroborated evidence from a witness who had not even been present during the events he was about to describe? Or would the bright lamp of justice burn during the proceedings, driving out darkness and hysteria? Weren't democratic institutions stronger than those who wished to subvert them?

Even though he didn't yet know who his accuser was, Pat began to feel he might have a fighting chance, after all.

"Well," Conroy began as they left Joan Magnuson's house, "I guess it was a wasted trip. When we go to Washington, we'll have no one but God on our side."

God's help would certainly be welcome, but Pat knew with certainty that he would have more than God on his side.

"I'm not afraid anymore, Robert," he replied.

360

The December hearings of the House Committee on Un-American Activities had as their primary purpose the exposure of criminal mismanagement of the Works Progress Administration, commonly known as the W.P.A. It was a New Deal program designed to give work to men and women who had been left jobless by the Depression, and some committee members were of the opinion that it had been infiltrated by Reds.

Witnesses were called upon to testify. One of them, Mrs. Hallie Flanagan, in attempting to defend the W.P.A.'s Theatre Project, made a reference to a gentleman named Marlowe, whereupon Congressman Starnes of Alabama interrupted.

"Is he a Communist?" he demanded.

Mrs. Flanagan was only momentarily flustered. He was a dramatist, she replied.

Congressman Starnes persisted. "Mrs. Flanagan," he asked, "tell us exactly who this Marlowe is."

"I'm speaking of Christopher Marlowe, who died in the year 1593, Mr. Starnes. So far as I know, he wasn't a Communist."

Patrick had read of the exchange in the newspapers during breakfast in his hotel room with Eva and Conroy. The public hearings on the W.P.A. would soon recess, and he and his accuser would at last meet each other face-to-face in executive session.

"Is Craig Lee in town yet?" he asked.

"If he is, he's not staying at any of the hotels under that name. I've already checked," Conroy said.

"Which one of us is going to be called first?"

Conroy wasn't sure. He personally hoped that Craig Lee would testify first, which would make a rebuttal easier. In the event that Pat was first to appear, Robert Conroy would be allowed to cross-examine Lee after he had given his own version of the events.

"I don't think I can eat any more breakfast," Pat said.

"Neither can I," Eva volunteered. "Why don't we go over there early and try to collect ourselves? Are you nervous, Pat?"

"I was," he answered, "but I'm not anymore. I'm mad

361

as hell. I'm already a Red, according to the newspapers."

Although it was to be a closed session, reporters had already gathered outside the committee room. Inside, five members were seated. They sipped coffee and chatted among themselves. Chairman Dies's place was still vacant, as was the chair assigned to Congressman Healey of Massachusetts.

Two clerks occupied seats in the room, pencils and notepads ready, prepared to record the proceedings. In front of the long, half-moon-shaped table at which the congressmen sat was a modest table with chairs for two. It was there that Pat would be invited to sit, Robert Conroy to his left, and face the committee. In the rear of the room were places for fifty or more spectators, but only three seats were taken. A guard stood inside the door.

"Why isn't he here?" Pat whispered.

"Dies has a reputation for coming in just a minute or so before the hearings convene," Conroy replied.

"I mean Craig Lee. If I'm called first, I still won't know who my accuser is."

"It doesn't make any difference," Conroy said soothingly. "If the committee accepts the testimony of a liar, then for all practical purposes they're your accuser. That's why you're going to defy the whole goddam committee."

"They'll hold me in contempt."

"They wouldn't dare."

"Here comes Martin Dies now," Conroy said as a youngish, pleasant-faced fellow entered the room, stopped at one end of the table, bent over, and whispered to a man whose nameplate identified him as Noah Mason of Illinois.

The Democratic congressman from Texas occupied the center chair, looked about him, then tapped a gavel against the table. In a southwestern drawl, he began, "This executive session of the House Committee on Un-American Activities will now come to order for the purpose of examining charges brought against Patrick Cassidy of the International Longshoremen's Association." He waited, then spoke across the room. "Mr. Cassidy, our proceedings will be quite informal. In sessions of this sort, the public has been barred in order that my colleagues and I can determine the veracity of charges found in this deposition"—he indicated a folder in his hand—"without pressure or hysteria. I shall take this opportunity to remind all of us here today that what transpires in our chambers is of a private nature, and premature reports are not to be issued to the news media." He turned to Congressman Dempsey and bowed his head. "I am indebted to the young congressman from New Mexico for bringing certain recent irregularities to my attention."

Pat knew for a fact that no love was lost between the members from Texas and New Mexico, and moreover that Dempsey had intimated that the chairman himself had been responsible for leaking unauthorized material to the press.

Eva tapped Pat's knee by way of commenting on the adroitness of Dies's speech. It was a joke among them that only Southerners could insult you without you ever knowing it.

"Are you represented by an attorney, Mr. Cassidy?" the chairman asked.

"I am, sir."

Martin Dies searched Robert Conroy's face, perhaps in hopes of determining his degree of competence or dedication.

"We have not yet been supplied with a copy of the deposition, sir," Conroy said as he and Pat took their seats in front of the half-moon table.

"The committee does not have your name. For the purpose of our records, it will be necessary for you to state that, please."

Though Conroy had already sat, he now stood and said, "Robert Conroy."

"And your place of residence?"

"Sacramento, California."

The name meant something to at least two committee members. Joseph Starnes whispered to Harold Mosier, who replied with an affirmative nod.

"The committee is pleased and honored to have a member of one of California's first families appear before it," Joe Starnes said with a strong Deep South accent.

"Thank you," Conroy replied. "I might add that I, too, am honored and pleased to represent Patrick Cassidy, who, though he is not from one of my state's first families, is most certainly from one of the most illustrious and venerated of them."

Chairman Dies smiled benignly. "In answer to your question, Mr. Conroy, it is not the custom of the committee to reveal the results of investigations by our staff members previous to our first executive session. If the committee feels that sufficient evidence is presented to warrant a public hearing, you and your client will be supplied with a copy of the charges."

Conroy had already explained to Pat that he was not appearing before a court of law and that many of the committee's rules had been tailor-made to suit its chairman. To challenge Dies at this point would only antagonize him.

"You have advised your client of his rights, have you, Mr. Conroy?"

"I have, sir."

In fact, Robert Conroy had suggested total defiance out of principle. The committee members would learn nothing from Pat. Instead, Conroy would attack Craig Lee's testimony in order to prove him a liar. It was risky, both agreed.

"If that is the case, we are ready to proceed," the chairman announced. "Mr. Cassidy, we have here a deposition that I shall now read to you." He cleared his throat. "It is dated September fifth, 1938, Los Angeles, California, and reads as follows: 'During the spring of 1932, while I was an active member of the Communist party of America, a meeting was arranged between me and a party member named Sarasohn, who was attempting to organize the farm workers of the Imperial Valley. A mutual friend had suggested that I might be interested in obtaining several pieces of jewelry, which Sarasohn hoped to convert to cash and use to support the farm workers. Understandably, I asked the seller how the jewelry had come into his possession, and he told me the following: in the year 1916, while he was a member of the party in New York City, a young Irish-American party member had infiltrated the shirtwaist workers for the purpose of organizing a strike and recruiting party members. Cell meetings which he attended were held at the union headquarters at Clinton Hall on Clinton Street. That man's name, Sarasohn told me, was Patrick Cassidy.' "

Chairman Dies removed a handkerchief from his pocket in order to wipe his brow, then continue. " 'I knew immediately that the jewelry, given to Cassiddy by a rich fellow-traveler, was a good investment, so I purchased what I could, and never saw Sarasohn again. Several years later, however, perhaps in 1934 or 1935, I became aware that Patrick Cassidy was an officer of the International Longshoreman's Association in San Francisco, and during a strike when charges were made against him that he was a Communist, he publicly denied them. At the time, I was still active in the party. Since then, in reaction to Stalin's reign of terror, I have left. Like many other Americans, I now consider communism to be the ultimate threat to our Western world and that every attempt should be made to quell it. Because of that, I am now volunteering the information that Patrick Cassidy, the president of one of the largest unions in the United States, is and has been since the year 1916 a card-carrying member of the Communist party.' " Chairman Dies paused, then added, " 'Signed: Craig Lee.' "

So those were the charges. There were truths in them, to be sure, but the falsehoods were electrifying. Sarasohn would have been the first to know that Pat was at no time involved in a Communist cell. He was a union organizer, no more and no less.

Craig Lee had made the rest up.

"Before a public hearing is convened, we should like to ask you a few questions, Mr. Cassidy. Feel at your ease." He then nodded to Congressman Thomas of New Jersey.

In a husky, stentorian voice, J. Parnell Thomas asked,

"Mr. Cassidy, are you now or have you ever been a member of the Communist party?"

Patrick looked first at Eva, then at Robert Conroy. "On Constitutional grounds, I refuse to answer that question."

The committee members sat up in their chairs.

"Mr. Cassidy," Congressman Starnes of Alabama began, "isn't it true that you attended cell meetings at Clinton Hall in New York City before becoming an official in the longshoremen's union?"

"I cite the Fifth Amendment to the Constitution," Patrick replied. "I refuse to answer that question on the grounds of self-incrimination."

Congressman Mason's eyes darkened. "You are aware, Mr. Cassidy, are you, that a witness during our August hearings testified that you are responsible for most of the labor strife on the West Coast. Is it not true, Mr. Cassidy, that this is a Communistic attempt to cripple American business and make this country ripe for a Communistic overthrow?"

"I value the American Constitution," Patrick answered. "On Constitutional grounds, I respectfully refuse to answer that question."

Congressman Dempsey, half smiling, asked, "You were described in the deposition, Mr. Cassidy, as being an Irish-American. Is that or is that not true?"

Pat met his eyes head-on. "I respectfully decline to answer that question on the grounds that I might incriminate myself."

Dempsey nodded with understanding. The others reacted more cholerically, turning to each other and talking heatedly. Chairman Dies was forced to sound the gavel once more to restore order.

"Is it true, Mr. Cassidy, that you intend to answer none of our questions?" the chairman asked impatiently.

Robert Conroy interrupted. "Mr. Chairman, my client so refuses until he is confronted by his accuser."

The chairman could not conceal his annoyance. "I repeat, Mr. Cassidy," he said shortly, "is it your intention to answer none of this committee's questions?"

Almost with a sigh, Patrick replied, "I refuse to answer even that question on the grounds that my Constitutional rights have been infringed upon."

"I trust that you have been advised, Mr. Cassidy, that the committee can hold you in contempt of Congress."

"I beg to correct the honorable chairman," Conroy said, rising from his chair. "The committee is empowered to do that only at a public hearing, at which time witnesses will be under oath. By then, it is to be hoped that my client and I will understand why Craig Lee has invented the most crucial part of his testimony."

"You are suggesting, sir," Congressman Mosier asked, "that our witness is something less than reliable?"

"We are, sir."

Chairman Dies looked from face to face at the table. "If that is the case, I see no profitable reason for continuing our interrogation of the very recalcitrant Mr. Cassidy. With the committee's permission, we shall dismiss him for the time being and call Mr. Craig Lee." To the guard who stood inside the door, he said, "We are ready for Mr. Lee."

Pat and Conroy returned to where Eva sat at the rear of the room. Once seated, they stared at the door, waiting for it to open.

In a minute, the guard held the door as Craig Lee's wife made her way into the room, occupying a seat across from the Cassidys and Robert Conroy. The door closed momentarily, then reopened, and as it did, there was the popping of flashbulbs and the grinding of newsreel cameras.

Craig Lee strode down the aisle toward the committee members. He was dressed in an expensively tailored gray suit and walked with a confident swagger. At his neck was a regimental tie. Yet covering his head was a paper bag, slit at his eyes, his nostrils, and his mouth. It was macabre: from the neck down, Lee appeared to be a banker, perhaps, but from the neck up, a kind of goblin, evil and nameless.

"Are they going to allow that?" Pat complained in fury and frustration.

"I'll object, but I'm sure they'll try to justify it, any-

367

way," Conroy answered. "You'll have to rely on your ears, Pat. Listen to him carefully. Let me know if you've ever heard his voice before."

Pat's skin crawled. Craig Lee's presence triggered a visceral reaction, but he didn't quite know why. As Lee took a chair at the table before the committee, Pat looked at his shoulders, the way he sat, and how his feet were placed on the floor, hoping to find something that would reveal the man.

"I *know* him," Pat said at last. "I've met him. I can *feel* him."

"Then who is he?" Eva asked urgently.

"I can't say. All I know is that the minute he walked into the room, I was sure that I'd seen that walk before. But I don't know where."

Quickly, Robert Conroy rose from his chair and went to the front of the room, positioning himself no more than four feet from the seated Craig Lee.

"Mr. Chairman?" he asked.

"I shall anticipate your remarks, Mr. Conroy," Chairman Dies replied. "Because our witness fears for his safety and perhaps even his life, we have permitted him to shield his face. Your client's associates in the longshoremen's union are well known for intemperance and violence, and the committee has authorized this unusual step in order to prevent reprisals."

Not only would the committee be listening to a second-hand account of events that had taken place more than twenty years before, but they were permitting Pat's accuser the luxury of anonymity. Patrick realized at once, however, that it was not being done to prevent possible reprisals—after all, Craig Lee lived in Brentwood and could not spend the rest of his life in hiding—but to make it impossible for Pat to recognize him during the hearings. Psychologically, Lee would have a tremendous advantage.

"For the record," Conroy declared, "I should like to protest."

"Your protest is duly acknowledged," the congressman from Texas replied blandly.

"Will I be allowed to question the witness?" he asked.

"Only when you have the approval of the chair," Dies answered, then turned his attention to the grotesquely concealed face in front of him. "Mr. Lee," he began, "we have here a deposition signed by you on the fifth of September of this year, charging that Patrick Cassidy of the International Longshoremen's Association is a member of the Communist party. Before we proceed, sir, have you any emendations or retractions to make?"

Patrick crouched forward in his seat to listen to Lee's first words.

"I haf not, sir," the lips within the bag said.

The intonation was Germanic. Had Patrick heard the voice before? Had it always spoken in this manner?

"Then we shall begin our questioning, Mr. Lee." The chairman nodded to Congressman Thomas of New Jersey.

"Will you explain to the committee, please, more fully than you have in your deposition, the reason that you have come forward with this information at this time," J. Parnell Thomas requested.

"To the fery best of my ability, I shall do so, sir," the voice within the slit bag replied. "It ist my confiction that the greatest threat in the vorld today is that of international communism. I say so mit the authority of a man who vas a party member for many years. I am now villing to admit, sirs, that I vas duped. I see Communists for vat they are: godless, savage, unprincipled men and vimmen who vill stop at nothing to achieve their goals. Ven I learned that such a man vas president of a great American labor union, I realized at once that it vas my patriotic duty to expose him for vat he ist."

Eva bent over to whisper to her husband, "I don't think he's German."

"I'm sure he isn't," Pat replied.

There was a quality about the voice that summoned up something in Pat's memory that was not unpleasant. What was it? Where had he met this man?

"And can we say, Mr. Lee," Congressman Mason suggested, "that you have no reason to misrepresent yourself at this executive session, and no reason to perjure yourself at a public hearing, should one be necessary?"

"Ve can say that mit confidence, sir," Lee replied.

369

"Then let us proceed," Chairman Dies urged. "Would you say, Mr. Lee, that you are an honest, law-abiding American who believes in Almighty God, and who is sincerely repentant for having thrown in your lot with the enemies of our fair and beautiful Republic?"

"I am all those things, Mr. Chairman."

"And is it your conviction, Mr. Lee, that an attempt is being made even now," the chairman continued, "to usurp our democratic institutions on the part of the godless hordes from the East?"

"It is my confiction," the witness answered.

"And you are aware, are you, Mr. Lee," Congressman Starnes of Alabama now asked, "that during our August hearings, a committee witness testified that there are more than six hundred and forty Communist-front organizations in America, and that more than six and one-half million Americans are engaged in activities designed to overthrow our system of government?"

"I am avare of that, sir," Lee declared. "Communists have infiltrated every phase of American life."

"And is it not true," Congressman Mason began, "that most of the longshoreman strikes in West Coast ports during the last eight years would not have occurred had it not been for the active leadership of Communists such as Patrick Cassidy?"

"I can go further than that, sir. Had it not been for the treasonable activity of Patrick Cassidy and others, there would have been no strikes in our ports at all."

Until now, Congressman Dempsey of New Mexico had been looking at the bagged face as if he were transfixed. Now he declared, "Must I remind the committee that it is not our function to put words in the mouths of witnesses? However knowledgeable Mr. Lee is—and for the time being, I shall give him the benefit of doubt—we have not asked him to appear before us in order to give his opinions. We are interested only in facts."

Chairman Dies accepted the admonition with surprising grace. "Once again, I am grateful to the junior congressman from New Mexico for reminding us of our duties." He paused, then returned his attention to the ghostly paper bag in front of them. "Will you be prepared

370

to testify under oath, Mr. Lee, at a public hearing to be held at some future date, and repeat your charges that Patrick Cassidy was a member of the Communist party in the year 1916 and, so far as you know, continues to be a member, though he denies it?"

Suddenly, the paper bag turned in order to watch Pat's expression as he replied, and as it did, Pat knew at once where he had last seen that head turn in just that manner.

"I vill sir!" Craig Lee cried.

Breathlessly, Pat whispered to Conroy, *"I know who he is, I know who he is! We have to get a recess! I know who he is!"*

Robert Conroy sprang from his seat. "Mr. Chairman!" he demanded.

"The chair recognizes Mr. Conroy."

Patrick slumped over in his seat, his eyes closed.

"I respectfully request a half-hour delay, Mr. Chairman. My client is ill."

The committee members peered at the writhing figure of Patrick Cassidy, held by his wife. His hand covered his heart.

Martin Dies smartly tapped the gavel. "Gentlemen," he said, "we shall reconvene in thirty minutes' time." To Conroy, he added, "It is our hope that Mr. Cassidy's indisposition is only temporary."

As Eva bent over him, Pat whispered, "It is mine, too, you bastards!"

Robert Conroy once said that a politician spent fifty percent of his life getting himself elected and the remainder paying off favors to those who had helped him. In his own case, as many debts were owed him as he owed others, and during the next thirty minutes, he called in three of the former for immediate repayment. In rapid succession, he telephoned the governor of California, the junior U.S. senator from California, and the chief of police of the city of Los Angeles.

The governor and the senator were asked to exert all the pressure they could to determine if the F.B.I. had a file on the accuser, and the Los Angeles police chief was asked if the man in the paper sack had ever run afoul of the law in that city.

Each was given the name that Patrick had supplied and told that they had slightly more than twenty-four minutes to return the telephone call.

While they waited, Pat revealed to Conroy everything he knew about the man who was testifying against him.

Thirteen minutes before the end of the recess, the telephone rang and Conroy was told that he had a call from Los Angeles. He talked excitedly for the next four minutes, at which time the second phone in the room began to ring. It was the governor's office in Sacramento advising Conroy that the director was giving the matter his attention, and that a reply could be expected before the eleven o'clock reconvening of the committee.

"In the event that the information is useful to you," the governor said to Conroy, "the director has asked me to remind you that under no circumstances are you to reveal the source of that information."

Robert Conroy agreed that it would be imprudent to introduce the director's name. What they were doing was against the policy of the F.B.I. and quite possibly even illegal, but it seemed to Conroy the only hope they had.

At five minutes to eleven, a guard tapped on the door of the room, then opened it to advise them that they were expected back in the committee's chambers.

Conroy still lacked the whole picture and was counting on the director to furnish it, but by ten fifty-eight he had not yet called.

"The committee is about to reconvene," the guard reminded them, and at the same minute the telephone began to ring under Conroy's hand.

"Yes," he said into the receiver. "Yes, sir. I am extremely grateful." In his fist, a pencil was poised over a sheet of paper. "Yes," he repeated, then began to write hurriedly. "I have that, sir. The year 1922, did you say?" Once again, he listened. "Yes. I see." Quickly, he began to write again. "That's astonishing. That's really astonishing." In seconds, half of the sheet of paper was filled with a barely legible scrawl. "In 1929, he disappeared? After that date, you have nothing in your files? I see. Yes, I see."

He looked across the room at Pat, even as the guard once again held the door open for them. At the other end of the hall, the committee members were filing into the chamber.

"You have no idea how indebted we are to you, sir. I hope someday that I'll be able to return the favor."

Conroy hung up, then hurried to the door. "We have the bastard by the short hairs," he whispered to Pat as they made their way down the hall.

When they entered the room, the committee members were already seated at the table. In the section set off for spectators sat the man known as Craig Lee, next to his wife.

Robert Conroy went directly to the chairman.

"It is the committee's hope," Chairman Dies began, "that your client has reconsidered the position he has taken and is now prepared to testify."

"With your permission, sir," Conroy replied. "I should first like to clarify one or two matters with Mr. Lee."

The Texan looked across the room at the eerie covering over Craig Lee's face.

"The chair recalls Mr. Lee to the witness stand."

Once again, Patrick watched his enemy make his way to the table directly in front of the committee members. He marveled at the man's composure. Had Pat been in similar circumstances, he was sure he wouldn't have been able to carry it off half so well.

Craig Lee sat in the chair and folded his hands in front of him at the table. As he breathed, the paper bag could be seen to inflate and deflate ever so slightly.

"Mr. Lee," Robert Conroy began in a deceptively pleasant fashion, "you have told the committee that in the year 1932, a member of the Communist party named Sarasohn positively identified Patrick Cassidy as having been a party member in the year 1916. Is that correct, sir?"

"It ist correct."

"It was not speculation on Sarasohn's part, or on

373

yours? He *positively* identified my client as a Communist. Is that true?"

"That ist true."

"And when Congressman Dies of Texas identified you as"—Conroy searched his notes—"an *honest, lawabiding American who believes in Almighty God,* can we assume that that is a fair and accurate representation of your character?"

The witness shifted his weight in the chair. "I think it is a fair and accurate description."

Conroy suddenly smiled. "And would you say, as an honest, law-abiding American, Mr. Lee, that patriotism alone has motivated you in making these charges before the committee, and that you have not acted through promise of personal gain?"

The man answered proudly, "As I haf explained to the committee, my solitary interest ist that Communists should be exposed."

"Thank you, Mr. Lee," Conroy replied, then addressed the committee members: "I merely wanted to remind the honorable members of the House Un-American Activities Committee that your witness's character is unimpeachable." He waited, then added, "With your permission, I should like to ask a few more questions."

With something between interest and suspicion, the Texan said, "Go ahead, Mr. Conroy."

"Thank you." Once again, Conroy turned to the witness. "Have you ever been employed by a shipping line, Mr. Lee?"

Without hesitation, the witness answered, "I haf not been."

"Let's put it another way, Mr. Lee. Under any name other than Craig Lee, have you ever been employed by a shipping line?" He paused. "May I remind you that at a public hearing you will be under oath and that the laws of perjury will govern your testimony."

The eyes behind the slits looked across the table toward Chairman Dies. "No, I haf not," he replied somewhat more hesitantly than previously.

Until now, Conroy had been easy and amiable. Now his approach changed. "Is it not true, Mr. Lee, that between the years 1922 and 1929, you were employed as an agent of the Comstock-Orient line in Honolulu?"

The witness did not volunteer an answer, nor did Conroy wait for one. "And is it not also true, Mr. Lee, that in November of the year 1929, you left your employment, without notice, and that in December of 1929, when an audit revealed that more than seventy-five thousand dollars of company funds had been transferred to your personal accounts over a period of months, a warrant was issued for your arrrest?"

"I don't know what the hell you're talking about," Craig Lee replied, and suddenly his Germanic accent had disappeared.

"And is it not also true that upon arriving in Los Angeles, you assumed your present name and identity, setting yourself up as a producer of films, using stolen money to do so?"

"It's a damned lie," Craig Lee stood at his chair. "Do I have to listen to this nonsense, Mr. Chairman?"

Chairman Dies did not immediately reply. "As Mr. Conroy has already suggested," he said at last, "the purpose of our executive session today is to determine if we have sufficient evidence for a public hearing. At the latter, Mr. Lee, you will be required to answer such questions under oath. We are meeting today in response to your deposition. I urge you to answer Mr. Conroy's charges."

Robert Conroy turned again to the witness. "In July of this year, Mr. Lee, in Los Angeles, California, a warrant was once again issued for your arrest on the charge of embezzlement. The complaint was signed by Peter Flynn of the Comstock-Orient shipping line, whose headquarters are in San Francisco. On September fifth, 1938, you signed a deposition charging that Patrick Cassidy of the I.L.A. was a member of the Communist party. On September seventh, 1938, the warrant for your arrest was withdrawn on authority of Peter Flynn, president of the Comstock-Orient line."

Conroy waited, then shouted, "Is it not true, Mr. Lee, that you exchanged a pack of lies for your freedom?"

Patrick watched as the shoulders of the man seated at the table pulled back with a start, as if he had been struck. In confusion, the face behind the paper bag turned first to his wife, then to Chairman Dies.

Conroy had not finished. When the man known as Craig Lee did not respond, the committee members looked anxiously across the table, and the witness's figure seemed to grow smaller.

"The question remains," Conroy continued, "why you have sought to ruin the reputation of an honest man. To be sure, by doing so, you induced Peter Flynn to dismiss criminal charges against you. Yet did you have no sympathy for your unknown victim, Mr. Lee?" Once again, he waited. "Or, in fact, was your victim known to you?"

"Have you nothing to say, Mr. Lee?" Chairman Dies asked.

In the silence that followed, it was Conroy who replied. "It might be a convenience, Mr. Chairman, if my client addressed your witness by the name under which he knows him."

Patrick rose from his seat, and from across the room, for the first time in almost a quarter of a century, he uttered the name of a man he had once considered his friend.

"Saul?" he asked. When there was no answer, he cried with indignation, "Saul Kaganoff!"

Slowly, the witness removed the paper sack from his head and let it fall to the floor. He buried his face in his hands.

Not a sound could be heard in the hushed room. At last, Congressman Dempsey rose from his chair. "Mr. Chairman," he began softly, "may I move that all allegations made today against Mr. Cassidy be stricken from our records, and that we adjourn."

Chairman Dies studied the witness, then said to his colleagues, "All those in favor of the motion set forward by the congressman from New Mexico, please say *aye*."

Five *ayes* sang out, followed by the chairman's own. As the gavel snapped against the tabletop, Saul Kaganoff hurried up the aisle toward the exit.

Suddenly, Eva was embracing Pat, and Robert Conroy was pumping his hand, but when he saw Kaganoff leave the hearing room, Pat broke away from them and rushed after him. Outside in the hall, a reporter shouted a question at him and a flashbulb popped.

Kaganoff was already descending the stairs, and as he looked over his shoulder and saw his pursuer, he began to run. Pat pushed past the newsmen and dashed down the stairs after him.

The first floor was empty, but a rest-room door still quivered ever so slightly. Patrick knocked it open with his fist.

Kaganoff was standing in the middle of the tiled floor. "So we meet again, Irishman."

Under his suntan, his face was bloated. Yet now that he no longer spoke with the absurd accent, there was that same warm and persuasive quality to his voice that had set Patrick's mind on fire the first time he had listened to it. He looked for traces of the selfless young man of high ideals he used to know, but saw only a thick-lipped, tired-eyed, middle-aged man.

"We are only human beings," his old friend apologized, "as much as we would like to be gods."

"Why did you do it?" Pat demanded.

Saul shrugged his shoulders. "After the strike failed, you left with Balaban's wife. You weren't the loser that I was. I had no job and no prospect of getting one. Then, when Sonia left the hospital, she told me she loved Sarasohn and was moving in with him. I had nothing."

Sweat poured from his forehead, and his face glistened under the lightbulb. "For the next two years, I bummed around the country. I lived in boxcars and hobo camps and listened to starving men talk about the coming revolution. I believed it all. Even when I shipped out for the islands, I still believed in the party and its goals. But then I got sick and wound up in the charity ward of a hospital in Honolulu. I had TB and a lot of time to think. And do you know what I decided, Irishman? I decided that I wasn't going to take any more shit from the world. Other people could wait for the revolution, but I was going to look after myself. So when I left the hospital, I got a job."

"Peter Flynn hired you."

"No. I never set eyes on him until a few months ago. An uncle of his hired me. I'd taken a few accounting courses at City College, and Comstock-Orient was looking for a bookkeeper who'd work for half nothing. I worked my balls off and gave them value for their money. But I also liked to gamble, so every now and then I dipped into the till, always intending to pay it back. But you know how it goes. I should have known by then not to expect anything out of life but disappointments. We were due for an auditing, and if I stayed in Honolulu, they'd put me in jail. What choice did I have? I ran away. When I got to the mainland, the first thing I did was change my name. Saul Kaganoff died, and Craig Lee was born. I bought some sunglasses and a few good suits and set myself up in Hollywood. I'd been told that anyone who could talk fast and loud could make money in the movie industry, and pretty soon I was rolling in dough."

Patrick interrupted. "Then you met Sarasohn again."

"No, I didn't. It was Sonia who came to see me at the office one day. She'd recognized me from a photo taken at a movie opening. She told me that I was a rich Red and that she and Sarasohn were poor Reds, and that it was my obligation to help them in their fight against the ranchers in the Imperial Valley. I said I couldn't do it because I'd already left the party. I left about the time that Stalin's collective-farm policy began to fail and we heard stories about millions of people dying of starvation and disease. If that was all the revolution accomplished, I didn't want to have any part of it. Sonia and Sarasohn were Stalinists right up to the end. So she asked me if I'd be interested in a purely business proposition. Sarasohn had a diamond brooch he wanted to get rid of because he needed the dough for the migrant workers. Did I want to buy it?"

"He kept it all those years?"

"Forgot he ever had it. After the strike failed, he and Sonia went back to Russia, and everything he owned was packed in a trunk and left with Sonia's family. In Russia they were caught up in the revolution, and it was almost nine years before they returned to America. By then Sonia's family had moved three or four times, and each time the trunk went with them. When Sarasohn finally opened it, he found the coat he'd been wearing the day the strike was broken, and the brooch was still in its pocket, just where he'd put it and forgotten all about it in the panic and confusion of that awful day. A little while later, he and Sonia set out for California, and the brooch went with them. When Sonia asked me to buy it, I offered her a fair price—I've got a good eye for precious stones, if for nothing else—and she accepted, said goodbye, and walked out. That's the last I've heard of either of them."

"Sarasohn is dead. He was killed with the Abraham Lincoln Brigade in Spain."

Saul writhed in pain. "And Sonia?"

"No one knows where she is. Somewhere in Europe, they think."

Kaganoff struck a fist into the palm of his hand. "They were fools, both of them!" He turned his face away. "You hate me, don't you, Irishman?"

Patrick couldn't find the words to deny it, so he said nothing.

When Saul spoke again, it was with the old passion and fervor that had once moved Pat and set him dreaming. "I tried to argue with Flynn! He wouldn't listen! When he found out where I was, he swore out a warrant for my arrrest. He didn't want money. He was going to put me in jail. I *had* to make a deal. Don't you understand? Everyone in California knew that the shipowners hated your guts and would give anything to get you out of their hair. So I told Flynn—that I knew a way—to have you deported. I told him I'd testify against you. I'm sorry, Irishman. I really am." Tears rolled down his cheeks. "I'm genuinely sorry. But it was bad luck that made me do it. Bad luck makes scoundrels of us all."

Was it true? Had Sarasohn ever had any luck that was anything but bad? Had Sonia or Annamarie? Bad luck had made heroes out of them, while it merely confirmed the baseness in Saul.

Saul was begging. He reached out for Patrick's hand. "What will happen to me now?"

Patrick turned and rushed from the room.

26

All week long, during the last torrid days of August 1939, the newspapers were filled with photographs of goose-stepping soldiers and of huge tanks lumbering along narrow roads beneath Lombardy poplars. In London, air-raid sirens wailed in a test run for the first time and gas masks were issued, while in Warsaw and Budapest, Jews tried desperately to settle their affairs and flee before the coming terror. Frenzied diplomats dashed from capital to capital, marshaling support for the defenseless Poles even as the *Wehrmacht* began to collect near their borders. Everywhere, people waited for the war that was now inescapable.

In New York City, the society wedding of the year was about to take place, or at least so it had been called by a headline writer for the *Daily News* who felt that in times of dire crisis people were in need of hyperbole. Though it could be argued that the site of the nuptials—St. Patrick's Cathedral on Fifth Avenue—was enough to cast doubt on the reporter's credibility, few readers were unmoved by the glittering cast of characters. Monsignor Fulton J. Sheen himself would officiate. In addition to the regular corps of New York City policemen, thirty-five private detectives had been hired to keep out the curious and ensure that the six hundred invited guests would not be annoyed. A second battalion of detectives would guard the tables laden with gifts at the Plaza, where the reception would take place. The Delanos' party would arrive by private train an hour and a half before the ceremony and be transferred by limousines from Grand Central to the cathedral. Many of the Molloys—Charles's brothers

381

and sisters and their familes—planned to steam into New York Harbor from Long Island on their yachts.

Whether the President himself would attend remained in doubt—Herr Hitler alone could determine that—but in the meantime an advance crew of Secret Service men had been sent to plumb the shadowy corners of St Patrick's Cathedral. Both Tom and Nancy hoped that he wouldn't come, as he would steal the show. It was their day, not his.

If it was not the society wedding of the year, it was at least the union of the most socially desirable young woman of that season with one of the handsomest and richest young men. Even the names of their friends were magical. Among Nancy's bridesmaids were a Biddle, a DuPont, and a Roosevelt. Two of Tom's ushers were a Phipps and a Morgan.

It was all very heady reading for subscribers to the *Daily News*.

Caitlin Molloy, however, tended to look at it rather skeptically. On the morning before the wedding, she read the newspaper account to her mother and father at the breakfast table in their house on East Seventy-first Street, then said, "Well, it appears that the Delanos have at last arrived. They're marrying into society."

More than that, they were marrying into the mysteries of the Roman Church, for, just the day before, Nancy had been confirmed at the church of St. Vincent Ferrer. Tom had not asked it, but Nancy had volunteered. It would help bind her to her husband, she said, and later there would be no quibbling about the religious instruction their children would receive.

Nancy's mother was something less than happy about the turn of events, but Benjamin Delano had persuaded her not to oppose it. By now, he had become a close friend and business associate of Charles Molloy, and he welcomed Molloy's freshness of outlook and boldness.

"These Irish are a damned sight nicer than one has been led to believe," Ben Delano mentioned at the Union Club when his daughter's engagement was announced at Christmas. "We could use a little excitement in our blood, and the Molloys are certainly exciting. Young Tom has a

382

splendid future. I'm really delighted with the whole thing."

For Nora Molloy, it had been a triumph in every way. During the course of Nancy's religious instruction, she had got to know her future daughter-in-law quite well, and Nancy and Caitlin had also become great friends. It was the Irish knack of overwhelming strangers with hospitality. Like John Phipps, who for all practical purposes had already been adopted by the entire clan, Nancy Delano became a daughter and a sister before she became a wife and a daughter-in-law.

"Sucked in by the fatal Irish charm," John Phipps said waggishly about it. "It's almost as if she were marrying all the Molloys, not just Tom."

But of course Nora Molloy would have had it no other way. From the very beginning, she had known that a wife of Tom's would end up doing Irish step dances and playing touch football on the lawn at the Southampton house. And when Nancy began to have babies and raise a family in the small place they had rented in Cambridge while Tom attended Harvard Law School, her children would be raised with Nora's own. After all, Nora's youngest was just barely two.

As for Nancy, she loved the gaiety and openness of the family, the noise, the confusion, the simple animal warmth of being in the same room with all eleven of them. They were so different from her saturnine mother and indifferent father, and their houses were so unlike the one she'd grown up in near Millbrook, where the only friends she'd had were servants.

So that when Nancy became a Catholic, it was as much through gratitude as out of respect for Tom's heritage. She was certain that she was the luckiest girl in the world, and surely *some*one had to be thanked. In her former religion, she wouldn't have known whom to address. But in the religion of the Molloys, God was an ever-present member of the family, and just as one expressed thanks to Edward or Deirdre when they passed something at the dinner table, one also offered gratitude to God for favors received.

She was not the only one. Nora had already brought

the match to the attention of God and requested that His undivided beneficence be directed toward it. Now, just twenty-four hours before the union was to take place, she hoped with all her heart that He would pay particular care, and be protective, too, especially during Tom's bachelor party that night.

John Phipps was hosting it at the Harvard Club, where he had rented rooms for the occasion. Nora had extracted a promise from Tom that he would be home by no later than one in the morning and that he would drink in moderation.

"Just what do they do at bachelor parties?" Caitlin Molloy asked at the breakfast table as her father finished reading the *Daily News* article and disdainfully laid it to one side of his plate.

"I expect they debauch," Nora replied.

"Tom is a very good drinker," his father boasted, it being his opinion that the world was divided between those people who could hold their liquor and those who couldn't.

Wistfully, Caitlin looked into space. "Oh, I wish I were being married tomorrow."

"Your turn will come, Caitlin dear."

"I'm really beginning to think that John likes me a little bit. I mean, he doesn't call me odious names anymore."

Charles Molloy smiled. "Well, that's an improvement."

"Wait until he sees you in your bridesmaid's dress," her mother told her. "He'll be swept off his feet."

"He's not dating that horrid Emily Thayer anymore, so he's available."

"Just don't push him too much, Caitlin," Charles Molloy advised. "A man always likes to believe that he makes the decisions." He waited, then added, "Even when he doesn't."

With absolute confidence, Caitlin said, "I really think he *will* marry me, sooner or later. After all, does anyone else like him as much as I do? I shall simply have to make myself more attractive to him."

"Why, Caitlin dear!" Nora cried in mock astonishment. "How conniving of you!"

384

Dryly, Charles observed, "I wonder where she got it." Then all three began to laugh.

By noon, Tom had telephoned Nancy in Millbrook four times, and in the end, her mother asked him to desist, as he was tying up the line and they were still waiting for a call from the White House, either confirming that the President would attend the ceremonies or, because the world was on the brink of war, sending his regrets.

"Doesn't make any difference to me," Tom said to John Phipps as they left the Harvard Club, where John had supervised the stocking of liquor for the party that evening. They were bound for Tiffany's to pick up the monogrammed sterling silver cigarette cases ordered for the ushers. They wanted to make sure they were ready for the party that night. The ring from Cartier's had been at home in the Molloys' safe for weeks.

"I think it would be rather nice if the old fellow could make an appearance. But I warn you: if he does, my father will probably corner him and start complaining about the New Deal."

It was the coming war that occupied Tom's attention, not Roosevelt's domestic policies. "I wish Nancy and I had done this early in the summer, before all this war fever began. This is not the same thing as Munich. This time, people are going to be killed."

With uncharacteristic gravity, Phipps asked, "And we'll be drawn into it, do you think? Roosevelt has promised to keep us out of it, Tom."

They walked east on Forty-fourth Street, until they reached Fifth Avenue, then turned north, passing pedestrians dressed in cool summer seersuckers and wearing straw hats.

"If the Nazis invade Poland," Tom replied, "Britain will have no choice but to declare war against Germany. And twenty-four hours later, the *Luftwaffe* will be flying over London, dropping bombs. This war is going to be different from all other wars in history because as many civilians will die as soldiers. We *can't* remain neutral. It would be immoral."

Phipps shook his head in confusion. "I really don't

know. The old man's an isolationist. He says that a European war is none of our business. It's tempting to believe him."

"Damn the isolationists all to hell! They won't even allow conscription in this country for fear of offending Hitler. And as a result, we're on the verge of war and we don't even have an adequate army or navy. That's patriotism, is it? Hell, that's madness."

They walked up the wide sidewalk in silence, each lost in thought. At last, Phipps began, "This is really an awful time to be alive. I was thinking that just the other day. First the Depression, now this. Our generation is going to suffer one hell of a lot before the war is over." He waited. "Some of us are even going to be killed."

Tom hoped that he wouldn't be one of them. No matter how hard he tried, he simply could not imagine himself dead. There were thousands of things in the world he hadn't yet experienced. Books he hadn't read. Places he hadn't visited. People he hadn't met. To die of old age would be quite tolerable, but to die young on a foreign battlefield—now that was something that was contrary to reason and fairness.

If he were dead, whom would he miss most? His mother and father, to be sure. Nancy, of course. His brothers and sisters. He could not even think of a hereafter without them. Death itself did not frighten him; it was the loneliness and friendlessness, like being locked in the huge main reading room of Widener Library for an endless night while life went on outside on Harvard Yard and no amount of entreating at the windows brought anyone to his aid.

"Have you talked to Nancy about the war?" Phipps asked.

"We try to avoid it."

It was a minute before his friend continued. "Have you ever—" He stumbled, then stopped altogether. "Does Nancy know anything about—that other girl?"

That other girl. Even Tom had tried to banish her name from his memory. For the first three months, it had been difficult, and sometimes when he was with Nancy—in Poughkeepsie, Cambridge, or New York—he had found himself making comparisons. You could not know a girl the way he'd known Peggy and ever forget her entirely.

"I told her," Tom admitted. "She knows all about it."

"That's very good of Nancy. It really is. Being so understanding, I mean. She's a wonderful girl. Everyone envies you." He wiped his eyes.

Tom turned to look at his friend and saw that his eyes were glistening. "Why the hell are you getting so emotional?"

"I don't know," Phipps replied. "Growing up and getting married and going off to war, I suppose. It's all so amazing."

It *was*. Even now, the day before his wedding, he was unable to see his future without amazement. What was happening to him seemed quite unreal. To be sure, there were real things: the apartment he and Nancy had chosen on Everett Street, the furniture they had picked out, the necessity for him to register at law school by the eighteenth of September. But it *was* amazing to think of himself as a husband and a scholar while the world was disintegrating.

Tiffany's was directly ahead of them. As they bore down on it, Tom asked, "What time does the party start tonight?"

"I said eight o'clock. We're having oysters first, in white wine, then roast beef. My mother attended to all of it. She's very good about such things."

"How many are coming?"

"I sent invitations to ninety."

"Good Christ! I'm not sure I know that many people."

"I could have invited the whole Class of 1938 and everyone would have come. There isn't anyone who doesn't love you, Tom."

"Bullshit," Tom replied as they sailed through Tiffany's doors.

Inside, two clerks looked up, and while one rushed to the rear of the store, the other approached them, his hands folded deferentially in front of him.

"Good afternoon, Mr. Molloy. The manager particularly asked to see you when you dropped by so that he could deliver his personal good wishes. All of New York is talking about your wedding. We at Tiffany's are praying for a perfect day."

As the clerk retreated to alert the manager, Tom sighed, "I'll be glad when all this is over."

Soothingly, Phipps replied, "You have nothing to worry about. After all, what could go wrong? You even have Tiffany's praying for you."

Caitlin was the first to hear the news.

She had turned on the radio in her bedroom, hoping for an amplification of an earlier weather report for the following day, Saturday, the second of September, but instead listened to a special news bulletin announcing that German troops even at that moment were pouring across the border into Poland.

She hurried downstairs to where her mother was in the kitchen, supervising preparations for the large dinner party the Molloys would be giving that evening for family members who had traveled great distances to New York for the wedding.

Somberly, Caitlin announced, "The President won't be coming."

Nora was not displeased. There would be enough excitement without him. "But Mrs. Delano was to have telephoned me the minute she heard," Nora complained.

"I expect she doesn't know yet. The war has begun."

For the past week, everyone had been waiting for it. It certainly came as no surprise. Yet Nora's hands trembled uncontrollably in her apron pockets.

She listened as her daughter recounted what she had heard, then said, "Well, we shall simply have to make the best of it. There is nothing we can do for Poland except pray. But we cannot let the war spoil Tom's wedding tomorrow. For one day, there can be no war."

The news, however, cast a pall over their preparations. There were tears on the part of some of the kitchen staff whose families still lived in Europe, and soon there were voices of paperboys in the street, hawking extra editions of the morning papers. The telephone did not stop ringing all afternoon. As soon as Nora hung up, it would ring again, and still one more friend would ask if the wedding were being postponed. Of course not, Nora replied. Life had to go on. Didn't they know that?

Tom was dour and gloomy when he and Phipps returned to the house late in the afternoon. He'd called Nancy the minute he'd heard the news, and they'd agreed that there could be no changes in their plans for the following day. Nancy felt guilty now that so much money was being spent on the affair, but she was not prepared to forfeit her elegant wedding for an austere wartime ceremony, and neither was Tom.

"The way I look at it," he said to her when he called from downtown, "is that it will be another two or three days before it really gets bad. Chamberlain has already told Hitler that unless Germany pulls all her troops out of Poland, Britain will enter the war."

"Maybe the Germans will withdraw."

"They're halfway to Warsaw." He waited, then added, "It gives you a funny feeling, doesn't it? I mean, your throat gets all dry and everything, just thinking about it."

"Mine was dry to begin with, just thinking about the wedding."

"Are you nervous?"

"Terribly. Aren't you?"

"A little."

In point of fact, he was more than a little nervous. He wished that it had not been necessary to invite such a huge crowd, many of whom he scarcely knew. All the Hudson River aristocracy were coming, as well as all the New York Irish aristocracy, their friends, and friends of their friends, some of them drawn only by the spectacle.

"I hope I can sleep tonight," Nancy said. "If I don't, I'll have bags under my eyes tomorrow. I don't know why they can't have spinster parties for girls the night before weddings. My mother and father are having a stuffy dinner party instead."

"Maybe it won't be too bad."

"I know it's going to be perfectly awful."

"Sunshine is forecast for tomorrow, and it's not supposed to be too hot. Mid-seventies. So at least we'll have a nice day for it."

"That's a blessing. Wouldn't it be terrible to be married in ninety-degree heat?"

"I'm going to take a nap now," Tom told her. "Phipps isn't picking me up till after seven."

"Have a good time tonight, Tom. But don't get drunk or you'll have a headache tomorrow."

"I'll probably have one, anyway."

"Are you going to call me in the morning?"

"Won't you be too busy?"

"I suppose I will be."

"Then I'll see you at the church. Okay?"

"Okay. Try not to laugh when I'm coming down the aisle."

"Why would I laugh?"

"I'll be so nervous."

Tom said good-bye, hung up, then left instructions that he was not to be disturbed until six-thirty. He would have time for a quick shower before he had to change for the party. In his bedroom was the cutaway suit he was to wear at the wedding and the tuxedo for the bachelor party. He had tried to talk his friend out of black tie, but Phipps was a stickler for formality. Suits would be bad form, he said. Only Yale men wore suits to celebrate their last evening of bachelorhood.

At seven-twenty, a taxi stopped in front of the house. It was Phipps calling for Tom. He was told that Tom had not finished dressing yet, but would be down in a minute.

Tom's face was flushed with excitement. Just as he pulled on his coat, his mother walked into the room from her bedroom, where she and Charles Molloy had been dressing for dinner.

"Let me look," she said, turning his shoulders and examining his tie. She made a minor adjustment, then brushed some imaginary lint from his shoulders. "You look so handsome, Tom," she said with pride.

"I wish I didn't have to go to the party tonight."

"It's custom. Anyway, you'll enjoy yourself once you get there and are among your friends."

In the hallway could be heard the ringing of a telephone, and shortly afterward, one of the maids who had been getting the youngest Molloy children ready for bed scurried past the door to answer it.

"Don't have too much to drink," Nora Molloy urged him.

"I won't."

"And don't stay up all night singing bawdy songs or whatever you do at bachelor parties, or you'll be hoarse tomorrow."

"I told Phipps that I wanted to be home by one. Don't wait up for me."

The maid poked her head into the doorway, then tapped against the paneling. "It's for you, Mr. Tom. Should I tell her that you've left?"

"It's Nancy. I'll get it."

"Have a lovely time tonight, Tom," Nora called to her son as he hurried down the hall to answer the telephone.

From the first floor, Phipps yelled, "Hey, are you coming or aren't you?"

"I'll be right down," Tom answered as he leaned over the banister, then picked up the telephone and said, "Nancy?"

He heard breathing at the other end, then: "Tommy? Is that you?"

He recognized the voice immediately and couldn't respond.

"I saw in the paper that you're getting married," Peggy Sweeney said timidly, "so I thought I'd call and—well, you know, wish you good luck and everything."

Tom turned his back to the opened door of his parents' bedroom and spoke softly. "Where are you calling from?"

"From here in New York."

"But you said you were going to Florida."

There was a pause while she tried to collect her thoughts.

"I never went," she replied at last.

"I don't understand," he cried. "You said—don't you *remember!*—you said that the guy you used to date was going to marry you. You told me that."

"I made it up, Tommy."

He crumpled into a chair. "What do you mean, you made it up?"

"I just made it up. No one asked me to marry him, and I didn't go to Florida."

"Then for the love of God, why did you tell me all that!"

"Because I knew I was spoiling things for you, Tommy. I knew you'd be happier with someone your family and your friends like better than me. I'm sorta rough around the edges. I know I am. This girl you're marrying—boy, she really sounds nice. I'm glad for you, Tommy. That's why I called. To wish you good luck and everything. I didn't want you to hate me."

Tom fought for breath. "Where are you?" he asked.

"I just wanted to wish you good luck. I don't want to spoil things . . ."

"Where are you!"

She gave him the address. It was on West Twenty-second Street.

"I'll be right down."

"Please, Tommy . . . I didn't mean . . ."

But he had already hung up and was leaping down the stairs.

As the taxi sped south on Fifth Avenue, Tom was only partly aware of his friend's cheerful monologue. So far as he could gather, he was telling off-color stories about other bridegrooms and horrendous accidents that had befallen them on their wedding nights. On more than one occasion, Phipps had to jab him in the elbow to get any reaction at all. "Precoital fright," he suggested by way of explaining Tom's silence.

Not until the cab had pulled up in front of the Harvard Club and Phipps was standing on the sidewalk and digging into his coat for his wallet to pay the driver did Tom have the courage to tell him.

"Look," he began, "if you don't mind too much, I'm going to be a little late. There's someone I have to see. Could you explain to the fellows?"

Phipps's normally ruddy face blanched. *"Whom* do you have to see, for Christ's sake?" he asked.

Almost in agony, Tom replied, "Peggy just called.

She's here in town. I have to see her to get something straightened out."

His friend reached in to yank him from the cab, but couldn't budge him. "Don't be such an asshole, Molloy! She's just trying to get her hooks into you again."

No, she wasn't, Tom protested. She hadn't even wanted to tell him where she was. But there was something he needed to know. "Apologize to the fellows," he said. "I won't be long."

Phipps stood on the sidewalk and watched as Tom pulled the door shut. "You're an asshole, Molloy!" he repreated mournfully.

"I'll never forgive myself if I don't see her. Please try to smooth things over with the fellows. I'll return the favor someday, John."

As the cab drew away from the curb, Phipps remained standing on the sidewalk, watching it disappear. Slowly, he shook his head. How would he ever get through the evening? How could he explain to eighty or ninety young friends that the bachelor for whom the fête was being given had run off to see an old girl friend?

Another taxi pulled up in front of the canopy. A group of black-tied young Harvard men began to spill out of it.

"Where's Molloy?" one of them asked.

Phipps gulped for air, then said with more equanimity than he'd thought possible, "Tom has been slightly delayed. Why don't we all go upstairs and get pissed?"

Tom searched the corroded mailboxes that lined the vestibule walls until he found her name, then entered a foul-smelling hall and made his way across the worn linoleum toward the stairs. From behind closed doors came the sounds of shrieking babies and men and women bellowing in foreign tongues. Between the first and second floors, it was necessary for him to step aside to allow a gentleman to descend who was dressed in an undershirt with his suspenders dangling over his trousers. Through habit, Tom said, "Good evening," but either the man did not understand or he did not share the sentiment, because there was no reply.

Tom found the door with a peeling number *3,* fol-

393

lowed by a penciled *D*. He knocked several times before a voice answered.

"Who is it?" Peggy asked, standing inside the door.

"It's me," he said, then listened as the bolt was released.

The first thing he perceived was that she had dyed her auburn hair a color deep enough to pass for black. It hardened her eyes and her face somehow, making her appear a good deal older than she was. She wore a black dress with a large piece of costume jewelry, and there were bright spots of rouge at her cheeks. Since the last time he had seen her, she had put on weight, just as she had always feared she would.

"Hello, Tom," she said. "Come on in."

There was no doubt that she was ill at ease, just as he was. She motioned him to a table at the center of the room where there were two chairs. She had apparently been occupying one of them when he knocked, because on the table in front of it lay a lighted cigarette in an ashtray and an opened bottle of beer.

"I'll get you a beer, Tommy," she said. "The fridge is on the bum, so it won't be too cold. Is that all right?" She studied his clothing. "That's a nice suit you've got on. It's a tuxedo, isn't it? I never seen you in one before. I saved the clipping from the *Daily News*. Did you read it?" She held up a section of a newspaper, neatly scissored, and Tom recognized it at once. It was that awful pap about "the society wedding of the year." Nonetheless, Peggy said, "It's a beautiful write-up. I cried when I read it." She hurried into the kitchen, and in a minute he heard a refrigerator door open and close.

"I don't want it," he declared when she returned with the beer.

"I'm sorry," she replied, misunderstanding the reason. "I'll get you a glass. I guess I wasn't thinking."

Angrily, he reached out and grabbed the shoulder of her cheap dress. "What the hell are you doing in this goddam place?" he shouted.

For a minute, beneath her heavy makeup, her face was almost the way it had been when he first met her: tender and vulnerable. "It's just temporary," she explained. "I

394

probably won't stay here too long. The place isn't much, but I've got a good job. I work as a hostess in a club, and I meet real nice people there. It's better than being a secretary, I'll tellya."

"Why did you leave me!" he cried.

"Maybe I wasn't meant to settle down. You know what I mean? A lotta girls are that way." She waited, then once again picked up the *Daily News* clipping. "What kind of life would you have had with me, Tommy? You got a real nice girl, it says here in the paper. She's a society girl. I mean, you'll never have to be ashamed of her, the way you was with me."

"I never was!" he shouted.

"Yes, you was, Tommy. I knew it all along. I wasn't the right girl for you. Now Eddy—he's the guy I live with sometimes—he don't care if I'm a slob. He likes me this way. That's okay with me. He's the one got me the job in the club and everything. He's a chef there. We have good times, Eddy and me."

Crestfallen, Tom asked, "You live with him?"

She stomped out the cigarette in the ashtray. "Maybe he'll marry me; maybe he won't. It don't matter the way it used to. He sees other women; I see other men. That's the way we are, Tommy."

"I loved you," he said in desperation.

"Did you, Tommy? But not enough, I bet. You got a real nice girl now. I can tell from her picture. I was going to try to sneak in to watch the wedding, but it says there'll be all kindsa policemen around to keep people out. So that's why I called you, Tommy. For old times' sake, I mean."

He sank on his knees and buried his face in her lap. "I loved you," he repeated.

"You can't change who you are, Tommy. You're what you are, and I'm what I am. But we did have some good times together, didn't we?"

"Please," he begged, "let me hold you."

She ran her fingers through his curly hair. "Oh, Tommy," she replied, "I was so hoping you'd want to."

All evening long at the Harvard Club, John Phipps

gave excuses for Tom's absence. He altered his story several times during the last four and one-half hours, and it wasn't until midnight that he dared suggest that his friend was ill with the flu, optimistically adding, "But we all hope that he can make it down the aisle tomorrow."

Tom's disappearance occasioned a good deal of whispering and speculation, and almost no one bought Phipps's explanation. One or two even suggested that the bridegroom had bolted.

"Of course not. He's nuts about Nancy," Phipps reassured them. "I'll call and see if I can get a progress report. I'll be right back."

It was nearly twelve-thirty when he placed the call to the Molloys' house. Because of their dinner party, he was fairly certain that they would not yet have retired for the night, but he didn't feel capable of breaking the news to Charles or Nora Molloy. Instead, when the maid answered, he asked for Caitlin.

"Miss Molloy has just this minute gone to bed, Mr. Phipps," the maid replied.

"Tell her it's urgent."

In a minute, Caitlin picked up the telephone and he told her the whole deplorable story. He had to share his concern with someone.

Caitlin gasped when he had finished. "Then it's possible he won't attend the wedding?"

It was quite possible.

"Good *God!*" she exclaimed.

For the time being, John advised her that no one else should be told. They would simply have to bear it themselves. As soon as he'd broken up the drunken brawl at the Harvard Club, he would be over to the Molloys' house and they would wait for Tom. If, by dawn, he had not appeared, they would have to break the news to the others.

"And I thought it was going to be a dull wedding," Caitlin observed. "I'll be waiting outside on the stoop for you."

By the time he returned to the party, many of the

guests had left. Others sat on chairs or in corners, very much the worse for wear, and had to be helped into cabs. Most were quite confused.

"Damnedest bachelor party I ever went to," one of them said. "Was Molloy here at all or did I just miss seeing him?"

For the hundredth time, Phipps repeated that Tom's prognosis was somewhat guarded. It was either the flu or the strain from all the wedding preparations. His doctor had advised bed rest, but for how long no one could say.

"Well, I certainly hope he makes it to his wedding," a classmate replied. "I would hate to see that Roosevelt crowd waiting in a Catholic church with all those graven images and no bridegroom."

Phipps's stomach sank even at the thought of it.

All night long, Phipps and Tom's sister sat disconsolately on the steps of the house on East Seventy-first Street. Caitlin was dressed in a robe and slippers, while Phipps was in black tie, and more than one late passerby stopped to stare. They slept intermittently and cried from time to time whenever one of them recalled that in just a few hours more than six hundred people would begin to converge on St. Patrick's Cathedral.

At six in the morning, when domestic servants were beginning to file into the houses along the block, Caitlin stood and said, "We must tell Mother and Father. The Delanos must be notified, too, and also the monsignor." Gloomily, they entered the house.

Nora was already awake and had been since five, ticking off in her mind a multitude of things that had to be attended to. From her bed, which she shared with a gently snoring Charles, she looked up and saw her daughter at the door. In the hall behind her stood John Phipps.

Noiselessly, so as not to awaken her husband, Nora slid from bed, wrapped herself in a robe, and hurried to the hall.

With remarkable composure, she listened as first Caitlin, then John attempted to explain. She felt giddy, almost as if she were going to faint, but knew that this was no time for that.

"Someone should notify the Delanos at once," Caitlin suggested urgently, "and also the cathedral."

"We shall do no such thing," Nora answered resolutely. "We shall wait for Tom, and in the meantime, no one else is to be informed of this."

"But *Mother*," Caitlin protested.

Nora refused to hear her out. She looked at the grandfather clock in the hall, then announced, "In fifteen minutes, I shall wake Charles and the children. We'll breakfast and dress for the wedding as if nothing has happened."

If Caitlin wasn't awed by her brazenness, John Phipps was. "But what if he doesn't come home, Mrs. Molloy?" he asked.

"Nonsense," Nora replied. "Of course he'll come home. This is his wedding day, isn't it?"

Phipps might have replied that last night was his bachelor's party, wasn't it, but was discreet enough not to.

But when John went home to wash and change and Caitlin went to her bedroom, Nora sank into a chair and held a hand over her thumping heart. She knew Tom well, his weaknesses as well as his strengths, and now she was afraid for him. Once before, the girl in North Cambridge had cast a spell over him. How could she stop her now?

In the quiet of the upstairs hall, she knelt and began to pray.

At six-thirty, the first sounds of activity drifted up the stairs from the kitchen below. Nora collected herself at once, then woke Charles with the joyous news that it was a perfectly lovely day for a wedding. Next, she hurried from bedroom to bedroom, pinching, pulling, cajoling, and threatening until each and every one of her progeny was more or less awake, urging them not to dawdle, as today was a very special day, and reminding them that they must be ready to leave for the cathedral by ten o'clock.

"Children, I'm depending upon you," she declared,

though the truth of the matter was that, as always, they were depending upon her.

Charles's first remark at the breakfast table was "Where the devil is Tom?" and Nora answered brightly that he had stayed over at John Phipps's house for the night. As she spoke, she looked sternly across the table at Caitlin, who was pale and silent, eyes red from crying. "Caitlin dear, eat your breakfast," she admonished. Privately, Nora debated whether or not she should telephone Monsignor Sheen. Perhaps he should be given some inkling of the problem so that the staff at the cathedral could be prepared for the worst. Yet to do so was to admit that such a possibility might occur, and Nora refused even to consider it. If Tom were alive—and she had no reason to suspect that he was anything but—he would appear before the family was due to leave for the church. If he did not intend to go through with the wedding, he himself would have to notify both Nancy Delano and Monsignor Sheen. Nora would not do it for him.

Yet there were problems in timing. The Delano party was due to leave Dutchess County by private train in order to arrive at Grand Central no later than ten-thirty. It seemed to Nora that it would be necessary for them to depart from Millbrook at least an hour before, which meant that the Delanos would have to be notified no later than nine-thirty if Tom had had second thoughts. The train could not be permitted to leave. It would be humiliating enough for Nancy without tying up Grand Central Station, then making a mess of traffic on Fifth Avenue, only to arrive at a church where no wedding would take place.

Tom had until nine-thirty, then, and because Nora knew everything else about her son, she was convinced that he was also aware of this. If he didn't appear, it would not be his own doing, but Peggy Sweeney's. Her flesh would be stronger and more persuasive than anything Nora had ever taught her son.

In the meantime, the children had to be fed and their dressing supervised. The younger ones were reminded that it would be difficult, if not impossible, for them to go to the bathroom once they reached St. Patrick's, and they were to make certain that it would not be necessary. As for Charles, he complained every second as he dressed in his cutaway, saying for the hundredth time that he hated whoever it was who had devised such sartorial torture.

At a quarter to nine, Nora finished dressing, then inspected Caitlin in her jonquil-yellow bridesmaid's dress and wide-brimmed hat. "You look lovely, dear," she said as tears rolled down her daughter's cheeks.

"What the hell is going on around here?" Charles Molloy demanded. "Am I the only one in this house who isn't crying? Where the hell is Tom?"

"Caitlin, dear, would you bring your father his bourbon, please?"

"I don't want any damn bourbon."

Nora rushed from the room to answer a telephone call from the caterer at the Plaza who had prepared the wedding buffet. Members of the orchestra and the armed guards watching the gifts had somehow or other got into the hors d'oeuvres, he told her, and now he'd have to add to the menu or there would not be enough to go around. It was nothing, Nora replied blithely. In fact, the caterer was to make certain that the off-duty detectives and the band members were fed.

At nine o'clock, John Phipps sneaked into the house, dressed in his cutaway. Once again, Charles Molloy asked where Tom was, and Phipps looked first at Nora Molloy, then at Caitlin, and answered, "He will be here momentarily, sir."

At nine-fifteen, four limousines pulled up in front of the house to carry the Molloys and all their servants to the cathedral.

At nine-twenty, Charles said, "Dammit, I want to know what's happening, Nora."

"Charles dear," she replied soothingly, "there is no need to get upset. Tom will be here by nine-thirty."

It was nine-twenty-five when she climbed the wide staircase to her bedroom, closed the door behind her, and fell on her knees before a statue of the Virgin Mary.

Hail Mary, full of grace, the Lord is with thee. Blessed art thou amongst women, and blessed is the fruit of thy womb, Jesus. Holy Mary, Mother of God, pray for us. . . .

Perhaps Nora had pushed Tom too far along the path she had set for him, pushed him well beyond his endurance, and that was why, once more, he had sought out comfort in the flesh of Peggy Sweeney. Perhaps she had misjudged both his strength and his needs.

Holy Mary of inestimable grace and mercy, grant me my prayer. . . .

But Tom was the hope of the family, the agent of its destiny, the carrier of its flame. Merely to be rich was nothing. To serve people and find a place in history for himself was what Tom was meant to do.

Grant me my prayer and let Tom be what he was destined to be. Holy Mary, Mother of God, pray for us sinners, now and at the hour of our death. Amen.

It was nine-thirty. Even now, the Delanos were preparing to leave their home in Millbrook for their journey to New York, and Nora could no longer deceive them—or herself, for that matter. She had failed, just as Tom had. Sadly, she picked up the telephone next to her bed and gave the operator the Delanos' number in Dutchess County, then listened as it began to ring.

As she did, something stirred inside her, something deep and primal that made her drop the phone and hurry to the window.

At the far end of the block, she saw a wraithlike figure hurtling down the sidewalk like a meteor, hair flying behind him, shoes clattering against the concrete. He was tieless and clutched his dinner jacket in his fist as he pushed past his brothers and sisters, dressed in their wedding finery, waiting for seats in the limousines, then bounded up the steps three at a time through the opened door and into the hallway to the stairs, then up them until at last he reached the second floor and flung open the door to Nora's room.

"I'm sorry," he cried breathlessly. "I'll be ready in ten minutes."

As he hurried toward his room, John Phipps and Charles Molloy ran behind him with his top hat and cutaway.

Blessed Mary, Daughter of the Father, Mother of the Son, Spouse of the Holy Ghost, thank you for granting me my prayer.

Outside, traffic was snarled on Fifth Avenue for several blocks in either direction as limousines stopped to deposit guests, and a glittering procession of people made their way into the cathedral. To the south, at Grand Central Station, the Delanos' private train had arrived and the first members of the party had already left the station in their cars and begun to move northward on Park Avenue.

Inside the great cathedral, East Side and Hudson River Valley patricians watched the Molloys' Irish friends dip their fingers into holy water fonts and genuflect toward the altar before taking their seats. It was most mysterious and Byzantine, yet moving somehow, too, that one's faith could be so absolute, and in the end, as the Delanos' friends and nieghbors waited, they were charmed by the merry Irish faces and by the pageantry of it all.

In the first row, Tom's family was seated, Charles on the aisle, Nora at his elbow, and next to her, arranged by age and height, those children who were not bridesmaids, ushers, ringbearers, or flower girls. They made a formidable delegation, and more than one guest marveled at the still-youthful beauty of the woman who had borne and raised them. There was no sign at all on her face of the strain she had been under earlier that morning.

Driving from the house, Tom had shared a car with his parents and best man, and after Charles had asked where the devil he had been all night, for one agonizing minute Nora had been afraid that he would blurt it all out. But John had come to his rescue.

"It's customary for a young man to say farewell to his youth the night before he marries," John answered, and wisely Charles had not pressed for details.

Nora was sure that John's assessment was correct. Tom looked very solemn indeed, and ennobled somehow, too. There was no doubt in her mind that the Sweeney girl had taught him a thing or two about sacrifice and love. He was lucky to have known her; he would be a better man for it.

As Nora sat in the rapidly filling church, waiting for the bridal party to arrive, she realized with a start that she, too, would now have to relinquish Tom, just as Peggy Sweeney had done. And for the same reason: for his own good. Until now, with and without his knowledge, she had protected him, both from external harm and from himself. But henceforth it would be Nancy to whom he would turn for help and guidance. Nora's work was done.

She regretted only that Thomas Cassidy couldn't be there on the day of his son's marriage. He would have been proud of Tom. Not because he was marrying into a family whose name ornamented history books, but because he was proof that what people *were* or *had been* was unimportant. What they *could be* was everything. It was that promise that had sustained Nora during the bleak and lonely days after she had set out from Ireland for the New World. And it was for that same promise that Tom's father had died.

No matter what else Tom was, he was an inheritor. Countless men and women before him had spent their lives on their knees, and he could now walk tall for them.

Charles nudged her gently. "They're here."

A sudden humming filled the church as the party from Millbrook entered and was seated. At the very end of the aisle, Nora spied a flash of bridal gown. From a door to one side of the altar, Tom now appeared.

Nora's eyes devoured him. He was so handsome, so vibrantly alive, so sure of himself. As Monsignor Sheen waited in all his medieval splendor to welcome the bride, for a second Tom's eyes met Nora's—they spoke to her with understanding and gratitude—then he raised them and watched spellbound as Nancy walked toward him.

27

Mr. Patrick Cassidy?" a voice asked from the doorway late one afternoon in November 1939. Pat looked up from his desk at union headquarters and saw a man in a double-breasted gray suit, carrying a leather briefcase and a fedora.

The stranger entered the room, closed the door behind him, then looked about the office to assure himself that they were alone. He settled on a straight chair in front of the desk, balancing his briefcase on his kneecaps and topping it with his hat. His posture was ramrod-straight, as if a hard maple board were riveted to his spine.

"My name is Sidney Rutherford," he announced in a clipped New England accent, "and I am with the State Department. Friends of yours in Washington have asked me to call on you."

Pat snorted, "I'm surprised I have friends in Washington."

"I assure you that you have several," Rutherford answered. "My superior, for one: Mr. Cordell Hull. And Mr. Harry Hopkins for another."

Pat made no attempt to conceal his astonishment. As a result of the hearings, he had achieved a certain notoriety, but he had not been aware that he'd attracted the attention of the Secretary of State or of Harry Hopkins, the latter described either as President Roosevelt's most trusted friend or as his Rasputin, depending upon one's political affiliation.

"It was Mr. Hopkins who brought your name to the attention of the Secretary, who in turn has asked that I make this journey to San Francisco in order to sound you out," his visitor said by way of explanation. "For some time now, we have been casting about for a prominent member of the Irish-American community to perform a service for us, and with Mr. Hopkins's urging, Mr. Hull has settled upon you, sir."

"Well, Mr. Rutherford," Pat began, "I am flattered. But I must remind you that there *is* no Irish-American community. There may be an Italian-American community, a Polish-American community, or a Jewish-American community, but we Irishmen despise the whole notion of community. We value our independence too much, and as a result, for every Irishman, there is an opposing point of view." He watched as Rutherford's face clouded. "As for my being a *prominent* member of such a community, may I remind you that if there is one way an Irish-American can earn the everlasting enmity of all other Irish-Americans, it is for him to become prominent."

The State Department official was not persuaded. "Be that as it may," he declared, "you are well known in Irish-American circles—I will avoid the use of the word *community*—and it has come to our attention that Prime Minister de Valera of Ireland knows you by reputation and is an admirer of yours." He didn't wait for the interruption that was on Pat's lips. "That is why Secretary of State Hull finds you uniquely qualified for the task I shall now, with your permission, describe."

Pat saw no alternative but to listen.

"What I am about to tell you, Mr. Cassidy, must be held in the strictest confidence. You are aware, I am sure, that the Irish Dáil recently voted to maintain neutrality during the war that is now engulfing Europe. As a result, English blood is being shed because Ireland has denied England the use of Irish ports."

"There is historical justification for the denial," Pat pointed out.

"We are not talking about history, Mr. Cassidy."

"It is impossible not to talk about history in matters that deal with Britain and Ireland. Never have two nations been so victimized by history."

Rutherford nodded solemnly. "You may have a point.

You *are* aware, I take it, what is happening off the coast of Ireland?"

How could anyone not be aware? On the third of September, Britain had declared war against Nazi Germany, and since then, the war had been largely fought in the waters of the North Atlantic. Toward the end of September, the British aircraft carrier *Courageous* had been torpedoed off the coast of Ireland; though it might have been saved had it been permitted to dash into Berehaven Harbor in County Cork, Ireland had refused sanctuary and there had been a heavy loss of life. Shortly afterward, the packet battleship *Graf Spee* had begun attacking British vessels as they neared the end of the lifeline across the Atlantic from America; by mid-October, seven ships had been sunk, more than one within in sight of Ireland's green shores.

It was hoped in Washington that Ireland might see fit to abandon its lofty neutrality and come to the aid of beleaguered and hard-pressed Britain.

Not all Americans, however, shared that hope, for not all considered England the mother country. There were Irish-Americans who could not forget that it was from Irish ports that English landlords had continued to ship grain for profit even while a million Irish peasants died of hunger in the 1840's; that those were the ports from which the dreaded "coffin ships" had set sail for America, their passengers dead long before the New World was sighted; and that through those ports black-booted English soldiers had arrived to quell any insurrection, answering with bullets every single Irish cry for freedom.

All over America, in Irish saloons where rebel songs were sung, there was unity on this subject, if on no other. The British could not be permitted to use those ports. And if Ireland's old enemy should suffer as a consequence, then perhaps at last the English would know what it felt like to be Irish.

Rutherford was now prepared to continue. "Within the past few weeks, sir, we have learned of two recent developments concerning the Irish ports and Irish neutrality. Herr von Ribbentrop and his minister to Dublin, Her Hempel, are about to mount a new effort to sway

407

de Valera to reconsider his position on neutrality and perhaps throw in his lot with the Third Reich."

Confidently, Pat replied, "He will not be swayed."

"That is our hope, too, sir. We fear, however, that the Germans may find other, more susceptible listeners to their arguments."

"If they exist, they are not pro-Nazi so much as they are anti-British."

Rutherford's eyes lit up. "Ah, but Mr. Cassidy, in this war it is the same thing. Like you, we at the State Department are confident that de Valera will resist such pressures, but we are alarmed that the Germans might find friends among members of the Irish Republican Army. And should the I.R.A. take this opportunity to perform mischief of one type or another, it's more than possible that Britain will react precipitously."

"Britain invariably does when dealing with Irish affairs."

The State Department official did not immediately resume, but when he did, there was a new gravity to his voice. "It has come to our attention within the last few days that Britain's First Lord of the Admiralty has privately suggested that the Irish ports be taken by coercion."

"Seized?" Pat asked incredulously.

"By armed force. The First Lord of the Admiralty considers the ports so strategic that an invasion of Ireland is justified."

It was madness! England had entered the war to protest Germany's invasion of Poland, yet Rutherford was now suggesting that an important member of its government was contemplating the same outrage against Ireland!

Pat sprang from his chair, too angry to speak. Why was it that every Englishman considered it his birthright to sail across the Irish Sea and attempt to vanquish the proud Celts? Was it something drummed into their heads as they sat at cold desks at Eton, Harrow, or Winchester? How could men of goodwill and probity stoop to such barbarity, and why was it that the English possessed a moral blind spot only when it came to Ireland?

"If British troops swarm onto the beaches of Ireland," Pat said darkly, "I assure you that they will meet with fierce resistance."

"It is much worse than that, Mr. Cassidy."

Gravely, Rutherford rose from his chair until he stood facing Pat. "It is our feeling in Washington that so long as Prime Minister Chamberlain remains in office, he will not set into motion such a course of action, but it is our belief that Chamberlain's government will fall the minute that Hitler strikes against the West."

Pat would agree. For better or worse, Chamberlain was a diplomat, and if England would soon be fighting for its life, there would then be little need for diplomacy.

"We anticipate that the *Wehrmacht* will march sometime after the first of the year, prhaps as late as spring. When it does, it is our opinion that Winston Churchill will be invited to form a new government."

"*Churchill?*" Pat repeated.

"Exactly," Rutherford answered. "He is presently First Lord of the Admiralty."

It was a moment before Pat recovered. "If Churchill, when he becomes prime minister, chooses to seize the Irish ports, he will have made a terrible error in judgment."

"No, Mr. Cassidy, a catastrophic one. And that is what brings me here today. For you see, sir, it is our considered opinion in Washington that should Churchill make good his threat, he will meet with far more than fierce resistance in Ireland. We believe that the outcry from Irish-Americans will be so great that it is unlikely that any American Congress will vote aid to Britain during its time of crisis. And if that should happen, Mr. Cassidy," he concluded, "we are convinced that Britain will lose the war."

Not since the Middle Ages would Ireland play such a vastly important role in history. Winston Churchill was a crusty old fellow, and Irish obstinacy brought out the worst in him. If de Valera defied the British Prime Minister, just as Irish peasants had for centuries defied their landlords, it was more than possible that Churchill would react with aristocratic rage.

Pat had denied that there was an Irish-American community. But there were millions and millions of Irish-American voices, and the call of blood was very strong indeed. If the British troops marched into Ireland, would Congress aid Britain in her fight against Germany? It was doubtful. There were too many *O's* and too many *Mac's* in the Senate and House of Representatives.

The State Department's scheme was a simple one. An attempt would be made to soothe Churchill after he assumed power. As it was well known that he was nettled by Irishmen, it was hoped that the present American Ambassador to the Court of St. James, Joseph Kennedy, would step down and be replaced by the former Governor of New Hampshire, John Winant, who would exercise a more restraining influence. The American Ambassador to Ireland, John Cudahy, who derived from Irish peasants, was thought to be too partisan on behalf of Irish causes, and in all probability he would be replaced by David Gray, a relative of Eleanor Roosevelt. It was thought in some circles, however, that Gray might be too evangelically pro-British, and that would be fatal in Dublin.

"President Roosevelt would be most pleased," Rutherford went on, "if the Irish could be persuaded to open their ports to the British. He is very much aware of the dangers of antagonizing de Valera if America presses too hard, however, and has come to believe that an appeal must be made to the Irish public before de Valera will alter his views. I needn't tell you, Mr. Cassidy, that the Irish—perhaps with justification—distrust government officials, and Dublin is already awash with them. Sir John Maffey is adroitly representing Britain's interests and may very well be able to charm de Valera into reconsidering. At the same time, Dr. Edouard Hempel, the German minister, has assured de Valera that the Third Reich will respect Irish neutrality, but has left the door open should the Irish prime minister see an advantage in allying himself with Germany. Also in Dublin are the Japanese consul, Satsuya Beppu, and the Italian minister, Vincenzo Beardis, cultivated and persuasive men waiting in the wings for a sign from de Valera that tells them that he has begun to waver. I assure you, Mr. Cassidy, Dublin is a viper's nest, and the foreign emissaries are playing on what they regard as the Irish weakness: a deep-seated, perhaps ineradicable hatred for the British."

At last, Patrick asked the question that had been on his lips since the State Department official had begun to speak. "And why are you telling me this, Mr. Rutherford?"

"I am telling you, Mr. Cassidy, because when Hitler makes his strike against the West, we are fearful that events may spring out of control between the British and the Irish. If Britain is driven against the wall, she may do something desperate. Similarly, the Irish Republican Army may choose that moment, with England on her knees, to try to break the yoke of partition. That is why we at the State Department have been searching for a widely known and influential Irish-American to make a moral appeal to the two parties the very minute that Hitler's armies begin to march and Churchill becomes prime minister."

"A moral appeal, Mr. Rutherford?"

Rutherford nodded. "We have in mind a radio address that could be beamed by shortwave to both a British and an Irish audience. Because of your prominence in American life, we are hopeful that de Valera and Churchill might be persuaded to listen to your argument."

"And what argument could I present that hasn't been heard a thousand times during the last seven hundred years?"

Rutherford shrugged his shoulders. "God knows, Mr. Cassidy. But we would like you to try. We are sure that you owe Ireland at least that much."

The State Department official did not press for an immediate answer. There would be time enough for that. Before he left, however, he urged Pat to consider it most carefully.

Ever since he had arrived in America, Pat had tried to sever himself from the maelstrom of Irish politics. During the Troubles in the early 1920s, he had never once dropped coins into the collection boxes in Irish bars because he knew that the money would be converted to

411

guns. For him, guns were not the answer; they were a part of the problem. Yet he had worked for people's freedom: for the women at the shirtwaist factory, for the longshoremen, and even for his own as recently as his appearance before the Dies Committee. He had not, however, worked for Ireland's freedom. Until now, it hadn't troubled his conscience.

Even while Hitler was at their doorsteps, it was quite possible that once again the British and the Irish would be at each other's throats. Rutherford hoped that Pat would be able to find the words to stop them. He had failed to save his own father and his brothers. How then, could he save Ireland? What were the words?

For the life of him, he didn't know.

28

The apartment on Everett Street in Cambridge was a small, one-bedroom place, furnished with discarded chests and tables and worn Oriental rugs from the attic of the Delanos' Millbrook house, along with brightly colored canvas chairs from a Brattle Street shop, and wedding gifts so ostentatious—a sterling silver punch bowl set for forty people!—that Nancy never removed them from their wrappers. A pair of silver candelabra from the Oyster Bay Roosevelts remained in tissue paper, as did the Haviland china, while Nancy stuck candles into the necks of empty Chianti bottles and they ate spaghetti off Woolworth plates. They hung cheap posters on the walls and consigned precious little sixteenth-century Dutch drawings to drawers. Books were the chief ornaments of the apartment; hundreds of Tom's merged with everything Nancy had brought up with her from Vassar, all arranged on simple boards held up by bricks.

They pretended obstinately that what they were doing had a kind of permanence about it, at least for the next three years. After all, Tom had gone to the trouble of arranging all their books by authors' last names and Nancy had spent four days scraping paint off the windowpanes, so why should they be required to leave their little nest just because the so-called master race was terrorizing the Continent?

They made love a great deal, on stomachs full of spaghetti and red wine, and that helped sustain their belief that their lives were magical and not subject to disruption. At first, Tom was very gentle with his new wife in bed, because of her innocence, but then he became experimental, and it was surprising how well she responded to corruption. Once the inhibitions were gone, she was filled with rapture, and often if Tom did not initiate lovemaking, she did.

He still confided in John Phipps. Late one afternoon at the end of November, as they trudged through newly fallen snow on Massachusetts Avenue, the buckles of their arctics clanging musically at their feet, he turned to his friend and said, "You know, she is the best girl in the world. I'm so damned lucky that people who loved me saved me from myself. And that includes Peggy."

Through a woolly muffler tied around his chin, Phipps answered, "You saved yourself, Tom. Don't you know by now that people are never rescued by others? They rescue themselves, or they destroy themselves. The choice is always theirs."

"Well, maybe so," Tom replied, unconvinced. "Anyway, I'm grateful that you were around. And my mother, too, of course." He waited, then added, "I've never confronted her about it, but I'm almost convinced that she had a talk with Peggy."

Phipps looked up with surprise. "Did Peggy say that?"

"No, but she hinted at it—the last night I saw her. At first I was angry at the thought of anyone interfering with my life. But Peggy convinced me it was right."

"Your mother's devoted to you, Tom. When I'm with the two of you, sometimes I see her look at you, and it scares me. It's like she's looking at—I don't know what."

"I know. She has such grandiose notions about what I should do. I'm not sure that I'll ever measure up to them."

"I don't know why the hell not," Phipps said with sudden conviction. "You're certainly the most promising fellow in first-year law."

"Sometimes I"—he fought for the words—"have to force myself to study. My mind is racing like crazy, and all I can think about are things thousands of miles away from here. It's like—you'll probably laugh—I'm possessed or something."

"The war?" Phipps asked.

"Mostly that. Do you know that Nancy and I never talk about it?"

"What's the use of talking about it? There's nothing we can do, one way or the other."

"But we all know—*you* know, *I* know, and everyone *else* knows—that within a year or a year and a half, we'll be in uniform. So why are we sitting here on our asses in libraries while people are dying? We're humanitarians, aren't we? Why aren't we doing something?" Angrily, he kicked at the snow. "We're a very selfish, pampered bunch, all of us here at Harvard. Where the hell are the Lord Byrons in our class ready to set out to fight for Greek liberty? Or the Hemingways willing to give up the soft life to drive an ambulance on the plains of Venice? Or what about our George Orwells? Why don't we have any? What's *wrong* with us!"

"Hell, anyone can shoot a rifle. They don't need a Harvard man to do that. You don't need a brain to fire a gun."

Tom turned to look at his friend. "You do to fly a plane."

John Phipps squinted and his mouth half opened.

"I'm taking lessons," Tom continued. "Twice a week since September. I'll have my pilot's license by Christmas."

Cynically, Phipps observed, "Oh, what a lovely Christmas present that's going to be for everyone." Then with absolute rage, he added, "What in hell do you intend to do with it?"

"I don't know," Tom replied. "I just felt—somehow—that I had to do something. Don't you understand?"

"No, I don't. You're being silly and romantic, and this is not a romantic war. I think—sometimes I think you're a maniac. I really do. You're not like anyone else in your family. Caitlin and I were talking about that a couple of weeks ago. You're not like your father, you're not like your mother, and you're not like anyone else in your family. You're some goddam *throwback*. You are also full of bullshit."

"You may be right," Tom conceded as they made their way to the two-family house where he lived. "Look. I'd appreciate it if you didn't mention it to Nancy."

"What? That you're full of bullshit?"

"No, the other thing. The flying lessons."

"I've already forgotten, and I'd suggest that you do the same."

On the porch, they stomped their feet and shook the snow from their hair. As Tom opened the door, an aromatic smell of spices and wine wafted into the cold air, and they quickly entered the hallway and stepped out of their galoshes.

"Hey, honey, we're home," Tom cried, pulling off his coat.

"Uhmmmmmmmm," Phipps purred as Nancy entered the hall. "Bay leaf and red wine, I betcha anything."

"Boeuf bourguignon," Nancy explained, wrapping an arm around Tom's waist and holding her face up to be kissed.

Nancy was wearing a peasant blouse with a long blue skirt and a matching band of velvet over her hair. Her skin was glowing, and her eyes were radiant.

"Gee, you look nice, Nancy," Phipps exclaimed. "Is this a party or something? You didn't tell me."

"We're sort of celebrating," Tom said bashfully.

Nancy began to rush into the kitchen. "Let me get our drinks. I made French seventy-fives."

She disappeared through a door as the two men entered the living room, rubbing their cold hands together. On the coffee table in front of the sofa was a plate containing intricately made hors d'oeuvres and on the phonograph was a rousing selection from *La Belle Hélène*.

Nancy hurried into the room with a tray in her hands. "I think I made them right, but maybe I used too much cognac."

"If so," Tom replied importantly, "we shall have to dispose of these quickly and mix a new batch." He held the tray as Nancy removed a tall goblet, then offered a second one to his friend. The last he took himself.

"Which one of us does it?" Nancy asked him.

"Why don't we do it together?"

"I think that's very appropriate," she agreed, then raised her glass. "We should like to propose a toast."

"A toast!" Tom grinned, holding up his drink.

Phipps looked from the one to the other in bafflement, but repeated their gesture.

"Here's to the youngest and the newest—" Nancy began.

"—the best and the brightest—" Tom contributed.

—"Molloy in all the world." She clinked the rim of her glass against her husband's. "To our baby."

"To our baby," Tom repeated. "May its life be long and filled with joy and wonder, and may it never know sorrow."

In stupefaction, John Phipps touched his glass against theirs. "A baby!" he cried, gulping from his glass. "That is the most goddam tremendous thing I've ever heard!" He placed his drink on a table, then hugged Nancy and shook Tom's hand. "It really is. I mean, it's mad. The whole universe is going to pieces, and you're having a baby!"

"But what better time?" Tom asked, reaching his arm around Nancy's back as she smiled beatifically.

Her eyes were enraptured, yet when Phipps looked into Tom's, he saw something almost like sadness. Or was it wisdom, as if he could divine what no one else could? But Tom recovered quickly, then bent over and touched his lips against Nancy's forehead.

One afternoon about three weeks later, Nancy was trudging through the snow on Brattle Street when someone called her name. When she turned, she saw one of Tom's former Lowell House friends. Like Tom, he was now in the first year at the law school.

"You're very agile for a pregnant woman," he said. "I've been trying to catch up with you for the last block."

Nancy explained that she was rushing in order to get home before Tom finished his classes.

"I wasn't aware that Tom had classes on Wednesday afternoons. I thought that's when he did his flying."

Nancy looked up with interest.

"In fact, I'm sure of it," he continued. "He was trying to bum a ride from someone out to the airport after his eleven o'clock today."

"I guess I have my days mixed up," she replied unconvincingly.

417

"You're looking just marvelous, Nancy. There is nothing like pregnancy to bring out rosy cheeks in a woman. When's it due, anyway?"

Nancy said that there would be a long wait. Early June.

"I admire you two. This is a hell of a year to have a baby. But if everyone felt that way, there wouldn't be any babies, would there? I've put off marriage for a while. I've decided that it's unfair to ask a girl to wait two or three years, or however long the war is going to last. I've enlisted in the Canadian Air Force. Has Tom enlisted yet?"

Nancy was shivering. It was an effort for her to say that Tom hadn't.

"Well, it seems to me that there are only three choices: Canadian Air Force, Royal Air Force, or waiting for the United States to get off its cowardly ass and enter the war. Tom was talking about the R.A.F. the other day. He was going to see someone at the British consulate. Did he ever do that?"

Nancy stammered, "I'm not sure."

"Well, whether it's Canadian or R.A.F., it's all the same in the long run. We'll both be fighting against Field Marshall Göring. Look, you don't want me to carry your packages, do you? I'd be happy to."

Nancy managed to say that they weren't heavy and that she really ought to be going home.

"Tom is something of a hero of mine," he said before turning to leave. "I won't conceal it. He's the one who's pricked the conscience of almost everyone in first-year law. I would say that at least six men have left our class since September to enlist because of Tom's missionary work. He's a very special fellow. I love him dearly."

Nancy was struggling to breathe. By the time she reached the apartment, she was shivering so much that she pulled a chair over the hot-air register on the floor and sat there wrapped in a blanket. As the winter sun left the sky, she didn't turn on any lights.

At six o'clock, Tom opened the door and saw her there. "How come the expectant mother is sitting in the dark?"

She couldn't answer for the fear she felt.

"What's wrong, Nancy?" he asked as he stood over her.

Tears washed down her cheeks. "I hate this war," she said. "I hate it."

"So do I. So does everyone. But hating it isn't going to make it go away."

She answered softly, "And taking flying lessons *is?*"

"Did John tell you?"

After she had explained, he said reassuringly, "I just didn't want you to worry. That's the only reason I didn't mention it."

"I don't have to be protected, Tom. I'm not weak. I'm not a sissy just because I'm a woman. I know damn well there's a war, and before it's over everyone on campus will be affected. But why do *you* have to be among the first?"

"The British need pilots. If they don't have them, no one will be able to stop the *Luftwaffe.*"

"But why *you?*"

He shrugged his shoulders. "Why not me? Someone has to."

"What about our baby?"

Almost angrily, he replied, "What good is it to have a baby if there's no world fit for it to be born into? Nancy, thousands and thousands, maybe millions of people are going to die in this war. I despise the war as much as you do, but someone has to take a stand."

It was a long time before she could speak. "Then you're going to enlist, aren't you?"

"If I wait, I'll be drafted, anyway. But I won't do it unless you tell me that I can."

"Please don't put the burden on me."

He was shouting now. "Well, then, please, for God's sake, don't make it so hard for me!"

He stood by the window, his back to her. In a minute, she was behind him and he felt the warmth of her hand on his shoulder.

"I'm sorry," she said. "I guess I'm being selfish. You should do whatever you think you have to do. That's the only way you can live with yourself, Tom. Whatever your decision is, I'll go along with it."

He turned to face her and with a superhuman effort said, "They want me over there by the end of January."

She buried her face on his chest.

"Okay," she said at last. "We'll have to make the most of what little time we have."

It was decided that the young couple would spend Christmas with the Molloys, then stay with the Delanos in Millbrook through New Year's. Nora and Charles were disappointed, but conceded that their own house was chock-full of people for the holidays and that Tom and Nancy would probably be more comfortable at the huge house in Dutchess County.

More than anything else, Tom wanted to avoid a confrontation with his mother and father because he knew that they would try to prevent what he was about to do. When Tom explained this to Nancy, she had difficulty in understanding.

"If I can accept it, I don't see why they can't, Tom."

It wasn't as simple as that. "You're not Irish," he said. "They are."

"What does that have to do with it?"

"Everything," he replied with exasperation. "My mother is the gentlest woman in the world. She has something kind to say about almost everyone, but mention the British in front of her and you might as well be talking about storm troopers. As for my father, he's third-generation American, but every year when the local Sinn Feiners come around asking for money, he gives a couple of hundred dollars. Do you know what it's for, Nancy? For the Irish Republican Army to buy guns to make life miserable for the British. And you think they'll understand why I'm doing what I'm doing? Hell, no. They're too Irish."

In bafflement, Nancy observed, "But you're Irish, too, Tom."

He shook his head. "I'm not so sure."

As a result, Tom and Nancy decided that they wouldn't break the news to the Molloys until the deed had been accomplished.

Yet Nora was aware that Tom was distracted and

restless and deliberately avoided being alone with her. She couldn't fathom it unless perhaps it had something to do with the press of studies and his impending fatherhood.

Charles, too, complained that Tom had become rather difficult to talk to. Was something bothering him? he asked Nora one morning during breakfast.

"I've felt it, too," she answered. "But I haven't wanted to pry." Even now, she was still ashamed for having used the private detective to ferret out the truth about the Sweeney girl. She would not stoop to that kind of behavior again.

"Perhaps I'll try to draw him aside before dinner, Charles, and ask him point-blank."

Yet that evening when Nora tried, she failed. She enticed Tom into the study in order to talk to him in private, but seconds later Nancy drifted in from the living room and began to praise the new Oriental rug from Sloane's. To Nora, it seemed almost as if Nancy were a confederate.

It was during that holiday season, however, that John Phipps showed that he had begun to think of Caitlin as something other than a brattish tomboy, and that helped deflect Nora's concern over Tom. War or no war, it was the debutante season, and John and Caitlin went to all the parties together, staying up all night and in the rosy dawn breakfasting on eggs benedict and champagne at the Sherry-Netherland or the Pierre.

The day before Christmas, while Nancy finished some last-minute shopping, Tom spent most of the afternoon at the British consulate. At five in the afternoon, he met Nancy in the lobby of the Plaza Hotel, and his first words were, "Well, it's done."

Nancy had to sit down then and there. She took a deep breath. "How much time?"

"Not as much as I thought. They want to send me someplace in the north of England. All I have is a pilot's license. I have to learn how to fly a Hurricane. I'm supposed to be in England by the end of the second week in January. I leave for Lisbon on the ninth, then fly from there to London."

"Then we just have a couple of weeks!"

"It looks that way."

Suddenly Nancy said, "I don't want to spend them at home. I mean, in Millbrook. Can't we go back to Cambridge and be alone?"

It was what he was going to propose. They would have to close the apartment and distribute the furniture they didn't want and move the rest into storage, anyway.

"Oh, Tom!" she cried. "Can't we keep our little apartment to use when the war is over?"

It was unrealistic, he told her. The war could last for four or five years.

"I don't care," she replied, and suddenly she was crying in the lobby of the Plaza. "We can keep it, can't we? We can find someone to use it while you're gone, and if we can't, I'll pay the rent out of my own money. Please, Tom! I don't want to give everything away. Can't we please keep it for after the war?"

It was absurd—he knew it, and she knew it—but in the end, he agreed.

Christmas dinner at the Molloy house was an ordeal for both of them. There was a huge crowd because of the children's habit of inviting strays from their schools. Father McNally from St. Vincent Ferrer was at the table in order to ensure that the religious significance of the day would not be forgotten, but after two predinner cocktails and wine with his meal, he was almost excessively mirthful. The noise in the sumptuous dining room, John Phipps said, was more like that of a rooming house than a New York town house. Two turkeys and two huge capons were sacrificed for their pleasure, and everyone at the table except two-year-old Megan drank Châteauneuf-du-Pape. Charles Molloy spent most of his time passing food and exhorting others to take more, so that a minute after the gravy boat had circled the table, he would once again set it in motion, followed by cranberry sauce, turkey, chicken, rolls, peas, and potatoes. Everything was ambrosial, Father McNally said.

And before the dessert was served, Deirdre and Edward were persuaded to do some step-dancing for the diners, with Maggie the maid at the piano. They did "The Shaskan Reel" and "The Lass on the Heather," and everyone commented that they danced like angels.

During it all, Tom and Nancy exchanged uneasy glances, and when they were not actively eating, they held hands under the linen tablecloth. After dinner was over, the children all declared that they would like nothing better than a romp in Central Park, and off they went with their sleds and their skates, supervised by Caitlin and John Phipps, who said that he would not take any gaff from them even though it was Christmas Day. Shortly after they left, Father McNally also departed, making his way down the sidewalk with a rolling gait and whistling a Gaelic tune.

When they were alone, Tom said, "Well, we can't stay too late. We're going back to Cambridge tonight."

"Tonight!" Nora complained. "But we thought you were going to stay in Millbrook through New Year's."

Nancy looked across the room at Tom waiting for his reply. "We wish we could, but there are a lot of things we have to do. Hey, Nancy, I'll get your coat." He vanished from the room.

Nora turned first to Charles, then to Nancy. "Something is wrong, I know it."

"There's been a lot of excitement the last week and a half. That's all," Nancy volunteered. "We don't want anything to happen to the baby."

"Well, if you think so," Charles said. "But it's a pity you have to go so soon. We'd hoped to have you around for a few more days."

Tom returned to the living room, dressed in his overcoat. He held out a tan polo coat for Nancy to slip into. He avoided looking into his mother's eyes.

"We could run into bad weather," he said to his father. "It's best that we get an early start."

"The dinner was lovely," Nancy said.

Nora hadn't been able to utter a word. She knew that she was being left out of something, but she didn't quite know what.

"Will you be getting down during the next month?" Charles asked at the door.

Perhaps. It depended on his studies, Tom replied. The work load was stupendous.

"You'll write, though, won't you?"

They assured Charles that they would. Nancy kissed her father-in-law, then Nora. "Thanks for the wonderful dinner."

It was Tom's turn. He shook his father's hand robustly. Quickly, he kissed Nora on the cheek.

"Thanks for everything you've done, Mom," he said. Then suddenly he and Nancy were rushing down the steps.

Nora stood at the opened door watching them.

"You'll catch cold," Charles admonished.

At last, the engine of the car started. Tom tooted its horn, then waved as he drove it past the house.

Nora continued to watch it until it had turned the corner.

"Here, let me close the door," Charles said to her, easing it shut.

Late in the morning of the ninth of January, Nora was supervising the housecleaning when Maggie answered the door and a minute later appeared with an envelope in her hand.

"It's special delivery," she said. "It looks like Mr. Tom's writing."

Nora tore open the envelope.

Dear Mom and Dad,

By the time you read this, I'll be on my way to England to serve in the Royal Air Force. It wasn't an impetuous decision, and it's been very painful for me to keep my plans from you, but I knew that you would try to stop me. Nancy has agreed to honor my decision, and I'm asking you to do the same.

I've tried very hard to study my motives, and it's tempting to say that I'm attracted by the ad-

venture of it all. But it's far more than that. I look at the war in Europe as a kind of religious war, almost—the powers of darkness against those of light—and I can't sympathize with Americans who pretend that it has nothing to do with them. You've always told me that I had certain obligations to society because I happened to be lucky enough to be born into a family with money and social position, and that it was my destiny to serve mankind in some special way. Well, maybe you were right, and my destiny is to do just what I'm doing.

It's only a matter of time before America enters the war, anyway, and until then, I can be of use to the British, who are desperate for men. I'll be trained to pilot a Hurricane, and the fact that I've already done some flying in Massachusetts will be a decided advantage. Hopefully, I'll be ready, and England will be, too, before the battle begins.

Nancy and I have sublet the apartment in Cambridge and kept all of the furniture there to use when I get home. Nancy's going to be staying with her folks in Millbrook until her confinement. We both think that it would be a good idea if she came into town and stayed with you for the last week or so because it will be easier to get her to Lenox Hill Hospital. I know that you'll be kind to her and love her as I do.

I'm sorry if you think that I've let you down. I sincerely haven't meant to. My prayers are with you always.

Love,
Tom

29

It was a paradox, a cruel paradox.

As never before, Nora found consolation in her religion. Every morning, she wrapped a scarf over her head and attended Mass at the church of St. Vincent Ferrer. Every other day, she was driven to Millbrook where she had lunch with Nancy and admired the wonderfully full and bourgeoning quality of her body.

They talked about Tom almost incessantly, yet neither said what was uppermost in her mind: Why was he doing this? Many times, Nora was tempted to tell Nancy about the true nature of Tom's birth and that his father had been hanged by soldiers of Britain, the very nation Tom was now serving. But each time, Nora refrained, knowing that it wouldn't help Nancy's understanding any more than it did her own.

During the long spring of the "phony war," while the world waited for Hitler to attack, Nancy and the Molloys lived for the letters they received from Tom. He liked the English boundlessly, he wrote them. They were the most generous people in the world. The minute one of them found out that he was a Yank, they did everything but give him the keys to their houses.

As soon as I complete my training, I'll be assigned to one of the groups in Fighter Command. Thus far, I've seen a great deal of the English countryside, but I've yet to see my first Kraut. I expect that he'll look like something like a cross between Bismarck, Beethoven, and Charles Lind-

*bergh. Everyone is waiting for Hitler to make his
next move, but the old boy is taking his time.*

I think of you constantly.

Other letters were filled with news about his training.
He even revealed the terminology of warfare. A takeoff
was a *scramble*. To land was to *pancake*. To fly at full
throttle was to *buster*. When the enemy was sighted, the
cry was *tally ho*.

As a result, the Molloy children scrambled from their
beds every morning, and in the evenings they pancaked
back into them. All day long, they lunged at each other,
crying, "Tally ho!"

Yet Nora still could not accept what he'd done. It was
an affront to reason. An enigma.

At Easter week, the gloom was lifted somewhat because the older children were home from their boarding
schools. John Phipps came down from Cambridge and
spent most of his time following Caitlin around the house.
On Good Friday, he stepped up to Charles Molloy in the
living room after dinner and said, "You know, sir, there's
something I've been meaning to talk to you about."

Brusquely, as if he were replying to a junior clerk at
his office, Charles said, "Well, go ahead, John. You've
got the floor."

"I was wondering, sir," he began, then faltered. "I
mean to say, Caitlin and I—well, you see, sir—"

Mercifully, Charles interrupted. "If you are asking for
my daughter's hand in marriage, you are welcome to it.
Ever since I first saw you around this house, I was sure
that you secretly wanted to be a Molloy, and since your
father will not allow us to adopt you, I suppose the
next best thing is for you to marry one of us." He wrapped
an arm around John's shoulder, then called everyone into
the room.

"Out of kindness, I have just proposed for John," he
announced. "He is about to marry your sister Caitlin and
become an official member of the family."

All the little Molloys shrieked hurrah.

On Easter Sunday, the Duesenberg was sent to Millbrook to fetch Nancy so that she could share the Molloys'

holiday feast. She was hugely and self-consciously pregnant and looked pale and distracted. Earlier, Nora had told Charles that Nancy had cried the last afternoon they'd been together after having received news that Tom's squadron had been on alert twice the week before.

As they finished dinner, the children squirmed uneasily in their chairs, looking over their shoulders from time to time toward the hall, where the telephone was located. When, at last, the telephone began to ring, Nancy was the only one who didn't jump out of her seat.

"It's Tom!" the children cried.

Charles had arranged for the call as a special treat, and as the family rushed into the front hall, the children were urged to stand in the background and refrain from coughing. Nancy was quickly instructed not to interrupt Tom's words, as the cable could carry only one transmission at a time.

"Hello?" Nancy said, her hands shaking. "Is that you, Tom?"

The overseas operator replied, "Your call from Portsmouth, England, is coming through. Go ahead, please."

"Nancy?" a voice said from thousands of miles away. "Can you hear me?"

"Tom! Oh, darling, how wonderful to hear your voice!"

"Are you all right, honey?"

"I'm fine, but I look very funny. I waddle around like a duck and can't even see my feet."

"I betcha you're more beautiful than ever. What does the doctor say about Charley or Kathleen?" They had decided that it would be Charles if a boy, Kathleen if a girl.

"No problems. He says if I'm a Vassar girl, I should be smart enough to have a baby." She listened to Tom's laughter. "I miss you so much, darling."

"I miss you, too, but I'll be home before you know it. You have to be real tough until I get there. I mean, no bawling or anything."

"I will be, Tom, I promise."

"Will you send me pictures as soon as the baby's born?"

"As soon as he looks presentable."

429

"I've been thinking it's going to be a girl. A girl would be great, Nancy."

"A boy would be great, too. Listen! Here's your mother and father. I'll be back later."

First, Charles took the telephone and everyone bent closely to hear Tom's words. "I've been meaning to ask, Tom. Do they taxi down the runways over there on the left-hand side or the right-hand side?" He then laughed at his witticism so loudly that no one could hear Tom's response. Nora scolded him.

"Are you there, Tom?" his father asked. "How are you?"

"I'm fine, Father, and I'm learning a lot about flying."

"What do you think of those new Spitfires?"

"They're marvelous machines. A hundred times better than a Messerschmitt."

"What kind of guns are mounted on them?"

"Browning machine guns, Father."

"They can slow you down, I hear."

"They have tremendous recoil. When we're firing, we lose forty miles an hour."

Nora did not approve of the turn of conversation. She reached for the phone with one hand and tapped her wristwatch with the other."

"Don't take any chances, Tom," Charles said hurriedly. "Let the other fellow take the chances. Do you *hear* me? Good luck. Here's your mother now."

Nora accepted the receiver, and when she spoke she was breathless. "Tom, we just have a few more seconds. They told us they have to keep the cable open. Are you all right, Thomas?"

"I've never felt better, Mom. Thanks for all the letters and for the cookies and sweets you sent. They're hard to get over here."

"Do you go to church, Tom?"

"Every chance I get."

"You must be careful. Promise me. There is no need to be a hero."

"I'll be very careful, Mom. I want to stay alive. But listen! If something goes wrong—you know what I mean

—please help Nancy get through it all. Will you do that for me, Mom?"

Why are you doing this? Nora wanted to ask. *Tell me!*

Instead, she answered, "I will, Tom, just as you've asked. But you must trust in God."

"I do, I do," he answered triumphantly.

"God bless you, Tom. Here's Nancy again."

As Nancy accepted the receiver, the overseas operator instructed her to conclude the call.

"Tom!" she cried. "I love you so much. I pray for you. Be careful, darling."

There was no answer. The connection was broken.

By the end of April, Patrick hadn't yet committed himself to Rutherford's proposal. The more he pondered it, the more convinced he was that he could not please anyone. If he were pro-Irish, he would antagonize the British; if he were pro-British, as the State Department no doubt hoped he would be, he would embitter the Irish.

Each time Rutherford telephoned, Pat continued to hedge, just as Hitler himself did in choosing the date to mount his offensive against the West.

During the first week of May, however, Pat received a call from Washington that propelled him to make up his mind.

"We've just learned of an alarming development," the State Department official told him. "Hitler's agents in Dublin have promised to end partition if the Irish open their ports to German battleships and U-boats and thus help defeat Britain."

The wished-for dream, a united Ireland at last! How cunning the Germans were. For a minute, Pat was too stunned to reply.

The Germans were promising what Britain would never willingly give. Even if, at some future date, the British Parliament advocated the rejoining of the north and south of Ireland, it was doubtful that Ulster would ever agree. The Germans, however, could deliver. Would the Irish be tempted?

With conviction, Pat declared, "De Valera will never do business with those Nazi murderers."

431

Rutherford deliberated before answering. "That depends, Mr. Cassidy. Though Prime Minister de Valera has attempted to keep the Germans at arm's length, it's our opinion that he might conceivably turn to them for salvation should he learn that Churchill is contemplating the seizure of Irish ports. The situation is exceedingly delicate," he continued. "Now more than ever, the Old World needs to listen to the voice of reason from the New. We should like to make tentative arrangements for your broadcast, leaving in doubt only the date, which of necessity will be determined not by us but by Hitler. Can we proceed, Mr. Cassidy?"

Pat saw no alternative but to agree.

On the tenth of May, Panzer divisions rolled across the frontiers into the Lowlands, while Stuka dive-bombers filled the skies overhead. The long-deferred attack had begun. Everywhere along a broad front, German troops swarmed into Holland, Belgium, and France.

In the British Parliament, it was feared that Chamberlain's government would not survive the day.

In Millbrook, Nancy telephoned the Molloys as soon as she heard the news and asked if she might move into town a bit earlier than she had planned. In a few hours, she was established in Tom's old room, its closet still filled with tweed jackets and dirty white buckskin shoes, its walls still plastered with Harvard and Portsmouth Priory pennants.

At six o'clock, London time, Winston Churchill became prime minister of England, and even as he did, the *Wehrmacht* continued to advance westward almost unimpeded.

At shortly before six in the evening, London and Dublin time—ten in the morning in San Francisco—Patrick sat before a microphone in a small, windowless studio and waited for an engineer to give him the signal to begin. His remarks, he'd been told, would be rebroadcast over the BBC and Radio Eireann within the hour, and both de Valera, in his tidy house in Blackrock near Dublin, and Churchill, already at 10 Downing Street, had been advised that the famous Irish-American labor leader

432

would be sending a message overseas on behalf of other Irish-Americans.

At the last minute, Pat had edited his speech down to the very bone. All night long, people in San Francisco had been listening to their radios as statesmen and kings, scholars and journalists gave their views on the rapidly developing events, and Pat was sure that brevity would be more appreciated than eloquence. As he now watched the engineer raise his finger to alert him, he quickly re-read his notes.

The engineer's finger chopped through the air, and a red light flashed on in the room.

Patrick began to speak:

"To all my former countrymen in the new Republic of Ireland, the ancient Inisfail, and to the brave men and women of Britain who are about to face their greatest peril in history, good evening from America."

Now that he had begun, the worst was over. Already he felt more comfortable.

"Tonight, as Hitler's armies begin their march toward the Channel, Britons from all walks of life are preparing to fight for their right to live as free men, not as slaves. We Irish-Americans wish you good luck and Godspeed. Yet we must also remind you that for seven centuries Ireland has been valiantly doing what you are only now about to undertake.

"Take courage, Englishmen and Englishwomen! In the end, good causes invariably triumph, and evil ones fail.

"For tonight, after having been threatened with extinction for seven hundred years, Ireland survives as a free nation.

"Yet seven centuries of bloodshed and horror have left their mark on the Irish character and on the collective memory of Irishmen everywhere. It is for that reason, as difficult as it is for some to understand, that tonight, while England braces for battle, Ireland has not held out a helping hand. Prime Minister de Valera of Ireland has steadfastly adhered to neutrality, although he has been tempted, and threatened, too, on all sides.

"It is much to ask of former slaves to be magnanimous when their old masters are in need. And just as freed

433

slaves never forget, masters sometimes never learn. For even now, while Britain fights for its very survival, it is said that some Britons in high office consider Ireland's neutrality illegal, just as they consider the Republic of Ireland itself illegal. To them, Ireland is, and will forever be, a vassal state.

"Let me say to those men that if they persist in their views and dishonor Irish neutrality—and if British troops once again occupy Ireland—then history will judge Britain accordingly. To value one's own freedom and disregard that of others is not the work of democratic people, but of despots. Should Britain seize the free and independent nation of Ireland, she will have lost her moral superiority in this war—and gained the everlasting enmity of Irish-Americans.

"And perhaps non-Irish-Americans as well. For we Americans are the outcasts of other nations, survivors of famines and pogroms, persecution and neglect. We are a nation of freed serfs and emancipated tenant farmers, a nation of people who have been set adrift because of religious intolerance and prejudice. We have little sympathy, most of us, for those who say that in this world some people are born to be masters and others are born to be slaves.

"So to Prime Minister Winston Churchill, who is about to guide Britain through the parlous days ahead, may I say: Spend your wrath wisely against Germany, which threatens you from the East, and look away from Ireland.

"Meanwhile, in Ireland itself, there are those who would use Britain's distress to press for the end of partition, the last vile remnant of serfdom, and they have been encouraged by Nazi hoodlums who have promised to end it for them should Ireland cooperate in bringing England to its knees.

"I implore members of the Irish Republican Army to turn a deaf ear to Herr Hitler's agents, however beguiling the prize. If Ireland cannot actively aid Britain in this war, then she must not impede her old enemy, either. If she cannot, for reasons of conscience, take up guns to defend the empire that once held her in subjugation, then she must not use them to help bring about its destruction.

"Such matters are better left to God.

"So on this dark, historic night, as the world appears to be disintegrating, I, an Irish-American, wish the good-hearted people of Britain boldness and fearlessness in their fight to survive; I stand in awe of the citizens of Eire, alone this evening, reviled by British and Germans alike, who have reminded the world that injustice can never be rewarded. Yet because here in the New World the loathing of injustice transcends race or religion or one's former allegiance to a country, I and many of my fellow Irish-Americans pledge our support, and even our lives, if necessary, to our old adversary Britain in her struggle against Nazi Germany. And in return, we ask that at some future date Britain help correct those ancient wrongs that still prevail in parts of Ireland, for until they are corrected, they unsettle the sleep of all Irishmen, wherever we may be.

"This has been Patrick Cassidy, an Irish-American. God bless you all."

As he finished, his shirt was sopping wet even on this cool San Francisco morning.

30

By the end of May, British and French forces were in full rout all across the front.

The letters to Millbrook and East Seventy-first Street from Flight Lieutenant Tom Molloy suddenly stopped. Searching desperately for an explanation, Tom's wife and his mother concluded that he was no longer stationed in England but at an airfield in France, and because fighter squadrons were in the air almost around the clock, he didn't have time to write. Yet they worried.

As Nancy neared her confinement, she kept more and more to her room, declining even to take the afternoon walks in the park her doctor had advised. And at the dinner table, she sat silent, scarcely eating, and once or twice ran from the table after someone had mentioned the war.

Nora was very concerned, as much about Nancy as about Tom. Charles said that he would try to enlist the aid of the American embassy in London to determine where Tom now was, and Nora pledged that she and the children would make an effort to cheer Nancy up.

But it was not easy, because Nora felt the same apprehension and despair that Nancy felt.

The last letter they received was posted on the tenth of May. If Tom was now in France, surely he would get in touch with them to allay their fears. Every evening, they huddled over the radio in the living room, and it was there that they listened in numb horror as Elmer Davis revealed that of sixty-seven British fighters in action that day in the air over Sedan, thirty-six had failed to return.

On the twenty-second, they learned that the R.A.F. was evacuating its last base in France and would conduct all its future operations from Britain. The children ran up and down the polished floors, singing to each other that Tom was back in England. Nancy was sure that he was now out of harm's way and would soon cable them and tell them that he was all right.

But no word came.

In desperation, Charles placed another call to the embassy in London and was told that they were trying their damnedest to determine if Tom had been injured or hospitalized, but that London was in chaos because it was feared that the entire British Expeditionary Force was about to be lost.

On the twenty-eighth, the Belgian Army surrendered and British troops were driven to the sea at Dunkirk.

"Where is Tom?" Nancy begged. "Please, someone, tell me where Tom is!"

But in the confusion, no one knew. The embassy replied that Tom had been attached to a squadron stationed at Merville in France, but during the withdrawal, communications had broken down.

Early in the morning of the last day of May, Nancy tapped on the door of the bedroom where Nora and Charles lay sleeping and breathlessly told them that the pains had begun. Charles slipped a suit over his pajamas and stuffed his sockless feet into a pair of shoes in order to drive her to the hospital. At his insistence, she sat alone in the center of the back seat of the enormous Duesenberg lest she be injured by his reckless driving while Nora sat next to him in the front, saying the rosary.

All day long, Nancy struggled to give birth as spasm after spasm of pain racked her frail body. The Delanos appeared, then Caitlin and John Phipps. The latter two took turns writing droll and irreverent cablegrams to be sent to Tom at the moment of birth, but rejected most of them for not having the right combination of solemnity and levity.

From time to time, Nancy cried out in agony, "Dear God, where is Tom!" and Nora turned away from her so that Nancy's fevered eyes would not see the doubt and sorrow on her face.

Again and again, Nancy cried out in frustration and grief, "Dammit! Dammit!"

A nurse said to her sympathetically, "It'll be over before you know it."

"I don't care, I don't care."

Nora searched for words to comfort her, but couldn't find them.

Suddenly, a terrible loneliness swept over her like a giant wave until she could scarcely breathe. Something had left her, she knew that now with certainty. Something rare and irreplaceable had gone away, and only memory remained.

Late in the morning, Charles rushed off to his office for an hour or two, and by noon hadn't yet returned. At twelve-thirty, Caitlin and John volunteered to see how the children at home were coping with the long wait, and urged Nora to accompany them, but she preferred to stay with Nancy.

As John turned the Packard onto East Seventy-first Street, he saw an unfamiliar automobile double-parked in front of the house. When Caitlin remarked that it bore a diplomatic license plate, he pushed his foot hard against the gas pedal.

Even as he drew up behind the car, the front door of the house was opened and Maggie hurried down the steps to the sidewalk. "An English gentleman is in the parlor with Mr. Molloy," she said excitedly. "He called him home from the office, sayin' as how it was most important."

They dashed into the hall and John flung open the door to the drawing room. Charles Molloy was sitting on the edge of the sofa, head bowed, and standing over him was a man they had never seen before.

"Has something happened to Tom?" John asked with apprehension.

Charles looked up at them, as he did, they saw the suffering on his face.

"Oh, no!" Caitlin cried.

The English gentleman stepped forward. "We are all profoundly sorry. On behalf of His Majesty's Government, we extend our heartfelt sympathy."

In disbelief, John asked, "Tom is *dead?*"

He waited for an answer, but none was given. When, at last, Charles spoke up, his voice was unrecognizable.

"Who will tell Nancy?"

Early in the evening, a baby girl was born.

After Nancy had been brought back from the delivery room, the Delanos were allowed to see her for a few minutes, and never in their lives had their marvelous self-control been put to better use. As they were leaving, Constance held Nora in her arms and quickly embraced her. Charles remained in the hall. He looked tired and worn, like an old man. Nora set a thin little smile on her lips, then entered the room.

Nancy's eyes were narrowed from pain, and her hair was matted against the pillow. "Tom has got his Kathleen, after all, Nora. He so wanted a baby girl."

Nora stood next to the bed and looked down at the woman Tom had loved. "We are all very happy for you, Nancy dear."

"Is she pretty?"

"Oh, a sight to behold! She has a headful of golden curls and a cry like a banshee."

Nancy grinned with satisfaction. "Did you send the cable to Tom yet?"

Nora caught her breath. "Not yet. Caitlin and John will attend to that. That's why they're not here tonight. They'll see you in the morning after you've had a good night's rest."

Nancy peered into the hallway. "And Charles?"

"He has a bit of a fever and thinks he might be coming down with a cold. He doesn't want to give it to you or the baby. He sends his love and will see you when you're stronger."

Nancy sank back into the pillows. "I promised Tom I'd send him a photograph as soon as she's presentable."

"Tomorrow will be time enough," Nora said patiently. "Or the next day."

Just then, a raucous howling filled the room as a nurse walked in with the bundled baby in her arms. "I can only let you have her for a minute or two, Mrs. Molloy," she said, handing it to Nancy.

Oh, the baby!

Nora looked down at its radiant face, and when she touched its rosy cheek, she felt the throb of life at her fingertips.

What Tom had done was right and proper, she knew that now. For him to have done anything else would have been craven and base. Nations rose and nations fell; the landless became lords of the land. Slaves became masters and masters were enslaved. In God's world, few things were permanent other than what existed in the hearts of brave men.

Tom had seen something dark and menacing and had cried out in defiance, just as Thomas Cassidy had done before him. It was right and proper; it was in the stars. For of all Thomas's gifts to his unseen son, none was more precious than that of indignation. Yet Tom had transformed it in some magical way, all his own, and instead of using it spitefully, had gone to the aid of his father's murderers.

It was a miracle.

Men deluded themselves into thinking that they could change the world, while the only miracle most would ever perform was to change themselves.

"It's such a lovely, lovely baby," Nancy sighed.

As Nora looked down at it, there was exaltation on her face. It was a link to the shadowy past and into the limitless future. In the baby, Tom's dreams would live forever.

Something else, as well. Whatever it was within him—strong and durable, stronger even than his Irishness—that had compelled him to do what he had done.

"Oh, the baby," Nora whispered to it as Nancy held it up for her to take. It was a rebeginning. It was hope and promise and continuity. "Oh, the darling baby, the sweet Kathleen."